"Despite everything, you still believed you were better," Muzien said. The tip of the sword lowered, the cold steel gently touching the skin of his neck.

"Every maneuver, every thrust and parry, carried that arrogance. Deep down, you felt your skill would overwhelm mine. Do you understand your error, Watcher? You will never defeat me. You will never even challenge me. There is so much you can learn at my hands, but only if you submit. Only if you humble yourself to one who is greater. Otherwise…"

The tip drew a single drop of blood.

"Otherwise you will die at these hands, having learned nothing at all."

Muzien withdrew the blade, sheathing it while walking away. He showed no fear at putting his back to Haern.

"Reconsider my offer," the elf said as he dismissed the rest of his guild with a single hand gesture. "Despite this poor performance, I still feel you are the most qualified to inherit my legacy."

"I won't," Haern said as he slowly rose to one knee. Blood trickled down his neck, and he had to grit his teeth against the continued pain from where Muzien kicked him. "I will never swear allegiance to someone like you."

Muzien cast a glance over his shoulder.

"Then get out of my city," he said. "You are unwelcome here."

With that he sprinted down the street, black coat flapping behind him. Haern watched him vanish, and the fear in his gut continued to grow.

By David Dalglish

Shadowdance

A Dance of Cloaks

A Dance of Blades

A Dance of Mirrors

A Dance of Shadows

A Dance of Ghosts

A Dance of Chaos

Cloak and Spider (e-only novella)

A DANCE OF CHAOS

SHADOWDANCE: BOOK 6

DAVID DALGLISH

www.orbitbooks.net

Copyright © 2015 by David Dalglish
Excerpt from *Skyborn* copyright © 2015 by David Dalglish
Excerpt from *A Crown for Cold Silver* copyright © 2015 by Alex Marshall
Map credit © Tim Paul

Orbit
Hachette Book Group
1290 Avenue of the Americas, New York, NY 10104
www.OrbitBooks.net

Printed in the United States of America

RRD-C

First Edition: May 2015

10 9 8 7 6 5 4 3 2 1

Orbit is an imprint of Hachette Book Group, Inc. The Orbit name and logo are trademarks of Little, Brown Book Group Limited.

The Hachette Speakers Bureau provides a wide range of authors for speaking events. To find out more, go to www.hachettespeakersbureau.com or call (866) 376-6591.

The publisher is not responsible for websites (or their content) that are not owned by the publisher.

Library of Congress Cataloging-in-Publication Data

Dalglish, David.
    A dance of chaos / David Dalglish.—First edition.
        pages ; cm.—(Shadowdance ; Book 6)
    ISBN 978-0-316-24257-8 (trade pbk.)—ISBN 978-1-4789-8527-3 (audio download)—ISBN 978-0-316-24255-4 (ebook)
    I. Title.
    PS3604.A376D36 2013
    813'.6—dc23
                                                                        2014045184

To you loyal readers,
who have allowed me to live a dream

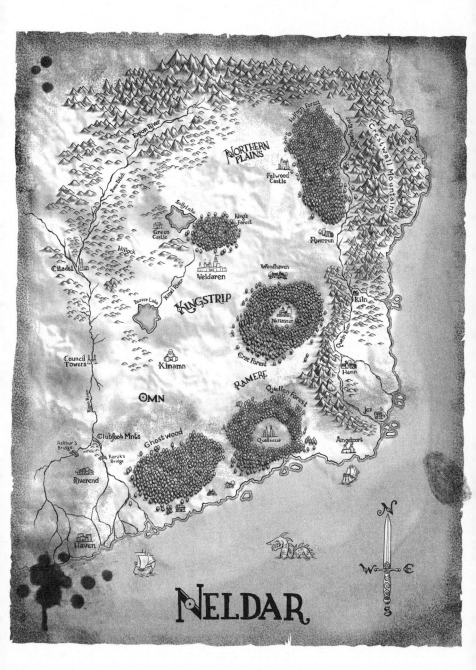

NELDAR

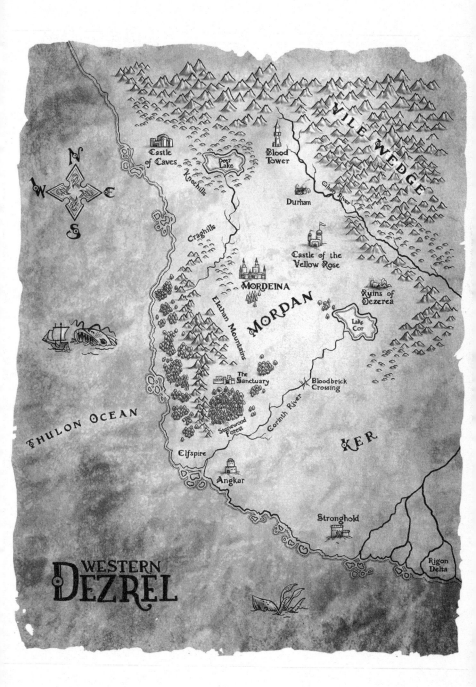

WESTERN
DEZREL

PROLOGUE

Into the secluded shrine below Palace Thyne walked Muzien Ordoth, and he was pleased to see he was not alone. He'd worried that the high priest of Celestia would be afraid to meet with him in such a clandestine manner, or worse, deem such a meeting beneath him. They met in a place long forgotten, accessible only through ancient tunnels cut into the granite beneath the palace. The shrine itself was lit with forever-burning torches that produced no smoke, their yellow light reflecting off the emerald walls.

"You should have been here before me, kneeling in prayer to our goddess," said Varen Dultha, rising from his knees before the statuette of Celestia that rested atop the oaken altar. When he turned, his smug distaste tested the limits of Muzien's patience, and control. "But then again, you've never been much for prayers and worship, have you?"

"I do not appreciate having my faith questioned," Muzien said. "My loyalty to the goddess has not wavered once over this past decade."

"I find that hard to believe," Varen said. "Living among humans? Trading with them? Keeping many in your employ? The goddess commanded us to watch over them, guide them, and remain neutral in their affairs if they would not listen. Pray tell me, how were you doing *Celestia's* work there in Mordeina?"

Muzien took in a deep breath, then slowly let it out. He needed to remain calm, and not let his disagreements with the high priest ruin all he'd done. In the secret records of their people, he would be called the savior of their city, perhaps their entire race. What did a few insults to his pride matter compared to that? But before he answered, he walked past Varen and put a hand atop the nude statuette. It was of their goddess, arms raised above her head, mouth open. Carefully carved to represent the delicate nature of balance, she could have been bound and in pain, or finding pleasure in freedom. Often the viewer's mood was what was reflected back, a subtle point Muzien wished more elves would understand. Above the statuette, carved into the emerald and filled with gold, was a four-pointed star, the fabled form Celestia had taken when coming down to speak with the brother gods before their war hundreds of years ago. It was as symbolic as it was historical, for that same star often represented the sun, showcasing the duality of the goddess, her watchful eye in both day and night.

After whispering a prayer for guidance, all while fully aware Varen impatiently waited, Muzien crossed his arms over his chest and met the stare of the priest. Varen was slender, even for an elf, his long hair so white it approached silver. He was young, nearly as young as Muzien. The two had risen in power together over the last century, but it had been Varen who won the position of high priest, the youngest elf ever to have done so. The wound to Muzien's ego had taken years to heal, the bleeding halted only when he'd realized there were better ways to protect his people than from within the isolated halls of their temples.

"I do Celestia's work by protecting her people," Muzien said.

"Are her people in danger?"

Muzien's jaw clenched tight, grinding his teeth.

"You're no fool, Varen," he said. "The humans' temperament toward us has worsened drastically over the past twenty years. They fear us now, that fear bordering on the insane. In their cities, men and women preach hatred toward us, a hatred so primal and raw no peaceful solution will ever suffice."

Varen's eyes narrowed.

"Is that why you've pulled me down to this forgotten place?" he asked. "To insult my diplomats before they may even speak a word?"

Muzien shook his head. Conflict between the races was growing; everyone could see that. Over the past year, as a way to counter the seemingly inevitable, Varen had championed an initiative to send dozens of trained diplomats to permanently live in Mordeina, the capital city of the human nation of Mordan. But Muzien had beat them there by a decade, and he knew the futility of such an attempt. His voice was absent during the debates, for he had no time for such things. He had a war to prevent.

"Your diplomats will be made to wait at the gates," Muzien said, stepping closer to Varen. "After a week or so, they'll be allowed in, only to be met with vicious crowds. They'll be cursed at, spat at. Little boys and girls will hurl stones at their heads. Whatever home you think they'll stay in will be burned to the ground. Should they go to speak with the king, they will be denied nine times out of ten, and whatever audience they find will be brief, and spent listening to the king inform us of our failures and deviousness. This anger the humans feel, it is a sickness, without base or merit or reason. It's founded on one thing, Varen: fear."

"If all this is true," asked Varen, "then how have you lived there so long?"

"Because I *want* them to fear me."

Muzien could feel the conversation slipping away from him, so before the priest responded he pressed on, letting his anger fuel his words.

"Listen well, Varen," he said. "You know war is coming, as sure as the rising sun. It is only a matter of time before the humans raise their banners and descend upon our forests. They'll burn every tree to ash if they must to satisfy their blood lust. If we don't do something to prevent it, our people will suffer terribly."

For once that smug look faded, revealing a very tired, frustrated Varen.

"Of course I know it," he said. "But too many consider the humans as curiosities to be ignored, not feared. They see the borders of our forest as impenetrable. To convince them to permanently station diplomats in Mordeina took more effort than you can imagine. Damn it, Muzien, it is easier for me to find an elf *eager* for war than one who will accept mankind as a legitimate danger."

Muzien reached out, put a hand on Varen's shoulder. He tried to remember a time when he'd considered the elf a friend. It felt like a different life, and a gulf of blood and coin lay between.

"There's still hope," Muzien said, and he felt his heart speeding up. This was it, the culmination of his plan. "In Mordeina, I have formed a guild of men and women loyal to my name. They're bound by greed and ambition, and for that alone they are both predictable and reliable. I've dipped my fingers into every bit of trade, particularly the vices their kings and queens have ruled illegal. The price was dear, Varen, and I've spilled more blood than I wish to see again in my lifetime, but I would gladly pay it a hundred times over if it means the safety of our people."

"I don't understand," said Varen. "How does a guild of humans spare us from a potential war?"

"By bringing the war to them. A minor noble from the southern nation of Ker has made repeated claims that he could conquer all of Mordan, usually under the guise of some bloated family history...a noble that is firmly in my pocket. From all across Mordeina and Ker I've secretly contacted mercenary bands, drawing them south to join him. Should he march upon Mordeina, and place it under siege, my guild will sabotage the defenses, overthrowing that wretched Baedan family line that has ruled Mordan for far too long."

As Varen listened, his pale face somehow grew paler.

"You would incite a rebellion against their king?" he asked when Muzien finished. "Even worse, you would have us explicitly responsible? Should the humans hear..."

"They won't," Muzien insisted. "I've used my guild's connections for every step of the plan, protecting our people from blame. When the fighting begins, it will be sudden, chaotic. We'll position the various mercenary groups all across Mordeina. At my word, they'll begin burning villages to the ground. The combination of chaos and surprise will prevent the king from properly mustering his troops, and that's when my puppet noble marches on Mordeina. The plan will succeed, Varen, I promise you."

Varen looked away, to the statuette of the goddess. Putting a hand atop it, he closed his eyes, shook his head.

"What is it you want from me?" he asked. "If you didn't need help, you'd have already put this plan into motion, consequences be damned."

Muzien felt relief sweep through him. If Varen was ready to consider the cost, then the hardest part was over.

"My guild's trade network is extensive, and has grown rapidly over the past few years, but it is still not enough to pay for an entire army's worth of mercenaries. I need the coffers of the priesthood opened to me. With it I can establish a puppet king loyal to my desires. Even if we fail, we'll plunge the human nations into chaos that will take years to recover from. All I ask is that you trust me."

"Why come to me?"

"Because what we do must be kept between just us. The fewer who know, the safer we are. You control the coffers, and you alone. I bring before you a plan to save our people. All you must do is give me the word to begin."

Varen opened his eyes, and his hand fell from the statuette.

"That coin is tithed to us so we may build statues and temples to our goddess," he said. "It is given to us so we may feed the hungry and clothe the naked. Come the midsummer festival, when we rejoice in the love of our maker, it is those tithes that pay for every instrument, every singer, every baker. And you would have me spend it on mercenaries to slaughter entire villages in the vain hope of replacing one human king with another?"

"I do what must be done," Muzien said, his temper flaring.

"And I do what the goddess says is right! The humans are flawed, but they hold as much capacity for good as they do evil. We will reason with them, Muzien. We will find ways to make them listen to us, to show we are not their enemy, and we'll do it without becoming the monsters they already think we are."

Varen moved to walk past him, and fighting off the beginnings of panic, Muzien stepped in his way and halted him with a hand on his chest.

"This is a mistake," he said. "Before us is a threat, and it must be met with full force, not delusions of peace! I do the goddess's work, restoring a balance so horribly broken only the most desperate of paths will save us. How can you not see that?"

The high priest grabbed his wrist and pushed it aside.

"Those years in Mordeina have corrupted you," Varen said. "And what I see is a sad shadow of my former friend. Conquest through coin? Death before peace? Celestia's blessing is not on your hands, Muzien. You're more human than elf now."

The words were a knife to his heart, and he felt his whole body tremble with rage. Reaching back, he put his hand on the statuette of the goddess, felt the cold stone against his skin.

"Varen," he said as the priest headed for the door.

"Yes?" asked Varen, turning about.

Muzien struck him across the head with the statuette, a corner of the square base crunching into his temple. Varen let out a single cry before dropping to the ground, his entire body limp. When he landed he splayed awkwardly, the back of his head smacking the hard floor with an audible crack. Dropping the statuette, Muzien stood there in the middle of the shrine, feeling panic nipping at the corners of his mind.

"Her will," he said to the body. "I did her will, always her will, yet you'd turn on me? You'd have my ten years of living among those wretched humans be for nothing? *Nothing!*"

He kicked Varen in the side, but there was no reaction. Blood continued to spill across the emerald floor, taking on a purplish hue. Trying to fight down panic, Muzien scrambled for ideas. There had to be a way to make his plan work. There had to be a way to salvage the situation. But everything involved coin he didn't have, and with Varen dead, there was little chance for him to obtain any wealth from his brethren.

Turning, he let his eyes fall upon the statuette, which lay on its side, the bottom stained with the priest's blood.

"I did this for you," Muzien said, voice dropping to a whisper as he fell to one knee and reached out to take it. "Tell me what to do, my goddess. My actions were just, I know it with all my heart. Please, tell me how to save our people."

The fingers of his left hand closed about the goddess's legs, and he bowed his head, eyes closed. He prayed for a voice, a sign, a whisper of wind in his ear...but instead he only felt pain. It grew steadily, burning, charring, but he refused to relent. Varen was wrong. Celestia would not abandon him so. She would not betray him. But why did his hand burn? Why did the pain sear into him, and why must he now be screaming?

At last he could stand no more. The statuette dropped to the ground, and when he opened his eyes, he saw a brief glow fading from the stone. As for his hand, he held it shaking before him, saw the blackened remains through the blur of his tears. His skin was charred, and with every twitch of his fingers fresh pain shot up his arm.

"No," Muzien whispered, tears falling. "No, damn it, no!"

Slowly he stood, his chest suddenly hollow as Varen's words echoed in his mind.

You're more human than elf now.

More human? Then so be it. Let the elven lands burn. Let humankind destroy the home of his former kin. Drawing a knife from his pocket, Muzien walked to the altar where the statuette had first rested. Dropping to one knee, he let his voice soften into prayer, let his whispers echo across the unseen void.

"If you would deny me, then I deny you as well," he told the goddess as he took the sharpened edge to the tip of his left ear. "If you would rebuke my attempts to save your people, then let them all perish."

He cut into the ear, removing the curled tip that set him apart from the men and women he'd walked among throughout the city of Mordeina. As the blood ran down his neck, he took the knife to the other ear. After two quick breaths, he cut it as well. Rising back to his feet, he sheathed his knife and clutched the bloody stumps of cartilage tightly in his darkened hand.

"If I am more human than elf, then let me become the greatest at being human," he swore to the heavens. "Their love of coin, their lust for power, their hearts ruled by pride and slaves to ambition...everything they cherish shall be my god, my only god. I need no other."

With that done, he kissed the burnt flesh of his hand, felt the heat of it on his lips, and then exited the hidden shrine. The severed tips of his ears he left atop the altar, just beneath the four-pointed star.

His final sacrifice to Celestia.

His first to a new god of blood and coin.

CHAPTER

1

Not since Alyssa Gemcroft unleashed her army of mercenaries upon the streets of Veldaren had Haern felt so at risk while racing along the rooftops. Before, he could use the cover of night and the blend of his cloaks to disguise his allegiance. Now those of the night belonged to the Sun, and they bore no cloaks at all. Before, the various politics and feuds among the guilds had kept his foes in check, and the Watcher's reputation alone had prevented most sane men from engaging him willingly. But times were no longer sane, and Haern could only guess how the master of the Sun Guild would react to the Watcher's return.

Haern slowed his run, then stopped completely at the edge of a home, careful to keep his footsteps light, his weight evenly distributed. He was nearing the castle, and there would be no densely packed homes to rely upon anymore. Grabbing the edge of the roof, he swung himself low, landed with but a whisper of sound on the cobbled stone. A quick glance up and down the street showed no one, not that that meant much. Eyes were everywhere in Veldaren, more so now than ever before. Noticeably absent were any patrols by the city guard. From what Tarlak had told him, the king had given the Sun Guild near-total immunity to any sort of punishment, and it seemed keeping the guard at home was the easiest way to accomplish that. Haern frowned, and for hardly the first time he wished a better man sat on the throne.

Before him loomed the castle, its large double doors shut and barred. Scaling the stone walls to the upper windows wasn't the hardest thing to do, but Haern had no need. Keeping to the shadows, he looped around to the eastern side of the castle, opposite the attached prison. There he found one of the many soldiers posted for patrol, an older man with a gentle demeanor that seemed to run counter to the armor he wore and the sword strapped to his thigh. Haern gave one last look about to ensure no one watched, then dashed toward the soldier.

Instead of being alarmed at the sudden approach, the man only nodded curtly.

"You're late," he said, putting his back to Haern and walking over to the stone wall of the castle. After a quick whistle, a rope fell from one of the battlements.

"Had to be more careful than usual," Haern said, grabbing the rope.

"Ain't that the truth," said the soldier.

Haern flew up the rope, easily scaling the castle and climbing onto the stone battlement, which was little more than a balcony overlooking that side, accessible through a single heavy door. Waiting for him, arms crossed and armor polished, was the man responsible for protecting the city of Veldaren: Antonil Copernus.

"You've been gone awhile," Antonil said as Haern pulled the rope back up. "Almost thought your note to meet was a trap or trick."

"By who, the Darkhand?" asked Haern. "He seems more the type to demand a meeting, not request it."

"Given past experience, it's more that if Muzien wished a meeting, he'd break into my bedroom to have it." Antonil shook his head. "Gods damn it, where have you been? The city's gone to shit in your absence, in ways we never could have anticipated."

Haern thought of his trek to the Stronghold with Delysia and his father, of how fruitless it had turned out to be, and he pulled his hood lower over his face.

"My reasons were my own," Haern said. "And I thought the Sun Guild was crushed when I left. I pray you'll forgive me the error, so long as I make it right."

Antonil rubbed his eyes with his thumb and forefinger. The man looked exhausted, and though they met just before midnight, Haern knew the late hour had little to do with it. The responsibilities of his station, coupled with his inability to fulfill them due to the terror Muzien inspired in the king, was clearly wearing on him.

"If you want to make it right, bring me Muzien's head so I can hang it by the ears over the city gate," Antonil said. "Hopefully that's the reason you've requested our little clandestine meeting, to let me know of the bastard's impending fate."

Haern chuckled.

"I wish," he said. "No, I have something far worse to share, Antonil, something I need you to swear to secrecy until we have a way to deal with it."

The man frowned, the dark circles beneath his eyes making him look more dead than alive.

"You have my word," he said. "Now what is it that could possibly be worse than an insane elf who's declared himself unofficially king?"

Haern almost didn't tell him. There wasn't much the man could do beyond spreading panic if he refused to keep his mouth shut, but Antonil was a loyal ally, and had proven his trustworthiness a dozen times before. Given the dire situation the city was in, he needed all the help he could get.

"Have you seen the tiles bearing the mark of the Sun that Muzien's placed all throughout the city?" he asked.

Antonil looked surprised at the question.

"I have," he said, brow furrowing. "What of them?"

"They've been magically enchanted with a spell, a very powerful and dangerous one. Last night Tarlak discovered just how powerful."

Antonil suddenly straightened his spine, his arms falling to his sides. When he spoke, it was as if his jaw didn't want to move.

"The explosion in the western district," he said. "I just thought it another mess caused by you or the Ash Guild. It was one of the tiles, wasn't it?"

Haern let out a sigh.

"It was," he said.

"That explosion leveled two homes and blasted a fair chunk out of the wall surrounding the city. A wall that has stood for years, a wall more than ten feet thick built with ancient stone."

"I know."

Antonil turned away, ran his hands through his hair, and then suddenly spun about, striking his fist against the door behind him.

"Do you know how many of those tiles have been buried against the castle's walls?" he asked. "Two dozen at last count, more than enough to level the whole damn thing. We have to get them out, and now."

"You can't," Haern said, and he felt a pang of guilt for his words. It seemed everything he said drained more hope and life from the man. "There's an enchantment upon them, something that messes with their weight and makes them nearly impossible to move by hand. If you do succeed, it will only break the magic and cause the tiles to activate immediately."

The weight of the words seemed to be settling on Antonil, and they were heavy indeed.

"These tiles," he said, "if they're magical, isn't there anything Tarlak can do to disarm them?"

"Perhaps," Haern said, after a moment's hesitation. Tarlak's rambling tirade about the differences between clerical and arcane magic, as well as the careful wardings built into each of the tiles, flashed through his mind. "It's complicated, though, and Tarlak's made little progress. Even trying to analyze one risks setting the spell off, killing anyone nearby. These tiles weren't buried in quiet little corners, I'm sure you've noticed."

"I have," Antonil said. He walked to the edge of the battlement, joining Haern, and put his hands on the short stone wall. Swallowing hard, he overlooked the city, and Haern knew he was remembering all the places he'd seen those tiles on his patrols, every intersection, every home, every shop.

"What does he want?" Antonil asked, his voice now a whisper.

"If you mean Muzien, I'm not sure," Haern said. "It's possible he was used by someone else to smuggle them into the city. So far he's made no threats and given no ultimatums. It may only be a final measure should he fail to retain control of the underworld. Honestly, I don't think we're supposed to know what they do yet. If we act quickly enough, we might be able to salvage the situation into something resembling a happy ending."

Antonil laughed, so tired, so bitter.

"A happy ending," he said. "I don't see that ahead of us."

Haern put a hand on Antonil's shoulder, patting the steel pauldron protecting it.

"Don't lose hope just yet," he said. "I'm here now, remember?"

He grinned, and despite his dour mood, Antonil grinned back.

"I guess there's always the chance you'll pull off another miracle," the guard captain said. "Stay safe, Watcher. Strange as it sounds, these streets are no longer yours."

Haern grabbed the coiled rope at his feet and tossed it over the side.

"They were never mine," he said. "But until I die, they will always be under my care."

Over the stone he went, using his cloak to protect his hands as he slid down, the rope curled once around his arm. The moment his feet touched ground, the rope ascended.

"I pray matters went well," said the lone soldier.

"Best as I could hope," Haern said as he returned to the dark streets.

It took less than thirty seconds to spot a man following him from the corner of his eye. Picking up his pace, Haern traveled the main road running south from the castle to the heart of the city. The tail, a younger man lurking on the rooftops, had to abandon stealth to maintain the chase, making it easy for Haern to get a look at the man's chest, and the four-pointed star sewn across it.

Will Muzien make his move against me already? Haern wondered, suddenly cutting right, his first deviation in several minutes. So far he'd had no interaction with the mysterious elf since returning from his trek west to infiltrate the Stronghold. A quick glance behind showed the tail grabbing the side of a rooftop and using it to swing down to the ground. Vanishing into an alley out of the man's sight, Haern turned, drew his swords, and began counting. At four he rushed forward, perfectly timing the man's arrival into the alley. Before he could even ready a dagger, Haern's sabers were at his throat.

"I pray you were hoping to talk," Haern said as the young man's eyes widened. "Because anything else is suicide."

"No, not, no..." the man said, and he looked ready to piss his pants. "Tracking your movements, that's all, I swear."

"That's right," said a voice behind Haern. "I'm the one actually looking for a fight."

Haern kneed the first man in the stomach, then kicked him to the ground before spinning to face his boastful challenger. Approaching from the other end of the alley, two long dirks drawn and twirling in hand, was a dark-skinned man with the Sun Guild's emblem sewn onto his shirt. The man's hair was long, and braided in a fashion Haern recognized as more common to the distant land of Ker.

"You should have used what little surprise you had," Haern said, settling into a stance, gaze flicking to the rooftops in case there were more ambushers. So far he saw none, but when it came to the Sun Guild, Haern had learned to expect the worst possible scenario.

"I don't want anyone claiming I was lucky instead of skilled," said the challenger. "You're a fool and a fake, Watcher. Whatever reputation you had, it's about to be mine."

With a sudden cry the man charged, dirks pulled back for a thrust. Haern dashed to meet him, easily recognizing an overinflated ego when he saw it. He'd grown up in Thren Felhorn's shadow, after all. Such an attitude meant overzealous aggression, and the easiest path to victory was to crush it immediately. The man thrust his dirks with admirable speed, but the placement was exactly where Haern had expected. Parrying both with a swipe of his left hand, Haern continued forward, lashing out with his right hand while twirling to deftly avoid the man's desperate charge. His saber found flesh, the man let out a gargle, and then he collapsed, a tangle of limbs and leaking blood.

Haern shook the blood off his saber and looked back to the man who'd first been tailing him. Instead of running, he stood in the alleyway, arms crossed.

"Shouldn't you have fled?" Haern asked.

"Why?"

The confidence with which he spoke alerted all of Haern's senses. Glancing back to the rooftops, he saw that this time he was not alone. Four men lurked at the edges, crossbows in hand. He spun to find four more emerge at the other end of the alley, blocking it off. Joining the first man were three more members of the Sun Guild, and they too held either daggers or small crossbows. The ambushers said nothing, and other than sealing the exits, they remained still, crossbows pointed but not fired, swords drawn but held low. There was something eerie about how silent they remained, these ghostly specters. Had Muzien ordered them to remain quiet? Haern had a feeling that was the case.

And then the wall of men parted before him, and in stepped Muzien the Darkhand. He was taller than Haern had expected, his thin body draped with a black coat. The front of his dark-umber hair was carefully braided and then tied behind his head, so not a strand dared interfere with his vision. His long ears ended at abrupt scars instead of upturned points, and true to his name, his left hand was blackened as if by fire. The elf smiled, and while Haern had expected him to be smug, instead he looked intrigued.

"The Watcher of Veldaren," Muzien said, and he extended his darkened hand in greeting. "I have longed to meet you, and witness your prowess with my own eyes." He glanced to the dead body at his feet. "The fool was a foreigner who insisted his skills were equal to yours. I hope you do not mind me letting him pay for his boast."

The elf was trying to be friendly, but his causal dismissal of a former guildmember's life, and the way he made everything seem like a harmless game, made Haern's throat tighten.

"I take no joy in killing," Haern said. "Nor do I appreciate being used for your amusement."

Muzien's smile grew, and this time Haern saw the smug satisfaction he'd expected.

"What makes you think you have a choice in the matter?" he asked, then continued without waiting for an answer. "This city, no, this *world*, is for our amusement, Watcher. We're here as playthings for gods, faulty toys that break at the slightest angry touch. You ended the life of an idiot and a braggart. You know nothing of him, of his family, could not even give me his name if I offered you ten tries. To you he was an opponent to be killed. To me he was a chance to behold your legendary skills. Now he is dead, and unworthy of remembrance."

Haern knew arguing was pointless, and he kept his hood low and his legs crouched. With so many watching, reaching Muzien would be difficult…but not impossible. Swords clenched tightly in his hands, he kept his instincts on edge, kept his eyes open for a possible opening for attack.

"No words?" asked the elf. "Fair enough. I only need an answer from you, so remain silent until then. Keep your hood low, your jaw locked in a frown. You've crafted an interesting persona, Watcher, and for years it has suited you well. But I hold no fear of a man whose face I cannot see. I do not dread finding your cloaks in my shadows. When you were but a thought in your father's mind, I was conquering the streets of Mordeina.

Bards have sung of my Red Wine since you were a babe suckling at your mother's breast. Whatever pride you have, whatever reputation you think you've built, know it means *nothing* to me. Do that, and perhaps you and I may come to an understanding."

"And what might that be?" Haern asked.

A bit of hope sparkled in Muzien's eye.

"That you belong as my champion, and as a potential heir to the Sun."

Haern wasn't the only one surprised. He sensed the shock and intrigue sweeping through the men surrounding him. No doubt many had once belonged to the various thief guilds native to Veldaren. They knew what it would mean if the Watcher joined the Sun Guild.

"You're insane," Haern said.

"Far from it." The elf drew a sword from his hip, and Haern braced for an attack that never came. "You were once this city's underworld king," Muzien said, pointing the blade at him. "Every faction, from the guilds to the Trifect, feared your wrath. Alone you conquered Veldaren, but you are not alone anymore, and you face an enemy you will never conquer. In a way you were my predecessor, but while you were willing to let others pretend to retain their power, I have neither the patience nor the goodwill to do so."

"I never sought to rule," Haern said.

Muzien laughed.

"Then unlike you, I am also unwilling to lie to myself. You ruled, Watcher, with a fist made of shadow instead of iron. I would offer you that position again. What we have now, is it not a peace greater than the one you fostered? No guilds are left to prey on one another. The Trifect continues to pay us for protection, and it is without need of the king's involvement or your constant overseeing. What you created was fragile, precarious. I have fostered something greater, something eternal."

At that, Haern slowly stood to his full height, and he held his sabers out to either side.

"Your creation is the same as mine," he said. "Each ends at our deaths. Forgive me if I find amusement in your claim to never tell yourself lies. You're as delusional as the dead man at your feet."

Muzien's amusement quickly vanished. The elf shook his head, and he slowly began to pace before Haern.

"A fate you may soon share if you resist me," Muzien said. "Whatever skills you have, they are not enough. I can train you, mold you into something unbelievable. Should I die, my creation will live on, for it will be in your hands, and then in the hands of whom you yourself choose. The Sun rises, the Sun falls, always and again. I need no truth beyond that."

Haern shifted, using his cloaks to hide the tensing of his legs. The men around him were growing anxious, unprepared for a discussion when they'd anticipated a battle. If he could keep the bantering going, make it seem he could be swayed...

"I'm not sure I share your truth, Muzien," he said. "No matter my actions, the sun will rise tomorrow. Your guild, however, can be broken, your men scattered to the four winds."

The elf's brow furrowed.

"Kneel before me, or die before me," he said. "You have no other fate, Watcher."

Haern's grim smile spread across his face.

"Then prove it."

He lunged, feet kicking up dirt behind him as he flew toward the elf. The gap closed in a heartbeat, and Muzien had time to shout only a single word before lifting his sword in defense.

"Don't!"

Two crossbows fired despite the order, both misjudging Haern's speed and punching holes through his trailing cloaks. Twirling his body for added strength, Haern brought his sabers slashing in, hoping to cut across the elf's shoulder and down his chest. Instead of falling back into a defense, Muzien stepped forward, sweeping his sword wide and into the way of Haern's swing. Despite all Haern's strength poured into the attack, the block succeeded with ease, and suddenly the elf was far too close. A slender hand shot out, grabbing him about the neck. Momentum halting with a jarring wrench of his spine, Haern tried to kick the elf in the stomach, but Muzien twisted, simultaneously avoiding the blow while hurling Haern to the ground.

Haern rolled, tucked his feet underneath him, and then exploded out in a double thrust. Muzien's blade looped about, something maddeningly casual about the way he parried the two hits, took a step back, and then smacked aside Haern's follow-up attack. Haern refused to relent, forcing Muzien to keep his sword dancing, batting from side to side against his flurry of blows. Haern's speed, his constant shifting of positions and attempts at disguising angles, never seemed to matter.

Haern hammered at the lone sword, three times in such rapid succession it sounded like a single hit, then used his right hand to attempt pushing the blade aside, his left thrusting toward what he hoped to be Muzien's exposed heart. Muzien's sword dipped beneath the push, swooped about, and then parried the thrust, all with such speed his blade was a blur. Haern tried cutting back in before Muzien could reset his position, but then the elf's leg snapped out, foot connecting with his abdomen. Letting out a cry, Haern fought through the pain to swing sabers lacking the strength they should have. Muzien batted them aside with ease, and too late Haern realized the elf had positioned himself close enough that his leg could loop behind Haern's left ankle. A step, a push, and Haern fell to his back.

Down came Muzien's blade, the tip halting an inch from Haern's exposed neck.

Haern remained perfectly still, knowing any movement could spell the end. Above him hovered Muzien, and staring into his eyes, Haern saw no malice, no anger...just disappointment.

"I've cut only your pride," he said. "Don't make me cut deeper."

To be beaten, and so easily, certainly wounded his pride, but the far more powerful emotion was the fear he felt growing in his stomach, squirrely and unwelcome. The elf held his life in his hands, yet the only thing that mattered to Muzien was how Haern had not lived up to his expectations. This was who now ruled Veldaren? This was whom he needed to defeat? True to his words, Muzien was not afraid of him in the slightest. No, just disappointed.

"Despite everything, you still believed you were better," Muzien said. The tip of the sword lowered, the cold steel gently touching Haern's neck. "Every maneuver, every thrust and parry, carried that arrogance. Deep down, you felt your skill would overwhelm mine. Do you understand your error, Watcher? You will never defeat me. You will never even challenge me. There is so much you can learn at my hands, but only if you submit. Only if you humble yourself to one who is greater. Otherwise..."

The tip drew a single drop of blood.

"Otherwise you will die at these hands, having learned nothing at all."

Muzien withdrew the blade, sheathing it while walking away. He showed no fear at putting his back to Haern.

"Reconsider my offer," the elf said as he dismissed the rest of his guild with a single hand gesture. "Despite this poor performance, I still feel you are the most qualified to inherit my legacy."

"I won't," Haern said as he slowly rose to one knee. Blood trickled down his neck, and he had to grit his teeth against the continued pain where Muzien had kicked him. "I will never swear allegiance to someone like you."

Muzien cast a glance over his shoulder.

"Then get out of my city," he said. "You are unwelcome here."

With that he sprinted down the street, black coat flapping behind him. Haern watched him vanish, and the fear in his gut continued to grow.

My city, Muzien had said. They were familiar words, an oft-made claim in the city of Veldaren. But for the first time, Haern believed them. As he stood and sheathed his sabers, he wondered if there was any real chance for him to challenge such a claim. His father had thought the city his, and in a night of blood and killing, Haern had wrested it away from him. But Muzien was not his father. Muzien was something greater. Something worse.

"My city," Haern whispered, words he himself had once believed. Glancing to his left, his eyes settled upon one of many stone tiles bearing the mark of the Sun Guild, placed just before the entrance to a home. He felt the threat they presented on his shoulders, unshakable, undeniable. The shame of his defeat burned in his heart, and he knew he had to be better. Knew he had to become stronger, fiercer.

Perhaps, he dared consider, to save the city, he needed to believe it his again.

Pulling his hood lower over his face, he ran back to the Eschaton Tower, hoping in vain that come daylight, Tarlak would have a better plan in mind.

CHAPTER

2

With her heart in her throat, Zusa returned home as the sun rose over the city wall. The soldiers at the mansion gate offered her strange looks, but they recognized her and did not dare comment.

"Welcome back," one said, and even that earned him a glare from the guard beside him.

Zusa crossed the yard at a clip, for despite her best attempts, she felt her nerves already fraying. Not since her argument with Alyssa the night before had she come back to the estate, or spoken with her beloved friend. She still wore the ill-fitting clothes stolen from Daverik after his death, and the bloodstains earned her another strange look from the armored man guarding the front door. A man whose tabard, she realized, signified him as loyal to Victor Kane, not Alyssa. Given their future marriage, perhaps that was a pointless distinction to make, but she made it nonetheless.

"Would you mind?" Zusa asked when the man refused to move from the door.

"Lord Victor needs to approve all guests before they enter," the guard said. "Your name, please?"

Zusa swallowed down a rock in her throat, and for a split second she debated cutting the man's throat and entering anyway.

"Zusa," she said instead. "And if you do not move, I will ensure Alyssa banishes you from these grounds forever."

The man grunted.

"No need for that," he said. "I've been warned of you."

Warned? The phrasing insulted her, but she rolled her eyes and did her best to ignore it. The man stepped aside and banged twice on the front door. It opened from within, and Zusa pushed on through into the mansion. Ignoring an offered escort, she hurried down the hall. She felt eyes on her from every soldier, every servant, and she tried telling herself it was just her imagination. It was her lack of wrappings. She felt strangely naked without them, even though she'd dressed in regular clothing during her time in Angelport with Haern. As ridiculous as it might sound, she felt as if everyone who looked upon her knew of her vow to never wear the wrappings again.

Turning a corner, she had to stop herself from running into a very tired, very pale boy.

"Nathaniel?" Zusa asked, kneeling before him and running a hand across his face. The boy blushed and turned away at her touch. "Are you all right?"

"I'm fine," he said, his words a mumble. "Not sleeping well is all. Bad dreams."

"I've not slept well, either," she said, forcing a smile. "Perhaps it is something in the air?"

That something was Victor, of course, and they both knew

it. Nathaniel smiled at her, offering a glimpse of the carefree boy he used to be. When she stood, he suddenly lurched forward, wrapping his arm around her leg in a hug.

"You're not leaving us, are you?" he asked.

She put a hand atop his head.

"That's not up to me."

Hardly the answer he was looking for, and Zusa chastised herself for such carelessness. Nathaniel had done nothing to earn her ire, and he was clearly handling the changes no better than she. The boy deserved far better. They both did.

"Hey, listen," she said, kneeling back down and putting her hands on his shoulders. "No matter what, I will never leave you. I'll never abandon you, Nathaniel. No matter what happens between me and your mother, you'll never be alone. Do you understand?"

He nodded and sniffled a bit.

"I do," he said, and he squirmed as if embarrassed.

"Good."

She kissed his forehead, then stood.

"Have you had anything to eat yet?" he asked. "I'm on my way to get something from the kitchen. You could . . . you could come with me."

Zusa smiled at him as she gestured to her clothes.

"Perhaps soon," she said. "But I must change first. Do you know where your mother is?"

"In her room." Nathaniel shuffled his feet. "She doesn't come out much. I don't think she's very happy."

Zusa let Nathaniel go before continuing down the hall.

"It seems no one is," she said, whispering so the boy would not hear.

At the grand doors to Alyssa's bedroom, Zusa paused. There were no guards, nor any servants waiting for orders. Had they been dismissed? And if so...by whom? Shaking her head, Zusa knocked twice, then leaned against the door, her forehead touching the sturdy oak.

"Yes?" she heard Alyssa say from within.

For a moment Zusa almost left. She remembered their fight, the painful dismissal, the implication she was nothing more than a servant...

"It's me," she said, memories be damned. Even if Alyssa refused, she was coming in.

"It's not locked."

That was enough for Zusa. She slipped inside, then shut the door behind her. Alyssa lay in the center of her bed, the curtains to her windows both raised, flooding the room with light. In one of those beams she lay, her red hair shining vibrant, her pale skin beautiful. Tainting the image were her missing eyes, the glass fakes still in a jar on a bedside table. Light spilled into those open cavities, the sight of veins and tissue enough to spoil whatever radiance Alyssa emitted. Zusa felt an ache in her heart, and she forced herself to move, ignoring Alyssa and instead going to the enormous closet and flinging it open.

"What are you looking for?" Alyssa asked, sitting up on the bed.

"Clothes."

Zusa pushed deeper into the closet, pulling open drawers, scanning the various shirts. She needed something practical, and of sturdier fabric than the silky things Alyssa had collected or inherited over time.

"What of your wrappings?" she heard Alyssa ask from behind her. Glancing back, she saw that Alyssa had left the bed and was coming to join her.

"I'll wear them no more."

Alyssa hesitated.

"Is there a particular reason?" she asked.

Zusa found a gray shirt and pulled it from the drawer. She told herself to stop caring about their last meeting. She told herself not to bother with Alyssa's affairs, whom she married, whom she trusted. She told herself not to be upset.

It didn't help.

"Yes," she said. "But I'd rather not speak of it."

Even in the best of circumstances, discussing Daverik's death would have been difficult. Worse would have been trying to explain why she'd continued wearing her wrappings after turning her back on Karak and his faceless, to explain it was her way of keeping the memory of her sisters alive, by flaunting her body in the clothing once meant to hide and shame it.

"Zusa," Alyssa said, taking another step closer. "We must talk. Last night…"

"Where do you keep your servants' clothes?" Zusa interrupted.

"Servants?" Alyssa asked. "Why?"

"Because you have only dresses to wear, and I need breeches that will not tear and rip after a single night upon the rooftops." And then, because she could not help it: "And if I'm merely a servant to you, it seems appropriate I dress like one, even if it is like the men instead of the women."

"Stop it, you know that isn't fair."

Zusa spun to find Alyssa blocking her way out of the closet. The woman faced her with those empty eye sockets, and it seemed they conveyed her anger and frustration far better than any glass ones possibly could.

"Fair?" asked Zusa. "I didn't know *fair* meant anything in this world, particularly yours. Now please, let me through."

"You're upset, I understand," Alyssa said. "Please, let me help."

"If you want to help," Zusa said, slipping past her and heading toward the bedroom door, "then procure me a handful of silver coins."

"Silver? For what?"

Zusa paused at the door.

"For my nine years of loyal service," she said. "I'd think myself at least worth that much."

She left, but it seemed Alyssa would not be so easily brushed aside. She followed her into the hall, her left hand touching the wall with each step.

"Zusa, stop," she said. "Stop, or I will have my guards make you."

Zusa did, turning and glaring at a servant who stood in the doorway of a nearby guest room with her mouth open.

"Give your mistress privacy," Zusa said, slamming the door shut. Before her fingers left the door handle, Alyssa's hand closed around hers, clutching her with intense strength.

"Zusa, enough of this," Alyssa said. "If you're angry, then tell me. If you're hurt, then tell me. Don't do this. Don't lash out like a child."

First a servant, then a child, thought Zusa, and she laughed despite her pain. *Can it get any worse?*

"If you want us to talk, then we shall talk," Zusa said. "But not here. Come with me. I still need to get dressed."

Left hand holding Alyssa's, she went down the hall to one of the servants' quarters. Barging in, she found several occupying the room, two playing a game of cards, the rest relaxing from duties they'd no doubt performed overnight.

"Leave us," Zusa said as she let go of Alyssa's hand and walked through the rows of double-bunk beds to four dressers stacked side by side.

"Please," Alyssa added as the others turned to her. "It will only be a moment."

The servants were wise enough, or trained well enough, to not ask questions, and they quickly filed out, the last one shutting the door behind him. As Zusa began pulling open drawers, Alyssa came up behind her.

"You're upset I likened you to a servant," she said. "I'm not a fool. I can tell that much."

Finding a pair of dark-gray breeches, no doubt for a man, Zusa held them to her waist. The length looked good, just a tiny bit too long, but it'd be easy enough to roll them at the ankle. Tossing them on a nearby bed, along with her shirt, she started searching for a belt. She found several, all thin and designed to hold up nothing heavier than the pants below. Ignoring Alyssa, she went to the door and yanked it open, not at all surprised to find two of Victor's guards lurking outside. The servants had likely summoned them the moment they left.

"Fetch me a sword belt," she told one. "Alyssa's orders. Find the smallest one you have."

She shut the door before they could protest. That done, she removed her cloak, set it atop the bed with the rest, and then began stripping down.

"It's not that you likened me to a servant," Zusa said as Alyssa stood in the center of the room, waiting for a response. "It's that you say it only because Victor demands it of you."

"Is that what this is about, my betrothal to Victor?" Alyssa took a step closer. "Or that you think I am putting him above you?"

Now naked, Zusa pulled the shirt over her head, pleasantly surprised by its looseness. Given Alyssa's smaller size, she'd thought it'd be tight, but the shirt must not have been originally hers.

"You *are* putting him above me," she said. "And even worse, putting him as your equal. You're a lady of the Trifect, Alyssa. He should be groveling at your feet for the privilege of entering your family's bloodline."

She pulled on the pants, and they were as long as she'd feared. Sitting down on the bed, she began folding them, forming small, tight rectangles along the bottoms.

"Don't act as if this is about me," Alyssa said, crossing her arms over her chest. "This isn't about my reputation, or my legacy as a member of the Trifect. It's something far more selfish than that. Tell me what bothers you, Zusa. Let me hear it so we can move on, and you return to the mansion like you belong."

"You wish to know what I want?" Zusa asked. She stood and crossed the room so she could grab Alyssa's hands. "I want you to trust me. End your betrothal to Victor, and banish his men from your mansion. Trust me to protect you. Trust me to keep Nathaniel safe, and to ensure no one dares interfere with his inheritance. You need no one else. Trust *me*, Alyssa. Trust me to be at your side...always and forever. Is that so wrong of me to desire? Is it really so selfish a request?"

"Always and forever?"

It seemed all the air was sucked from the room. Alyssa's hand reached up, and softly she trailed a finger along Zusa's face, trembling only when her fingertip brushed a tear that drifted down her cheek.

"I would have you nowhere else," she said. "But what you want, it *is* wrong, because I don't think you can, Zusa. It's too much for your shoulders to bear alone. Right now I ask that you trust me to know what I'm doing, and that what we do is best."

"Yes," said Zusa, bitterness in every word, "because your judgment in men has never once been in error."

It was a hateful thing to say, and she knew it. So did Alyssa.

"Perhaps not just in men," Alyssa said, and she pulled her hand back and clutched it into a fist.

Apologize, now, thought Zusa. *Before the wound is too deep.*

But the hurt moved both ways, and it gave her an easy stubbornness to rely upon. Biting her tongue, she returned to the door and opened it. On the other side, looking confused, was one of the house soldiers. In his hand he held several sword belts.

"I pray these are sufficient?" the man asked.

Zusa grabbed the smallest one, shut the door, and then began looping it about her waist. It also had been designed for a man, and she had to use a dagger to pierce a hole in the leather so she could cinch it tight enough. That done, she brushed past Alyssa into a closet, found a pair of boots, and pulled them on. Meanwhile Alyssa said nothing, only stood listening to her prepare. She resembled an animal in waiting, poised to strike. When Zusa tried to pass her for her cloak, Alyssa reached out, grabbing her by the shoulder and clutching her tight.

"Stop," she said. "Please, just stop. I cannot do this. I won't. I'm sorry I can't trust you like I should, Zusa, but doing so would only get you killed. To let that happen...for years I've asked everything of you. For once, let me spare you that burden. Veldaren is crumbling, and while I am bound to its destruction, I will not carry you down with me. Victor is but a flailing fool, the thinnest hope in a world where I truly believe there is none. If his plans fail, let him be the one to suffer, and I at his side. But not you, and not Nathaniel."

"You don't need to do this," Zusa insisted. "Leave Veldaren. Put this damn place behind you, and let us build a life in Riverrun, or Angelport. We don't need Victor to find happiness. Just you, Nathaniel...and me."

Alyssa closed her eyelids, head tilting, frown growing.

"A wonderful dream," she said. "But just that, a dream. I won't flee from this. It's not in me to do so. Whatever legacy I carry with me to my grave, I would rather it be one of blood than of cowardice."

That was it, then. Zusa didn't know what else to say. She felt her heart breaking, felt the friend she'd rescued from a damp dark cell suddenly becoming a woman who knew only death and hopelessness.

"I love you, Alyssa," she said. "Does that not matter?"

Alyssa took a step back, eyelids still closed. For a moment she debated her words, a long, interminable moment for Zusa.

"In a different lifetime, a better lifetime, it would matter," she said, so softly, so carefully. "But not this one."

Zusa grabbed her daggers off the nearby bed and jammed them into her belt. She clasped the cloak around her neck and shoulders, and it folded about her, a meager comfort to the aching cold she felt spreading throughout her chest.

"How do you look?" Alyssa asked.

Zusa glanced to her gray shirt, her dark pants and boots, and the cloak wrapped about her.

"Like him," she said.

Alyssa needed no more explanation than that.

"There are worse you could resemble," she said.

A strong need to cover her face overcame Zusa. For once she felt she understood why the Watcher kept his features in shadow. The intimidation was useful, but being able to hide, to become something different from yourself to escape the hurt and turmoil . . .

A knock on the door, and then in stepped Victor without waiting for an answer. If he was taken aback by Zusa's new outfit, he hid it well.

"I was told you'd returned," he said. "I'm glad. I've been wishing to speak with you."

"If this is about me obeying your orders, you can stop," Zusa said. "Once Alyssa pays me, I am leaving."

Victor stayed in the center of the doorway, denying her the possibility of an easy exit. There was a look on his handsome face she couldn't quite read, something dangerous in his blue eyes that told her she should get out before he spoke another word.

"Actually, it is a far more delicate matter I'd have us discuss." He glanced to Alyssa. "Assuming you two have a moment, of course."

"Go ahead," Alyssa said, sitting down on one of the servants' beds. "Zusa was just finding herself some new clothes."

"Ones with less blood on them, I see," said Victor, glancing at the pile near Zusa's feet. Something about it seemed to mildly amuse him.

"If you have something to discuss, then let's discuss it," Zusa said, having no patience for trivialities. She wanted out. She wanted away from Alyssa and the hurt tearing into her gut.

"Very well. I've been thinking of ways for us to strike at the Sun Guild without letting our resistance be known. If Muzien brings his entire wrath down upon us, we'll be crushed in a night. Difficult as it will be, we must outwit him, and use his own tricks and secrecy against him until we know exactly when and where to attack."

"What does this have to do with me?" Zusa asked.

Victor crossed his arms, any remnants of a smile on his face quickly vanishing.

"We want you to infiltrate the Sun Guild as our spy."

"We?" Zusa asked, nearly laughing at the ludicrousness of it. So much for Alyssa keeping Zusa free from her perceived downfall of the city. So much for relying on Victor to save her from the dark corners of Veldaren that they'd have her infiltrate.

"It wasn't my idea," Alyssa said, and her neck flushed red.

"There's no reason it would fail," Victor insisted. "Muzien will have no reason to know who you are, nor of your allegiance to Alyssa."

"Unless he's looked into her past," Zusa argued.

"And knows what? A woman in wrappings once guarded Alyssa? You'll be anything but to them, Zusa. You'll be a pretty face that knows how to kill. I daresay you'll fit right in."

It was crazy. She almost pushed past Victor, then decided it might be better to move to a corner of the room where the shadows were deepest. Diving in, she could reappear outside the mansion, be free of them forever. But to leave Alyssa helpless, to leave her and Nathaniel's lives in that oaf Victor's hands...

"You don't have to do this," Alyssa said, interrupting her thoughts. "I don't want you to."

And that was it, enough to change her mind. In the end, Zusa was more stubborn than she realized.

"I'll do it," she said.

Victor's smile blossomed anew.

"Excellent," he said. "Once we discover where he sleeps, where he eats, where his men stay...we'll find a weakness and exploit it. When Muzien's dead, the entire Sun Guild will come crashing down, ending their threat to us once and for all. Who knows, perhaps you'll be able to kill him yourself, Zusa, should he let his guard down in your presence."

"I think you underestimate the danger of our foe."

The man shook his head.

"Or you underestimate your own skill. This will work. I'm sure of it."

Zusa was far less convinced, but her word was given.

"Very well," she said. "Come tomorrow, I will find a recruiter for the Suns and make myself known to them. Once I have, any contact between us will be done solely at my discretion. Is that understood?"

"Perfectly," said Victor.

Zusa lowered her voice as she slipped past Victor.

"I die, or Muzien dies," she whispered. "Either way you win, don't you, Victor?"

His smile was his only answer, but it was answer enough.

CHAPTER 3

Thren Felhorn was on his way to the graveyard when he spotted two members of the Sun behind one of Muzien's new whorehouses bickering with one another over the body of a prostitute. It was too dark for Thren to make out whether or not she lived, but the men were clearly debating who would get the first turn.

"Fuck off," said one to the other. "If you're so worried about where my cock's been, choose yourself a different hole."

Thren's hand drifted to his side, where his short sword remained hidden by a long ratty coat he'd stolen. Every remnant of his former guild he'd tossed aside, for Muzien had declared a death penalty on his head, and being recognized was the last thing he needed. His hair he hid beneath a flattened cap, his face behind the high collar of his coat. His shambling walk was that of a drunk, his downcast eyes that of a man who'd spent a life beaten and trodden upon. No one would think him burdened with money or respect. To those two behind the whorehouse, he'd be a mark at best, or a bit of fun at worst.

But given Thren's sour mood, and the two's secluded location, a bit of fun seemed like a fine idea.

"If you can't decide, I'll take the girl so neither of you have her first," he said, leaving the road. The two men snapped their heads about, glaring. The one on the left reached for a blade but didn't draw it yet.

"This one's paid for," said the man on the right. He was handsome enough, with long dark hair, and Thren knew he could have found himself a pretty lass by lingering around the various taverns throughout the city. No, he wanted the violence. Glancing down, he saw the woman did indeed still breathe. By the end of things, Thren doubted she would. His instincts told him the man wanted her to do a bit of screaming first. The other man, however, was ugly enough it'd take a stunning personality for a woman to overlook. Given the way he kept leering down at the unconscious whore, Thren found that highly unlikely.

"Have you now?" Thren asked. "Mind if I ask your lady friend if you're telling the truth?"

They both drew their weapons, the ugly one purposefully pulling down his shirt to reveal the four-pointed star tattooed onto his neck. As if that would intimidate him.

"Get lost if you want to live," the man said.

Thren held his hands out wide, making it seem as if he were unarmed.

"Come make me," he said, grinning.

The ugly one acted first, pulling a dirk from his belt and slashing at Thren's face. Such a simple, basic attack, one a child might use if handed a blade. Thren leaned back, the edge just barely missing his nose, and then shot forward, grabbing the man's arm with his right hand and ramming down on it with his left elbow. The man screamed. Bone snapped. Twisting his arm, Thren elbowed the man in the face, splattering blood from his shattered nose. A kick to the groin weakened his stance, allowing Thren to pull the ugly one to the side, shoving him in the way of his companion's desperate thrust of his short sword.

A scream punctuated the blade's entry to the man's belly, coupled with Thren's mocking laughter.

He violently shoved the dying man into the other. Entangled and unable to pull free his blade, the man let it go and drew a dagger instead. Again Thren held his hands out, showing himself unarmed.

"You can still run," he said.

"You'll just stab me in the back."

Thren grinned.

"You're right."

The frightened man suddenly leaped forward, trying to shove the dagger into Thren's chest. In a single smooth motion, Thren drew his short sword from his waist, parried aside the thrust, and then buried his blade in the man's chest. Momentum carried him forward, pushing the tip out his back. The man let out a gasp, blood gushing from his mouth. Smile fading, Thren twisted the blade, then kicked the dead man off it. Cleaning the blood on the man's shirt, he looked to the prostitute. The woman was awake, a dazed look on her face, no doubt the lingering effects of the blow that had knocked her out. Thren knelt before her, helping her to sit up against the wall of the whorehouse.

"Thank you," she muttered, causing Thren to shake his head.

"Do you serve him loyally?" he asked her.

The woman frowned, and she held her head as she grimaced against a wave of pain.

"I don't...what do you mean?"

Thren pulled a slender dagger from his belt and pressed it against the soft skin of her neck. Her eyes widened, her confusion replaced with fear.

"Muzien," he told her. "The Darkhand bastard. Do you serve him loyally?"

Hardness overtook her features, a toughness earned by the life she led.

"I lie about how much I earn," she said. "Why else would I be out here instead of inside?"

Thren smiled, and he put away the dagger.

"This city needs more like you," he said. "Have a pleasant night, milady."

He dipped his head in respect and then returned to the road. The woman glared, not that he cared. Saving her had been for amusement, and nothing more. A pleasant diversion before a meeting he could only wish would be as pleasant, or as productive. When it came to Deathmask and his Ash Guild, the only consistency was in knowing he'd leave annoyed and in a foul mood. Still, in a city so thoroughly conquered by the Darkhand, any ally could mean the difference between life and death.

Digging his hands into the pockets of his coat, he lowered his head, put his gaze to the ground, and hurried toward his destination. Into the wealthy eastern district of Veldaren he went, gradually drifting south. At one point every towering home, with its sharp rooftop and fenced property lines, had belonged to his Spider Guild. The owners had delivered a small but consistent sum each month to keep their homes free of fire and vandalism. Now only a single marking dominated them all, the symbol of the Sun carved into stone tiles. To many they were signs of allegiance, but to Thren they carried a far more dire meaning. They were signs of death, and while the Sun might have been carved into them, it was the Spider who controlled their fate.

His hand brushed the amulet around his neck through his shirt, felt its presence. It was both comforting and terrifying having it there. Terrifying, for a single touch coupled with a single word could level all of Veldaren to the ground. Comforting, for he was the one who possessed it, and no one else.

At last he arrived at the tall iron fence that surrounded the cemetery. When Thren had made his initial rounds through the city, trying to take account of all the changes that had occurred in his absence, he'd gone to the Ash Guild's former headquarters. While he was there, one of the guild's few members, Veliana, had spotted him. She'd said nothing, only hurled him a note tied to a dagger: *Roseborn Cemetery, Gemcroft tomb*, it'd said. Thren passed by that cemetery now, looking for any who might be watching from windows or rooftops. When he saw none, he abruptly turned around and dashed through the open gates. The soft dirt sank beneath his feet as he hurried toward the larger crypts in the heart of the cemetery. He went to one in particular, and as he entered the tomb marked with the Gemcroft family name, it put a smile on his face.

"First I try to kill you when you're but a little girl, and then I keep you alive while in the guise of my son," he said, thinking back to mostly better times, and his interactions with Alyssa Gemcroft. "At least you kept things interesting. More than I can say for your father."

A childish notion of vandalizing Maynard's coffin came to him, and he dismissed it with a shake of his head. Thren's scheming had brought about the Bloody Kensgold and the attack on Maynard's mansion that had driven an arrow through his chest. To mock him in death, after killing him in life, was beneath Thren.

But not, apparently, beneath Deathmask.

The coffins were placed into holes carved into the stone walls, the names of their owners cut into tiles and then nailed above them. When Thren came upon Maynard's, he found the coffin open and removed from its hole. Maynard's body, a desiccated corpse that was mostly bones, hair, and a thin black layer of what had once been flesh and organs, stood in the center of his open coffin. One hand was above his head, the other curled before him as if clutching a dancing partner. Without a sound, Maynard's corpse dipped to one side, turned, dipped again. Thren watched, baffled, torn between amusement and disgust. Maynard Gemcroft was dancing, quite slowly and poorly, in his own grave.

"Like what I've done with the place?" asked Deathmask, appearing from the deeper darkness of the crypt. The man wore dark-red robes, his usual gray mask and cloud of ash missing. It'd been a year since they last met. How much older the man looked, and how tired, was shocking. Even his dark skin appeared paler than usual, and his long black hair was stringy and wet.

"You have a strange sense of entertainment," Thren said, gesturing to the dancing corpse. "I didn't know you held animosity toward Maynard."

"Oh, him?" asked Deathmask. "No, no animosity. His corpse was the freshest, that's all. These are the things one does to pass the time when forced into hiding for far too long."

"I'd say there's a simple enough solution to that," Thren said. "Stop hiding."

Deathmask leaned against the stone wall, and he laughed.

"Ever the blunt, simple one," he said. "Of course you'd never hide. So proud, so mighty. Except you don't appear to be wearing the cloak of the Spider. Why's that, Thren? Is it because, perhaps, you know it'd be suicide to openly flaunt your opposition to the Darkhand? But surely that's not it. That'd make your mocking my hiding both arrogant and hypocritical, something you've *never* been in your sordid history."

"I have little patience for sarcasm," Thren said.

"And I for pointless pride. If you wish for us to talk, then let's talk, but keep your comments to yourself if you won't acknowledge reality. I know more about the state of this city than you do, and trust me, it isn't pretty."

Thren had to hold back his grin.

Oh, I know one secret you don't, he thought, arms crossed over his chest, fingers casually brushing the hidden amulet.

"Very well," Thren said. "I sought you out for a reason, one you can likely guess. I seek an alliance between us, one that shall last until Muzien hangs from the city wall by his entrails."

"A noble pursuit," Deathmask said, drumming his fingers atop another coffin. "But I fail to see how you will help me. What exactly do you bring to such an alliance?"

"I bring my name, my reputation, and all who would seek to overthrow Muzien and return to the better days of old."

"Ah yes, those better days…" Deathmask ceased drumming and instead began to pace back and forth beside the dancing corpse. "That's the tricky point, Thren. You see, the past few years have been rather lean for most. You may remember the glory days during the height of the war with the Trifect, but what's going to stick in the minds of any you try to recruit will be the recent years of peace you forged, and the dwindling coin that entered each of their hands."

Thren did his best to ignore Maynard's rotted skeleton, instead meeting Deathmask's mismatched eyes and doing what he could to convey his conviction and determination. It was cold down there in the tomb, and he wanted their conversation over as fast as possible.

"We promise them an overthrowing of the old agreement," Thren said. "The destruction of the Watcher, and an end to all truces. Together we can bring anarchy back to Veldaren, and in its chaos, we will thrive."

Deathmask grinned.

"Now you have my attention. Muzien's men from the west are worthless to us. They worship him as a god, and I've learned to just leave the fanatics be. But the members who once belonged to the Wolf Guild, the Spider Guild, the Shadow and the Serpent? They're the ones who can be persuaded to turn. That's the tricky part, Thren. We have to convince them we can make a difference. We have to make them believe Muzien can be killed."

Thren thought of the many training sessions he'd had with his former master. He had never once won any spar, any competition. Deep down, he wondered if the elf actually could be beaten, but he kept those cowardly words to himself.

"He can be killed," he said instead. "But it won't be easy. What is it you suggest?"

Deathmask put a hand on Maynard's corpse and whispered something Thren could not make out. The corpse turned, bowed to Deathmask, and then changed dances so that it swayed from side to side, arms limp, head rolling.

"Killing Muzien will be impossible until we strip him of his followers," Deathmask said. "But there are other ways to show he isn't the inhuman god he's made himself out to be. His second-in-command, a man named Ridley, would be a fine example. Capture him, execute him in a very public, very gruesome manner, and we'll have made our point."

Thren drew his sword, and before Deathmask could react, he lopped off Maynard's head. To his disgust, the corpse continued to dance, even with the head lying behind it in the coffin.

"Make it stop," he said, sheathing his blade. "I'm tired of looking at it."

"If you insist."

Instead of seeming bothered by the demand, Deathmask only looked amused. He snapped his fingers, and the body collapsed instantly.

"If we kill Ridley, we'll make our opposition known," Thren said. "He won't take kindly to it. I've heard what Muzien did in the marketplace a few weeks back. If he thinks he's losing the city, what will stop him from performing a similar spectacle?"

Deathmask's grin spread wider.

"That's the point," he said. "I *want* him to try another spectacle. When he does such things, he's elevating himself above us mere mortals to declare himself superior. If we knock him down at that exact moment, if we toss egg on his face and mud on his clothes, it'll show the entire city that Muzien isn't perfect. He can be mocked. He can be stopped. He can be killed. After that, we let this city descend into anarchy. We'll set fire to the businesses most loyal to Muzien, we'll burn down the buildings where his men sleep, and we'll execute anyone willing to wear the pointed star. Chaos, Thren, it all comes down to chaos. Make it terrible enough, and even the king will realize he has to make a choice. When it comes to who he fears most, you or Muzien, well…"

"If forced to make a choice, the king will act against the elf instead of me," Thren said. "In the end, I'm human, and Muzien's not. That alone will suffice. But what you're suggesting is going to take more men than we have. How do we recruit without giving ourselves away, or bringing in traitors who will turn us over to Muzien?"

"We do it by being careful, and selective," Deathmask said. "And I have already made an...unusual ally, whose name I'd rather keep to myself for now. This ally alone grants us many men who know how to use the sharp end of a sword. The question is, what of you, Thren? Is there someone you trust to aid you in taking down that blasted elf?"

Thren thought of the various members of his guild, and he shook his head remembering how one of his most trusted, Martin, had likely turned on him within a day of his return to Veldaren. No, there was no one he could trust without doubt. He'd led by fear, and now that Muzien ruled, there was no way he could inspire fear so thoroughly that the Darkhand held no sway.

Of course, outside his Spider Guild, there was one who could be a powerful ally, one whom Thren could trust to never work with Muzien.

"Only one," he said, pulling his coat tighter about him. "But he's the only one that will matter. We'll bring the Watcher into this war, Deathmask, and we'll make sure he's on our side. Once we do, even the most loyal of lapdogs will start to wonder if they made a mistake."

Deathmask rubbed his chin as he mused aloud.

"Interesting," he said. "But the Watcher's always had his own rules and code. Compared to Muzien, he's predictable, he's safe. Do you think he can inspire the fear we need?"

Thren felt excitement building in his chest at the idea of him and his son facing off against his former master.

"It doesn't matter," he said. "Whoever the Watcher was, he's different now. Faced with the loss of his city, he'll become who he needs to be to win it back."

Deathmask bowed low.

"Then consider him your recruit," he said. "I doubt your success, but I'm eager to see your results nonetheless."

After hesitating, Thren extended his hand to the strange man.

"Allies," Deathmask said, clasping his wrist and shaking it.

"Allies."

"This city isn't lost to us yet," Deathmask said as Thren turned and walked toward the crypt's exit. "Not if we revel in chaos so great and wild only we know how to endure the dance. If the Watcher's to join us in it, he better learn to embrace the darker side of things."

"Trust me," Thren said, quickening his step as he ran plans through his mind. "At our side, he'll become the killer we need."

That, and more, thought Thren as he stepped out into the graveyard and gazed upon the rooftops his son called home.

The killer he was always meant to be.

CHAPTER

 4

Haern awoke in his room to the thoroughly unpleasant sight of Tarlak hovering over him, arms crossed, pointy hat tilted to one side. A grin was on the wizard's face, and that just made everything worse.

"You could knock on the door to wake me, you know," Haern muttered.

"My tower, my rules. Time to rise and shine."

"I'd rather sleep."

Tarlak let out a snort.

"You've had four hours, that's plenty. Antonil sent us a messenger requesting our presence, and it seemed urgent."

Haern let out a sigh. He should have known the guard captain would attempt to take matters into his own hands after learning of the threat that'd been smuggled into the city right under his nose. But if Antonil wanted to talk to them, then talk they would. In all reality, Antonil was one of the very few good people left.

"Fine," he said. "Let me change, and then we'll go."

Tarlak clapped his hands, then paused, as if confused.

"You have more than one outfit?"

"Out, wizard, or I swear to Ashhur I will cut off your beard and shove it down your damn throat."

"Fine, fine," Tarlak said, exiting the room and shutting the door behind him. From the other side, still audible as he descended the stairs, the wizard's rant continued. "Someone needs to start sleeping more and skulking rooftops less, I swear."

"Couldn't agree more," Haern said, sliding out of his bed and beginning to disrobe.

Five minutes later he exited the stairs to the bottom floor to find Tarlak sitting in his favorite chair beside a dormant fireplace, wineglass in hand.

"Is Delysia coming with us?" Haern asked, and he felt slightly awkward in doing so.

"She's already in the city with Brug," Tarlak said, finishing the last of his sparkling clear drink and then making the glass vanish with a snap of his fingers. Hopping up from the seat, a bundle of energy that inspired a mixture of annoyance and rage inside Haern, the wizard hurried to the door. "Hoping to see what the priests of Ashhur can make of those tiles, since their sworn enemy had a hand in making them. I've already sent Del a whisper spell telling them to meet us when they're done."

Haern nodded. He had yet to talk to her since returning, and was hardly looking forward to it.

"All right then," said Tarlak. "Let's go."

According to Tarlak, Antonil's messenger had requested that they meet him in the far south of the city, just off the main road. After stopping by a stall so Haern could buy something to eat, they made their way south. With Haern in his cloaks and Tarlak in his yellow robes, they were an easy pair to spot, earning themselves plenty of strange glances from those they passed.

"You'd think they'd never seen the color yellow before," the wizard mused after a woman glared at the two.

"The people here must endure the guilds, the thieves, and the corrupt guards of the city, all to scrape together enough to afford their daily bread," Haern said. "You, however, can summon yourself a glass of wine with the snap of your fingers. I don't think it is the color yellow they dislike."

"Aren't you cheery this morning?" Tarlak said, thrusting his shoulders back so he stood taller as they walked.

Before Haern could retort, he spotted Antonil waiting in the center of the road, a trio of soldiers with him. He looked calm enough, his demeanor belying whatever urgency the messenger had insisted upon. Tarlak saw the man too, and he straightened up his hat and then quickened his step so that he could greet Antonil first.

"I'm glad you're here," Antonil said, seeing the two approach and stepping forward to offer his hand. "You two have my thanks for coming so quickly."

"Your thanks is hardly what I'm doing this for, but I'll accept it nonetheless," Tarlak said, shaking the soldier's hand. "Care to share what you needed us for?"

Antonil ignored him, instead nodding curtly to Haern.

"It's good to see you in the daylight for once," he said.

"It's hardly the safest for either of us," Haern said. "I pray this is important?"

"It is," Antonil said, gesturing to his left, where a dead-end street was blocked off by multiple city guards. "There's one of the Sun Guild's tiles in the center of the street. Since Tarlak can't work on the tiles without the risk of hurting innocents, I've done you the favor of removing everyone along the entire street."

"I doubt those living there were too happy about that," Haern said.

"True, they'd probably be happier dead," Antonil said, "but I'm willing to endure their angry words. I've got soldiers posted all about the area, and if anyone tries sneaking in to watch, they'll let us know. You have your privacy, Tarlak, and a reasonably safe environment. This is the best I can do. The rest is up to you. Do you think you can find a way to render the magic within them harmless?"

Tarlak cracked his knuckles, and he offered the guard captain a smile Haern immediately knew was fake.

"I'm willing to try," he said. "Beyond that, no promises."

As Tarlak strolled down the street to where the tile was buried, Haern found a spot of shade against one of the dilapidated homes and nestled into it, pulling his hood low over his face.

"Not sure why I have to be here," he shouted to Tarlak as the wizard knelt in the center of the street, his back to him.

"Emotional support," Tarlak shouted back. "That, and in case someone doesn't like what I'm doing, you're here to save me. I'm sure Antonil's soldiers are fine men, but they're no match for someone like Muzien."

Haern wasn't sure he considered himself a match for Muzien either. He hadn't told Tarlak of his meeting with Antonil the night before, and he didn't feel like doing so now. Sleep sounded wonderful, and while Haern didn't think he could, at the least he could shut his eyes and do his best to relax. The empty street was eerily quiet, with just the soft whisper of a wind that had picked up over the past two days, plus Tarlak's occasional mutters and curses as he examined the tile. Time drifted along, and twice Haern had to shift his weight to remain comfortable.

"Anything yet?" he asked Tarlak.

"I'm not sure."

The wizard sat on his rump before the tile, chin resting in the palms of his hands. Though Haern couldn't see his face, he had a feeling Tarlak was drilling holes into the tile with his eyes.

"What do you mean?" Haern asked. "It's magical. You know how to manipulate magic. Just...remove whatever's on it."

Tarlak slowly turned his head, giving Haern the worst glare he'd ever seen in his life.

"Just remove it?" he asked. "Is that it? Is it really that easy? Thank you, Mister Stabby Sword Man, for telling me how to do my job. I'd have *never* figured that out without your help. If you would, though, please humor me. Have you ever picked a lock? Imagine doing that, except instead of using thin strips of metal, you only have a piece of string, a chicken bone, and a rock the size of your head. Oh, and the lock is surrounded by mirrors, and if you accidentally break one of the mirrors, you get the privilege of dying in a great fiery explosion. Just remove whatever's on it? Praise Ashhur for sending us your brilliance and wisdom."

When he was finally done ranting, Haern offered him his biggest grin.

"Happy to help," he said.

Haern wondered which was more likely to explode in the next few minutes, Tarlak or the tile he was working on. So far, his gut said the wizard.

"I see I haven't missed much," Delysia interrupted, and the two men turned to see her passing between Antonil and his soldiers to join them. She looked radiant in her white priestess robes, though her face lacked any of the humor her words implied.

"Come, have a seat," Haern said, tapping the dirt beside him. "Where'd Brug run off to?"

"To use his words, 'I'd rather find something to eat than get blown up by that fool wizard,'" she said, smoothing out her dress and then sitting down next to Haern. "Though his language was a bit more...colorful."

Haern laughed, glad for something to smile about to hide his unease. The last he'd talked to her, Ghost had been dying before him. Having her so close, acting as if nothing were wrong, nothing troubling between them...could it be so? Might they put behind them the horrible trials they'd endured on the road to the Stronghold? Much as he wished that were true, he knew it wouldn't be that easy. Things rarely were.

"Did you learn anything from the priests?" he asked, trying to keep the conversation going, and on anything other than themselves.

"I spoke with Calan himself," Delysia said, shaking her head. "The magic upon the tiles is incredibly powerful. Worse, they were specifically warded against Ashhur's faithful. Given the seriousness of the matter, he's pledged the aid of the temple in any way we need it, but when it comes to removing their danger, they cannot help us."

Haern tapped at his lips with his fingers, thinking. The priests of Ashhur were powerful allies indeed. If he could find a way to turn them against the Sun Guild, perhaps...

"Well, I'm glad I'm not the only one who thinks these things are difficult," Tarlak said, wiping at his eyes. "Gods damn it, this is giving me a headache. What I'd give to shake the hand of whoever came up with such clever protections."

"Thren killed him, remember?" Haern said.

"Right. Well. Shake the hand of his corpse, and then burn it to a cinder. He's equally deserving of both, the bastard."

The wizard stood, popping his back and letting out loud groans. His pointy hat fell from his head, and muttering, Tarlak swept it off the ground and put it back on. As he did, he paused, staring at the tile as if seeing it for the first time.

"You said it was warded against Ashhur's followers, right? I think I can spot that inscription. If I can, I wonder..."

He knelt before the tile again, putting his fingers on the edge.

"Discover something?" Haern asked.

"Divine magic is not my specialty, but I'm thinking if I can remove that specific protection against Ashhur's priests so they can take a crack at this instead, just maybe..."

He ignored them for a moment to instead begin whispering the soft, peculiar words of magic. A silver light shone around his hands, the edges of it creeping down into the tile like a living mist. Beside Haern, Delysia straightened up, the worry plain on her face.

"Tar?" she said.

Tarlak whispered a few more incantations, then abruptly halted.

"Oh fuck."

The tile cracked, Haern caught the briefest flash of lightning, and then the shock wave hit him, stealing his breath away. The sound was intense, like the roar of a lion larger than the city itself. Haern had thought himself far enough away, but in the split second the purple fire blasted toward him, he knew he'd made a grave error. When it rolled across his body, he felt no heat, only pressure, and an ache in his ears. No burns. The fire vanished, and when Haern looked down, he saw Delysia clutching his hand, white light shimmering from her fingers.

"Tarlak!" Delysia screamed, and after such an eruption, her voice sounded so thin, so hollow. She let Haern go to dash toward the crater in the center of the street, and she wasn't alone. Soldiers from up the road came running, Antonil in the lead. Haern rose to his feet, lost his balance, struggled to stand again. His head ached, his eyes still filled with the afterimage of the explosion, and his stomach was performing loops. Delysia had protected him from the flames, he knew, but the blast had struck him in a way he couldn't quite understand, leaving him sick and dazed. Fighting through it, he staggered after Delysia while offering a desperate prayer for his idiot wizard friend.

Fires burned on either side of the street, adding a rumble to the cries of the soldiers and Delysia. Haern stumbled into the crater, which contained patches of dwindling purple fire that billowed smoke. At the sight of Tarlak sitting on his rump, hat in his hands, Haern let out a breath he hadn't known he'd been holding. The wizard's eyes were wide, and he looked like he'd taken a few punches to the face, but other than random burnt spots on his yellow robes, he appeared no worse for wear.

"Least I knew what was coming this time," Tarlak said as Delysia threw her arms around him. The wizard looked past Haern, let out a grunt. "Someone should do something about those fires before they spread."

"My men are already on it," Antonil said from the crater's edge. The soldier's face was locked in a frown so stiff it looked made of iron. "And is it safe to say you've made no progress?"

With Delysia's help Tarlak stood, and he leaned on her heavily.

"Quite the opposite," he said, and despite his obvious dizziness, he smiled at the guard captain. "I've learned a *second* way to make these things explode."

Antonil certainly saw no humor in the situation, and without responding he turned to take charge of the cleanup.

"Come on," Haern said, taking Tarlak by the arm and shifting his weight onto him and off Delysia. "You might not have been burned, but you're not well. That much is obvious."

Through the patches of smoke they led him, then farther down the street so they could be away from the commotion of the scrambling soldiers. Tarlak more collapsed than sat when they stopped in the middle, and he let out a loud groan.

"Had protections against fire on me from the beginning," he said, and he touched his stomach as if in pain. "Guess I should have put on a few more. Felt like I was hit with a brick when that damn thing went off."

Haern looked back to the crater and the burning homes and suppressed a shudder. Tarlak had told him what the tiles did, but seeing it...seeing was something else entirely. Over three hundred of those tiles were scattered throughout the city. Should they be activated at once, the only thing that'd remain would be the greatest common grave in the entire history of Dezrel. A chill ran up Haern's spine at the horrid thought, and he did his best to push it away. Dwelling on such things would only paralyze him into inaction.

"Sit still," Delysia said, putting her hands on either side of her brother's face. "Let me see if I can help."

She closed her eyes and began to pray. White light surrounded her hands, flashing briefly before sinking into Tarlak's skin. When she was done, the wizard did appear more together mentally, and he kissed his sister on the cheek.

"Thanks, Sis," he said, earning himself a smile.

As Tarlak put his hat back on, he looked to where the tile had been, and Haern brought his attention to it as well.

"It doesn't make sense," Tarlak said. "If Muzien wants to destroy Veldaren, why hasn't he done so already?"

"How do you know it's Muzien?" Delysia asked.

"He's the one who smuggled them in, and it's his guild's symbol on their front," Haern said.

"But Luther, a priest of Karak, helped make them," she countered. "And don't forget, Thren was the last to see Luther alive."

"Perhaps," said Tarlak, "but Luther's dead, and he's not giving us any answers as to why he did it. If Thren has the key, why hasn't he said or done something about it? They're Muzien's tiles, and it makes sense that he's the one holding the key. Question is, what does he want? Maybe they're his backup plan in case someone defeats him."

"He does seem like one to hold an entire city hostage," Haern said. "That might be why no one's heard anything of these tiles. With Muzien's takeover progressing so smoothly, he's had no reason to need them. That might change if we directly challenge him."

Tarlak stood, brushing dirt and ash off his yellow robes.

"Then if we do challenge him, we need to do it before he knows he's in danger," Tarlak said. "Killing him in his sleep sounds like the best plan to me. Give him no chance to activate these tiles, however it is he does it." He turned Haern's way. "Question is, are you capable of finding out where he sleeps? Where he eats? Where he might be vulnerable in any way?"

Haern thought of how he'd been guided into an alley to fight a member of the Sun Guild for Muzien's amusement, thought of how easily he'd been defeated in a direct fight. Muzien, the ruthless killer...vulnerable?

"I don't know," Haern said. "The elf is a legend for a reason, Tar. What you ask for may not be possible."

Tarlak shook his head.

"You damn well better try," he said. "Right now, we've got little else to go on. Whatever hope we have, it's resting on you."

The wizard stormed off, yelling for soldiers to clear the way from the homes so he could douse the fires with his magic. Frustrated at his fears being so callously dismissed, Haern turned to leave, but Delysia reached out and caught his wrist.

"Haern," she said. "Please, we should talk."

He glanced to her, saw her resolve, and knew he could not bear to challenge it at that moment.

"I'm sorry," he said. "I buried Ghost's body as you asked. Other than that, I'm not sure I'm ready to talk about it."

His words cut into her. True to her nature, she refused to let it show.

"I see," she said. "Then let me say my own piece until you are ready. I'm sorry, Haern. About your father, and you...I never should have said it."

The remembrance only added guilt to his already shaken mind. *Your father would be so proud*, she'd said. Comparing him. Condemning him. He pulled his hand free of her, slowly, not wanting to offend her or hurt her more than he already had. She was waiting for him to respond, and he saw the hope in her eyes that her apology would shake him free.

"I'm sorry, Del," he said, this time his voice far softer. "I really am sorry. Beyond that, I have nothing to say."

She brushed a hand across his forehead, pushing a bit of blond hair away from his face.

"Well, when you do have something to say, I'll be waiting for you."

She went to kiss his cheek, but when she did, the image of Zusa climbing on top of him flashed in Haern's mind, and he turned his face away.

"I need to sleep," he said, feeling a sudden surge of guilt. "Tonight will be a long, long night."

She watched him leave past Tarlak, past the burning homes, past the crater left by Muzien's tile on his way back to the Eschaton Tower. She said nothing, but he heard her voice anyway, chasing after him in his mind.

Back when the city had been ruled by the various guilds, if Haern wanted to find a member of the Serpent Guild, he went to the Serpent Guild's territory. As he crouched in the rooftop corner of an inn, listening to the boisterous laughter within, he pulled his hood lower over his face and frowned. Now, though? Now the whole damn city was Muzien's. Where was he to even start?

Inside were several members of the Sun Guild he'd stalked to the inn under the cover of night. They gathered on the second floor, in a large common room where they sat playing cards at a table. Near them was the window Haern hung above, easily listening in. The men and women were loud, they were drunk, and they'd said not a damn thing useful the whole hour he'd been there.

"Patience, Haern," he told himself as he rolled onto his back and thumped his head against the rooftop. "You're not going to solve this riddle in a day."

Haern had been convinced one of them was a higher-ranking member of the Sun Guild, and hoped an overheard conversation would give him what he needed. It appeared not to be. If he wanted information, it'd involve the edge of a blade and a bit of blood. Killing them might alert Muzien that someone hunted him, but deep down Haern knew it'd been naïve to hope he could discover the elf's location without cutting a few throats.

Rolling onto his knees, Haern drew one of his swords and crouched before the rooftop's edge. The window was just barely large enough for him to fit through, though he'd need to shatter it thoroughly to not get stuck. Grabbing the edge with his free hand, he prepared to jump, then froze. A creak of wood behind him, that of someone landing on the rooftop. Pretending he hadn't heard, Haern lowered more, as if tensing for an assault on the room below, then spun, drawing his other blade and holding them out in a defensive formation. Instead of an assault, he found a painfully familiar figure standing on the other side of the inn's rooftop, arms crossed over his chest.

"I hope you weren't thinking of torturing those six down there for information," Thren Felhorn said, shaking his head in disappointment.

"Why's that?"

"Because it'd be a waste of time. None of them are beyond the second rank. At best, you'll find where they've stashed a haul of crimleaf or stolen goods. Nothing truly valuable."

Haern slowly lowered his sabers, though his fingers still gripped the handles tightly. The faintest of scars marked his chin where his father had cut him the last time they met. *We're all murderers*, Thren had said. *Some just better than others*. It was the clearest window into his father's soul he'd ever had, and it made his heart ache as much as it enraged him. Seeing Thren on the rooftop with him, disappointed as usual, face passive and bored as if nothing between them existed, did little to help matters.

"Why are you here?" Haern asked. "What is it you want?"

Thren tilted his head to one side, as if analyzing an animal.

"I want your help."

Haern didn't know whether to laugh or cry.

"Is that so?"

"It is. The city has changed in our absence, as I'm sure you've discovered. The Sun Guild rules, but that rule cannot last. Veldaren was my city once, and it needs to become that again."

"You'd have me help restore you to power?" Haern asked. Even for his father, this seemed too audacious.

"I'd have you prevent the destruction of the entire city by the tiles Luther created."

Haern froze, and Thren smiled at his surprise.

"What do you know?" Haern asked, hoping to glean some information from his father, information he'd refused to share at their last meeting.

"I know what Luther told me," Thren said. "I know the destruction those tiles are capable of, and I know who currently holds the amulet to activate them."

"Muzien."

Thren nodded.

"A wise guess. Which fate would you choose for this city, Watcher? To thrive in my hands, or collapse into rubble and flame? Muzien was my teacher once. I know how he thinks, how he plans, and what he's capable of. Work with me. Together, we can bring that elf low."

"An alliance," Haern said, and he felt a knot forming in the center of his chest. "Because it worked so well when we went after Luther."

"Together we entered, and together we left," Thren said with a shrug. "Karak's paladins died, not us."

Thren was conveniently leaving out Delysia's role in the events, as well as Thren's betrayal in between the arrival and the escape, but Haern knew he still had a point. If there was anyone who might know of a chink in Muzien's armor, it was Thren. Much as he disliked the idea of working with him again, he knew of no better way.

"I'll aid you only in killing Muzien," Haern said. "Nothing else. I won't help you reform the Spider Guild, nor attack other guilds."

"As if I needed your help in such matters," Thren said. "It's Muzien, and only Muzien, who surpasses my own skill. I fear no one else, not even you. Together we will return Veldaren to the world we both know and rule."

Haern tried to ignore how such language made the knot in his stomach worse.

"I want to make this perfectly clear," he said. "I'm with you only to save this city from the threat of the tiles, nothing else. The moment I feel you're leading me on for your own agenda, I'm on my own. Got it?"

Thren looked merely amused at his insistence.

"Of course," he said.

"Good," Haern said, and he sheathed his swords. "So let's get started. If those below us are worthless, then where do we actually start?"

Thren grinned.

"I don't know where Muzien is, but there is someone we can find who I believe will. His name is Ridley, Muzien's right-hand man when it comes to affairs in Veldaren..."

CHAPTER

5

Zusa walked through the dark streets, doing her best to ignore the tiny worm of nervousness swimming around in her belly. She'd endured the strength of the underworld a thousand times before; becoming part of it should prove no more daunting, nor dangerous. Finding a member of the Sun Guild was hardly difficult. Someone who might be able to induct her? That was a different matter. She needed someone she could impress, someone who would put her in a position of significant worth instead of on her back in a brothel or picking people's pockets in the marketplace.

To her right she passed two men quietly talking with one another at the entrance of an alley, one of them holding a dim lantern. Their clothes were new, and they bore the mark of the Sun Guild on their breasts. No good, thought Zusa. She needed to find men and women from Mordeina, members of the Sun who would have no idea who she was. Zusa very rarely interacted with the guilds, but after so many years protecting Alyssa, there was still the odd chance someone might recognize her face despite the rather drastic change in her clothing.

Continuing, she kept her head up and eyes alert. Should anyone spot her, the confidence in her posture would do wonders to keep her safe. Thugs sought out downcast gazes and hunched shoulders, not those who moved without fear of their surroundings. She spotted another group, this of three, but one of them had a spider tattoo across the center of his face. Telling herself to remain patient, she shifted east, toward where the houses were finer and the streets more evenly paved.

At last she spotted a group of three huddled under a lamp, laughing and joking with one another. Their clothes were worn, their left ears decorated with several rings, and most importantly, all three sported the wide-brimmed hats currently in fashion in Mordan. They were selling something illicit, crimleaf most likely. Zusa strode up to the three, and their laughter died as they spotted her approach.

"Which guild did you used to belong to, sweetheart?" said the biggest of the three, a burly man with a dark-gray beard. He alone appeared armed, with a long sword strapped to his waist. Appearances were deceiving with the others, of course. Zusa had no doubt they kept slender daggers hidden somewhere on their persons.

"No guilds," Zusa said. "But I am hoping for the Sun Guild to be my first."

More snickering. The middle man gestured to Zusa's daggers. "Are you any good with those?"

"I wouldn't wear them if I wasn't."

The bearded man crossed his arms, and while the others appeared amused, he looked mildly interested.

"Show me," he said.

Before the man could draw his own sword, Zusa's dagger was at his throat. For good measure she pointed the other toward the snickering man, the sharp tip an inch from poking into his stomach. All three swore.

"Not bad," said the bearded man. "And gods damn are you fast. What's your name, girl?"

"I'm no girl."

"My apologies. Your name, milady?"

There was an edge of sarcasm to his voice, but at least Zusa was making progress.

"Are you capable of bringing me into the guild?" she asked, pulling back her daggers and jamming them into her belt.

"No, I'm not."

Her turn to smirk.

"Then you don't get to know my name," she said. Deciding that being quick might not be enough, she chose to use another weapon in her arsenal. She locked her gaze on the bearded man, letting a soft smile spread across her lips. When she spoke next, she curled her fingers around the man's face and delicately drifted them down to his neck. "But I wouldn't mind knowing yours."

"And why's that?" he asked, eyebrow lifting.

She leaned in closer, opened her lips so that her warm breath softly blew against his ear, but then pulled back instead of whispering. Her eyes flicked away, just for a moment. Flirty, risky. As if he intimidated her the tiniest bit.

"No reason," she said, flashing him a smile while tilting her head to one side.

His sudden laugh sounded hearty and honest.

"The name's Hal," he said. "And you've certainly made this night an interesting one." He turned to the quiet man who'd said nothing, only watched. "Alex, take our mystery woman to see Ridley."

"You think it's a good idea?" Alex asked, then, turning to her, "I mean no offense, of course."

"I'm sure none is taken," said the bearded man. "And yes, I do think it's a good idea. Our little woman here seems capable with both blade and beauty. Ridley should appreciate us sending him such a fine recruit."

Alex shrugged.

"Your call, not mine. You can take the heat if she wastes Ridley's time."

Zusa smiled at him as sweetly as she could.

"Would you be my escort, dear sir?"

It earned her a laugh, and shaking his head, Alex turned up the street and led her north.

"You can cut the act," he said. "I'm not the one you need to impress."

Zusa's smile faded, and she dropped the flirtatious tone.

"And I take it Ridley is?" she asked.

"Ridley's as high up as you may ever meet," Alex said, running a hand through his long brown hair as he talked. "Impress him and you're set. Claim all you want you've never been with a guild, but the way you dress and carry yourself says otherwise. Don't worry. It don't matter who you used to be with. I was a member of the Serpents before Muzien arrived. Thankfully he's shown no bad blood toward anyone, regardless of who they once served, not even the old Spider Guild members. So if Ridley asks you who you once worked with, just tell him the truth. It'll be better for you in the long run, all right? Telling lies is a good way to find yourself facedown in a ditch somewhere, choking on your own tongue."

"I'll keep it in mind," Zusa said, walking alongside him.

She could only guess where Alex was taking her. Along the way she debated whether to use an alias when she met with

Ridley. To the bulk of the city, Zusa did not exist. She was an oddity to those who worked in the Gemcroft mansion, and only a few, like Victor, knew how dangerous she truly was. For Muzien to know about her, he'd have to have looked extensively into Alyssa's history. In some ways he seemed like someone who would do that, but on the other hand, if the elf did not think of Alyssa as a threat, he might not have done but the most cursory of digging.

Of course, if he'd done extensive research, he might recognize her on sight, making her name of little relevance when he could just look upon her face.

Alex took her to a nondescript home, stopping before its unguarded door. The front had a single window, and through its dirty glass she saw the light of a candle burning within, obscured by the thick curtain blocking the entirety of the window. Above the door, small but finely cut, was the symbol of the Sun Guild. Despite the lack of any lamps or torches, the symbol seemed to shine in the moonlight. Alex knocked on the door, waited a few seconds, then knocked several more times. When the door cracked open, he stepped back and bowed his head in respect.

"Someone wishing to join the guild," Alex said to whoever was within.

"Send him to the recruiters," said a rough voice within. "It's their job, not mine."

"It's a her," Alex said, and there was no hiding the sudden nervousness in his voice. "And she's ... unusual. I figured it best you meet her."

The door swung all the way open, and out stepped a stocky man with short hair and pockmarks on his face. He glanced Zusa up and down, seemingly unimpressed.

"Ridley," he said, not offering his hand.

"And I am Zusa. I wish to become a member of the Sun Guild."

"Why us?" Ridley asked.

"Because there is no one else, not anymore."

The man cracked a half-smile. Leaning back against his door, he crossed his arms and seemed to regard her a second time. Beside her Alex fidgeted, clearly uncomfortable and wishing to leave.

"In that you're correct," Ridley said finally. "And we did it through sacrifice and determination. We did it shedding blood, not through luck and laziness. If you accept the symbol of the Sun, you're devoting your entire life to our cause. Every breath of air you take into your lungs, every beat of your heart in your chest, it is done to further the servitude to the whole. Members of the Sun will become your family, your friends, your entire reason for existing. If you are willing to embrace our teachings, if you are willing to bleed for us, and die for us, then you will share in the tremendous wealth and power we wield, wealth and power that grow every single day. Is this something you're still interested in joining?"

It was bondage, Zusa realized, a unique form of it, perhaps, but bondage nonetheless. The chains were made of gold and blood, and they would have her enter it willingly, but that mattered little in the end. She had a feeling Karak would be proud.

"I am," she said, standing tall and meeting Ridley's eye when she answered.

Ridley scratched the side of his face, clucked his tongue.

"Alex says you're special," he said. "Prove it. Kill him."

Alex paled.

"Wait, what did—"

No hesitation. No second thoughts. To show humanity or

hesitation would only betray her. She drew her dagger and cut across Alex's throat before he could try to defend himself. As the blood flowed, Zusa slid to the side, avoiding its spray. To the ground Alex dropped, clutching at his throat as he made noises that might have been attempts at words. Zusa refused to look at him, instead watching Ridley. If the man held the slightest sympathy, he did not show it. A special kind of monster, Zusa realized, but when she looked to the body she felt no remorse, either. How different from him could she truly pretend to be?

"You've killed before," Ridley said, tilting his head to one side, analyzing her, judging her. "Did you belong to one of the former guilds here, or are you a mercenary?"

"A mercenary," Zusa lied. "From Angelport. I've come here for work, and for coin. The Sun Guild seems the perfect fit."

"You are a killer then? Not a thief of coin but of blood?"

It might take her down a dark road, but she knew it best suited her skills.

"I am," she said.

"So be it. Follow me. Your test isn't over just yet."

Without waiting for a response, he left his home, assuming it was his home, and began backtracking along the route Alex and Zusa had taken. He walked with a purpose, and a distant dread built in Zusa as she anticipated the reason. Behind them Alex's body remained, though she had a feeling members of the Sun would deal with it shortly...which meant Ridley's home was being watched at all times.

Back to that lamplit street corner they went, halting a hundred feet away. The remaining two men saw Ridley and Zusa approaching, and they stood up straighter, with Hal nodding in greeting.

"Your speed is great," Ridley said, softly at first so only she could hear. "But let's see how you handle a more prepared enemy. Todd! Hal! This woman comes for your life. Defend yourselves!"

Zusa drew her daggers as the two men readied their blades. Hal looked calm, but Todd reckless and angry. Instead of rushing them she slowly approached, each step measured. She wanted to frighten them with her certainty. She wanted to unnerve them with her lack of fear. Taking a cue from Haern, she leaned forward, letting her cloak wrap about her. Halfway between them she crouched down, tensing the muscles in her legs in anticipation of her charge.

"Is Alex dead, too?" Hal asked as he held his sword with both hands.

"He is," said Zusa.

"Then it's on my head. You better kill me, girl, or I'm taking every bit of my guilt out on your corpse."

Zusa smiled.

"Consider it done."

She burst into movement, a charge at Todd instead of Hal. Fear was in the smaller man's eyes. There'd be no competition, no dance, no risk of his plunging a blade in her back with a coward's bravery. Just a quick death. Todd swung at her, as did his fellow rogue, but Zusa rolled to one side, recovered her footing, and then lunged. Her daggers found purchase, plunging through Todd's ribs. Driving the weapons harder into him, she pushed him back, then retreated when Hal's long sword slashed for her neck. She twirled so she could set her feet and reposition her blades. In came the bearded man's thrust, but he'd rushed the attack in hopes of catching her unprepared.

With a simple twist and shift of her left arm, she parried the attack wide. Having overextended himself, there was nothing he could do, not compared to Zusa's speed. A step, a thrust, and to the street he dropped, blood gushing from the hole she'd opened in his chest. Steeling her heart against his cries, she stood above the dying man with her daggers in her hands. Despite the sudden fight, despite her pounding heart, they did not tremble.

Behind her Ridley clapped.

"Well done," he said. "Not even a challenge, I daresay. You will be a fine addition to our guild."

Zusa watched the man die, saw the life leave his eyes as he breathed his last. He was scum, she told herself. Just a foe worthy of death. The lives she saved by bringing Muzien to justice easily outweighed a few dead guild rats. Easy, cruel words, and she repeated them in her head so no guilt might dare surface within her breast.

"They broke the rules," Ridley said, coming up beside her and seeing how she focused on the dead man. "If you were an assassin, they'd have brought you right to my doorstep instead of a recruiter's. For such a mistake, they deserved death."

"Even though I'm not an assassin?" she asked.

Ridley grinned at her.

"Oh, you're an assassin, just our assassin now. Besides, I wanted to see how well you killed men you'd spoken with. So far, so good. Come with me. It's time to make your entrance official and get you your star."

Back north they walked, again leaving the bodies where they lay. *Is all of Veldaren their personal burial ground?* thought Zusa grimly.

At first she thought they were going back to Ridley's home, but instead he veered west, through a row of carefully lit stores. At the far end he stopped and gestured at the door of what seemed a simple little shop. With a gentle push, the door cracked open.

"Through here," he said. "Know that once you enter, your life is sworn to the Sun."

She brushed past him, pushed the door open all the way to reveal an empty, dark space. After a single step, the floor creaking beneath her foot, a sharp, brutal pain struck the back of her head. The world spun, she was falling, and then came only darkness.

When Zusa awoke she sat upright in a wooden chair. Her arms were bound behind her back, the rope about her wrists looping up and around her neck before trailing back down to bind her ankles as well. The moment she struggled she felt the knots tighten, choking off her breath. Gasping, she tried to relax and take in her surroundings, not that there was much to see. She was in a pitch-black room, without window or lantern for light. If there was anyone else with her, she could not hear them. The back of her head throbbed where she'd been struck. If that was the worst of it, she considered herself lucky. She was fully clothed, which was a relief, though her daggers were missing.

"Damn it," she muttered, throat feeling raw. She'd made a mistake, but could still recover. They'd left her alive, and in darkness. With shadows being doorways for her, she could be free in moments. However, not killing her meant one of two things. They wanted either to torture her, or to question her. If she remained, and endured the questioning, her task might not yet be a failure...

"I see you're awake," said a man's voice in the darkness. Zusa froze, frightened, but only temporarily.

Calm down, she told herself. *You still have this under control. Keep your head, and play along with their game.*

"I hope I didn't keep you waiting long," Zusa told her captor.

A lantern burst alight directly above her head, bathing her in a dull yellow glow. It took all of Zusa's concentration not to swear, and she hid her panic in the general discomfort of the sudden brightness. With the lantern so close, the darkness was gone, the shadows she could use as doorways distant. From what she could see, her chair was in the center of a grand room, for the light did not reach a single wall. At best, she might be able to roll the chair into the darker recesses, but doing so would leave her horribly vulnerable.

Blinking away the colored spots in her vision, she looked to her captor, who stood opposite her with arms crossed. His left hand was black, his ears scarred along the tops. His face, while youthful, was sharp and angular, his blue eyes full of curiosity. There was only one man who might be before her. More correctly, one elf.

"Muzien," Zusa said.

"Indeed," Muzien said, eyes sparkling. "Ridley told me your name was Zusa, though I have plenty of reasons to doubt its authenticity. Would you care to tell me your real name?"

"Zusa is my real name."

Muzien smirked.

"Is that so? Let's find out for certain."

He drew a blade from his belt, and with slow, almost casual ease, he put the sharpened edge to her throat, teasing her skin as it slid up and down. His face was mere inches away, eyes boring into hers.

"I've had many, many years to practice and learn," he said. His breath smelled like mint leaves, Zusa realized. She didn't know why it unnerved her, but it did. "I know how to read a man's, or woman's, reactions. The way the eyes dilate. The way they look to their feet, or twitch their fingers, or stress the wrong word when trying so very hard to insist they never lie.

There's many more, of course, and a definite art to picking out the lies. Informed intuition, you might say. So let me ask you again, woman...what is your name?"

She refused to look away, and she didn't dare dwell on her own reactions. The more she tried to ensure her hands remained still, or her face expressionless, the more likely she'd come across as unnatural. Her entire body was a mask, she told herself. *Pretend you are in your wrappings. All he will see is your eyes, and you know how to control a man with them.*

"My name is Zusa," she said.

"Did you ever carry a name before that one, Zusa?"

It was a needle to her heart, but she answered anyway.

"Before I was Zusa, my name was Katherine."

"Katherine," Muzien said, tilting his head from side to side. She felt like a piece of meat before him. "Katherine, what a beautiful name, far more so than Zusa. So tell me, Katherine, who are you spying for?"

Her immediate instinct was to deny it, and she forced it down. Play the game, she had to play the game.

"Just a spy?" she asked. "How do you know I'm not here to kill you?"

Muzien paused, just long enough for Zusa to know she'd won him over.

"A person of your skill does not simply appear," he said, stepping back and pulling the blade from her throat. "Ridley assured me you could kill the finest of my men with those daggers of yours. That impresses me, Katherine. More importantly, it means I should have heard of you by now, yet I don't believe I have. Would you care to explain why?"

The opening was there, so simple and perfect it almost made Zusa smile. Almost.

"Because no one was to know of my existence," she said. "I

was a faceless of Karak, trained to be my god's blade in the night."

The elf turned and walked to the edge of the lantern's reach, not once taking his eyes off her. Beyond her sight he grabbed a wooden chair similar to hers, carried it back, and set it down in front of her.

"You *were* a servant?" Muzien asked as he took a seat. "Are you no longer?"

"Cut these ropes off of me," Zusa said. "Only then will I give you my answer."

"You're still in a rather precarious position to issue demands."

"It's a condition, not a demand. Cut my throat if you wish, but you still won't get my answer. That only comes when the ropes are off."

The elf smiled at her.

"You're a rare flower, aren't you?"

"Those who know me would say I'm more thorns than flower."

Muzien rose, and after two quick cuts, the ropes fell slack. Zusa pulled her arms free, rubbed a sore stretch on her neck. As the elf sat back down, she straightened in her chair and tried to settle on the right words to detail her past in the temple.

"I was once a priestess," she said, figuring to start from the beginning. "We were under strict orders to have no physical contact with the opposite sex, especially fellow members of the temple. I broke that rule, and because of that I was forced to become a member of the faceless."

"There are no faceless in Mordeina," Muzien said. "Who, or what, are you?"

"We were Karak's shameful, forced to wear dark strips of cloth across our entire bodies, hiding even our eyes with thin white silk. Every day was a penance, our bodies a thing of sin, our killings our atonement. We were trained to move through darkness, and to remain unseen when we wished it so. The wealthy in good standing with the temple could pay for our services, bringing death to their enemies. The only difference between us and you was that the coin we earned for our killings went to our god instead of our pockets."

Muzien chuckled.

"There are more differences between you and me than just that," he said. "But this imprisonment to your god...how long ago did you escape it?"

This was tougher to answer, and she almost lied. Still, pretending she had just left Karak's temple would involve too many potential chances to be found out.

"Nine years," she said. "I escaped them nine years ago. As far as I know, they believe I'm dead."

It was strange how excited the elf seemed to become. His eyes were wider, his smile brighter. Eager, she realized. Learning of her loathing of her god made him eager to hear more, and to join in himself.

"To repress your sexuality is unnatural," he said, rising to his feet and beginning to pace. "What sin is there in your fornication? Your pitifully short-lived race would have already died out long ago without it. But Karak wants control, doesn't he? He wants defeated men, twisted, bent, heads down, eyes to the ground. What the gods call humility, I call slavery. What the gods call worship, I call indulging vanity. They're no different from each other, none of them, no matter what their followers insist. In the end the gods want puppets who will willingly hand over their strings, begging to be made to dance. So tell me, Katherine, deep down in your heart, are you still one of their dancers?"

Zusa rose to her feet, and she pulled her shoulders back wide and stood tall.

"I will never bow to Karak again," she said. "And my name is Zusa. Katherine died years ago when those priests lashed her naked and bleeding body."

Muzien's darkened hand flexed, unflexed.

"You are a stunning beauty," he said. "I cannot wait to witness your blades in action."

Just when Zusa was finally ready to relax, to let out the breath it seemed she'd been holding since she awoke in that room, Muzien suddenly exploded in motion. An elbow slammed into her stomach, a fist into her cheek. A kick dropped to her to one knee, and she let out a pained cry as she heard the ringing of metal. Muzien's hand was on her throat, his sword pressed against her gut. His speed, his fluidity of movement...it was incredible. In a mere heartbeat he'd shown her how easily he could defeat her. Despite the sudden violence, when he spoke there was no anger in his voice, just simple truth.

"You're skilled in many things, and lies may be one of them," he said. "I don't believe you have come to me for work. Perhaps Karak sent you to investigate me, or a lord of the Trifect to spy upon me, or a former thief guild to assassinate me. Whatever the reason, I do not care. Cast it off, Zusa. Free yourself of your old life, and embrace the light that has come to Veldaren. If you remain loyal, I can make you a queen. Imagine wielding power unmatched, and possessing wealth beyond anything you were ever promised. Your new life began the moment you awoke in this room. All else before is shadow and smoke, so let it fade into nothing, let yourself embrace my call. Loyalty, Zusa. That's all I ask, and I shall reward it in return, freeing you from the chains Karak placed upon your life the moment he deemed you faceless."

Zusa's jaw clenched tight, and she could not hold back her glare.

"If I must bow to you, how am I any freer than when I bowed to Karak?" she asked.

The hand left her throat, the sword her belly. Muzien's words were ice in her veins, his voice strong as iron, terrifying as fire, seductive as wine.

"I'll never want you broken. I'll never want you as a fool, or with your true self hidden behind white cloth and black lies. The world is a joke, and so we laugh in the face of its delusions. Freedom comes from truth, truth I would have you see with your eyes, profess with your lips, and embrace with the edge of your blades. Forget Karak, my dear Zusa. I am your god now."

A chill swept over her, shockingly powerful. Zusa bowed her head and closed her eyes, and as she felt Muzien place his hand lovingly upon her, she found herself wishing for the comparative safety and sanity of Karak's vile temple.

CHAPTER

6

Morning was an hour away when Ridley finally came home. They'd waited for what felt like the entire night, and several times Haern had questioned the accuracy of Thren's information.

"It's a trustworthy source," Thren had said as the two of them crouched atop the roof, waiting for Ridley to return home. They'd already broken inside through the upper floor's window, verifying the house's emptiness.

"And who is that source?" Haern had asked.

Thren shrugged.

"I'm not sure telling you would help."

Hardly what Haern had wanted to hear.

"If we're waiting, I'd like to know whose word is keeping me here."

"Fine. It's Deathmask."

Haern didn't bother hiding his surprise.

"You're right," he said. "It doesn't."

"Just remember, you're not the only one who wants Muzien gone," Thren had said, and he'd left it at that. Now, as Ridley approached, his marked face matching the given description, Haern crouched lower as they peered off the rooftop. Beside him, Thren tapped his shoulder, then motioned for him to remain still. Haern nodded in response. They'd wait until Ridley was inside, then sneak in after him. There'd be no chance of witnesses, plus they could more easily limit his avenues of escape.

Ridley himself seemed in a jovial mood as he stepped off the road toward his door. Reaching into his pocket, he pulled out a key, put it to the keyhole, and then paused. Haern felt his heart skip a beat, and he frowned. Had they been spotted? Surely not. The two were practically legends at remaining unseen. Hands drifting down to the handle of his swords, Haern wondered if there was some defense mechanism they'd failed to account for. They'd come through the window of the second floor, so no thin string or hair on the door could be broken, no prints left in the dirt. Yet as Ridley stepped back, looked straight up to the rooftop, and then smiled, Haern knew their ambush was blown.

"How?" Thren whispered beside him.

As Haern prepared to move, he saw that Ridley wasn't grinning at them, not exactly. The man's eyes flitted left, right, almost as if . . .

Haern rolled to one side, then shoved to his feet. His sabers were in his hands in a flash, and his father mirrored his actions. Back-to-back, they watched as men in long dark coats landed on either side of the rooftop, the moonlight reflecting off the naked steel of their daggers and swords. An escort, Haern realized. Ridley had never spotted them, but the men tasked with keeping Ridley alive had.

"Only six?" Thren asked as the members of the Sun closed in.

"Four more than we need," said one, lifting a small hand crossbow that had been strapped to his side. Before he could fire, Haern leaped straight for him. The sudden burst of speed prompted the man into firing without aiming, and before the man's finger could even finish pulling the trigger Haern had already dropped to a roll. The bolt sailed above him, and pulling out of his roll, Haern plunged his saber deep into the man's belly. As he died, his body collapsed onto Haern, gushing blood across his hands and legs. Shoving it away, Haern flung his arms out to the sides, blocking hit after hit as two others of the Sun flanked him. Dictating the flow of the battle, Haern shifted back and forth, as dependable as the pendulum of a clock. He never let either go on the offensive, always slashing for their necks and faces so they must parry or retreat. Behind him he heard vicious collisions of steel, no doubt his father battling the other three.

The men were good, Haern had to give them that. Twice he had openings for a kill that he could not take, for the other attacker would leap to the threatened man's aid by pressing the offensive and forcing Haern's attention his way. Still, no matter how good they were, Haern was better. Pulling back to the edge of the roof, he put the two men before him, then crouched low. They'd anticipated it, of course, but he trusted his speed. Leaping forward, he spun once, spinning his cloak in a wide flourish to hide his movements. As his sabers came slicing in, the two scattered to either side, fleeing his attacks and once again putting themselves into flanking position. Haern ducked beneath a stab, parried a slash from his right, and then swore.

These men weren't just good. They were Muzien's best.

But Muzien's best or not, he was the Watcher. He couldn't let them believe they had a chance. He couldn't let the city know the gap between his skill and that of his enemies was closing. On the balls of his feet he twirled, positioning his sabers through gut reaction and the briefest glimpses from the corners of his eyes. His left hand batted aside a killing thrust, his spin continued, and then he finally managed to draw blood by slicing across the face of the other man. As the man screamed, Haern jammed his right leg into the rooftop to halt his spin, and like a midnight predator he launched himself upon his wounded prey. Sabers sinking into flesh, Haern pulled them free and turned to the other man, blocking the anticipated attack. It'd been a desperate attempt, for they both knew that one-on-one there would be no contest.

Steel sang as Haern batted away the attempted flurry of blows, then stepped forward. The two were incredibly close, their weapons awkwardly positioned, but Haern had been ready, the other man had not. His knee rammed the man's groin as he simultaneously head-butted him. Dazed and struggling to stand, the man could do little when Haern's sabers came racing in, cutting across his belly and inner thigh, spilling blood and intestines across the rooftop.

As the Sun Guild member collapsed, Haern turned to help his father. Of the original three, one was dead, the other two pressing him hard with flanking maneuvers. Haern broke into a run, hoping neither had realized the other fight had ended. He slammed into one of the men with his shoulder, then rolled to halt his momentum, coming up just shy of the rooftop's edge. His opponent was not so lucky, sailing off the side and landing headfirst in a bloody heap at the feet of a no-longer-smiling Ridley.

"You should have run," Haern told him.

Ridley turned to do just that as Haern grabbed the side of the rooftop and swung down. Reaching into his belt, he grabbed two small, slender daggers weighted for throwing. As Ridley dashed for the street, Haern hurled the first, then the second. The first he'd sent purposefully wide left, and as it whisked past, Ridley instinctively jerked to the right...and into the path of the second dagger. It sank up to the handle into the man's right leg, and with a scream he crumpled. Haern rushed to where Ridley lay, and in his haste he nearly lost his foot. Ridley rolled onto his back, lashing out with a short sword he'd drawn while Haern could not see. At the last second Haern leaped over it, landed on the other side of Ridley, spun, and then kicked him in the head as hard as he could.

The connection made an audible crack, and Haern nearly screamed at the pain it caused his foot. The weapon dropped from Ridley's limp hand, and falling to one knee, Haern put a hand on Ridley's chest to feel for a heartbeat.

"Is he dead?" Thren asked as he came up behind him. Haern glanced his way and saw him wrapping a torn piece of his cloak around his left arm. No doubt his father had finished off his final opponent, but given the amount of blood dripping down his arm, it looked like it hadn't been without cost.

"Still breathing," Haern said, gingerly rising to his feet. It felt like he'd jammed several of his toes, if not dislocating one of them as well. "We need to get him out of the open."

"We can't use his house," Thren said, finishing up tying his makeshift bandage. "Too many dead bodies lying around."

Sheathing his sabers, Haern bent down and grabbed Ridley by the arms.

"Help me," he said. "We don't have much time."

Thren grabbed the other arm, and as if carrying a drunken friend they hurried down the street, both on the lookout for other members of the Sun Guild.

"Here," Thren said after crossing several streets. They were before a home that looked like any other, perhaps on the smaller side. There was a single window at the front, covered with a thick wooden shutter.

"Where are we?" Haern asked.

"All this used to be my territory," Thren said as he let go of Ridley to kneel before the closed door. "This home here is owned by a fat merchant who cheated on his wife at one of my...well, what used to be one of my whorehouses. She left him about a year ago, and I don't think there's been a day since where he actually falls asleep in his own bed instead of a tavern or a whorehouse."

It took his father less than a minute to pick the lock, but it still felt like an eternity. Haern kept his eyes to the rooftops, alert for unwelcome visitors. Nothing. It seemed luck was now on their side. As Thren shoved open the door, Haern hefted Ridley back into his arms, dragging him inside. Given the nature of their intended conversation with Ridley, and the likely screaming that would accompany it, Haern moved on past the initial living room and to the bedroom in the back. With a grunt he plopped Ridley down onto the bed, then turned to his father, who entered the room holding his injured arm.

"Will you be all right?" Haern asked.

"I'm fine," Thren said. "Didn't tear muscle, only skin, now let's get this bastard tied up before he wakes."

Since they had no rope, they made do with the sheets on the bed, using their swords to cut ragged but usable strips. As they worked, Haern realized how easy it all was, how natural. For the third time in recent memory he would torture a man for information at the side of his father. He knew, deep down, that this should give him chills...but it didn't. Instead he felt the weight of the city upon his shoulders, the lives of hundreds of thousands who would die if Muzien's tiles erupted, blasting the city with fire and destruction. Staring down at a miserable human being like Ridley, he found it difficult to summon any empathy or guilt.

Delysia wouldn't approve, Haern thought as they waited for Ridley to return to consciousness. Then again, that seemed to be an all-too-familiar occurrence as well. He'd always used her as his guide, but perhaps she was right to say she could no longer be that for him. The world was filled with dark places, and ruled by people like Muzien. To stand against it, he had to dwell in those dark places. Still, should it really feel so satisfying to cut down the Sun Guild's men?

"He's waking," Thren said, stirring Haern from his thoughts. Drawing a dagger from his belt, Thren knelt over Ridley and put the blade to the man's face so it'd be there when he awoke. Just the flat edge, no risk of drawing blood. Haern crossed his arms, willing to let his father do the dirty work. As if emerging from below water, Ridley awoke coughing and gagging. The makeshift ropes easily held him. Thren calmly waited, showing no real hurry. Haern steeled himself against the brutality that would surely follow.

We do what must be done, Haern told himself. It felt like the words weren't for him, but the specter of Delysia he felt watching them. *That's all. What must be done. Like putting down a rabid dog, or amputating a rotting limb. Sometimes the real world has to be messy.*

"Welcome back," Thren said as Ridley opened his eyes. His gaze flicked between the two of them, and there was no hiding his panic. *Good,* thought Haern. The more the man was afraid, the easier it'd be to break him. Thren saw this as well, and a smile blossomed on his face.

"You two are dead men for this," Ridley said, putting on a brave front.

"Is that so?" Thren said. "Your leader's already condemned us, yet here we both are. Seems like Muzien might not be quite so godlike as he pretends."

Ridley swallowed hard, and Haern caught him subtly testing the limits of his bonds. They would not give, of course. Both Haern and Thren knew how to restrain a prisoner.

"What do you want from me?" Ridley asked after letting out a deep breath.

Thren removed the dagger from Ridley's face, twirled it in his hand.

"Well now, this might be easier than I hoped," he said. "Less interesting, but that's a sacrifice I'm willing to make. We want to know where Muzien sleeps, Ridley, and when."

"He's an elf," Ridley said. "He doesn't sleep."

"He does, maybe not longer than a few hours, but I know he sleeps. Tell me where, Ridley, if you want us to remain on friendly terms."

At the word *friendly* Ridley let out a short laugh, and something about the resignation in the man's voice made Haern's stomach uneasy.

"I don't know," he said.

Thren shook his head.

"Well," he said, "it looks like we may get to have some fun after all."

Before Ridley could react, Thren took the dagger, grabbed Ridley's jaw with his free hand to hold him still, and then carefully slid the dagger into the man's left eye. Ridley's entire body went rigid, his teeth clenched tight as he breathed in and out using quick, shallow gasps. He tried to shut his eyes, but that pressed his eyelids against the sharpened edges of the dagger, forcing him to leave it open, blood and tears dripping down the side of his face.

"I'm going to make this very clear," Thren said as he slowly twisted the dagger by the handle, rotating it back and forth by nearly imperceptible degrees. "The more I move this dagger, the more you'll feel the muscle and tendons holding your eye in place start to tear. Trust me when I say this will hurt very, very much. If you lie to me, I'll keep going until I finally rip the whole bloody thing out down to the stem. Tell me the truth, and answer my questions without any games or deception, and I'll push the dagger in instead. The blade will go into your brain, and you'll be free from this life and move on to whatever follows. Have I made myself clear?"

Ridley's entire body had begun to shake, and he fought it with admirable control.

"Yes," the man said, trying hard not to move his head when he spoke.

"Very well. Let's try again, shall we? Where does Muzien sleep?"

"I don't know."

Thren rotated the dagger ninety degrees. As Ridley screamed, Haern fought down his repulsion.

What must be done, he told himself, though it was now harder to believe. This time, the specter of Delysia hovering over him wasn't disappointed. It was furious.

"No lies, remember?" Thren said. Despite Ridley's screams of pain, Thren sounded calm, almost bored. "You're his second-in-command here in Veldaren, are you not?"

"Yes!"

"He trusts you more than anyone else in the Sun Guild, yes?"

"I . . . yes, yes he does."

Thren rotated the dagger ninety degrees in the opposite direction, bringing the eye back to its original position.

"Then answer me," Thren said. "Where does Muzien go to sleep? Where is he when he's most vulnerable?"

"I . . . don't . . . know!" Ridley screamed.

"Damn it, Thren, enough," Haern said, grabbing his father by the shoulder. Thren pulled free, and he glared until Haern stepped away.

"You both disappoint me," Thren said as he pulled back the dagger. The eye came with it, accompanied by a burst of blood and an audible pop. Ridley screamed, and now free of the dagger, he jerked back his head, clenching both eyelids shut. Blood and tears continued to weep. Haern watched, torn between his desire to learn what he needed to save his city, and the sheer gruesomeness of the torture the man endured. *Rabid dog*, he told himself again and again, but it no longer carried the same strength.

"You fools," Ridley said in between his gasps of pain. "I might be his second-in-command, but that means shit to someone like him. Muzien doesn't trust *anyone*. No one knows where he goes at night to rest. We don't know his routine. We don't know when he'll come to us with orders. You think he's lived as long as he has by being *predictable*? By being *trusting*? For fuck's sake, aren't you two supposed to be the greatest threat that's left to fight him? Then the city's his. Just give up already. You don't stand a chance."

When he ceased, the room filled with an angry silence. Thren stood over the bed, one hand clenched into a fist, the other clutching the dagger with the eyeball still pierced by the tip.

"Thren," Haern said, voice soft. "I think he's telling the truth."

Thren shook his head, and without a word he climbed onto the bed, straddled Ridley, and held his head once more in a vise grip.

"I've seen the loyalty Muzien inspires," Thren said, and somehow, something had changed. He seemed to glow with cold loathing. Each word dripped with disgust and hatred. "I've seen men bow to him as if he were a god. He's no different than Karak, no different than Ashhur. He wants to be worshipped as a divinity. He wants to build a legend to rival anything accomplished by humanity's hands. You've screamed and begged, Ridley, but you haven't made me believe you."

"You know nothing of him," Ridley said, panic creeping into his voice.

"I was his heir," Thren whispered, dagger slipping beneath the remaining eye. "Who's the damn fool now?"

The door to the bedroom opened, and Haern felt his heart leap in his chest. Spinning, hands falling for his sabers, he expected members of the Sun Guild. Instead he found a fat man with a receding hairline and alcohol stains on his shirt. The home's owner, Haern realized.

"...The fuck?" the man asked, eyes bloodshot, brow furrowed.

Before either could answer, Ridley flung his body forward, straining every limit of his bonds. His head snapped forward, plunging Thren's dagger deep into his other eye, burying it up to the hilt. Immediately afterward his body began to seize, head flopping up and down, arms flailing against the tied sheets.

"Gods damn it!" Thren said, ripping out the dagger. Furious, he turned to the interloper, yanked off the eyeball, and then flung the dagger across the room. It sank into the throat of the fat man, who stood there, stunned. Haern watched just as stunned, knowing he should have done something to stop it, yet he'd not. With two men now dead, the room began to stink of blood and evacuated bowels. Pulling his hood lower, Haern stepped over the homeowner's corpse.

"Time to go," he said. "It's almost morning, and there's nothing left for us here."

"You're wrong," Thren said, retrieving his dagger. "We may not have learned anything, but we're fighting a war, and must take every victory we can."

Haern turned back around, shrugged.

"Then what do you want?" he asked.

Thren glared down at Ridley's body.

"To leave a message," he said, and then he began to work.

Using the sheets of the bed, they tied his arms together and then hung him naked before the door of his home. His eyes were gone, as were his fingers, his ears, and his tongue.

Across his bare chest, carved deep into the skin, bled the symbol of the Spider.

CHAPTER 7

Muzien stormed into the guildhouse, between the guards who snapped alert in near terror, and into the main foyer. Nearly a dozen men and women stood waiting, their ears full of rings. They were his best, his brightest...what was left of them, anyway. Those whom Thren Felhorn hadn't butchered the night before.

"What do we know?" Muzien asked as they gave way, allowing him access to the large round table in the center of the well-lit room. On the table was a grand map of Veldaren, accompanied by multiple bottles of wine and ale. Muzien grabbed one, accepted a glass immediately offered by a man to his right, and poured himself a drink.

"Ridley was attacked at his home," said Haley, a woman with blond hair and fifteen rings and studs in her left ear. She was one of the few from Veldaren's old guilds to rapidly rise in rank, all fifteen kills having come after her joining the Sun

Guild. "His guards were ready for it, not that it seemed to matter. We found dead bodies all about both the rooftops and the ground below. After that, best guess is he took Ridley, dragged him to a nearby safe house, and then got to work."

Muzien glanced around to the others, and none looked eager to disagree with the assessment, or add anything of note.

"That's it?" Muzien asked. "That's all we know?"

"The spider makes it pretty clear who is responsible," said Roddick, the other recruit from Veldaren in the room, and a former member of the Spider Guild, no less. "At least, who we're supposed to think is responsible. Thren Felhorn doesn't appear to be too frightened of your threats, Muzien."

Having finished the glass, Muzien poured a second and downed it as well. It burned his throat, but it felt like appropriate punishment given his mistakes.

"I should have killed the bastard when I had him," he muttered. "Thren's pride is far too great to hand over Veldaren without a fight. Question is, did Thren do this alone, and what was he hoping to gain?"

"It's obvious what he wanted," said Haley. "He wanted to send a message."

Muzien was hardly convinced. They could have wanted information from Ridley as well, the man having had his fingers in nearly everything that transpired within the city. He let the matter drop as another of the group spoke up.

"Is Thren good enough to handle six men at once?" asked Owen, a bald man with a slight lisp. Of everyone there, he bore the most rings in his ears, at twenty-seven. Since the death of Ridley's guards, Muzien considered Owen the most competent of his men when it came to battle, with only the newcomer Zusa as a possible challenger.

"Thren would certainly say he is," Roddick said.

Muzien shook his head.

"No," he said. "Not those six. I expected someone to make an attempt on Ridley's life, and those six were the best I had. Three he could handle, four at most. Someone helped him."

"Former members of his guild?" asked Haley.

Letting out a sigh, Muzien put his hand on the map of Veldaren, analyzing it.

"Ridley's body was left hanging in the heart of what used to be the Spider Guild's territory," he said. "That wasn't an accident. He wants the rest of his guild to know he's alive and resisting. Haley's right. This was about a message, which means we must send one in return."

Muzien glanced about, checking faces as he came to his decision.

"Everyone but Haley out," he said. The men and women exchanged looks, then obeyed, heading outside or up the stairs to the various gambling rooms and private bedrooms. Standing opposite him at the table, Haley waited with her hands crossed behind her back. He could see the fear in her, the way she struggled to maintain an image of calm. Fearful, but controlled. Excellent.

"How well did you know those of the Spider Guild?" he asked her when they were alone.

"I . . ." She hesitated. "I know of many, Muzien, mostly by name, and only those with a respectable rank. Wilson Ket liked to keep track of those in power among all the other guilds, Thren's in particular."

Muzien walked to one of the far walls, on which hung a painted landscape featuring the four-pointed star. The star dominated the skyline so that no other stars might shine, and so that the light of the rising sun looked weak in comparison. Beneath was a dresser with many slender drawers, and yanking open the one on the bottom, he reached in and pulled out a book bound in fine leather. Dropping it before Haley, he opened it to the halfway mark, skimmed a few pages, and then stopped and pointed.

"Can you read?" he asked.

"Yes," she said, nodding.

"Good. Here is every addition to my guild since our arrival to Veldaren. Find me six who once belonged to the Spider Guild. The higher their former rank the better."

Haley swallowed, and he could tell she was relieved. Now knowing his ire would not be aimed at her, she pored over the pages, tapping at names. Muzien grabbed a sheet of paper from the same dresser where he'd gotten the enrollment list, and he jotted down each name Haley listed. When she was done, he added Roddick as the seventh, then went to the door of the foyer and yanked it open.

"Give this to Owen," he told the man on guard, handing over the list. "Tell him I want all seven brought here to me at once. Oh, and that Zusa woman as well. He'll know who I mean."

"Of course," the man said, bowing low and then hurrying away. Muzien slammed the door shut and caught Haley staring at him from across the room.

"Is there something you'd like to say?" he asked.

"No," she said.

"Then leave. Your part in this is over."

Haley dipped her head in respect, then left. In her absence Muzien moved about the large table in the center, pulling away several chairs and stacking them at the far wall so that only seven remained. That done, he poured himself another drink and waited. The former members of the Spider Guild, five men and two women, arrived in scattered bursts, and he greeted each one in turn with the same quiet order.

"Take a seat and say nothing," he told them. That was all.

It took nearly thirty minutes of awkward silence, worried glances, and muted coughs before the last arrived, Zusa and Roddick striding in together. Unlike the last time he'd seen her, Zusa wore a long coat instead of a cloak, and sewn onto her pale shirt was the four-pointed star.

"Have a seat, Roddick," Muzien said after ordering Owen to remain outside. "Zusa, beside me, please."

The two exchanged a look, and then obeyed. As Zusa joined him at the wall, he turned so his back was to the table, and he lowered his voice so only she might hear.

"Thren killed someone important to me," he whispered. "And for every one he takes, I will take seven from him. These are the seven. Go kill them where they sit."

He stared into her eyes with each word he spoke, watching for signs of weakness, hesitation, or refusal. Upon her hearing the order, there was none, only the slightest of nods.

"As you wish," she said. "But before I start...which of the seven should I fear most?"

The question alone improved his opinion of her immensely.

"Roddick," he said.

Zusa nodded, turned toward the table. Casually she walked toward the seven. Crossing his arms and leaning against the wall beside the painting, Muzien watched, eager to see for himself the skill Ridley had insisted Zusa wielded.

Well, he thought. *At least I shall have myself some entertainment. A shame you could not watch it with me, Ridley.*

As Zusa curled around the table, heading for Roddick, Muzien felt his anticipation building. It had been a very long time since he'd witnessed a fighter of any intriguing skill. But a former follower of Karak, taught by the dark human god how to kill? This...this had promise, and it put a small smile on his face.

The seven watched her, unsure what Muzien wanted of them and clearly wary of Zusa's role in the matter. Zusa, however, appeared unconcerned, and it wasn't until she was directly behind Roddick that her hand dropped to her waist.

"Roddick," she said, causing him to turn her way. Doing so exposed his neck, and with beautiful smoothness she drew a long dagger, sliced it across his throat, and then flipped the dagger blade-downward so she could jam it into the eye of the woman who sat beside him. Just like that, two were dead, and the others had yet to leave their seats.

Muzien's smile doubled in size.

The final five lurched to their feet, drawing short swords and daggers to defend themselves.

"Slay her and live," Muzien called out to them, wanting to ensure they gave it their all. "Flee, and you die by my hand instead of hers."

Even at their superior numbers Zusa remained undaunted. With no hesitation, no fear, she jumped onto the table, toes barely touching the wood before she pushed herself off, leaping straight at the man on the opposite side. Unprepared for the sudden assault, he lifted his blade while falling back. It accomplished nothing, Zusa flying at him like an arrow that would never miss. Her daggers slammed aside his defense, she sidestepped left, then pirouetted. Arms lashing out, she blocked a strike from the woman near her while simultaneously slicing open the jugular of the first man. Blood splashed into the air, hot and sticky as it sprayed her cheek and hair. Undeterred, she finished the pirouette with both feet planted firmly on the ground, allowing her to leap at the woman with all her strength. They collided, a tangle of steel and limbs.

To her foe it might have been chaos, but Muzien's eyes saw

the control, the way Zusa positioned her blades to ensure a killing thrust as they rolled to the floor.

The remaining three moved to surround her, a man named Renley shouting orders to the others in a frantic attempt to coordinate. This was it, Muzien knew. Zusa's advantage of surprise was lost, and the rest had positioning as well. Forming a triangle, they closed in as Zusa separated herself from the dead woman's bleeding corpse.

"Which of you three is the bravest?" Zusa asked, head constantly on a swivel.

"Don't need to be," said Renley. "Just need you to make a mistake."

Zusa smiled his way.

"You'll die last," she said.

At his smirk she dove into a roll, directly toward the table. The two men she dove between swung, their blades slashing the air above her. Shouting out cries to follow, the three rushed the table, hoping to trap her underneath. Muzien thought she might spin about, perhaps attempt to hamstring one, but instead he saw her reach the center of the table…and then fall straight into the shadowed floor, vanishing completely.

Instead of confusion, Muzien felt only elation as Zusa reappeared, falling from the very ceiling. Her opponents had no idea she'd even vanished as she came crashing down, one dagger jamming into a man's back. As he screamed, Zusa yanked it free, dashed two steps, and slammed both blades into another's chest as he turned to see the reason for the scream. He toppled, and Zusa twisted her daggers on their way out, then faced the lone survivor: Renley.

"You got anything besides tricks?" he asked, holding his short sword up in defense. "Come on. Let's see you kill at least one man face-to-face."

With no urgency, Zusa carefully stalked Renley. She feinted an attack, just a quick flinch, but enough to make Renley hop backward. Muzien laughed in open mockery of the final survivor. At the start Zusa had resembled a wild panther unleashed. Now she was a cat playing with a mouse. Zusa swung a single dagger, hitting the short sword, making its metal sing. Then came the other, back and forth, each stroke accompanied by a step forward. With every block Renley retreated, her attacks coming with such a maddeningly consistent yet rapid pace he found no chance to counter, no way to break her cycle. There were ways, of course. Muzien could list off several solutions to take control of the battle. But Renley was not Muzien.

When his back touched the wall, Renley panicked, at last attempting to counter one of the cuts during the brief window between it and the next. His sword chopped for Zusa's head, but she twisted her body, the sharpened edge swishing through the air. A step, a thrust, and Zusa's dagger plunged to the hilt in the man's chest, piercing his heart. As Renley let out a pained gasp, she put a foot on his sternum and kicked him off her weapon so he could tumble down and die.

From his wall, Muzien clapped in approval.

"A splendid display," he said.

"I do only what must be done," Zusa said, cleaning blood off her daggers using one of the dead women's coats.

"Tell me, the trick you used to vanish and reappear...you both came and went from the darkest parts of the room, where the sunlight could not reach through the windows. Is that a power Karak granted you, a way to make doorways of the darkness?"

Zusa eyed him from across the room. Her hesitance lasted but a moment before she stood and jammed her daggers into her belt.

"It is," she said, elaborating no further.

Muzien grinned at her as he thought of their first meeting.

"You could have left the chair I bound you to at any time," he said.

"Yet I didn't."

Muzien nodded.

"Indeed, you didn't. I shall remember that, Zusa."

As I shall remember your trick should you ever turn against me.

Muzien walked to the door of the guildhouse, stepping carefully around the bodies so no blood stained his boots, and opened it. Owen waited outside, back purposefully to the entrance as if he was trying to show he'd been in no way listening to the carnage within.

"Back inside," Muzien said, and Owen followed. Returning to the bodies, he gestured to the seven dead.

"Hang them somewhere public," he told Owen. "For every one Thren kills, I shall send him seven in return."

"The rest who belonged to the Spider Guild won't be happy with this," said Owen. "Getting killed for something Thren does? They won't see it as fair."

"Then they best pray that when Thren inevitably comes recruiting, they turn him in to me before anyone else might die." Muzien let out a bitter chuckle. "Fair? When in any of their miserable lives has the world been *fair*?"

As Owen left to gather men to help him carry out the order, another man entered, one of his veteran members, named Cole. He was on the shorter side, face covered with an uneven growth of blond hair.

"Muzien," he said, bowing low.

"What is it?" Muzien asked.

The man cleared his throat, and the troubled look on his face put a damper on Muzien's fragile good mood.

"We need you outside the city," he said.

"For what?"

Cole pointedly glanced to Zusa.

"I think it best that only your ears hear this for now," he said. "I assure you, Muzien, I'm not wasting your time."

That serious? Muzien let out a sigh, and he beckoned Zusa over. When she came, he took her hand and raised it to his lips.

"Thank you for a brief moment of sunshine this morning," he said, kissing her across the knuckles. "Wash the blood off you, and find yourself a change of clothes. Once you're done, see if you can hunt down Thren Felhorn for me so that these seven are the last who must die because of his stubbornness."

A quick nod was her answer, and bracing himself for more bad news, Muzien turned to Cole and gestured for him to lead the way.

"I'll explain when we're free of the city," Cole said as they shut the door to the guildhouse behind them. "I mean it when I say your ears should be the only ones hearing this."

"Your confidence in the importance of this matter is admirable," Muzien said as they walked down the main street toward the western entrance through the wall surrounding the city. "For your sake, I hope you are right."

"I think in this matter, I'd rather be wrong than right," Cole said.

Muzien raised an eyebrow.

"I'm not kind to those who waste my time."

At that, Cole let out a laugh.

"Well aware, Muzien, but when you see what I'm afraid of, I think even you will be relieved to find out I'm worrying over nothing."

Suddenly the last vestiges of his good mood from Zusa's display were gone. Cole wasn't nervous over something minor.

No, this had him worried down to the bone. Not good. Not good at all.

They kept to themselves as they neared the gate, and they passed through without inspection, the star on their clothes all that was necessary to prevent questioning. Down the well-worn dirt path they walked, putting the city behind them.

"Would you consider us alone?" Cole asked, giving one last glance around. There were a few walking the same road, but they were either several hundred feet behind and falling farther, or much too far ahead to hear anything but shouting.

"Safe enough," Muzien said. "Now tell me where we're going, and why the secrecy?"

As they crested a shallow hill, Cole pointed up ahead, to where a covered wagon remained stationary a quarter mile away.

"We were bringing in the final shipment Luther sent us," Cole began. "Was the smallest by far, just four of the tiles bearing our mark. Because of it, we loaded up some crates of crimleaf along with it before leaving Ker, hid 'em beneath stacks of wheat. Filled up the wagon pretty good, probably too much given the shitty condition that rotting piece of junk is in. Broke an axle coming down the hill, and we didn't have a replacement seeing how it was the third damn time it'd broken on the trip here. Anyway, since Veldaren was so close, we just sat tight and sent Daryl out to get us what we needed to fix it."

"All of this is fascinating," Muzien said, his patience starting to thin. "But I hope you did not bring me out here because of a broken wagon."

"Give me more credit than that, Muzien. While we were waiting, we decided to unload everything to make it easier to lift up the wagon and get it fixed. That meant dropping a couple of those tiles onto the dirt, and there they stayed for a good hour while Daryl wasted all our time haggling, no doubt hoping to pocket whatever coin he saved. Well, he came back, we fixed our wagon, and then started loading everything back up...and that's when we stumbled upon our little discovery."

Muzien didn't like where this was going in the slightest, but he asked anyway.

"Luther's tiles," he guessed. "Something's not right with them."

"That's right," Cole said. "The one that'd been pushed into the dirt by the weight of the others atop it, to be specific. We couldn't get the damn thing out. Tried prying it up, digging it out, but nothing. Wasn't budging. Lifting it was like trying to lift a boulder. Last we got ourselves a long bar of iron and jammed it underneath real good. Daryl's the biggest of all of us, so we had him give it a nice strong push."

"What happened?"

"Daryl collapsed to the ground, flopping like a fish out of water." Cole shook his head. "He didn't seem hurt too bad, just real surprised. Said it felt like his hands got stung by bees, only it went through his entire body. Wasn't but a few seconds before he was able to hold himself still. No mark on his hands, no injury that we can tell, but given the circumstances, we figured it best we go and bring you over to handle the matter yourself, all things considered."

All 337, you mean, thought Muzien, the number of tiles they'd buried throughout the city at Luther's behest.

"It may just be a simple protection," Muzien said as they approached the wagon. Three men waited there, sitting in the grass or in the back, and they hopped to their feet once Muzien was only a minute away.

"Protection?" asked Cole. "By who?"

Muzien glared at him.

"No more questions," he said, refusing to answer. Things were already spiraling out of control. The last thing he wanted was Cole's wagging tongue making it worse. Given Luther's secrecy, and how the burial of the tiles had been his only requirement for aiding the Sun Guild in taking over Veldaren, he'd known the man had ulterior motives. The question was what exactly they were. His assumption had been that the tiles bore some use against Ashhur's faithful, perhaps weakening their power or alerting Karak's priests to their presence should they pass by. That the tiles had protections built into them to prevent removal, while displeasing him, did not surprise him.

Still, now that he knew for certain magic was involved, it was time to discover what exactly those tiles might do.

"Has anything changed with the tile during Cole's absence?" Muzien asked as he stopped before the three.

"Not a thing," said the biggest of them.

"Are you Daryl?" Muzien asked.

"I am."

"Good. You still have that piece of iron?"

"That I do. You want to take a crack at it?"

Muzien shook his head.

"No, but someone else will."

Looking none too pleased, Daryl followed him around to the back of the wagon, where in the grass not far off the road was one of the tiles bearing the mark of the Sun Guild. Muzien stared at it, starting to regret ever agreeing to cooperate with Luther. At the time, invading Veldaren had looked to be an incredibly difficult task. When Grayson had died, that pushed him into agreeing with Luther's plan. Being able to smuggle in so many goods and men, all with the city guard turning a blind eye at the gates, had given him the initial foothold he'd needed. How did the placing of a few stone tiles bearing his own symbol compare to that? Easy work, and though he'd known there was more to them, he'd considered it a mild curiosity, something pertaining to gods and faith and other matters he could not care about in the slightest. But now? Now he'd get to find out how greatly he should regret that decision.

"Cole, head back to Veldaren," he said. "Find yourself some hired labor, the dimmer the better, and then bring him back here. Just one man, you understand? If anyone asks, you need help getting the wagon fixed and loaded. Oh, and procure a nice heavy sledge, too."

"Understood," said Cole.

As the man returned to the city, Muzien found himself a comfortable patch of grass a suitable distance away from the other men, lay down, and waited for Cole's return. It took over half an hour, and all the while Muzien ran through scenarios of what the tiles could do, and how he would react when he knew for certain. He could challenge Luther about it, act furious, or pretend he knew nothing at all. It depended on the game the priest played, and how that game affected him.

When Cole returned, a gargantuan of a man walked alongside him. His arms stayed in a locked position as he walked, his footsteps strangely stiff and uneven. As he walked, his eyes remained focused on the ground, his head slightly bent.

"So who is this?" Muzien asked, rising from the grass to meet the two on the road.

"Caretaker said to just call him Boy," Cole said. Boy looked up, and he smiled once in greeting. "The guy said he'll do whatever we ask so long as it don't hurt him."

"That'll work," Muzien said. Boy seemed an appropriate-enough name, for the way the big man looked about, Muzien doubted he had intelligence beyond that of a five- or six-year-old human child. "Give him the sledge."

Cole did, and leading the way, they circled around the wagon to where the tile lay buried in the grass.

"See that?" Muzien told Boy. "When I yell for you to start, I want you to break that thing into as many pieces as you can. Do you understand me?"

"Yeah, I got it," Boy said, each word slow and carefully spoken.

"Excellent."

Muzien turned and walked back toward the road. He had enough experience around magic to know that the best way to observe unknown occurrences of it was at a very, very safe distance. His hope was that it all meant nothing, and that even if the tiles were protected, it'd just break a few bones or give Boy a nasty shock. Cole followed him, hands in his pockets and a frown on his face. Meanwhile the other three lingered at the wagon, watching.

"That tile nearly knocked Daryl out," Cole said. "You sure it's a good idea doing this?"

"No, I'm not," Muzien said, turning about to watch after ensuring there were no nearby travelers on the road west. "But unless one of you four feel like volunteering, that's why we have our idiot over there doing it for us. Speaking of, tell him to start."

Cole cupped his hands to his mouth and yelled for Boy, who'd remained still as a statue before the tile, to begin. At first Boy stared at the tile for a moment, then lifted up the sledge by its long wooden handle. With a motion akin to that of chopping firewood, a task Muzien had a feeling Boy had performed many, many times, the enormous man lifted the sledge up into the air and then swung it down with all his impressive might.

The metal head cracked the tile, and with the crack came a sound like a great release of air. Silence followed, incredibly brief, and then the explosion rocked the ground. Purple flame rolled in all directions, consuming the wagon and turning the grass to ash. The loudest stroke of thunder Muzien had ever heard struck him like a physical blow to the chest. Staggering a step back, he watched with mouth open as the fire slowly dwindled, revealing an enormous crater in the earth where the tile had been. All that remained of the wagon was broken wood and scattered, burning wheat. Of Boy and the other three he saw nothing, not even bodies.

"Holy shit," Cole said, eyes wide as saucers. "Shit, shit, shit. What was that, Muzien? What the fuck was—"

Muzien slashed open a red smile beneath Cole's blond beard, twisting to dodge the sudden flow of blood. As Cole dropped to the grass, body convulsing, Muzien let out a sigh.

"I'm sorry," he said, turning back to the smoking remnants, "but no one can know, not even you. It's a matter of trust, Cole, and right now, I trust no one but the dead."

He doubted the man heard, but he felt better offering that parting wisdom anyway. Watching ash flutter about, listening to the crackle of dwindling fire, Muzien felt his stomach harden into an iron ball. Luther had been tricking him, that Muzien had always known, but to accomplish this…madness? This insanity? If every tile could erupt in the same way, then all of Veldaren was an idiot with a sledge away from becoming ash and rubble. It went beyond anything logical. Anything sane.

Plan forming in his mind, Muzien turned to the city and began trudging back, chastising himself along the way. He should have known better. He should have seen this coming. When dealing with a fanatical man of faith, what meaning did logic and sanity hold? But at least he still had a chance to correct things, even if doing so meant visiting with yet more fanatics.

That night he would have a word with Karak's priests in Veldaren, and he knew just the woman to show him the way.

CHAPTER

8

Three hours. That was all Haern had slept in the past day and a half, and he felt the effects of it wearing on his nerves. After they'd hung the mutilated body, Haern had insisted he and his father lie low for a while to rest and plan. Finding an inn on the opposite side of the city, they'd crashed, Thren in the bed, Haern on the floor. Pretending not to notice the cockroaches skittering in the corners, Haern had closed his eyes and slept, though not nearly long enough.

"Get up," Thren had said, pushing the tip of his boot into Haern's chest to wake him. "It's almost midday. Enough rest."

Haern had disagreed, but he would not appear weak before his father, who acted as if sleep were something he occasionally flirted with. Unwrapping himself from his cloaks, he'd risen, rubbed his eyes, pulled his hood lower over his face, and then prepared to face another day of hunting and bloodshed. Neck aching from the uncomfortable sleeping position, Haern pushed the pain into a far corner of his mind and tried to focus through the groggy fog on the task at hand.

"Ridley's death is bound to upset Muzien," Thren said as he led Haern through the open market and its buzzing crowd of men and women. Stomach grumbling, Haern swiped an apple and tossed a copper all without the seller, a young girl, noticing until the coin landed in her lap.

"Good to know our efforts will annoy the bastard," Haern said after taking a bite. "But I'm still not sure how that helps us."

"Ridley was important, which means he'll need to be replaced," Thren said, twisting sideways to slide between two big men who stood chatting in the middle of the pathway as if oblivious to the traffic on either side of them. "Until then, Muzien will need to be more hands-on when it comes to his various enterprises...and that means someone might actually know where he is."

So that's why we're in the market, Haern thought as he glanced about. His father was searching for members of the Sun Guild, no doubt hoping to take another for interrogation as he had Ridley. His gut said the result would be a similar dead end, but it wasn't like Haern had any better ideas, so he followed.

"We're getting an awful lot of strange looks," Haern whispered to his father as they neared the center of the market.

"Most cloaks have turned themselves over to the patches, coats, and earrings of the Sun," Thren said softly back. "Soon the style of the west will become highly fashionable among even the noble bloods. You and I, we're walking relics of a dying past. Plus, you're wearing that damn hood. You might as well write 'thief guild' in blood across your chest."

"You're cheery in the morning, you know that?"

"It's midday. Keep up."

Throughout the stalls, Haern saw young street rats trained

to pilfer the pockets of the wealthy and unaware. Nearby would be a taskmaster in charge of them, and to whom they'd bring their score immediately in case they were later caught, and more importantly, so they didn't sneak off to spend it themselves. That taskmaster would be on the lower end in terms of rank, but at least it was a place to start. Near the northern corner of the market, back to a wall with arms crossed and eyes alert, Haern spotted such a taskmaster. The symbol of the Sun was sewn proudly onto the front of his shirt, and folded at his feet was a long gray coat. Haern made sure to not meet the man's eyes, instead nudging his father's elbow.

"There," he said, nodding his head slightly.

"I saw him," Thren said. "His name's Halloran, used to belong to my guild. Muzien would never let someone like him know anything of the slightest importance. Keep moving. We'll find someone else."

"How about we let Halloran lead us to that someone else?" Haern asked, and before letting his father answer he turned about, looping past a stall of blueberries to get a closer look at the former Spider. The man's garments were clean, yet his hair was long and ratty, his hands dirty. It made him resemble an ugly animal stuffed into fine clothing, and he looked fittingly uncomfortable. Taking one last bite of his apple, Haern flung it sideways, aiming for the man's forehead. It smacked him straight between the eyes, eliciting a furious howl.

"Get back here, you piece of shit!" Halloran shouted, wiping at his face with one hand while drawing a dagger with the other. Haern turned, and he spread his arms out to either side as if confused.

"Oh, sorry, I didn't see you there," Haern said as Halloran came rushing toward him.

"The fuck you didn't," the other man said, and he punched

his free hand into Haern's stomach. Letting it connect, Haern doubled over, exaggerating the pain while keeping an eye on that dagger. The second he looked ready to use it...

"Damn it, I said I didn't see you!" Haern cried, taking an uneven step backward. A glance about showed those passing by only mildly intrigued. Good. Halloran punched again, a roundhouse that might have impressed a foe in a bar fight. For Haern, who'd endured blows from men like Ghost and Grayson, it was an easily ignored tap to the jaw.

Not that he let it show. No, Haern sold the punch the best he could, stumbling back another step and then falling to his rump. Halloran pointed his dagger at Haern and then spit.

"Watch what you're doing," he said. "I might not be so nice next time."

"Now, now, no need to lose your temper," Thren said, stepping between them and grabbing the wrist of the hand that held the dagger. Before the man could react, Thren had pushed him to the wall, then to an alley that formed a shaded exit from the market. Wiping blood from his swelling lip, Haern rose to his feet, giving another glance about to ensure they'd gotten the proper reaction. To anyone casually observing, Thren was just someone preventing a beaten foe from enduring more punishment. After fixing his hood, Haern followed them into the alleyway. Thren stood before Halloran, a huge grin on his face.

"How's life been treating you in your new guild, Hal?" he asked.

"I didn't know you were back, I swear," Halloran insisted, eyes wide, hands shaking. Thren had drawn no weapons, but the way the former guildmember stood with his back to the wall, arms raised, there might as well have been a blade to his throat. "You disbanded, that's what everyone said, you were gone and we were free to do whatever. So I did. I did what everyone with half a brain would do and joined the Darkhand."

"But you only have a quarter of a brain," Thren said, leaning closer so all Halloran would see was his eyes. "So I hope it doesn't tax you too terribly when I ask where I can find Muzien."

Halloran swallowed.

"You know I don't know that," he said. "Muzien keeps to himself, always does."

As Haern kept watch on the alley entrance, Thren reached into Halloran's pants pocket, pulled out a pouch of coins, and held it before the man's nose.

"Who do you take these to?" Thren asked.

"Leoric," Halloran said. "Leoric Goldear. One of Muzien's men he brought with him from Mordeina."

"Where is he?"

The man looked over to Haern as if noticing for the first time he was there, and his eyes widened further.

"The Watcher?" he asked. "You're working with the Watcher?"

"Strange times make strange bedfellows," Thren said, grabbing him by the front of the shirt and shoving him hard against the wall. "Now where's Leoric? I'm not asking a third time, Halloran..."

"Corner of West and Bronze. He'll be waiting there for money from people like me, I swear!"

"How will I recognize him?"

Halloran tapped his left eye.

"This eye's all white, with a scar running along here toward his hair."

"Excellent," Thren said. "For once, Hal, you were helpful."

Halloran's smile lasted only a heartbeat before Thren yanked the dagger out of his hand, flipped it around, and jammed it into the same eye Hal had tapped. Muffling the death scream with his arm, Thren guided him to the ground, then let him plop onto his stomach. The brutality of it left Haern shocked. He should protest, he knew. Demand the unnecessary killings cease. A bad taste filled his mouth. Given the many of the Sun Guild he'd slaughtered the night before, did he really have much of a leg to stand on?

"I thought he was one of your own?" Haern asked, trying to dismiss his confusion.

"I hardly wanted him even when he was," Thren said, wiping a bit of blood and fluid from his hand onto his pants leg. "When I reform the Spider Guild, no one will miss him, least of all me. Now would you like to stand here and mourn for that idiot, or come with me to Bronze Street so we can have a chat with someone of much higher intellect?"

Spotting Leoric was simple enough, the older man with a clouded eye waiting on the street corner, his long coat sporting the symbol of the Sun just shy of the front left pocket. A second man was with him, smaller, his body nearly enveloped by his coat and the wide-brimmed hat he wore. Thren and Haern spied on the two from farther up the road, using the uneven jut of the buildings to hide.

"They're both in the open," Haern said. "Grabbing Leoric and getting him out of sight won't be easy."

"There's a little space between the two buildings behind them," Thren said, nodding toward the small glover's and milliner's shops. "We can drag him there."

"I see. And what will you do when Leoric starts screaming from your persuasions to talk?"

Thren glared his way.

"Less sarcasm, more ideas, if you wouldn't mind."

"It's your idea to do this in daylight, so you come up with the solutions."

Haern looked up and down the street, knowing that to the few who passed by they had to look obscenely guilty of something. Time was not on their side, and neither was the daylight. What he'd give for a blanket of stars and the quiet danger of Veldaren's night hours...

"We have no choice," Thren said, shaking his head. "Wait until it's clear, and then we go. I'll take down Leoric before he can cause a scene, you kill the one with him. We'll drag him into the alley, gag him, and then make sure he knows anything other than the answer we want will get him killed when we finally ungag him."

"Simple enough," Haern said, again glancing about to take in the locations of those walking the street. He did everything he could not to dwell on what "work" Thren planned on doing.

"Sometimes simple is best," Thren said. "After those two women there are gone, we go."

Another thirty seconds, and then the street was clear. Thren stepped out from behind the building and walked as if in no real hurry. Haern followed, keeping his head down, face obscured by the shadows of his hood. The two would stand out, there was no doubt about that. The question was how Leoric and his companion would react. If fate was kind, confidence and ego would outweigh caution.

Leoric was talking with the other man, unbothered by their approach. When Haern was just within earshot, the man let out a laugh.

"I swear I'm seeing ghosts," he said, finally turning their way.

Thren continued without hesitation, a calm, steady approach that hid well his lethal intentions.

"Just men wishing to have a friendly word," Haern said, tilting his head and willing the magic within the hood to pull back, dispelling its permanent shadows to reveal just enough of his face for them to see his smile…a smile he hoped was convincing.

"Everyone's friends in this city, if the coin is right," Leoric said.

Beside him his companion turned, and Haern saw his initial assumptions had been horribly incorrect. Not a man, but a woman, with deep-green eyes, dark skin, and a frighteningly familiar glare. Haern felt his heart sink into his chest moments before Thren attacked.

"Oh shit."

Once Thren was close enough, he leaped forward, elbow leading. It connected with Leoric's forehead, who reacted far too late to get out of the way. As the man fell, Haern drew his blades and dashed to put himself between Zusa and Thren. He offered only the lamest of swings, which Zusa easily blocked. The movements knocked aside her hat, revealing her hair pulled back from her face.

They knew we were coming, Haern thought. Her eyes met his, and she glanced just once to her left, down the street, before leaping toward him. Their weapons met, interlocking, and as she pushed she gave him a smile.

"I suggest you run," she whispered, then twirled away, avoiding an attempted spearing by Thren from the side. Thren made to chase, but Haern yelled for him to wait. The man looked back a half-second, glaring, and then all along the rooftops rose members of the Sun, loaded crossbows in hand.

Now it was Thren's turn to curse.

Remembering the way Zusa had looked and praying he had interpreted it correctly, Haern shouted for his father to follow and then sprinted left, keeping his body low and flinging his cloaks wide to make himself a harder target. From up above came the distinctive twang of bowstrings, followed by the clacks of the bolts striking the stone street. Haern continued weaving from side to side, pushing his legs to their limit.

When he reached the end of the street, somehow not filled with holes from the crossbowmen, he glanced behind to see a dozen more members of the Sun rushing from the opposite direction. If he and Thren had fled right instead of left, they'd have crossed the guildmembers' path in seconds.

"Follow me!" Thren shouted, zipping past him, curling left, and bolting down the street. Haern followed, cursing the sun that denied him a dozen hiding spots he could have used otherwise. He'd wondered why one direction had been guarded and the other not. That question was answered when eight men, half with swords, half with crossbows, cut them off at the end of the street.

"To the rooftops," Haern said, rolling to the side as bolts flew through the air toward them, one hitting close enough to punch a hole through one of his cloaks. Wishing he could soar into the air as easily as Zusa did, Haern jumped, kicked off the wall, and caught a bolt of iron holding up the sign of some store. Rocking backward first, he then flung his legs forward, gaining enough momentum to release, curl around feetfirst, and catch the side of the roof with his hand. Doubting his father would be able to re-create the maneuver, Haern pulled himself the rest of the way up, ignored the unnerving sound of a bolt thunking into the building inches away from his arm, and then lay flat on his belly, arms hanging over the side. Thren jumped, caught him by the wrists, and used them to join Haern on the rooftop.

"Why are we running?" Thren asked as he crouched low to prevent anyone on the ground below from having a clean shot.

"Because I don't feel like dying?"

Seemed obvious enough to Haern. He vaulted into a sprint, leaping from rooftop to rooftop as the shouts of their pursuers followed. Thren wasn't far behind, his eyes more often on the streets than on his path.

"Too many," he said, suddenly grabbing Haern's arm. "This way."

Turning back the way they'd come, he ran to the side, grabbed the rooftop, and then swung down through an open window. Haern followed without question, tumbling into an empty bedroom. Opposite the window was a closet, and Thren dashed into it and wedged himself to one side. Haern did likewise, pushing his back against the closet interior and then grabbing the closet door to yank it mostly closed, leaving but a tiny crack for him to peer out of.

"We'll be trapped if they find us here," Haern said as he hunkered down deeper into his side of the closet.

"They can't search every home in Veldaren," Thren said. "They'll scour a bit more, then assume us gone. Just be patient."

Haern pulled his legs up closer to his chest, trying to get comfortable given the meager room for the two of them. Only a tiny sliver of sunlight made it to his eye when he peered through the crack. Even if someone were to glance inside, it'd be a miracle for them to spot the hiding place.

"We shouldn't have run," said Thren, earning a glare from Haern.

"Why not?"

"It sets a bad precedent. I don't like letting Muzien think we're scared."

Haern let out a sigh, very much not wanting to argue the point. His head ached, whether from hunger, lack of sleep, or the sudden exertion, he could only begin to guess.

"We were outnumbered over ten to one," he said. "And I know the woman who led them. She's a match for either of us, Thren. Add her to the mix, and it was only a matter of time before we ended up dead."

"No one is a match for us, Watcher."

The comment elicited a chuckle from Haern.

"You may be right," he said. "But truth be told, I wouldn't want to face her to find out for certain."

"You held your own just fine not moments ago."

"She wasn't trying. It looks like we're not the only ones playing games with the Sun Guild."

From the window came a soft thud, and both immediately fell silent. Haern peered through the crack, watching as a man in a long coat knelt into the bedroom, gave a cursory glance about, and then dropped back down to the street. Slowly letting out his breath, Haern gave thanks to Ashhur that their whispers had gone unheard.

"It's dangerous thinking," Thren whispered after a moment. "Believing it possible that woman could defeat you in a fight. Muzien is the most dangerous foe there is. If there's another soul alive you cannot defeat, then Muzien has already won."

"Muzien may be able to defeat me in a fair fight," Haern said, "but I didn't think we planned on fighting fair. The better question is whether or not he can take down the two of us in a chaotic melee. No matter how good he is, no one is *that* good. We'll defeat him, Thren. We have to. We'll tear at his guild, piece by piece, until there's nothing left. Victory will soon follow."

Thren seemed to consider this, and then he shook his head, frowning deeply.

"Have you heard the story of Muzien's Red Wine?" asked Thren.

"No, I haven't."

Thren shifted again, thumping his knees against the side of the closet as he tried to get comfortable.

"The story's more common the farther west you go. When Muzien first started his Sun Guild, it wasn't much in terms of numbers, just a small piece of Mordeina that he carved out for himself. A few times the other guilds tried to crush him, insulted by this elven upstart that dared to play their game. Muzien made them pay, every single time. It's how he lived so long when others had more coin, more power, or more influence. He didn't need to be the strongest. He just had to ensure the cost of destroying him was greater than anyone was willing to pay.

"Then something changed. He vanished for a few weeks, and when he returned, he bore the blackened hand that gave him his name. With that hand came vicious expansion. No longer happy with his little corner of Mordeina, he sought dominion over every single street. Suddenly he wasn't a curiosity or a minor player, but a major force threatening to topple the other guilds as street after street fell to the Sun. To have an elf usurp them all? Preposterous, and that alone helped unite the thief guilds against Muzien. They struck back, hard. They killed over half his members in a single night, robbing his warehouses and burning what they could not carry. Complete and thorough humiliation, Watcher, of the like that would have made any sane man or woman surrender. At first it seemed even Muzien himself saw the hopelessness of his situation. He called for a meeting between him and the seven other guildleaders, and they agreed to attend once he allowed a priest to oversee the meeting."

"A priest?" asked Haern. "Why would they involve themselves?"

"Things aren't like here in Veldaren, Watcher. The priests of Karak wield far greater power in Mordeina, and they do not remain neutral in affairs like they do here. Should a man call for a priest to oversee a matter, the weight of the temple would ensure no promise was broken. So Muzien swore, under penalty of retribution by Karak's temple, that no guildleader would suffer harm. And so they came, one after the other, expecting to hear Muzien's terms of surrender." Thren laughed. "I can only imagine the smug looks on their faces, their self-congratulatory remarks to one another at toppling the heathen elf. 'Start the meeting,' they said once they were all there, but Muzien begged for a few minutes more.

"'I'm waiting for the wine,' he tells them. A gift, you see, they all thought it an offered gift as part of his request for peace. And then sure enough, in comes a man holding this giant barrel of wine, pops it open, and then Muzien takes the first drink. 'Excellent,' he says. 'Now bring in the rest.'"

It was strange listening to his father tell the story. He was a natural storyteller, as men who demanded attention at all times often were. But what put Haern's hair on edge was not the story he told, but the way he spoke of the elf, the way he delivered those lines accompanied by grand gestures of his hands. Thren didn't just admire Muzien. No, as Thren continued his tale, Haern sensed the bond between them was far stronger than mere admiration or respect. The wounds were there, but as Thren's words cast a spell over him, he knew that Muzien had once been someone his father loved. On their trip west to the Stronghold, a man of the Sun Guild had called Thren "the heir of Muzien." Listening to the story,

Haern realized how much was hidden there that he did not understand.

"And so they bring in the rest," Thren continued. "Seven women and children, wives, lovers, sons and daughters... Muzien's men dragged in at knife-point one for each of the leaders. Then the rest of Muzien's guild, hiding high above in the rafters, fired their crossbows, killing the various guards those fools had brought. All acceptable to the priest of Karak, of course. If those bastards are anything, it's loyal to the letter and not the spirit of a law.

" 'Bring me the first,' Muzien says. Some say it was a man's wife, others his gay lover, but most agree it was his daughter Muzien called over. Cup in one hand, dagger in the other, he cuts this little girl's palm and then squeezes drops of blood into the cup. After that he fills the rest with wine from the barrel and hands it to that girl's father. And then he gave his edict, Watcher, solidifying himself as a terror they would never defeat, as an enemy that would forever endure."

Thren hesitated, and Haern sensed the manipulation of it, the building of anticipation. But in truth, Haern did want to hear.

"What did he say?" he asked.

" 'This is the cup I offer. Surrender to me, drink of my wine, and you shall live. Refuse it, deny my authority, and all of my men and women shall share a drink instead. One cup, or a hundred. Make your choice.' "

Haern felt a chill sweep through his veins.

"How many resisted?" he asked.

There was no hiding the smile on his father's face when he answered.

"Only one. Muzien made sure they all watched the drinking of every single cup. After that no one dared refuse him. They knew how far he would go, much farther than they would ever dare. And unlike them, Muzien had no loved ones, no ancestors, and no children. Just his guild. By harming his guild, they'd harmed the closest thing he had to loved ones, so he hurt their loved ones in return. They thought they'd cowed him, humbled him. Fools. They only made him that much more desperate. All men are dangerous when backed into a corner, but Muzien turns it into a damn art form."

Haern shot another look through the crack of the closet at the daylight beyond, and it felt as if he searched for the monsters that used to hide underneath his bed when he was a child. Again he thought of Thren's supposed title, and he had no choice but to ask.

"You told Ridley you were Muzien's heir," Haern said. "What does that mean? What is your connection with him?"

Thren fell silent for a moment, and when Haern looked his way, he was stunned to see his father subtly shifting his gaze to not look him in the eye.

"I was just a street orphan," Thren said. "My mother worked at a tavern, and I never met my father, only knew he was a soldier she slept with for a few days. When she died, I had nothing, no one, and so I stole to live. Muzien came upon me one day, and he…saw something in me, as well as my only friend, Grayson. He tested us, made us prove ourselves, and when we succeeded, he adopted us as his heirs. He was the closest person I ever had to a father, teaching me how to kill, how to hide, how to command attention and respect. It was his lessons I tried to emulate the best I could with my own sons…"

Again came the heavy silence, and with it came a thousand childhood memories, each one tainted by the haunting specter of Muzien the Darkhand.

"When did you turn against him?" Haern asked, unable to bear the silence.

"Only when Grayson returned with the Sun Guild a few months back. Coming to Veldaren was our final test. I was to conquer the underworld to prove my worthiness as his heir. Apparently I failed, and you're largely considered the reason why, Watcher. Consider that another of your accomplishments, if you wish."

"I'd rather be remembered for stopping Muzien. You're a has-been at this point, old man."

He grinned at Thren, who shockingly enough grinned back.

"My time is not yet passed, Watcher. We'll take down Muzien, but we won't do it how you suggested, not piece by piece. It must be complete and thorough, the cutting off of a head with a single clean stroke. A gradual defeat will give him time to recover, to plan, or even worse, to destroy the entire city with those tiles. Muzien will never surrender. The thought will never enter his mind. But if he thinks the city is lost to him, he'll burn it all to the ground before letting it fall into anyone else's hands."

"Reminds me of someone else I know."

From the dark corner came Thren's laughter.

"So true," he said. "So very true."

Haern looked once more, then pushed open the closet door.

"They're bound to have moved on by now," he said.

"Not quite," Thren said. "Scouts will remain behind, but we can handle a few scouts, can't we?"

He led the way, shifting so he could peer left and right without sticking his head out the window.

"One, to the right," he whispered. "Follow my lead."

Thren turned about, reached through the window to grab the roof, and then yanked himself up. Haern did likewise, and once both were on the rooftop, Haern did a quick scan of his surroundings. Scouts did indeed remain, two that he could see. The one Thren had spotted lurked with his back to them on the edge of a rooftop, scanning the street below. The other was several hundred feet away, just a brown outline in the distance.

"Move fast," Thren whispered.

Together they ran across the rooftop, leaped across the street, and grabbed the roof on the other side. Twin images, they pulled up, bounded forward, and drew their weapons. Their passing made no noise, gave the scout no warning. Haern fell back a half-step to let his father take the lead, and like a bull, Thren slammed into the man, his horns the two short swords he wielded in his hands. Blood spilled as they toppled over the roof, Thren shifting so his knees were braced against the scout's chest. When they hit the ground, the wet, crunching noise of lungs and ribs mashing together was the only death cry the scout would make.

Hooking a hand on the side of the roof, Haern used it to swing low, hung for a moment to kill his momentum, and then released so he could fall silently beside the mess. A glance about showed they had not yet been noticed by those passing on either side of the alley. Meanwhile Thren pulled himself free of the body, unfazed by the gore on his clothes. Instead he took his sword, covered it with fresh blood, and then started sliding it along the brick wall of the building they'd just leaped off of. With the smooth precision of a painter, Thren dipped his sword in and out of the blood as he drew.

"You counter fear with defiance," his father said, voice soft, resolve hardened. "You counter arrogance with mockery. It's been a long time since someone truly challenged Muzien, and even longer since he had his nose bloodied. But this is my city, and he's going to learn the hard way that I will never drink from the cup he offers."

When he was done, he stepped back to examine the mark of the Spider scrawled across the wall. Haern stared at it, remembering how that symbol had given him pride when he was a child, then fear and loathing when he was a homeless vagrant rebelling against the underworld. After he assumed his role as the Watcher, the Spider had become something weaker, something managed and controlled. But what was it now? Defiance? Rebellion? Why did it no longer fill his stomach with dread?

Haern knelt down beside the body, and he drew his own dagger to dip into the bloody mess. They were fighting a war, he realized. War had casualties, both on and off the battlefield. He couldn't keep dreading doing the wrong thing. They had to win. For the sake of everyone. What had he told Ghost once? *I'm the monster this city needs.* Not its protector. Not its savior. Its monster. Which meant no longer feeling guilt at the killings, wincing at the pain of his enemies. It was time to embrace a far darker part of his past.

Four strokes in and out of the blood, that was all it took for him to draw a symbol he'd not used in years.

"We should find the other scouts," Haern said when he was done. "Muzien's fond of messages, so let's send him one in return. He'll learn to fear us equally in both day and night."

Thren agreed, and back to the rooftops they climbed, leaving behind the message that would grace many other walls that day. Two marks drawn in blood, Thren's spider and the Watcher's eye.

Two marks, side-by-side.

CHAPTER

9

It was a day Alyssa had thought would never come, despite having dreamed of it for years while growing up a child of the Trifect. Back then she'd imagined extravagant parties, exotic food, and distinguished guests gathered from all four corners of Dezrel to witness her take the hand of a handsome man of noble birth, stare lovingly into his eyes, and declare herself his wife until the last breath upon this world. But there would be no guests, no parties, and when she gazed up into the eyes of her betrothed, she would see darkness, not love.

"You look lovely," one of her servants said as they finished tightening and tying the last of the strings upon the back of her corset.

"You tell me that every morning."

"More lovely than usual," she said in a vain attempt to correct herself.

Stop being cruel, Alyssa told herself, and she forced a smile.

"If you say so, then I believe you," she said. "Given how long it's taken, it'd be insulting for me to think you've not given me your best efforts."

There were three servant girls applying her cosmetics and aiding in dressing her, and she sensed all three let out sighs of relief. Of all parts of the day, Alyssa treated the ritual of primping and preening with the least amount of patience. But this was the day of her wedding. If any day was worth the time and effort, this was it.

"If you're finished, leave me be," she told them.

"Yes, milady," they said in unison, quickly filing out and leaving Alyssa alone in a grand washroom. Before her was a mirror, and she pretended to see herself in its reflection. Every time she failed. Her skin and hair she could picture easily enough, a soft smile on her lips, but her eyes ruined the illusion. They were always solid black orbs, lifeless, dead. *Windows to the soul*, she thought. *If that's true, what soul is left within me?*

A knock on the door stirred her from that grim thought.

"Yes?" she asked.

"It's...it's me, Terrance. I was hoping I could have a word with you before the ceremony."

Alyssa felt a tingle in the back of her mind, one of warning. Terrance was a distant cousin of hers, a kind, intelligent young man who'd aided with the management of her finances and trade for over four years. Terrance rarely came to her unless he wished to talk business, and only then if it was important. So what was so important he must discuss it prior to the wedding?

"Come in," she said, and the door opened and then shut. "Though there's not much ceremony to speak of, Terrance. We'll be wed before one of the king's lawyers, not a crowd of friends."

She heard Terrance clear his throat, and unable to endure his lurking behind her like that, she spun around on her seat and crossed her arms over her tight, grossly expensive dress.

"What is it?" she asked. "Even without eyes I can tell you're shifting about as if holding in a piss."

A crude joke might have relaxed most people and pried open their lips, but with Terrance it seemed only to make things worse. Wishing she had eyes so she could roll them, Alyssa uncrossed her arms and adopted a more nurturing tone.

"Whatever it is, don't be afraid to tell me. You know how much I trust you."

"It's about Victor," Terrance blurted out.

Of course it is, thought Alyssa.

"Oh?" she said, pretending to be surprised. "And what of him?"

The young man cleared his throat, and by his footsteps she could tell he'd begun pacing.

"Well, after your engagement, he came to me about integrating his property, as well as his debts, into the Gemcroft family holdings. All fair, of course, but his debts…"

"I know Victor's holdings were not great," she said, hoping that was all Terrance fretted over. It wasn't.

"No," he said. "It's not just that. He's been taking coin from our savings to pay his mercenaries. He claimed it part of his debts, but I've had discussions with the leaders, and it's clear what's going on, especially when looking over his holdings. We're paying for both his family soldiers and his mercenaries. All of them, for work both the past six months, and six months from now."

Alyssa felt her throat tighten. A large part of why she'd agreed to an engagement with Victor had been his loyal soldiers, and the respect he commanded. But if she could have gained all of that just by contacting the mercenary guild and throwing around a mess of coin...

"Why did you not speak with me about this sooner?" she asked him.

Terrance cleared his throat, a nervous tic of his she was well familiar with.

"Victor strongly implied it would be unwise for me to bring this to your attention."

I'm sure he did.

"You've done the right thing," she told him. "Please, have a servant fetch Victor so I may speak with him."

"As you wish, milady."

As she sat there in her chair, Alyssa's mind raced over what she might say, what she might do. Did it matter if he was spending her coin? Come their marriage, she'd assume all his debts, all his costs, and be paying for the men just the same. Something about it unnerved her, though. It felt like a portent of things to come, of deals made behind her back and servants threatened in the dark. Worse, though, was how Victor saw himself as an honorable man. No doubt everything he'd done, everything he'd one day do, he'd justify to himself as necessary.

No, she decided. She was entering into the marriage under promises of future greatness, and for a pretense of stability and power she no longer had. To go in blind...

Alyssa laughed at herself.

Of course she was going in blind. But at least she could try, however vainly, to open her eyes to the man Zusa had feared he was.

A knock on the door, no doubt Victor.

"Come in," she said, folding her hands on her lap. She heard the door open and close, then heavy footsteps as Victor entered the room, crossing the distance. Gently she felt him take her hand, and she did her best to smile.

"By the gods," said Victor. "Your beauty is stunning, truly stunning."

"So my girls tell me."

"They were not lying, I can assure you of that. With but a smile, I'd wager you could make yourself queen."

"Was that not what our marriage was for?" she asked, deciding there would be no dancing around the issue. Truth be told, such games didn't suit her. *Strength*, she told herself. *You once relied on strength. You can do so again.*

She sensed Victor's disapproval of such questioning, but he smoothly attempted to deflect it.

"Today is a day of happiness," he said, patting her hand. "Not a time to discuss such serious things."

"But we will discuss it, Victor. I've forfeited my happiness for the Trifect before, and I'll do so again if I must. You promised me my son would be king. If you wish to kneel with me before a priest later today and take on the name of Gemcroft, you'll tell me exactly how you plan to make that come to pass."

Victor sighed, and if she could see and be certain not to miss, she'd have slapped him for it.

"Such a thing will take time and patience," he said, his footsteps letting her know he had begun pacing. "In a sword duel, sometimes the way to victory isn't by hacking and slashing at your foe, but instead letting them make a mistake, perhaps an errant swing or an overextension, and then taking advantage of that mistake. Deposing King Edwin successfully will involve perfect timing and expert manipulation of the people, and until certain...factors line up, we cannot make our move."

"What factors?" she asked. "What is it we are waiting for?"

Another damn sigh.

"The king to die, of course. It's only a matter of time. He has no heirs and no wife. While the noble bloods only grumble and mutter about it under their breath, it won't be like that for much longer. No clear successor means war upon his death, and a throne dozens may attempt to seize. Someone will kill him in hopes of taking it for themselves; it doesn't have to be us. For Karak's sake, even Muzien may end up doing us the favor. He's already threatened to. It may just take a few well-placed rumors and lies to convince the elf to carry through on his threat."

The whole time he spoke, Alyssa felt her throat tightening and her heart beginning to pound in her chest.

"Is that so?" she said, struggling to keep her tone neutral. "And when the king dies...?"

"Then we seize the castle. Between your house soldiers and my growing army of mercenaries, we can storm its gates with ease. With the king dead, it's possible no one will be there to resist us. Power is all about image, Alyssa, and once we declare ourselves king and queen from the throne, much of the battle will already be won."

It was enticing, of course. A wonderful dream. A beautiful suicide.

"Armies will march on us," she said. "We won't have the man-power to guard the walls, and your unprotected lands will be conquered in days. Someone with a better claim..."

"Listen to me, Alyssa," Victor said, pacing halted. "You are Alyssa Gemcroft, she with fire in her veins. When you declare yourself queen, tell me, who in their right mind would dare challenge you, when challenging you means challenging the entirety of the Trifect? Not a coin passes through this land your empire hasn't touched. You control the mines, the

Conningtons the farms and merchant guilds, the Keenans the ships that sail the waters...and the boats little Tori Keenan doesn't control, the Merchant Lords do, and now they themselves are your allies. Turning against you would be financial suicide. No, every lord and lady will line up to kiss our asses in hopes of benefitting from the new rulers of Veldaren... married rulers, strong, wise, and with a named heir."

Alyssa could sense the threads of possibility woven throughout, but intermixed was desperation, even insanity. The Trifect had remained in power since the departure of the brother gods precisely because it refused to accept the responsibility of the crown. Better to manipulate those in power than to bear such a burden oneself. To take up that burden now, when the Trifect felt more fragile than it had in decades, with Tori so young and the Conningtons still bickering over who would replace the dead Stephen? Madness.

But she'd told Zusa she saw no hope in any other future, and she still felt that helplessness hanging over her. Steeling her jaw, she swore to cast it off, and heart pounding harder, she vowed to make it all work, to endure even Victor's foolishness while gaining from him what she could.

"I understand," she said. "Are they ready for us outside?"

It took Victor a moment to realize what she meant.

"I...yes, the priest is here, as is the lawyer, but the kitchen's just started preparing the feast, and I don't know if Nathaniel's dressed yet."

"I don't care." Alyssa rose from her seat and offered Victor a hand. "This isn't about love, Victor, just power and respect. Take me to my garden. Let's sign our names, and before both god and king, declare you a member of the Trifect."

"Not quite the sweet words I imagined hearing from my

betrothed on our wedding day," he said, taking her hand in his. At that, Alyssa could not help but laugh.

"Whatever expectations you have of me, Victor, I suggest you lower them. You're my husband now, and it won't be long before you discover how far less noble I am than you."

"I'm not your husband yet," he said as he tightened his grip and led her from her room toward the garden. On their way they encountered Terrance, and Alyssa tensed when she heard Victor call out his name.

"The wedding begins now," Victor told him, hardly slowing as he guided Alyssa through the hall. "Send only those necessary into the garden."

"Of course," Terrance said, and she sensed his unease in the slight quiver of his voice.

Onward they went, passing through doors, until a gust of fresh air blew against her skin. Reflexively closing her eyes against it, Alyssa pretended she could see the colors of the flowers, the golden light shining down through swaying leaves, and the carefully managed carpet of green grass. She had her memories to guide her, to aid in the pretending, and for one brief moment she was happy.

"They should be ready soon," Victor said, shattering the illusion.

"Good," Alyssa said, swallowing down the lump in her throat. "Very good."

Awkwardly she stood there, holding Victor's hand, waiting for the ceremony, or what little there would be, to begin.

"Ah, the lovely couple," said an older voice, and Alyssa turned his way. "Forgive me, but with such haste this will be a most unusual ceremony. Are you sure you would rather not wait?"

"Are you the priest?" she asked.

"I am."

"Then say only what you must. I care not for the ceremony."

The older man cleared his throat, and she sensed him turning his attention to Victor.

"The lawyer is here as well. We may begin whenever you wish."

Victor squeezed Alyssa's hand tight.

"We are ready," he said.

Some shuffling, the older man coughed, and then without pomp he began.

"I ask the each of you, Lady Alyssa Gemcroft and Lord Victor Kane, do you promise your love, your trust, and your faithfulness to one another, to become in union something blessed and holy before the sight of our god, Ashhur?"

"We do," said Victor.

"We do," said Alyssa, and she felt the tightening of invisible ropes about her neck with each syllable.

"Then before Ashhur, as witnessed by a representative of His Majesty, King Edwin Vaelor, I declare you husband and wife, Lord and Lady Gemcroft. May you know only happiness in your years together, from this first moment of new life to the grave and the life beyond."

"If you'd sign here," said another man, younger, sounding bored and even a little annoyed. The lawyer, she decided, the guess confirmed when a quill was placed in her free hand. Victor released her other hand, took her wrist, and guided her to the line, where she signed with a quick scribble she knew was getting worse every day. That done, she handed over the quill, felt her husband take her hands.

"My lovely wife," he said, leaning closer, his voice dropping. "It is such an honor to become a member of the Gemcroft family. I pray you trust me always, and I promise you, I will never, ever let you regret this day."

"Such grand promises," she said, doing her best to smile. She sensed him dipping lower, felt his lips upon hers. She kissed back once, lips pressed tightly closed together, her back arching away from him ever so slightly. From all around she heard soft, scattered applause from the few servants in attendance. As Victor pulled away and squeezed her hands, all Alyssa could think of was how glad she was Zusa hadn't witnessed that cold mockery of a kiss.

CHAPTER

10

As the sun set behind the walls of the city, Muzien waited for Zusa at the entrance to his guildhouse, having sent runners to find her half an hour before. Despite the seriousness of the night, it still put a smile on his face to see her come strolling up the road. So much confidence in her step, conveyed with every swing of her hips and the daggers belted to them. To think servants of Karak would wish her smooth skin hidden, her green eyes veiled...

"You summoned me?" she asked once she could speak without shouting.

"I heard you had a run-in with Thren and the Watcher," he said.

"I did. They escaped, but I promise not to let them do so again."

"They're skilled foes," Muzien said, shaking his head. "Make no such promises, for they are beyond even your control. In time, though, they'll make a mistake, and you will be there to ensure they pay for it."

Zusa waited before him, arms crossed over her chest. She tugged at the collar of her coat, and Muzien wondered how much she might prefer a cloak instead.

"They'll grow bolder with each day they live," she said. "Such confidence is dangerous. Will you not go after them instead?"

Muzien stepped close, and he ran his fingers through her short dark hair.

"For such skill and beauty, you've lived only in shadows and secrecy," he told her. "If you kill Thren or the Watcher, your name will be envied throughout the underworld. But should you kill them *both*? My legacy is already set in stone. Yours? Yours is young, and I would give you the chance to make it something beautiful."

It was impressive, if not a little disappointing, how controlled she remained at his touch. No excitement, no tilting of the face. No disgust, either, nor repulsion. Simply put, he didn't know what he was to her. Given her skill, her beauty, he decided that come peaceful times he would put far more effort into investigating the riddle that was the former faceless woman.

"Walk with me," he said, and she joined him as he traveled down the road.

"Do you wish something of me?" she asked.

"Besides your lovely company?"

He lifted an eyebrow, but again she gave him no clue, no reaction. The cloth may as well have never left her face, she was so guarded and unreadable.

"Besides that, yes," she said.

Muzien let out a sigh, and he forced his mind to more pressing matters.

"I know the priests of Karak have a strong presence in the city," he said. "But what I do not know is where their temple is located. I've scoured this entire city and found nothing, yet those in power insist it is real, yet also insist they cannot bring me to it lest they suffer greatly. This troubles me, for I need to discuss matters of importance with Karak's followers."

"You wish me to lead you to the temple," Zusa said. It was not a question.

"I do."

For once that perfect visage cracked, and he saw the barest hints of an internal debate raging within.

"I will lead you there," she said. "But I will not enter. Should they recognize me, there will be blood spilled, and I will not risk becoming their prisoner again."

Silence fell over them as they walked, and Muzien debated how to react. By refusing to enter the temple she was refusing him, regardless of whether he had actually given the order. Part of him wanted to break her for it, to let her know her life depended on accepting his wishes no matter how strongly they risked her life or filled her with repulsion. But she was clearly different from his other guildmembers, something special, and given the wounds of her past as well as the risk of complications should the priests recognize her, he decided to let the matter slide.

"Very well," he said. "Lead me to their temple doors, and I shall force you to travel no closer than that."

That appeared acceptable enough, and she nodded.

"All right," she said. "Follow me."

She led him to the eastern district of the city, where the homes were built tall and guarded, revealing the power and wealth of those who resided safely away from the poverty of the other districts. Amid the affluence was a somber-looking mansion with heavy iron gates surrounding it. Zusa paused before it, and she nodded in the building's direction.

"Is this the temple?" he asked.

"It is, but not quite," she said. "Put your hand on the gate."

He did, his eyes not on the mansion but on her.

"Repeat after me," she said. "I see through your illusions."

"I see through your illusions."

At that the mansion shimmered, then changed into an impressive structure of black stone, the front smooth, decorated only with pillars and the enormous skull of a lion hanging above the doorway. The gate opened a crack on its own, and Muzien pushed it farther so they might pass. On the obsidian walkway he stepped, but Zusa did not follow.

"This is as far as I go," she said.

Again he thought to rebuke her, then let it pass.

"I understand," he said, thinking of at least one way to exert some measure of control. "Wait just outside, though, and do not leave until I come back for you."

"If you insist."

She bowed low, and he dipped his head in return. Putting his back to her, he crossed the obsidian to the imposing double doors set in a deep recess behind the dark pillars and carved lions. Before them he paused, unsure of what he would ask. He was forced to decide quickly, for the doors cracked open, and a young man stepped out and bowed.

"How might we help you?" the man, little more than a boy, asked.

"I wish to speak with whoever wields the greatest power within this temple," Muzien said.

The boy didn't seem too impressed with the request.

"That would be our high priest, Pelarak," he said. "But

he must agree to speak with you, which is doubtful, for the high priest is a very busy man with many important duties. There are others who may hear your confession, or accept your tithes, should you wish to kneel before the altar and wait for attending."

Muzien smirked at the word *tithes*.

"I doubt your priests would so readily accept any tithes I might offer," he said. "Go tell Pelarak that Muzien the Dark-hand stands at his door. I assure you, the high priest will find time to meet with me."

"Very well," the boy said, bowing. With a deep thud the doors shut, leaving Muzien alone between the pillars. Leaving him there was disrespectful, but Muzien knew enough of the gods and their servants not to be surprised. They obeyed but one lord, and all others, no matter how much wealth and power they wielded, would always be treated as inferior.

After several minutes the doors reopened.

"Follow me," the boy said, then turned to lead the way without waiting to see if Muzien followed.

When he stepped into the temple, Muzien felt a shiver shoot up his spine.

This is not the home of a sane god, he thought, an almost instinctual decision. Everything seemed fine to his eyes, just humans making their meager attempts to worship and make offerings to the divine. As he followed the boy, he passed by rows of little candles, as well as numerous paintings of their god, Karak, as his worshippers guessed him to have looked when he first walked the land. The entry hall had rows of hardwood benches, the carpet a soft red. The feel in the air made him uncomfortable, he decided, the quiet anger that seemed to echo from every wall.

And then he stepped before the great statue of Karak in the

grand foyer, and he knew his instinct had been correct. Karak's visage carved of stone towered over the few priests kneeling before him. A bloodstained bowl lay at its feet, former contents splashed across its legs and chest. The god stood with sword in one hand, fist raised high to the heavens in the other. Deep-purple light shone across him from all sides, coming from braziers at the statue's feet that burned the same somber color. The very sight of the statue filled Muzien with a momentary desire to kneel, immediately followed by complete revulsion. He would bow to no god, not Celestia, and certainly not one of the failed, pathetic human deities that had come to Dezrel fleeing their own failures on another world.

From there they passed through a door, Muzien's guide pausing to dip his head in respect to the statue. Muzien ignored it the best he could, and was glad when they were deeper in the temple, out of sight of the horrible thing. They passed by several doors, none of them marked, before the boy stopped and knocked on one of them. The moment the door opened, the boy stepped aside, bowed his head, and took a position waiting, leaving Muzien with no choice but to introduce himself to the high priest of the temple.

"Greetings," he said as the pale man stepped out. "I am Muzien the Darkhand, and I have come to talk."

"Come in," said Pelarak, swinging the door open wider. "I am honored to have you as my guest."

The bedroom was plain, simple, a padded bed, a desk, a chair, and a filled bookshelf were all that decorated the room. Given the grandeur of everywhere else in the temple, Muzien found it a nice change of pace. Pelarak himself was unimposing enough, though he carried himself with the air of one with absolute authority. When he spoke, every syllable came out as if he were declaring the immutable law of the heavens.

"I thank you for allowing me this visit," Muzien said, deciding there would be no harm in attempting civility at the start.

"Believe it or not, this is a historical occasion," Pelarak said, dipping his head in respect. "You are the first of Celestia's children to ever set foot within our temple."

"Perhaps I am the first to ever desire to," he said, flashing his most charming smile. "Though perhaps *desire* is too strong a word for my situation. No, I come because I must, Pelarak. There are traitors in your midst, and they must be dealt with before the damage they deal cannot be undone."

Whatever pleasantness had been in Pelarak's smile and voice immediately vanished. He shut the door behind Muzien so they might have total privacy, then stepped away.

"Tell me," he said. "And do not mince words. I am not one for games and riddles, and your tongue will bring death upon the names you offer... or upon you, should you come into our home spreading lies and chaos."

"You're a man of power, Pelarak, but I assure you I am one of very few you should never threaten."

Pelarak smiled at him, the smile of a king on his throne leering down at a penniless servant.

"You are inside Karak's most sacred temple, and are surrounded by his faithful," he said. "I make no threats, only simple statements of truth. Speak lies to me, and you will die, Muzien."

Already Muzien could tell his entire visit to the temple would be distasteful. Still, he had more important things to worry about than a few petty stabs at his pride.

"From before my arrival, I have been working with members of your priesthood," Muzien said. "Two men in particular, Luther and Daverik, both seeking to keep their efforts hidden from you and your ilk."

Upon hearing the names, Pelarak swallowed hard and sat down in his plain chair.

"What did they offer you?" he asked.

"Daverik ensured my men could enter the city without hassle from the guards, smuggling in supplies, weapons, and merchandise to sell on the streets. In return, I was to position stone tiles bearing the mark of my guild throughout the city."

"I've seen them," the priest said. "Was that all they wished of you, the smuggling of those tiles? It is a strange payment to demand."

"It was," Muzien said. "Which meant the tiles hid something. Not that I was surprised, but I expected something… mundane. But they're not, Pelarak, and that is why I'm here. I've come for an explanation to the madness I've discovered."

Pelarak's eyes narrowed.

"Explain yourself," he said.

Muzien put a hand on the desk and leaned closer, staring the priest in the eye so he would see he spoke no lie.

"The tiles have been filled with fire and thunder. Upon their breaking, they destroy anything in the vicinity, be it stone or wood or flesh. Karak's magic is at work, and I need to know what goal could possibly be served by leveling the entire city."

Pelarak took in a deep breath and then let it out.

"The destruction these tiles can accomplish," he said. "You've seen it?"

The elf nodded.

"I had one broken with a sledge. The ensuing eruption left a crater in the grass, and turned four men, plus my wagon, into a pile of ash. Given how many are scattered throughout the city, someone out there has the power to turn this entire city into a monument of fire and ruin."

The priest rocked back and forth a moment. He was shaking, and when he spoke, Muzien realized that he shook with rage.

"I assure you such action was never once condoned by our order," he said. "Whatever Daverik and Luther have done, it was done behind our backs, making them traitors to our order."

"It's still not too late for it to be rectified," Muzien said. "Bring Daverik here before us, and we shall hear the answer from his own lips why he has put your entire city in danger."

Pelarak sighed.

"It isn't that simple," he said. "Daverik is dead, murdered five days ago."

"Murdered? By whom?"

The priest hesitated.

"This is a matter that does not concern you, only members of the faith."

"Priest," Muzien said, his voice dropping lower, "I would prefer to be the judge of what does and does not matter when it comes to the destruction of my city. I have been used by a madman, so if you wish to help me undo the damage, then keep no secrets from me. I am not your enemy here, now tell me all you know about Daverik and why he was murdered."

The priest thought it over a moment longer, then finally relented.

"So be it," he said. "Two of Daverik's students witnessed his murder at the hands of a former lover and traitor to our faith, Zusa the faceless. A personal matter, I'm sure, with nothing to do with your...arrangements."

Despite the many years Muzien had spent learning to control his reactions, he nearly let his surprise show at hearing Zusa's name.

That explains why you refused to enter the temple, he thought, vowing to investigate that curious tidbit further when he had more time.

"Then that leaves Luther for us to receive our answers from," Muzien said. "Last I heard he was in Ker. I know your kind has ways to communicate across long distances, and surely this is an occasion worthy of that ability."

Pelarak shook his head, and he seemed to sink farther into his chair.

"I received a scroll ten days ago from the Stronghold," he said. "It warned against potential intruders, for it seemed a man by the name of Haern had broken into the Stronghold and slain Luther in his room. The paladins captured him, but the next night he broke free, though whether alone or not, the high paladin could not say for certain. As for the reason, none was given, and we had nothing to go on as to why Haern might have done so. Now, though..."

Pelarak looked back up at him, brow furrowed, cold eyes piercing his.

"Now it seems we have a reason. There are others involved in whatever game you and Luther were playing, Muzien. As for the intruder, Haern is likely the one known as the Watcher of Veldaren, and the attack on the Stronghold matches up with the weeks he went absent. An absence your own guild used well to its own advantage, I must say."

Muzien's pulse had begun to race, and he forced down his smile, kept at bay his growing excitement.

"So do you think the Watcher was working with Luther?" he asked, even though he knew the answer. Better to ask, though. Better to let Pelarak think answers eluded him.

"I don't know," Pelarak said. "We have been debating how we shall respond to such a grievous insult. The proof is meager, with only a name given under duress, and it easily could have been a lie. Taking down the Watcher would involve casualties, of that we are certain. A vocal group of our temple insists we let the paladins come here to seek their own vengeance, given how their failures let him escape in the first place. But if the Watcher was indeed behind the placing of these tiles, any attempt to take him could prove disastrous. The tiles erupt in enormous fire and force upon activation, yes? I fear whoever placed them will be able to activate them upon demand, granting this person frightening power."

"This doesn't feel like something within the Watcher's capabilities or morality," Muzien said.

"Then who else, Muzien? Under normal circumstances, given your placing of the tiles, I would assume *you* the one with the key to activating them. And if you are not, we have no other guesses."

Muzien had one, not that he would let the priest know it. After all, during the Watcher's absence, there'd been another man mysteriously absent . . .

"Can you see if your priests can disarm them?" he asked.

Pelarak rose to his feet.

"I will see what I can do. If it is beyond the power of our temple, I will find you and inform you so you might discover a different solution."

Such candor struck Muzien as humorous, and as the man led him to the door, he said so.

"By your words, you make it sound as if we are friends, if not allies," Muzien said.

Pelarak paused, hand on the door handle.

"We are not blind to your arrival," he said, glancing over his shoulder. "You seek power and domination, and you can have neither unless the city stands. So long as you keep your focus on the people's pockets, we will remain out of your affairs. Their hearts and souls are ours, though, elf. We heard of your display in the marketplace. Be careful declaring yourself a god. You might make true gods jealous, and there is little more dangerous than that."

Muzien flashed him a smile, and he lifted his darkened hand.

"I know better than most the touch of an angry god," he said. "And even so, I am not afraid. Good day, Pelarak. For all our sakes, I hope you find a way to remove the teeth from these tiles."

Exiting the room, Muzien refused the offered escort back to the front door from the boy in robes. Past the statue of Karak he walked, and this time the effect was far weaker, its gaze no longer focused on him, the purple glow of the fires casting strange shadows upon its sides.

Other than fear and demand for obedience, there never was much to you, was there? the elf thought, and he grinned at the statue that could not answer back.

Once he was outside the temple, the iron gate surrounding it slamming shut on its own after his passing, he glanced back to see the dark, deserted mansion once more. Several hundred feet down the road, arms crossed over her chest as she leaned against the side of a home, waited Zusa.

"I hope the trip was worth the time," she said.

"It was," Muzien said as she joined his side. His mind raced over all he knew. The Watcher would never hold the entire city hostage. Everything Muzien had learned of him showed him to be someone with a strong sense of morality, however misguided it might be. Plus his truce had appeared to be one made to protect the people, those he viewed as innocent. Killing those innocents? Preposterous. Muzien's former apprentice, however...

"It seems I have not taken things as seriously as I should," Muzien continued. "Thren Felhorn must be found and eliminated at all costs."

"We can put a bounty on his head," Zusa suggested. "Not that it'll do much good. Too many are still afraid of him, and those who aren't I doubt have the skill to take him down. Worse, he's homeless and guildless, just a single man lurking within the hundreds of thousands between these walls. Finding him without his revealing himself will be difficult to say the least."

"All true," Muzien said, "which means we must work with what we have."

She frowned.

"What does that mean?" she asked.

Muzien shrugged as he led them toward the guildhouse so he might gather more of his men for the task at hand.

"Tell me, Zusa, the markings drawn in blood that were left to mock you this morning…were there two symbols, or one?"

Her eyes seemed to shimmer. With fear or excitement, he could not tell.

"Two," she said.

"Exactly. I may not know how to find the Spider, but my gut says the Watcher does. Now come. The night is young, and I have a legend to capture."

CHAPTER

 11

Tarlak's eyes snapped open moments before whoever was at his tower door knocked their fist against it.

"This better be important," he muttered, rolling off his bed, grabbing his hat from the nightstand, and stumbling down the stone staircase in his bed robes. When he closed his eyes, he saw a glimpse of his doorway as if he were standing outside, though he kept it up for only a second. The last thing he needed was to break his neck rolling down the steps of his own tower. What he saw was enough, though. A soldier in the armor and tabard of the city guard was ramming his fist against the tower door as if he were a barbarian come to loot and pillage.

Just . . . ugh, thought Tarlak as he reached the bottom floor. *Good news never, ever comes at night, and certainly not from the lips of the city guard.*

"What?" Tarlak asked, flinging the door open. The soldier nearly lost his footing, having been in the process of knocking again. Taking a step back, the man began to mutter something of an apology, but Tarlak cut him off.

"Look, I'm sure you're a nice young lad," he said, "but it's far past midnight, I'm tired, and whatever wisdom you've heard about not interfering in the affairs of wizards applies doubly when they're cranky and sleep-deprived. So ignore the pleasantries and tell me why you're here."

"Antonil sent me," said the young man after overcoming his surprise. "Please, you have to hurry to the city. Muzien's taken the king hostage."

The wizard blinked a few times, then dug a finger into his ear to clear out whatever was surely interfering with his hearing.

"Could you repeat that?" he asked.

The soldier's neck flushed red, and he glared with impatience.

"Muzien has the king held hostage," he said. "He's demanding the Watcher turn himself in."

"He is?" Tarlak asked. "Did he say *why*?"

"If I knew I'd tell you. All I have are the words Antonil told me, that either the king's head or the Watcher's would be on a pike over the city gates come morning."

Tarlak knew his ears weren't at fault, but he was still having trouble believing what he was hearing.

"And I take it Antonil's hoping that I'll hand the Watcher over to save that sorry excuse of a royal brat, may Ashhur bless his reign?"

The soldier crossed his arms and looked unsure how to react to such an insult to his king. Deciding it best to ignore it, he shook his head and cleared his throat.

"Uh, no," he said. "Sir Antonil said to tell you he wanted Muzien turned into a hoofed animal he could send to the butcher's shop, and if not that, then your help killing the bastard would still be appreciated."

Tarlak raised an eyebrow.

"Did he now?"

"He did," said the soldier. "And he said to tell you that you'd be paid well for such service to the crown."

The wizard finally smiled.

"See," he said, "that's what you need to open with. Tell Antonil we'll be on our way to join him in a few."

"Thank you," the soldier said, bowing. "We're gathering at the western gate. Antonil will be waiting there for your—"

The soldier was still bowing when Tarlak slammed the door in his face. Holding a ring to his lips, Tarlak spoke into it, knowing his voice would be repeated in every bedroom of the tower.

"Brug, Del, wake up," he said. "We have a job to do."

As they dressed and prepared, Tarlak sat in his chair before the fireplace, still in his bed robes, and scratched at his goatee. He'd not seen Haern for some time, not since he'd tried and failed to disarm one of Muzien's tiles. Such a long absence was worrying, but Tarlak trusted his friend to still be alive. Given the dire circumstances the city was in, and Haern's search for a way to kill Muzien, it made sense for him to be absent for long periods.

"Well, we're ready," Brug said, leading Delysia down the stairs, he in his plate mail, she in her white priestess robes. "Care to tell us what we're doing?"

"Traveling to the city gate," Tarlak said. "Someone's set a trap for us, and we're going to spring it."

Neither looked rested enough to handle such news.

"Could you explain further?" Delysia asked.

Brug was less diplomatic.

"Fuck that, I'm going to bed."

"Get back down here," Tarlak said before the short man

could climb a step. "This isn't a game. My gut says Muzien wants us captured, though I can't begin to guess why. Well, I can guess, but it'd be irrelevant. Thing is, if he wants us, that means he won't stop trying until he *does* get us. We avoid him now, it makes things dangerous later, and it also means I can't ever trust you two to go out alone. Besides, this is our one chance to get the jump on that elven piss bucket, and I have no intention of letting it slip past."

"What about Haern?" Delysia asked. "Shouldn't we wait for him to come with us?"

"No clue when he might return," Tarlak said, rising from his chair. "The longer we wait, the more likely Muzien realizes we're onto him. I told the soldier, or the man pretending to be one, whichever it is, that we'd be leaving in a few, so that's what we're doing."

"Could we pretend you meant a few hours, not minutes?" Brug grumbled, eliciting an eye roll from Tarlak.

"You're not going out in that, are you?" Delysia asked, ignoring him and gesturing to Tarlak's bed robes. Tarlak glanced down at them, grunted, and snapped his fingers. Instantly they changed into his long yellow robes. Patting his multitude of pockets to ensure the various reagents were there, he nodded, then cracked his knuckles.

"I'll take us to a clearing just outside the west gate," he said. "From there, just play it loose and aggressive. Supposedly the king's being held hostage, and we're meeting Antonil's men to prepare for a rescue. My gut says it's at that gate we'll be attacked, so we need to be the ones getting the jump on them, not the other way around. Muzien's priority number one. Either of you see a chance to cut him down, you take it. Well, maybe not you, Brug. You just focus on keeping the two of us alive and kicking."

"I'll do what I can, smartass."

Tarlak clapped his hands, took a deep breath, and then prepared to open the portal. Before he could continue the motions, Delysia reached out and put her hand on his, preventing him.

"This is serious, Tarlak," she said, staring up at him. "If you're right, and Muzien's planned an ambush, every one of us may be killed. Are you sure you want to do this?"

Tarlak wrapped her hands with his own.

"Sis, we might save the life of every man, woman, and child in Veldaren if we pull this off," he said. "Of course we have to do this."

"At least we'll get paid, right?" Brug asked as Tarlak tore open a swirling blue hole in the fabric of reality.

"No guarantees, but I imagine Muzien's head should be worth a sizable reward. Eyes on the prize, Brug. I like your thinking."

With that he stepped inside, felt his stomach churn, felt the world shift, and then he was standing outside the western gate of the city. Behind him Brug and Delysia followed, and he felt a tug on his mind with the passage of each. Once both were through, he clenched a fist, banishing the portal.

"What makes you so certain it's an ambush?" Brug asked as the three approached the city gate. "Muzien seems like the type of fellow who'd kidnap a king to get what he wants."

Tarlak glanced back toward Brug, tossed him a wink.

"If Muzien wanted Haern, he wouldn't kidnap the king to get him. He'd kidnap *us*."

Brug, already in a poor mood, soured even further.

"Lovely," he said, hands resting on the handles to the punch daggers tucked into his belt. "Just lovely. The things I do for my friends."

"At least I'm not making you skip a meal."

"Yes, because food is so much more important than losing

sleep or walking into a certain ambush. My priorities must be so damned confused."

"Shush now," Delysia said, stepping between them. "Or you'll announce to Muzien's men we know of their ambush."

"I'd think if me and Brug weren't bickering it might tip them off something was amiss," Tarlak said. "But point taken." He nodded ahead to the gate. "I count twelve waiting. Want me to roast them, or wait until the trap's sprung?"

"I doubt Muzien's one of those twelve," Brug said, scratching at his beard, no easy feat given his plate gauntlets. "If you want him, you'll need to let him show himself."

"We might be dead or unconscious before that happens."

Brug rolled his eyes.

"Then just piss him off so much he appears anyway. I think you can manage that, too."

Tarlak drummed his fingers against his thigh, debating. Seeing the twelve armed and armored men waiting in a circle tempted him to blast them apart before they knew battle was upon them... but there was always that slight chance the guard had been telling the truth, and Antonil had actually summoned their band. Killing innocent men on a hunch? The wizard let out a sigh. No, he couldn't do that. He'd have to let the trap be sprung.

"Just stay sharp," he said as they passed through the open and unguarded western gate. "This will get ugly fast."

Many of the twelve were watching their approach, their group gathered in the center of the wide road leading deeper into the city. Given the darkness, and how the twelve were jumbled together, it was hard for him to know for certain, but seeing no hint of Antonil's golden armor made him all the more convinced of the ambush. If only they'd do something to confirm it...

"Tarlak?" one of the men shouted, taking a few steps toward them.

"Yeah?" Tarlak asked back.

That was all it took. The front-most of the group stepped aside, revealing five of the imposter guards holding small crossbows, the tips of their bolts no doubt coated with paralyzing or sleeping toxins. Tarlak's hands were already moving before they could fire. The bolts flew with a chorus of twangs, shooting through the air only to come to a sudden halt a few feet in front of their intended targets.

"Thanks for that," Tarlak said as the bolts dropped harmlessly to the ground. No longer worried about killing honest guards, the wizard clapped his hands, then spread them forward. Fire surged from his open palms, a wide spray that crossed the distance between them in a heartbeat, bathing the soldiers. As they screamed, Brug drew his punch daggers and clanged them together. When the fire dissipated, he rushed forward, where the few who'd survived cried out in pain from the burns.

"Get back here, you idiot!" Tarlak cried, but it was too late. On the rooftops of the fine homes on either side emerged dozens of men wearing long coats and the four-pointed star. Summoning another wall of force, Tarlak blocked a second barrage of arrows. Brug, beyond reach of the shield, shrugged off the few that hit him, the thin, slender shots unable to pierce his heavy armor. Less easy to shrug off was the kick to his head from a woman who leaped from the rooftop, attacking before all the others. As his friend dropped, Tarlak put his back to Delysia's and prepared another protective wall in case their ambushers should fire more arrows.

"This might have been a mistake," he muttered, praying Brug would somehow survive out there alone.

"Now's not the time to doubt yourself," his sister said, and he heard a soft ringing, saw light shining from her hands.

Abandoning their crossbows, the members of the Sun drew their blades and leaped from the rooftops. Hooking his fingers into the necessary formations while incanting the enacting words, Tarlak surrounded the two of them with a wall of fire, the flames blazing hot and taller than a man. He thought it'd slow the attackers down, but the men and women leaped through anyway, crossing their arms over their faces and enduring the burns. Tarlak blasted the first two with bolts of lightning, and the third he gave an icicle straight through the eye. From behind him he heard another loud ringing, followed by a blast of air as his sister fought with her own holy magic.

Trusting his sister to handle her own, Tarlak bathed his hands with fire, a welcome for the next to assault him. They came in a group of three, two men and a woman, using their long coats to protect themselves from the flames. Pushing his wrists together, he unleashed a giant spray of fire, its accompanying rumble and recoil forcing the wizard to brace his legs and dig in his heels. The man in the middle had no hope, his body consumed within the blink of an eye. The other two dove sideways, one crossing into the existing wall of fire, the other curling back around just within its reaches and then lunging with weapon drawn.

Trying not to panic, Tarlak twisted to the side, electricity sparking from his fingertips. He brushed the woman's extended wrist, releasing the power into her. For a brief moment her body locked in place, every muscle rigid, and then she collapsed, dead or unconscious, he didn't know.

"Tar!" he heard his sister shout, and he turned to find her backpedaling toward him, her hands a blur of light, blinding and disorienting the two men chasing her.

"I got them," Tarlak said, pulling his hand back to hurl a ball of fire. Movement from the corner of his eye made him pause. A woman sailed through the air, vaulting upside down over his wall of fire as if it were a simple matter. Tarlak froze, for though the clothes were different, he recognized that face, and those twin blades.

About time something went our way, he thought as Zusa landed between Delysia and her attackers, but his relief was short-lived. Before his sister could issue a word of gratitude, Zusa rammed an elbow into her stomach, then whipped about to strike her temple with the butt of a dagger. With a meager whimper, she crumpled, her body turning limp.

The fire around Tarlak's hands tripled in size.

"You lost your damn mind?" he cried, flinging two balls of flame. Zusa retreated, twisting her body like a dancer to avoid the attacks. The balls continued, detonating against one of the nearby homes, but he was too furious to care. Preparing to see if Zusa could dodge lightning as easily as she did fire, Tarlak only barely noticed another attacker leaping over his wall of flame. Whirling at the last second, Tarlak unleashed the great barrage of swirling lightning...at least, it should have been, only a ring on the man's hand flared with a sudden red light, preventing the spell from activating. Unimpaired, the man landed before Tarlak, then leaped forward, his feet seeming to never touch the ground.

Only it wasn't a man, Tarlak realized as he cast a desperate defense. It was an elf.

Twin lances of ice shot from his two hands, each one sharp enough to skewer Muzien where he stood. The elf was prepared for such an attack, and he leaped out of the way...both left and right, his body seeming to split into two copies. Tarlak realized it was an illusion, but his half-second of confusion was more than enough for someone as fast and deadly as Muzien. From both directions the elf closed in. It seemed he wanted Tarlak alive, for neither copy swung his blade, instead leading with elbow and knee. Defending against one or the other could mean picking wrong, so Tarlak did what he did best: improvise.

Dropping to his knees, he slammed his fists against the ground, unleashing his power in a shock wave rolling in all directions. To his left Muzien vanished as if he'd never existed, while on his right the elf let out a groan as his body halted in midair, then tumbled backward several feet. The wave continued, rattling windows and knocking loose shingles from the roofs of nearby homes. His ring of fire dissipated, and gasping for air, Tarlak rose to his feet, fingers dancing. It seemed the rest of the Sun Guild was content to let its master deal with him, and he couldn't be happier.

"Come on," Tarlak said, hurling a bolt of lightning as the elf raced back toward him. Light flashed with its release, and in that flash, Muzien shifted aside, just far enough to let the bolt fly harmlessly past. Two more Tarlak fired, and each time, in that briefest flash, Muzien shifted positions. Putting his hands together, Tarlak prepared to unleash a blast so gigantic no dodge would be possible. As he pooled his power, Muzien now frighteningly close, the elf shimmered, then vanished from view.

A second later, something hard cracked against the back of Tarlak's head. He dropped to the ground, his legs suddenly too weak to keep him standing. His hat tumbled free before him, landing at the feet of Zusa, who carried an unconscious Delysia.

"A shame you weren't better," Zusa whispered, just before shoving him with her foot so he rolled onto his back. Muzien towered over him as the world weaved uneasily from the blow to his head. Trying, and failing, to summon one last spell, Tarlak waved an ineffectual hand toward the elf in his long dark coat. Muzien pulled a rag from one of his pockets, a bottle of fluid from the other. As two other men grabbed Tarlak's arms and pinned him to the ground, Muzien dabbed some of the liquid onto the rag and knelt.

"Sleep now," Muzien said. He smothered Tarlak with the rag, punching him in the gut before he could think to hold his breath. Gasping in, Tarlak was overwhelmed by a sickly sweet smell. Pressure built in his forehead, he tasted copper, and then the growing darkness left him no choice but to obey Muzien's command as the fumes carried him away.

CHAPTER

12

It had been a long night, but Zusa expected no relief come the dawn, only an even longer day. She vaulted over the fence of the Gemcroft mansion, stealing Karak's power to float across its spikes and gently down to the ground on the other side. The number of guards on patrol actually impressed her. Perhaps Victor's insistence on his ability to protect Alyssa was more than idle boasting.

Not that it'd stop her. Across the grass she ran, keeping to the shadows, having no need for doors or windows. A bare wall was her goal, and crossing her arms, she leaped into its darkness. She felt a moment's dizziness, then emerged on the other side into a poorly lit hallway. Zusa let out a relaxed breath, glad to see no soldiers. Victor had been pulling in new men every day. Some might not recognize her, instead thinking she was an assassin. Her clothing would certainly do her no favors. She'd ditched the long coat Muzien had given her, but the four-pointed star was still sewn onto the front of her blouse.

Glancing around the corner, Zusa caught sight of the door to the master bedroom, and two men stood bored stiff at either side. Pulling back, Zusa debated the best way to go about getting inside. The last thing she wanted was a commotion, given the secrecy and urgency of her matter. Instead of knocking the two men out, she drew her daggers, put them on the ground, and then stepped around the corner with her arms raised above her head.

"I'm unarmed," she said as the two men jolted in surprise at her arrival. "My name is Zusa, a friend of Alyssa's, and I just wish to talk."

The man on the left drew his sword, but the other reached out and grabbed his wrist.

"I recognize her," he said to his fellow before turning toward Zusa. "Though that star on your chest makes me think we should send you to a cell instead of the lady's bedroom."

"A disguise, and nothing more," she said, arms still raised. "Let Alyssa know I'm here."

The first soldier pulled his hand free of his companion's, then banged on the door, the noise obnoxiously loud. He was trying to alert other soldiers without making it seem obvious, Zusa knew. Telling herself to be patient, she gritted her teeth and waited.

"Yes?" asked Alyssa's voice from the other side.

"A woman's here, says her name is Zusa."

A pause.

"Let her in."

Zusa smiled sweetly at them both as they opened the door, and then into the master bedroom she slid, the doors promptly shutting behind her.

"Forgive the intrusion," Zusa said. Alyssa sat before her in her bed, blankets bunched at her waist and her hair ruffled from sleep. "I know it's late, but we have little time to act before dawn, and the executions begin. Where is Victor?"

Despite her glass eyes being in a jar on the bed table beside her, Alyssa blinked a few times and rubbed her forehead, struggling to make sense of Zusa's words.

"Victor? Executions? What are you talking about, Zusa?"

Zusa took in a deep breath, and she forced herself to calm down as she sat at the foot of the enormous bed.

"Muzien's decided to draw out the Watcher," she said. "To do so, he's captured several of his friends, and come dawn, he plans on creating another spectacle like he did in the marketplace. We have to be ready. This is our chance, the best chance we could ever hope for. Now summon your betrothed so we can prepare."

Alyssa seemed almost embarrassed, and it baffled Zusa.

"He's not my betrothed," she said. "We...we married earlier today, Zusa."

Zusa tilted her head, and she started to gesture about her before feeling foolish upon realizing Alyssa would not see the motions.

"Then where is Victor?"

"Down the hall, in his quarters."

"It's a strange wedding night that has the newlyweds sleeping in different beds," Zusa said.

"I think tonight has seen stranger," Alyssa said, sliding out of bed, walking three careful steps, and then grabbing a waiting bed robe that hung from the side of a dresser. "Do you know exactly what his plans are?" she asked as she put on the robe.

"An excellent question," said a man's voice from the corner, and both turned toward the source. Haern stood beside an opened window, a window Zusa had long been displeased with for the exact reason before her. There should have been guards positioned beneath...but of course, it was stupid to think the Watcher would not have been able to handle them.

"I pray you didn't kill anyone to enter through there, Watcher," Zusa said, purposefully using his name to ensure Alyssa knew the identity of the stranger invading her bedroom.

"They'll wake," Haern said. "Now what is the meaning of this?"

He tossed a rolled-up letter onto the bed, the letter she'd written and left hanging from the door of the Eschaton Tower earlier that night. *They are gone*, it read. *Come to Alyssa's for answers*.

"We've...the Sun Guild has captured three fellow members of your mercenaries," Zusa said. "It will be a simple exchange, your life for theirs. Muzien will cry it out to the entire city to ensure you know, then begin killing them one by one until you show."

Haern's face, already clothed in shadow by that magical hood of his, somehow seemed to grow darker.

"Where?" he asked, his voice nearly a growl.

Before Zusa could answer, Alyssa interrupted, putting a hand on Zusa's shoulder to gain her attention.

"Not yet," she said. "Victor should be here for this."

Hardly an opinion Zusa shared, but she knew it was pointless to argue. Walking to the door, she yanked it open, startling the two soldiers who still stood guard.

"Fetch Victor for us," she said, then slammed it shut.

"I don't care about your plans, nor if you agree," Haern said from the corner. "Tell me where my friends are, Zusa. I won't leave them in that madman's hands for another second."

"You will if you want to kill him," Zusa said, matching the

Watcher's icy glare with one of her own. "I've risked everything to infiltrate Muzien's guild, and now we finally have a chance to catch him off guard. If you run off before dawn, alone and reckless, you'll ruin all I've worked for. Getting yourself killed won't help your friends, Watcher. Only patience will."

Haern's hands balled into fists, his rage as palpable as the warm night air, but Zusa stared him down without fear. She was the one in control here, not he. The door opened behind them, and Victor stepped inside. He looked strange without his armor, instead wearing a loose shirt and worn pants. His sword, though, he kept with him, carrying it in its sheath with both hands. Looking none too pleased, he glanced among the three, then joined Alyssa's side.

"What's going on here?" he asked, taking Alyssa's hand. It should have meant nothing, given how they were now husband and wife, but the sight of it still made Zusa's stomach twist.

"Muzien's planning another spectacle, this time at the fountain in the center crossroads of the city," Zusa said. "He's kidnapped friends of the Watcher, and hopes to use them as bait."

"When will he start?" Victor asked, and there was no hiding his eagerness.

"When else?" Zusa said. "At the rising of the sun. He's not one to pass up a chance for symbolism."

Victor glanced about the room again, squeezed Alyssa's hand.

"I take it we're discussing how to respond?" he asked.

"Glad you're caught up," Haern muttered. "And the solution is obvious. I'll wait with Zusa near the fountain, and the moment we spot my friends, we attempt our rescue. If Muzien dies during it, then all the better."

"A reckless waste," Zusa argued. "We have a few hours until dawn, and I say we use them. Gather every house soldier and mercenary, and prepare them for battle. Deathmask and his

Ash Guild have also offered to help, though how, he insisted be left up to him. With our combined might, we can leave Muzien with nowhere to escape, dealing the Sun Guild a mortal blow. Let him give his pronouncement. It'll be the last one he ever makes."

"So you want to wait?" Haern asked. "How long? Until there's a blade hanging over my friends' heads? And worse, you'd bring Deathmask into this?"

"I've worked with the Ash Guild before," Victor said. "I wouldn't call him trustworthy, but he will be when it comes to this. He wants the Sun Guild gone just as strongly as we do."

Haern turned away. He didn't argue the point, which Zusa saw as a good sign.

"The night is wasting away," Zusa said as the four stood awkwardly in the expansive bedroom. "We need to reach a decision while there is still time to act."

"It's a trap," Haern said. "A trap, purposefully set for me, and you want us to walk right into it."

"Of course it's a trap," Alyssa said, speaking up for the first time. For much of the discussion she'd appeared distant, lost in thought, but not now. She looked to the three with her vacant eyes, as if she could still see them. "But Muzien's arrogant, and he thinks himself infallible. If we overwhelm him from all sides, his preparations will mean nothing. A trap for a rabbit cannot catch a bear."

"Except it's not a rabbit he's after," Haern said. "It's me. He won't come unprepared, and even if we can surprise him, we're putting a lot of lives at risk. Innocent men and women will die, you have to know that."

At that Victor laughed, and he made his way to the door.

"Innocent men and women die every day," he said. "It's a poor reason to let a vile man go unpunished. I'll prepare our mercenaries for battle. For once, we'll be the ones getting a jump on that elven bastard. It doesn't matter what you say, Watcher. This is an opportunity, and we're going to seize it."

He pushed open the door, and before it could shut behind him, Zusa heard him issuing orders to the guards waiting there. Zusa stared after him, torn between relief that he had agreed with her and a gut desire to bury a dagger between his shoulder blades.

He wouldn't be the first of Alyssa's suitors I've killed, she thought, momentarily allowing herself to entertain the fantasy.

The opening of a window turned her back around. The Watcher was halfway out, feet braced on the windowsill.

"Where are you going?" she asked him, suddenly worried Haern would ignore their requests and attempt to find and rescue the rest of the Eschaton anyway.

"You, Victor, and now the Ash Guild?" Haern said. "It seems we're gathering help from all walks of life, so I know of one more who would love a chance to bury a blade in Muzien's throat."

"Who?" Zusa asked.

Haern only shook his head.

"I'll be back before sunrise," he said. "And don't worry, I'll play along. I hate this, Zusa, I hate it so much, but for the sake of this city, the Sun Guild needs to be broken, and this is the best chance we might ever have."

With a flourish of cloaks, he leaped out the window. Zusa slowly walked over to it, grabbed it with both hands, and slammed it shut as hard as she dared without risking breaking the glass.

"Zusa?" Alyssa asked, and she turned to face her. Her dearest friend sat on the edge of the bed, hands fiddling with the hem of her robe. "Many people will die this morning, won't they?"

A strange question to ask, and one that made her wonder. Something troubled Alyssa greatly, that much was obvious... but what?

"You know the answer," Zusa said, walking over to her side. She almost sat down next to her, changed her mind. That closeness, that trust, appeared to be over. So instead she stood before her, arms crossed. "What is bothering you, Alyssa?"

"Are we alone?" she asked.

"We are."

Alyssa swallowed, and she took in a deep breath. With her slow exhalation, the trembling of her hands vanished, the droop leaving her shoulders.

"Zusa... do you trust me?"

She was taken aback by the question, and it took a moment for Zusa to decide her answer. Kneeling down before Alyssa, she reached out and wrapped the woman's hands with hers.

"No," she said. "But if you'd ask it of me, I would trust you again."

Relief flashed across Alyssa's face, so swift, so brief.

"Thank you," she said, and she brushed her fingers across Zusa's cheek. "Thank you so much. Because come the morning, there's something I need you to do..."

CHAPTER 13

Haern could only guess at what tortures awaited those in the Abyss, but they had to be akin to what he felt as he watched Muzien's men drag Tarlak, Brug, and Delysia to the fountain. All three had been stripped naked and bound with rope around their wrists and ankles. By those ropes they were dragged, scraping the flesh of their backs along the hard ground. They were placed side by side, arms above their heads, thick white gags shoved into their mouths. To his minor relief, they did not appear to have been beaten. Despite the dozens of members of the Sun swarming the streets from all directions, Haern nearly jumped out the open window he watched from. Only Zusa stopped him, grabbing his arm and clutching his sleeve tightly.

"Wait," she said. "You won't save them by dying. Wait until the signal."

The two of them hid on the upper floor of one of the many stores within sight of the main crossroads through the center of

Veldaren, the meeting point of the west and south roads that ran from the two city gates. To the north and south, Victor's men waited in multiple groups, positioned far enough away to ensure none of Muzien's men saw their coming. They would wait for a runner sent by Victor from his own hiding spot on the opposite side of the street, a runner Haern prayed was already on his way.

"The moment he threatens any of the three, I'm going out there," Haern said, fingers drumming the hard metal of his sabers' hilts.

"And I'll be with you," she said. "Now endure. They won't be in danger until Muzien shows. He'll want their blood on his hands, and only after demanding your surrender."

"Small comfort," Haern whispered as members of the Sun sealed off the four exits around the crossroads and fountain, trapping at least a hundred innocent men and women within, herding them like cattle closer to the center. As he watched, more and more members of the Sun appeared from alleys and down the roads, some even crawling down from rooftops.

How many serve him now? Haern wondered, stunned by the sight. At least two hundred bore the four-pointed star, an army of blades and arrows awaiting its king.

"Still no sign of Muzien," Zusa said, keeping herself close to the wall and peering only as much as necessary, to prevent being spotted. To disguise her identity from Muzien, she wore a black bandanna across her mouth, a gray hood over her head, and long gloves so that very little of the color of her skin might be seen. Given better circumstances, Haern might have spent more time wondering how purposeful were the similarities to his own outfit.

"He must be waiting to make his grand entrance," Haern said. "Do you see any of the Ash Guild?"

"No. I don't see Thren, either. Do you fear they changed their minds?"

Haern shook his head.

"They'll be here. Neither would be willing to miss out on something this important."

"You're probably right," Zusa said, shifting so she could peer farther. Haern caught her tensing, and he felt his heart skip a beat.

"There," she said, and Haern slid beside her to watch.

With an entourage of four, positioned so they formed the points of his guild's symbol, Muzien arrived from the south. The wall of his men and women parted for him, followed by a scattering of those innocents trapped within. To his three prisoners he strode, looking so smug and confident Haern couldn't wait to bury his sabers in the bastard's face. Zusa tapped his shoulder, and when she pointed, he leaned out as far as he dared to look north. From the other direction came more members of the Sun, pulling a cart. Inside it, as best he could tell from that distance, were many heavy stones.

Muzien hopped up onto the side of the fountain, lording over his three prisoners with his arms spread wide.

"People of Veldaren," he cried, and the way he projected his words struck a memory so distinct it chilled Haern to the bone. The stance, the tone, the force of his voice...after slaying Tarlak and Delysia's father, Delius Eschaton, Thren had addressed the people the same way. The same contempt. The same sense of absolute mastery and power.

"Your faithfulness has pleased me," the elf continued. "But there is one who still fights against the inevitable dawn. A man who once ruled, and refuses to accept that his head no longer bears a crown. You know him as the Watcher, and it is to him I now call. Before me are your friends, people I know are close to you. We have crossed blades before, Watcher. You know you are powerless to save them. If you wish to spare their lives, only one option remains: surrender."

Murmurs spread throughout the frightened crowd. How many of them had waited for him to challenge Muzien, Haern wondered. How many had pinned desperate hopes on the symbol of his bloody eye scrawled over the star? Now came the long-awaited challenge. Shaking his head, Haern had to laugh. Surrounded by nearly two hundred members of his guild? Not exactly the fairest of battlegrounds.

It seemed Muzien's proclamation was finished, or at least had momentarily paused. He gestured to one of the men beside him, who went running to the cart. Eyes narrowing, Haern watched the cart roll up beside the three. Among the stones he saw thick planks of wood. Heart leaping to his throat, he realized what they were for.

"We go, now," Haern said.

"Not yet," Zusa hissed. "We have to wait!"

He could ignore her. A large part of him wanted to. Just leap out the window, assault every man and woman bearing the symbol of the Sun, and then pray reinforcements came in time. Only the tiniest sliver of control held him back. As the guildmembers began lifting out the planks of wood and heavy stones, Muzien turned and gave them an order Haern could not hear, but reading the words on his lips was easy enough: *Start with the girl.*

Two men pinned her down, one holding her ankles, the other her arms above her head. Brug began to struggle beside her, earning himself a kick to the face. On the other side, Tarlak only lay there staring, and Haern had an inkling the wizard was drugged. One of the wood planks settled over Delysia's body, covering her from her neck to her knees. That done, Muzien's men took the first of the blocks, heavy pieces of granite used to repair the wall surrounding the city, and set it down on the wood.

"Every moment I wait, we place another," Muzien shouted to the city. "The weight will crush her, breaking her bones and choking the life from her lungs. What is she worth to you, Watcher? Your friends here, are they less important than your pride?"

Another stone atop the wood.

"How many broken bones will it take to teach you humility?"

Haern's blood was on fire. Muzien bent down, yanked Delysia's gag free, and then motioned for them to place a third stone. The crowd had fallen silent at the display, making it all too easy to hear Delysia's pained cries. When they set down the stone, and she let out a horrific shriek, Haern felt Zusa grab his shoulder.

"Go," she said. "But not with blades drawn. Give him what he wants."

Sickening as it was, Haern knew she was right. Taking in a deep breath, he stepped on the edge of the open window, leaned out, and then dropped to the ground. Immediately the people who saw him scattered, giving him an open path to the fountain. He kept his hands at either side, balled into fists to prevent himself from drawing his sabers. The shadow of his hood lightened, Haern keeping its magic weak so they could all see the fury in his eyes.

"I'm here," he told Muzien, and his voice carried like the winds of a tornado.

The elf turned, and his grin was from ear to ear. He hovered his foot a moment over the pinned Delysia, then shifted so he stepped down from the fountain just beside her instead. His arms were open, as if he moved to greet a long-lost friend. The sickening amusement in his eyes betrayed his true desires.

"At last," Muzien said, still projecting so all the crowd could hear. "You have fought against me, but it is time to accept the changing winds. Kneel, Watcher. Bow, remove your hood, and beg for forgiveness. Only then will I remove the weight and spare your friends' lives. You need not die this morning, and neither must they. All I ask for is a single act of humility."

All eyes were upon them, and Haern realized he had never been witnessed by so many simultaneously. Here he was, their midnight specter, in plain sight beneath the morning sun. Most of Muzien's men had belonged to the Spiders, the Serpents, the Wolves...they had all feared his wrath over the past years. What Haern said now, what he did...it would carry throughout the city. It would define their memory of him, perhaps forever. Trusting his friends and allies, he let his cloaks fall across his body, hiding his hands, which dropped to the hilts of his sabers.

"I will never kneel," he seethed, the magic of his stolen hood ensuring all for hundreds of yards heard his whisper. "I will never bow. I have bled for these people, and I will die for them, all so they might know a measure of peace. This city is not yours to rule, Darkhand, and it never will be. You're not a king. You're not a god. You're a leech with a crown, and it's time we ripped you from our flesh."

It seemed a shadow fell across Muzien's face, though his smile remained.

"Draw your blades, Watcher," he said. "Let us see whose crown breaks this day."

An open path was all that separated the two, but just as Haern moved to leap forward, a brilliant red light flashed between them, followed by a gust of air and a thundering boom. Stone cracked, and Haern turned his head to the side to protect his eyes from the thin slivers of stone that flew in all directions.

Into the silence that followed came laughter, stealing attention to the rooftops nearby. Atop them stood Deathmask, his face covered by his gray mask and a swirling vortex of ash. At his left were the identical twins, Mier and Nien, twirling their daggers, while at his side crouched the crimson-haired Veliana.

"Come now," said the leader of the Ash Guild, a sparkle in his eyes. "You weren't thinking of having fun without me, were you two?"

Muzien glared up to the rooftop.

"Bring me his head," he ordered his men.

"That's funny," Deathmask said, not afraid in the slightest. "I was about to give the same order."

And then the horns sounded, coming from all four directions of the crossroads. Panic spread through Muzien's men as they turned to face the roads they guarded, only to see squads of armored soldiers approaching in formation. Haern spared only a moment's glance before turning his attention back to Muzien. If the elf held the key to the tiles, and he felt the day lost, he might activate them all. The air was thick with tension and screams and the sound of swords being drawn. Through it all Muzien stood perfectly still, unafraid. If anything, he looked disappointed.

"This city could have had peace," he said, staring straight at Haern. "Know that these deaths are on your hands."

He put his blackened fingers to his lips and whistled. Haern dashed forward, pushing aside any remembrance of their previous fight, and the humiliation he'd suffered. This was it, their best chance to defeat him. He would not dare lose it now.

Muzien's blades were drawn by the time Haern crashed into him, unleashing a barrage of cuts and slashes. Each one rang against steel as Muzien wove his defense, fluid as a dancer, strong as a lion. Haern slashed thrice, leaped back to gain distance for another charge, and then the explosions hit. In all four directions they roared, that horribly familiar sight of purple flame rising up from the demolished streets. Stone flew, and from all about came screams of the wounded. Some were of soldiers, some of Muzien's guildmembers, but oh so many were not.

The cries of battle heightened tenfold. From what little Haern could see, the explosions had struck Victor's men on their approach. He couldn't begin to guess the casualties. The remnants fought on, slamming into Muzien's lines, while Deathmask descended upon them from up high, shadow and flame bursting from his hands. The rest of his guild followed, the expert fighters cutting through the group of fifty attempting to secure the north road. Amid all the fire and chaos, innocent men and women tried in vain to flee to safety.

"You bastard," Haern said as the sound of steel on steel overwhelmed the screams.

"On your head, remember," said Muzien. "You could have knelt."

The elf charged, his speed incredible. Before his sabers first made contact Haern was already retreating, batting them from side to side in rapid cuts to prevent Muzien's sudden flurry from overwhelming him. It almost didn't matter. Muzien's strokes, while seemingly random, were guiding Haern's hands, manipulating his blocks, and it was only when he fell for a feint, leaving his chest wide open, that he realized his error.

But instead of going for the kill, the elf somersaulted backward. Haern's confusion lasted only a half-second, and then Zusa came slamming in from the sky, daggers piercing the dirt. She recovered instantly, and she did not attack alone. Together she and Haern rushed the elf, shifting to either side so they might flank him.

"To me!" Muzien cried to his guild as he spun. With one

hand devoted to either, he kept shifting, twisting, and to Haern's shock, he even stayed on the offensive. Back and forth between them he bounced, slamming aside Zusa's daggers, then missing a killing thrust by only an inch as the woman arced her back and fell away. Haern rushed to protect her, only to find himself screaming as the edge of a sword sliced through his arm, Muzien having predicted the move and swung blindly behind him. Praying the cut wasn't deep, Haern blocked the next few attacks Muzien unleashed against him, the elf ignoring Zusa as if she were no longer there. From the glimpses he saw of her, it might have been true. Three members of the Sun had rushed to the aid of their master, and they surrounded her.

"All for your pride," Muzien said, shaking the blade that had scored the cut so the blood on it would fleck away. "I had no desire to kill you, Watcher. You were merely bait."

"Bait?" Haern asked. "Bait for who?"

In answer, Muzien's eyes flicked to something just beyond Haern, and his grin hardened.

"Him."

Haern risked the glance, trusting his reflexes in case it was a trap. Cutting his way through members of the Sun, his short swords performing butcher's work, was his father. Amid such chaos, none could stand against him.

"No more games," Thren said, stalking forward like a predator, no hesitation, no delay, just drawn swords caked with blood at his sides. "Kill him, and end this farce."

Each step gained him more momentum, so that by the time he reached Haern his father was in full sprint. Haern dashed with him, heart pounding, blood pumping in his veins. His focus narrowed, and it seemed time slowed as his sabers slammed into Muzien's blocking sword. Twice more he cut in while moving in a semicircle, putting him to the elf's back. On the other side his father crashed in like a mad bull, blasting his swords in with all his strength. Muzien kept his feet moving, shifting between them so they could never have him fully flanked. Haern thrust with his left hand, pulled back with his right, and then instead of attacking with the other he leaped forward, hoping the sudden burst would surprise the elf.

Surprise, however, was with Muzien. His body shimmered, then vanished, immediately reappearing behind Thren. Haern dodged right, only barely avoiding impaling his father, and then dashed around Thren so he might hurl himself between Thren and Muzien's killing thrust. He batted the first aside, blocked a second coming from up high, then retreated before the two looped around and knifed past his defenses. Haern halted after only a few steps, for Thren was with him, and together they launched another offensive.

A ring on Muzien's dark hand flashed red, and then there were two of the elf, one leaping left, the other right. Haern and Thren reacted on instinct, each taking a direction. Haern extended in mid-run, hoping to slash one of Muzien's legs to hobble his movement, but his blade cut only air. The image of Muzien vanished, and the moment it did, Haern dug in his feet and then burst into a run in the other direction. Momentarily alone, Thren and Muzien tore into one another, feet firmly planted, their swords ringing and dancing with awe-inspiring speed. When their blades connected, challenging each other's strength, Haern came racing in from the side, hoping to thrust a saber through the elf's ribs.

The rest of the carnage was but background noise to Haern as his swords came knifing in. Again he felt time slow, felt his heart leap when Muzien suddenly flung back his father as if he were a child, then whirled in place. The motion gave him speed, and his arms extended, lashing out with his swords. A trap, Haern realized, the weapons a split second away from his neck. A sudden hard tug on the back of Haern's cloak spared him, killing his momentum so that Muzien's blade slashed an inch from his throat. Stumbling to regain his balance, Haern saw Zusa leap back into the fray, joining Thren's side.

They were masters, all of them, and when Haern came to their aid from the other side, Muzien could only retreat. Still they could not entrap him, his movements too quick, his awareness so great he would leap away at the last minute, twisting and ducking beneath what should have been fatal blows. Haern raced after, only for the elf to step onto the fountain and then leap to the statue in its center. Kicking off it, he sailed higher, back toward the three. Haern thought him preparing one final desperate assault, but then he shimmered, vanishing into nothing.

"Damn it," Thren said, spinning and pointing. Muzien had reappeared fifty feet directly forward, tumbling onto a rooftop. Before they could even think to chase, the elf was gone, rushing madly to the south, long coat flapping behind him.

When the elf was out of sight, Haern rushed to the only other thing that mattered: his friends.

During the chaos, it looked like the three had been left alone, Muzien's men having far more important things to do than watch over the prisoners. Haern wrapped his arms around the first of the stones and lifted it up just enough to move it, letting it thud down beside Delysia. He did the same with the other two, working as fast as his tired body would let him. With the last gone, he flung aside the wood plank and lifted Delysia up against him, wrapping his cloaks about her naked body.

"Are you all right?" he asked her as she clutched him tightly. He'd tried not to look upon her in such an indecent state, but his quick glimpse had shown enormous bruises growing all across her body. His rage burned anew, his jaw trembling and his hands shaking as he held the softly crying Delysia.

"I thought he'd kill you," Delysia whispered. "You should have left me, Haern. You should have..."

"Enough of that," Haern said. With her finally safe, he dared take stock of the surroundings. Bodies of men, women, and children filled the center square. Some were cut, some burned, some wore the four-pointed star, some wore mercenary armor. Far too many wore neither, just simple clothing that could not protect them against the rising chaos of daggers and unholy magic. Muzien's men were fleeing in all directions, their lines broken by Victor's soldiers. Deathmask stood amid a circle of bodies to the north, laughing as he flung a dart of fire into the face of a man in full retreat from Veliana's wicked daggers. Before him was a crater caused by the detonation of one of Muzien's tiles. Victor's men had been hit particularly hard there, and dozens of armored men lay about, their bodies mutilated by the power of the explosion. Though they were only four, the Ash Guild had massacred their opponents just as well as the other squads of forty. As for Thren and Zusa, neither was to be seen.

We won, thought Haern, letting out a sigh as the high-pitched keening of an abandoned child punctuated the ending of the battle. *Such a high cost, but at least we won.*

Haern detached one of his cloaks so Delysia could keep it about her. Kissing her forehead, he gently separated himself, then reached down and ripped the gag from Brug's mouth.

"About damn time you remembered we were here, too," the captive man grumbled.

Haern had no heart for the banter. Two quick cuts with his knife removed the bindings around the man's wrists and ankles.

"There's plenty of dead around," Haern told him. "Go find a cloak or something for you and Tar."

Turning his attention to the wizard, he frowned, not liking

what he saw. Tarlak's eyes were wide and glassy, but when Haern touched his neck, he still felt a pulse.

"They drugged him," Delysia said, kneeling down beside her brother. "They were afraid of what he could do if he awoke and used his magic."

Haern removed the gag, then cut the ropes. He noticed Tarlak's eyes were able to follow him slowly, as if the eyeballs were moving through ice.

"This should do until we get home," Brug said, returning with one of the Sun Guild's long coats. He wore a pair of breeches, the front stained with blood. Haern doubted he cared.

"Thanks," Haern said. Looping an arm underneath him, he raised the wizard to his feet. The man cooperated, but sluggishly, as if he were struggling to emerge from within a deep sleep. Haern put the coat on him and buttoned it shut as Delysia reached a hand out from her cloak, putting a hand on her brother's face. Tears in her eyes, she closed them and whispered the words of a prayer. Light shone across her fingers, dim but consistent, before sinking into the wizard's skin.

Tarlak blinked a few times, straightened up a bit, and then spoke, his speech heavily slurred.

"Did we win?"

"Yeah," Haern said, shifting the man's weight on his shoulder to have an easier time walking. "I guess we did."

"Good," Tarlak said, smiling drunkenly. "That's good."

"Del, let's go," Haern said as they started to walk west. When she remained put, Brug slid his shoulder underneath Tarlak's arm.

"I got him," Brug said.

Haern had to speed up to a jog to catch up to Delysia, who was rushing toward one of many injured lying about.

"Delysia, we need to get you home," he said, grabbing her arm. "You're hurt."

"They are, too," Delysia said, spinning about. "I have to help them!"

"You can barely stand," Haern said, holding her and doing his best to ignore the ache in her eyes. "The priests of Ashhur will be here soon. Come home. You're what matters now."

She was crying, but her resistance was meager. Haern held her firmly as she shuddered.

"Can't you hear them all?" she asked.

He could. Dozens crying out in pain, their wounds bleeding, their bones broken. One nearby man was pleading for someone to bring him a drink of wine, as if that would put his intestines back into his abdomen. The little girl with raven hair had wandered to the fountain and was sitting on its edge while she shrieked, ignored by all passing by. Two soldiers behind her were struggling to help each other stand, blood seeping over their armor from knife wounds that had failed to kill. Yes, he heard them, but Haern would sacrifice every one of them to spare her, and he hardened his heart against their agony.

"I do," he said. "But you're going to worry about yourself for once."

He put his arm about her, and thankfully she did not fight him. With her body leaning against him, Haern led her away from the remnants of battle. Tarlak's words echoed in his mind, the question far more poignant than the addled wizard's brain could have realized.

Did we win?

Hundreds dead, with several buildings on fire, huge chunks missing from the roads, and their main target, Muzien, still escaping with his life.

"Ashhur save us from another victory such as this," Haern whispered as he and Delysia returned home to their tower, and to safety.

CHAPTER

14

Few times had Alyssa yearned for eyesight as badly as when the battle raged, and she could rely only on what Victor told her.

"Don't worry," he told her as the explosions rumbled, shaking the building and making her eardrums ache. "We have this, we still have this."

More explosions followed, adorned by panicked cries and screams of pain. She heard horns, the marching of feet and armor, and then a near-constant chorus of ringing metal. It was all below her, for she and Victor watched and waited from the second-story window of the shop of a wealthy shoemaker, whose owner they'd bribed to let them enter. Victor had given a halfhearted argument that he should accompany his men when the battle started, but Alyssa had quickly disabused him of the notion.

"You are my husband now," she'd said. "I won't let you turn me into a widow a mere day after we are wed."

And so they waited, and Victor watched, as the battle continued. From time to time he'd describe the ebb and flow of the battle to aid her.

"The bastard set off an explosion using those tiles of his," her husband said. "Magic of some sort, it has to be; it's too big for anything else."

"How many were caught in the explosion?" Alyssa asked.

"Too many," was Victor's grim reply.

More screams, and a sudden heightening of the sounds of battle.

"The Watcher's fighting him," Victor said. "Zusa too, they're trying to surround him."

Alyssa felt her heart skip, and the seconds passed by at an agonizingly slow pace. Was it possible the two could kill the elf who had taken over their city? Or would she lose Zusa now, when she needed her most?

Victor swore, and it took all Alyssa's willpower not to immediately assume the worst.

"He escaped," Victor said, after what felt like several minutes of combat. "The elven shit escaped, but it doesn't matter. I'd say sixty members of his guild lie dead, probably more, and all three of the Watcher's friends survived."

He took Alyssa's hand in his and squeezed it, and Alyssa squeezed back.

"Do your men give chase?" she asked.

"They were ordered to do so," Victor said, and she sensed him turning his attention back to the window. "Every life we take reinforces our victory. In the end it won't matter that he escaped. We've made a mockery of his prideful spectacle. After today no one will dare think he's the god he's claimed to be."

Alyssa smiled, hiding the incessant pounding of her heart.

"Good," she said. "Very good."

There was a lone door leading into their small room, and Alyssa heard it open, the sound followed by a rattle of plate mail.

"Sir," said a voice, that of one of the two guards stationed just outside the door. "Zusa wishes to—"

His words ended with a sudden gargle, then a rattling cacophony of plate mail striking the ground. Victor flung an arm across Alyssa's chest, pulling her behind him, as she heard his other hand draw his sword.

"Zusa," he cried. "What madness is this?"

"One of your guards was a traitor in the pocket of the Sun Guild," Zusa said from across the room.

"Andarin? He's served my family for twenty years. He can't be a traitor."

Alyssa could only imagine Zusa's smile.

"I know," she said. "But that is what we will say when asked what happened here."

In a hidden pocket of her dress, Alyssa carried a dagger, and with his back still turned to her, there was nothing Victor could do. She plunged the blade into the side of his neck, then released as she felt warm blood flow across her fingers. It'd gone in deep, and if it wasn't enough, Zusa would fix that. Retreating until her back reached a wall, she steeled herself against Victor's weak cries of pain, which came low from the floor. He'd collapsed, Alyssa realized. Good. She heard a sword slide across the ground, a repositioning of the dead guard's body. Moments later Zusa was before her, wiping away Victor's blood splashed across her hands.

"The wound is fatal," Zusa whispered. "When his movement stops, scream for soldiers. The one outside the door is dead, but I'll make sure others are beneath the window to hear you."

"Thank you," Alyssa said. "Now hurry. Make sure others see you taking part in the chase."

Lips pressed against her forehead, and then Zusa was gone, vanishing down the steps. Heart still hammering, Alyssa slid to a sit, back still against the wall. Victor was across from her, and to her surprise, she heard him force out words.

"Why?" he asked. The question came out labored, and she tried to imagine what he looked like. Did he clutch at his bleeding throat? Did he lie on his stomach, or his back? As badly as she'd wished to witness the battle outside, she felt relief at being unable to see the hurt and betrayal in Victor's eyes.

"Why?" she said. "Because you're a fool, Victor. Overthrowing Edwin, declaring ourselves king and queen... it's a fool's dream, and shame on me for having believed it for a second."

"We..." Victor coughed, and she heard a splashing of liquid, followed by a scraping sound as he dragged himself closer. "We could have done it. You're strong... strong enough for this... then for anything."

Alyssa looked away, despite her blindness. She kept seeing the man's face, seeing his blue eyes. There'd been a glimmer of fanaticism when he'd come to her, there was no denying that. But he'd been a good man... hadn't he?

No. She couldn't believe that.

"You could have said no," Victor continued. "You... you could have just said no."

"And you'd have only betrayed me," Alyssa said. *Remember his threats*, she told herself. *Remember his insanity, his single-minded destructiveness. He doesn't deserve your pity. He doesn't!*

"I wouldn't," he gasped, and Alyssa found herself wishing he'd die faster. She didn't want to hear his words. She didn't want to answer his questions.

"Everyone has," she whispered. "Yoren, Arthur, Bertram, Graeven, my own mother...you would have too, Victor. It was only a matter of time."

The room went silent for several long seconds, and when Victor spoke again, he was disturbingly close.

"Never," he gasped. "I...never..."

There was no doubt in her mind that he believed he told the truth. She felt his hand touch her leg, and she held back a shiver. Despite all her insistence that her actions were necessary, all her mental berating for entertaining such weakness, she still felt tears running from her glass eyes, and she reached down to hold that hand clutching her with dying strength.

"I'm sorry," she said, a lump growing in her throat. "But I can't believe that. I can't...not of anyone. Not anymore. I'm sorry, Victor. I'm so sorry."

Into the city he'd come, banner held high, and as Alyssa cried, she heard him gasp his last breath, dying betrayed and alone at the hands of his wife. At that moment she felt only hatred for the cruel, miserable world, and all the things it would demand she do to secure a future for herself and her son.

Alyssa crawled along the floor, blood smearing across her fingers and seeping into her dress. Arms sweeping, she continued until she found the body of the guard, which Zusa had moved deeper into the room and then laid on its stomach. Still holding her dagger, she felt along his neck until she located the wound, then jammed her blade into it. More blood spilled, and she made sure it got across her hands. Finished, she crawled back to Victor.

Let them think he died in my arms, she thought. *It's true enough.*

His body was starting to stiffen, but she lifted it enough that she could place his arm over her legs, then knelt over him.

Blind, bloodied, she knew she must look a pathetic sight. It was exactly what she was hoping for.

"*Guards!*" she screamed. "*Guards, help! Help!*"

Distant shouts came from the window, followed by her men rushing into the building. Alyssa waited, staring down at Victor's face. His eyes, she wondered. Were they as glassy and lifeless as her own? She thought to close them, but her hand trembled too much, and she feared she would miss.

More shouts, curses as heavy footsteps reached the stairs and the dead guard. The door burst open, mercenaries pouring in like stampeding cattle.

"What happened?" asked one of the soldiers.

"He killed him," Alyssa said, needing little effort to summon fresh tears, or to add a quiver to her voice. "One of the men, I heard him draw his sword, and then Victor started screaming in pain. I didn't know what else to do, so I just took my dagger..."

She let her voice trail off. The blood from the guard's neck, and all over Alyssa's clothes, would tell the rest of the story. Who would think a blind woman responsible for the murder? They might have guessed Zusa's involvement, but she'd been seen by dozens fighting Muzien's men in the battle outside, and her slip inside the shoemaker's had lasted mere moments during the chaotic aftermath.

No—the blood, the bodies, it'd all tell a story they'd seen countless times before. They began searching the guard's body, and she heard a rattle. One of them had found the coin purse Alyssa had given Zusa to plant on him.

"Fucking traitor," the soldier said.

"We need to get her somewhere safe," said another voice.

"Take me to my mansion," Alyssa said, gently removing Victor's arm from her leg so she could stand. "I need to be with my son. If there are traitors here, they may be elsewhere as well."

"What do we do with . . . you know?"

Victor's body, of course. Many of the men in that room had never pledged allegiance to her, only to Victor. They didn't know how to respond, what sort of protocol to follow. As a gloved hand took hers, Alyssa straightened up, showing the resolve they all expected of her, fostered by her bloody years of ruling her household.

"Wrap him and bring him with us," she said. "He was a Gemcroft, and he'll be buried with every privilege that deserves."

Her escort led her down the stairs as she heard men behind them discussing ways to carry the body. Despite Muzien's failure, despite her inheriting control of all of Victor's men, despite her telling herself again and again today had been a good day, her walk to her mansion felt like the long, suffocating procession of a funeral, one where the body inside the coffin was not Victor's, but hers.

CHAPTER 15

Tarlak was mostly himself again by the time they reached the tower, which meant Haern had to endure a lengthy tirade of curses the final few minutes of walking.

"I'll turn him into a frog," said the wizard. "No, a toad, a gods-damn wart-covered toad I can hang by its legs from a tree until the vultures come for an easy meal."

"I'll tell you what," Haern said, Delysia still in his arms. "If I catch the son of a bitch, I'll try to leave him alive so you can do just that."

Tarlak cocked an eyebrow his way.

"I'm half-drugged, naked, and pissed off. Please tell me you aren't mocking me."

"I'd never dream of it."

Once inside the tower, Haern collapsed beside the fire, which Tarlak reignited with a snap of his fingers. The other three climbed the stairs, to their rooms to dress and clean themselves. Finally given a moment of respite, Haern closed his eyes and tried to massage away his growing headache. He'd hardly had any rest, for when he'd come home from a long day of tormenting the Sun Guild and scrawling the symbol of the Watcher alongside Thren's spider, he'd found the note left for him by Zusa telling him to come find answers at the Gemcroft mansion. When he'd scoured the tower, finding the rest of his friends gone, he'd immediately rushed over. Now that they were safe, he wanted nothing more than to lie down, close his eyes, and sleep. Sadly, it seemed it would be hours before he would have such a chance.

Tarlak was the first to come down, a drink already in his hand. Brug followed, the squat man taking a seat in a rocking chair while Tarlak plopped down onto their couch facing the fire. As he sank into the cushions, the wizard let out a groan of appreciation.

"Bastards kept us tied up all night," he said. "Feel like every single muscle got pulled and twisted a totally wrong direction."

"Least you were out of it because of whatever they made you drink," Brug grumbled. "Me and Del, however..."

He trailed off, and Haern had to repress a shudder. The three had been dragged naked through the streets of Veldaren to their intended execution. Mocked. Humiliated. Whatever remnants of exhaustion Haern felt faded away under a fresh wave of fury.

When Delysia came down from her room a few minutes later, changed into a comfortable white robe, she assured them her wounds were not serious.

"Just bruises," she said as she sat down next to her brother. "You revealed yourself before... before there was too much."

Haern clenched his jaw tight, fighting away the horrible image of her screaming as the rocks were placed upon her one by one. It seemed that every passing moment, his need for vengeance grew.

"Did you get a look at how Victor's men fared?" Tarlak asked, rubbing at his eyes as he had often over the past half hour.

"They were hit hard," Haern said, thinking on what little he'd seen; his attention had been so heavily focused on Muzien. "When those tiles exploded, I think the bulk of his forces were either directly on them or just beyond."

"Those tiles," Tarlak said, and he shook his head. "That confirms it. They must be under the elf's control. Even with far superior numbers, he had a solution ready. Given what happened today, we might need to consider the very real possibility he turns all of Veldaren into a giant smoking crater."

"It's always been a possibility," Haern said, holding his head in his hands as he sat on the floor.

"Except we figured if the city was in Muzien's hands, he had no reason to blow it up," Tarlak argued. "Well, today's asskicking may make him reconsider just how securely that crown sits upon his head."

"Then what do we do about it?" Haern asked, exasperated. "We can't move them. We can't break the magic in them. If Muzien's holding the key, he's still out there, and most likely furious. What solution is there beyond evacuating the whole damn city? Maybe you haven't noticed, but this tower isn't big enough to hold hundreds of thousands of people."

"No, but we can handle one more," Tarlak said, voice rising. "Bring the king here if that's what it takes to convince him he'll be safe. Even given how cowardly that little shit is, he'd be insane to ignore something this ridiculous. For Ashhur's sake, we're fighting a war within a stone's throw of his throne. He has to act. I don't care if every soldier in the entire realm of Neldar must be housed in these walls, it's time to bring Muzien down for good!"

"If armies arrive, Muzien may declare this all a lost cause," Delysia said, shrinking into the cushions. "He doesn't seem the sort to leave without one last grand act, and we all know what it'd be."

Her soft statement quieted them all. Letting out a sigh, Haern said good-bye to any chance for rest within the next few hours.

"I'm tired of letting our fears guide our actions," he said, rising to his feet. "Despite the risks, we have to start countering Muzien with everything we have. If there's anything we've learned today, it's that our only hope of peace comes with his death."

"Where are you going?" Tarlak asked as Haern headed for the door.

"The castle," Haern said, pulling his hood over his head. "The king cannot turn a blind eye to this chaos any longer, and no matter what it takes, I will convince him of that."

"Are you sure it's safe to go out there alone?" Brug asked, tilting back his chair so he could look over his shoulder at him.

"Safe?" Haern asked, pushing open the door to their tower. "No one's safe, not anymore, and that's why this must be done."

Many times Haern had sneaked into the castle, and as on many occasions before, his message for Edwin would not be delivered to the king directly. No, there was another who was far easier to reason with, the one who truly controlled the city, tugging at whatever strings he must to make the frightened, immature puppet that was their king dance the proper dance. To his room Haern went, scaling the walls of the castle and crawling in through an open window, using extra care given the daylight.

Haern had expected guards to be posted at the door of Gerand Crold's room deep in the heart of the castle, but he'd expected wrong. Pushing it open, he was once again surprised to find Gerand actually within, instead of hiding elsewhere or rushing about the city trying to make sense of the craziness.

"Do you have a death wish?" Haern asked the middle-aged man, who sat in a chair facing the door, a bottle of wine in his left hand, a glass in his right.

"I've come to certain conclusions over the past decade," Gerand said, taking a sip. "If people like you, or Thren, or that Muzien fellow wish to have me dead…well, then I'm dead. After today, I thought I'd be getting a visit from one of you three. Must admit, I'm happy you're the one to show."

Haern shut the door behind him, then leaned his back against it. Arms crossed, hood low over his face, he stared at the king's adviser, trying to get a read on him. The man seemed broken somehow, a far cry from the confident bastard Haern was used to dealing with.

"Why aren't you at the king's side?" he asked.

"Veldaren's glorious king?" Gerand asked, pouring more wine into his glass, then lifting it in a toast. "You mean that cowardly, spoiled, infantile snot of a boy, whom Ashhur has ordained through the luck of being from the right set of testicles to be our lord and master? Fuck him."

He downed half the glass, then set it aside.

"He's hiding in his room," he continued. "Possibly crying into a pillow, or maybe ranting and raving at whatever guard is stuck listening to him. He's convinced he'll be blamed for what happened at the city center, which means his paranoia's about to go through the castle roof. Gods damn it, what I'd give for a good insurrection, so long as my head didn't join Edwin's on the chopping block."

Under normal circumstances Haern would have been amused, but his exhaustion and anger kept the smile from his face.

"We don't have time for this," he said. "That display earlier should make it clear Muzien cannot be ignored. You've relied for too long on people like us to do your dirty work. It's time for the city's soldiers to attack the Sun Guild. Order the four-pointed star banished, and have your men sweep the city."

Gerand laughed, first softly, then louder and louder, his shoulders rocking violently by the end.

"Ah, Watcher," he said, rubbing a tear from his eye. "What city have you been living in the past few years? There's a greater chance of pigs falling from the sky on a clear day than what you're requesting."

"I'm not requesting," Haern said, letting an edge enter his voice.

"Spare me. You think your threats matter? The king is terrified for his life, and unlike the lions who have ruled before, he's more of a turtle. He's going to pull into his castle here, close his eyes, and pray that everything just goes away."

Haern pulled back his cloak to show a hand resting on the hilt of his saber.

"Put down that glass," he said. "You're drunk enough, and I need you to listen. Either the king comes out of his shell, or he dies. Have I made myself clear?"

"As clear as this glass," Gerand said, lifting it up to him in another toast. "But the moment he moves against Muzien, as you demand, Muzien will execute him. So you're threatening to kill the king if he doesn't go and voluntarily get himself killed. See the conundrum? And honestly, when it comes to which one he'd rather be killed by, well, Muzien pulls a more intimidating presence than you. No offense, of course, but you don't seem the type to enjoy torturing a man. That elven bastard? Trust me, the king's heard the story of his Red Wine. You're not winning this competition."

Haern lunged forward, grabbing the man by the front of his shirt and yanking him to his feet. Struggling to control his anger, he flung Gerand against a wall, knocking over the bottle of wine in the process. The red liquid poured across their feet as Haern leaned in close, pinning the man.

"Have my years here meant nothing?" he asked him, seething. "How many bodies have I left in my wake? How many challengers and upstarts have I beaten down with my sabers? Muzien was the one who fled our ambush, not the other way around. Our boot is on his neck. We'll break the Sun Guild if we keep up the pressure. You say the king fears him more? Then I will go to him myself, and let him see the fury in my eyes."

He shoved Gerand once more, then turned to leave.

"Wait," the adviser said, grabbing Haern by the arm. The act, while brave, was also stupid, and Haern whirled about on instinct, breaking his grip and ramming him back against the wall. Gerand let out a groan from the pain of the contact, but he did not relent.

"You don't understand," Gerand said. "You've been in our shadows so long, we know you. We know you protect this city. We know you'll do everything you must to keep us safe. Even the king, in all his stupidity, knows it. That's why you can't win this through fear, nor through intimidation. You would protect us; Muzien would *destroy* us. He calls himself a god, and do you know what gods do to followers who turn on them? It isn't pretty. It isn't kind. Edwin will make whatever deal, and sacrifice whatever lives necessary, to spare himself that wrath."

"You fear what Muzien would do to you if you betrayed him," Haern said. "What you should truly fear is what this city would become if you served him loyally. We cannot let him win. Please, Gerand, you know that, deep down, you have to know that."

Gerand looked down to the wine spreading across the stone floor. Letting out a sigh, he retrieved the bottle and set it atop his desk. It seemed his entire body sank as he turned away, fingers still clutching the bottle's neck.

"I do know," he said. "And though it's tantamount to treason, I will order the city guard to no longer turn a blind eye to the Sun Guild's dealings. It won't be the war you want, Watcher, but after that debacle at the fountain, it is the best I can do."

Haern reached out and put a hand on the man's shoulder.

"You're doing the right thing," he told him.

"Perhaps," Gerand said, looking over his shoulder and offering Haern a half-smile. "And we all know what happens to those who do the right thing in this fair city of ours. Now leave me to drink what's left of this bottle in peace."

Haern bowed low, offered his thanks, and left.

When he shut the door, he heard the bottle smash against its other side, heard the softest of sobs.

CHAPTER

 16

The dreams had come every night, but this night, Nathaniel sensed they were different. As the world shifted and took shape around him, he felt a greater awareness to its movements, its textures, sounds, and tastes. The ground beneath him was hard and black, as if burned by a great fire. The sky above was a massive blanket of stars, with not a single cloud to mar the image. Wind blew from the west, sticky and hot like the breath of a giant beast. Spinning about, he saw only barren wasteland, no trees, no grass, no homes or walls or signs of life. Amid it all, a rumble shook the land ever so slightly. It was the growl of a lion, of such size Veldaren was but a flea compared to a single claw on its paw.

The time approaches, spoke a voice like thunder. Panic spiked through Nathaniel's chest, and despite spinning on his feet, he could not find the speaker. The dreams, no one had spoken to him through the dreams since...since...

"Since you asked how you might serve," said another voice, deep, powerful, and directly behind him. Nathaniel spun, and his jaw dropped as he stared up at the enormous man. He wore black plate mail, and strapped to his side was a gigantic sword. He was unquestionably handsome, short hair a deep brown, skin like bronze, jaw square and firm. Emblazoned across his chest piece was a roaring lion reared up for battle, stunning in its minute detail. With every movement the light shifted, making it seem like the lion's fur blew in the wind.

"Who are you?" Nathaniel dared ask.

"You know my name, yet you ask anyway," said the stranger to his dreams. "Why do you not trust what you know to be true?"

Nathaniel swallowed, throat so dry he had to fight down a cough. The man's eyes... there were stars shifting within the eyes, spinning, twinkling...

"Karak," he whispered. "You are Karak."

The god smiled.

"I am, child. Come. Sit with me. We do not have much time."

Nathaniel was about to ask where they might sit when a slab of stone tore up from the cracked ground, dirt slaking off it. Its surface was wide and impossibly smooth, and when Nathaniel put his hand on it to climb atop, he was surprised by the chill it had despite having just come from beneath the ground. Granted, he was in a dreaming land, so why should he expect it to make sense?

Karak sat down beside him, and he lifted his divine gaze to the heavens.

"It's peaceful here," he said.

Nathaniel looked about the wasteland, held back a shiver.

"It's so empty," he said.

"Aye, it is. But when you look up at the stars, child, does it matter? Stare at their beauty, and then let your ears listen, and your heart feel across the void. Do you sense it? No neighbors curse one another. No man seeks to take what belongs to his friends. No woman seeks to poison her enemies. There is no hunger. No suffering. Close your eyes, and feel the comfort that comes from belonging in a place of proper Order, a place free of chaos, pain, and sadness."

It felt as if the world were glassing over. Nathaniel stared at the stars, seeing them for the first time, and not just them, but things shimmering behind the stars, colors and shapes and whole worlds beyond his understanding. His awareness expanded, and for the briefest moment he felt himself one of thousands, in a land full of men and women soaking in the beauty of the heavens, without need for sleep, or food, or warmth. No movement, no drawn breaths, just statues of thought and wonder. In the soft silence, Nathaniel felt the faintest touch of that peace Karak offered, a place without fear or doubt or failure. In that tide of humanity, he was like all others, neither greater nor worse. His future responsibilities weighed nothing, for no longer did faceless, nameless men and women circle his family like vultures, seeking to tear away everything that might be his. A painless existence. A hateless future lost in the void of an eternity that stretched on and on, promising something new with each shift of the sun.

"This is what you want?" he asked. Before his eyes the stars whirled past, as if he were hurtling into the deep black skies, and lost in wonder, he watched a swirling nebula of red collapsing into a burning yellow orb of such a size he could never comprehend.

"It is," Karak said. "Life leads to sin. Humans are broken, their failure inevitable, their flaws built into the very core of their souls. There will be no perfection, not in their current forms. I merely seek to offer them the closest resemblance they might ever achieve before the collapsing of the days. To do that I need your help, child."

"My help?" Nathaniel asked, and he felt himself pulled back down to the blasted heath, and to the god sitting beside him. The fields of men and women were gone, and he wondered if he'd ever truly seen them. "Why do you need my help?"

"Because I am imprisoned," Karak said. "There are cracks, tiny and fleeting, that my strength might slip through, and to my faithful I deliver all the power I can. Through servants I must act, Nathaniel, through the faithful and the brave. One such servant comes for Veldaren, and you must help him. I catch glimpses of the future through my prison, and I see the importance you will play, if you would only obey."

It seemed so strange to be asked to carry such a mantle. Karak was a god. He could surely see how young he was, how frightened and helpless. What could he possibly do? But as another warm wind blew, he glanced to the stars, and in them he saw moons dancing, saw giant orbs each surrounded by a dozen rings that revolved in perfect synchronization. Breathtaking, truly breathtaking.

"What must I do?" he asked.

Karak's giant hand settled onto his shoulder.

"The gems of the chrysarium," he said. "You must find them, and keep them close. They once adorned the hem of my cloak when I walked the land of Dezrel centuries ago, and my power still dwells within them. They will keep you safe, and should you cry out my name in faith, they will strike down those who would do you harm. Do you understand?"

Nathaniel nodded.

"I do," he said.

"Good. Now wake, child. Your life is in danger."

*　　*　　*

Nathaniel's eyes snapped open, and despite the depths of his dreaming, he felt wide-awake. Scanning the darkness of his room, he saw nothing, heard no one, but there was no denying the pounding of his heart in his chest, nor the warning Karak had offered.

The chrysarium, he thought. As he slid from his bed, he felt certain he must find it, the collection of gems the most important thing in all the world for him to protect. But where was it? It'd belonged to his grandmother, so where might it have been put? In her room? Padding across the carpet to the door, he paused, hand on the knob, and felt paralyzed by indecision. He must find it, he knew he must find it, but *where*?

An idea came to him, and it felt troubling to even consider it, but what else was there? Doing his best to remember the way his grandmother had prayed, he closed his eyes, bowed his head, and whispered the words.

"Karak... I am your servant. If... if you would, if my dream wasn't just a dream, then show me where it is."

Nathaniel jerked backward as if a needle had stabbed his forehead. For the briefest moment he felt he could not breathe, and flooding the space before his eyes he saw flashes of images: Victor stumbling to Melody's dead body, her fingers curled about the chrysarium, her blood leaking over it—then Victor taking it from her—then Zusa demanding it be destroyed, her voice warbling and distant. The last image was of Victor promising his mother she would never see it again.

As suddenly as they'd come, the images vanished, and Nathaniel let out a gasp as he recovered.

Victor's room, he thought, and he felt so certain he might as well have been the one to put it there. Given how they'd yet to bury him, they'd not decided what to do with his possessions. Pulling open the door, Nathaniel stepped outside, and was immediately stopped by the guard positioned there.

"Whoa there, little master," said the guard, a friendly man named Argus who'd been guarding his room for the past several nights. "What are you up to at so late an hour?"

Again he felt a moment of panic. No one could know of the chrysarium. He knew that as he knew the sun was yellow. But what excuse could he use to wander the mansion unescorted?

"I'm hungry."

Argus lifted an eyebrow.

"You're hungry?"

It felt like such a lame excuse, but Nathaniel nodded anyway.

"I just wanted a snack from the kitchen, that's all."

The tall man shrugged.

"I probably shouldn't, but I'll tell no one if you don't," he said. "You're not going alone, though. Follow me."

As the guard led the way, Nathaniel felt his mind at odds with itself.

Tell him, he thought. *Warn him you're in danger!*

But to do that would mean explaining himself. That would lead to questions, perhaps losing the chrysarium, and he felt a gut panic at the idea of his mother's learning of his dreams of Karak. Fear paralyzed his tongue, and fear kept his feet moving. Maybe if he got there quickly, everything would be fine. Maybe simply leaving his room would save him from whoever would dare break into their mansion.

But what about Mother? asked his pounding heart. *She's in danger, too!*

Karak's face flashed before his eyes, that peaceful smile, but accompanying it was the earth-shattering growl of the lion. He felt it in his belly, felt it rattle his bones, and he pulled his arm across his chest, clutched the stump of his other arm, and shivered.

"You need a blanket or a robe?" Argus asked, keeping his voice low as they turned a corner. "I'm hot as the Abyss, but I've got all this armor, so it's not right for me to judge."

Nathaniel's teeth chattered, just once before he could clench his jaw tight.

"I'm fine," he said, and he offered no further explanation beyond that. They were just passing by the door to Victor's room, and it cried out to him like a wailing child.

"Wait," he said, halting. Argus took another step, then turned about, confused.

"This is hardly the kitchen," he said, raising an eyebrow.

Nathaniel's fingers drummed across the stump of his arm. What to do? Lie? Pretend he had some sort of authority and demand to be left alone? Swallowing down a growing lump in his throat, he decided to appeal in the only way he knew: with honesty.

"I . . . I need something from Victor's room," he said.

"Do you now? Should I ask what it might be?"

"No, you shouldn't. And I don't want you telling my mother, either. This is really important."

Argus frowned, and Nathaniel endured his stare as he waited for the man to reach a decision.

"You just want in and out?" he asked.

Nathaniel nodded, earning himself a sigh.

"Fine. I'll wait out here. Just make it fast, all right?"

Nathaniel barged through the door without acknowledging him, his head pounding with urgency. Victor's old room was incredibly dark, and stumbling to the opposite side, where he saw the vague outline of the curtains, he opened them fully so he might see by the strong moonlight. So strange, he thought. Everything was neat and tidy, and belonged to a man who mere hours ago had been alive, and a new member of his family. Nathaniel hadn't even figured out how he felt about having Victor as a new father before the man had died. Deep down, he couldn't decide if it was a blessing or a curse.

"Where are you?" Nathaniel wondered aloud as he searched. The bed had been stripped of sheets and not remade, the only visible acknowledgment of Victor's passing. The stand for his armor was empty, for he'd died wearing it. At the foot of his bed was a chest, and when Nathaniel put his hand on its side he felt a surge of electricity spike from his fingertips to his shoulder. When he opened the lid, he was disappointed to see it largely empty, and containing only meager things: belts, cuffs, books, and a razor for shaving.

Hurry up, he thought, fighting down panic. It had to be somewhere in the room. It had to be, why else would Karak have shown him Victor taking it?

The gems were valuable, he realized, and it felt strange, for it seemed the thought was not his own, but someone else's lingering in his mind. *What do you do with valuable things?*

"Hide them," Nathaniel mumbled. Somewhere easy to access, merely out of the way and safe from the prying eyes of servants who might be tempted to pocket them. Under the bed wouldn't work, for they'd be found when the floor was swept. Same went for the sheets, the mattress, and the pillows. A glance into the closet revealed it barren but for a few changes of clothes and an extra pair of boots.

Hidden…hidden…where could they be hidden?

Two soft knocks sounded from the door.

"I'm getting nervous out here," Argus said softly from the other side. "Whatever you're doing, make it quick."

Nathaniel returned to the chest, and he dropped to his knees before it. He'd felt so certain it was inside...

Leaning in closer, he put his hand on the interior of the lid, feeling. There was a give to it, not much, but noticeable. Sliding his fingers around the edge, he found a slight groove. Nathaniel grinned. *There.* He pushed his finger in and then pulled. The false lid popped free, and tucked neatly into the hollow was the chrysarium, with the nine gems pooled atop it.

Just the gems, Nathaniel thought, again with that strange feeling that the idea was not quite his own. Taking out the chrysarium, he set it on the floor, put a foot atop the plate, and then one by one yanked the gems free, easily breaking the thin silver chains that held them. Once finished, he replaced the silver plate in the false lid, shut it, and closed the chest. Nathaniel turned his attention to the nine gems, scooping them one by one into his hand. There'd be no way to hide them from Argus, not when they were bulging from his fingers like that. Bribing the guard would be equally futile. Instead he sat on the bed, placed the gems on his stomach, and then wrapped them in his shirt. Argus would know he was carrying something, but that was already a given. *What* he carried was all that mattered, and so long as the guard did not know, Nathaniel felt certain he'd be safe from the man's telling his mother.

Returning to the door, he paused, then tapped his elbow against it.

"My hand is full," he whispered.

Argus opened the door for him, and he looked none too pleased.

"Got what you wanted?" he asked, glancing at the wrapped bundle made of his bunched shirt. When Nathaniel nodded, the guard shook his head. "I take it you're not actually hungry, are you? Come on then. Back to your room, before anyone gets worried."

Together they padded down the hall, Nathaniel lingering slightly behind his escort. His heart was still pounding, and despite holding the gems of the chrysarium, he felt no safer than before. When they turned the corner to see two hooded men creeping open the door to his room, Nathaniel's first reaction was not horror, but relief that he'd not lost his mind, and Karak had truly given him warning.

"Intruders!" Argus screamed, drawing his sword. "All men, inside, intruders!"

Each of the men wielded long daggers, and the first rushed toward Argus while the second dashed inside, no doubt hoping Nathaniel was still in his bed. Argus stood his ground, blocking the hallway, sword clutched tightly in both hands.

"Run, Nathan," he said. "Fast as you can, now run!"

Nathaniel stepped backward, unable to take his eyes off the two combatants. The hooded man also wore a long coat, and sewn onto its breast was a four-pointed star. His daggers gleamed in the meager light as he whipped them back and forth, hammering them into Argus's sword. To the guard's credit, he did not balk at such speed, nor did he let the quicker man guide the combat. John Gandrem had often talked about the advantages of having the longer weapon, plus that of heavier mail, and Argus used both well, willing to let some of the weaker hits through so that he might attempt his own killing thrusts or cuts.

Several times Nathaniel saw a dagger rake the armor, doing little but scratching the plate. Argus's sword cut through coat and cloth twice, using high, slanted chops to limit how much his foe could dodge in the hallway. Nathaniel dared think Argus might win, but then the other hooded man came racing out of Nathaniel's bedroom. Two against one…could Argus endure such odds?

The instinct to run pulsed inside him, but Karak's words echoed in his mind, devouring his fear.

Cry out my name in faith…

Unraveling his bunched shirt, he let the gems fall into his hand, and upon their touching his skin he saw hints of light glowing from their centers. Closing his fingers, Nathaniel turned his attention back to Argus. The man was bleeding from cuts on his hands and face, and he was steadily retreating against the combined onslaught. The guard spared a glance over his shoulder only once, and seeing Nathaniel still standing there, his eyes bulged.

"You dumb shit!" he yelled. "Run!"

Before Nathaniel could do something, not that he knew what that something was, Argus suddenly rushed forward, showing no care for the daggers, no fear for his own life. The cuts came in, slender blades stabbing through the creases of his armor, but at last Argus scored a hit of his own. His long sword came crashing down on the shoulder of one of the men, smashing through bone and slicing to the ribs. As he died, the other hooded man plunged his dagger again and again into Argus's side, blood pouring through the underpadding.

Argus collapsed, and twirling his dagger, the remaining intruder stepped over his prone body toward Nathaniel.

"Thanks for not running," the man said. "It'll save us both a lot of trouble."

Hand shaking, Nathaniel stared into the shadow of the hood and did his best to hide his fear.

"Another step, and you'll die," he said.

The man laughed, then dashed forward, dagger thrusting for Nathaniel's stomach. With confidence that stunned even himself, Nathaniel outstretched his hand, the various gems clutched tightly between his fingers, and let out a cry that would have seemed insane to him six months prior.

"Karak!"

The gems flared with life. Before the hooded man could cross the distance, a beam of fire burst forth from their combined center. It struck him square in the chest, slamming him to a halt. The fire surged through his clothes, as if melting into him, then spread. It crawled across his skin like liquid, a steady, inevitable creep. He could not scream, his lungs were so quickly consumed. The coat, his clothes, his flesh: it all burned. As Nathaniel struggled to stand against the steady force pushing against his arm, the power of the gems flared once more, then faded. Of his would-be killer, only the two daggers remained, even his bones consumed. The weapons hit the carpet with soft thuds, but Nathaniel barely saw them. His mind was far away, lost in a powerful flood of emotions.

Power. Pleasure. Elation. They'd all surged through him, and for once, he was not slave to his protectors and his nightmares.

Snapping out of it, he rushed to Argus, who was still alive despite his wounds.

"What...?" Argus asked, coughing. "What the bloody Abyss was that?"

"Nothing," Nathaniel said, feeling the gems warm in his hand. Staring into the guard's eyes, he let Karak's power flow. "There was only one assassin, and you killed him. Do you understand?"

"I understand," Argus said. "Just one, and I killed the son of a bitch."

Nathaniel smiled at him.

"That you did."

Cries of alarm were sounding all throughout the mansion,

and Nathaniel knew he had seconds to act. Before anyone else might arrive, he rushed through the open door of his room, hurled the gems of the chrysarium beneath his bed, and then returned to Argus's side. Zusa arrived only moments later, coming from his mother's room farther down the hall.

"Are you all right?" she asked. She wielded daggers in each hand, and fresh blood dripped from their blades.

"He needs help," Nathaniel said, putting his hand on Argus's shoulder. "He saved me."

Argus tried to smile, but the pain and blood loss were too much, and he slipped into unconsciousness. Zusa shouted for others to come, then put her hand on Nathaniel's shoulder.

"Go to Alyssa," she told him. "Get to where it's safe."

He obeyed, and when he entered his mother's room, which was rapidly filling up with soldiers, she flung her arms around him.

"I'm so glad you're all right," she said, holding him tightly against her.

"I'm fine," Nathaniel whispered, and despite everything, he felt perfectly calm. "Really, I am."

She wouldn't understand, of course, and as she planted kisses on his cheek, he let his mind wander to the gems. Waiting for him. Protecting him.

"We're safe," he told her, voice soft but firm. "We're safe, I promise."

The freedom was invigorating, and a terrible weight left his heart. His family was no longer at the mercy of the underworld and all its cruel masters, for it was safe in Karak's strong hands.

CHAPTER

17

Night had fallen, and with it came a sense of change, an electric tension that made the tips of Thren's fingers tingle. Muzien had failed, his grand display of power crumbling under pressure from all sides. The people sensed whatever war was being waged in the shadows was not yet done, and the increased tenacity of the guards only verified that fact. For once, men and women kept the four-pointed star hidden as they went about their lives.

Good, thought Thren as he approached a quiet portion of the southern wall. *Let them remember who Muzien fled from. Let them remember who once ruled the underworld before the Sun Guild's rise.*

The rumor had floated throughout dozens of the city's taverns, a message that eventually reached Thren's ears: Muzien sought an audience with the former master of the Spider Guild.

"Tell him I'll meet him along the southern wall, just shy of the gate," Thren had told a member of the Sun. "And tell him to come alone."

On his way he passed through the rubble and ruin of the city center. Hanging from the ancient statue in the middle of the fountain, a rope about his neck, was the king's adviser, Gerand. The symbol of the Sun was carved into his naked chest, the blood dried and flaking. Thren paused only a moment to watch the body swing before continuing.

Casualties of war, he thought. *Such a shame. He was useful.*

As Thren stopped before the wall, he scanned its upper reaches, unsure if Muzien had met his demand to keep the rest of his guild away. Not that the elf would feel the need for help. If it came to a battle, both of them knew Muzien would win. Tapping the amulet beneath his shirt for confidence, Thren smiled, reminding himself that not all battles were won or lost by the edge of a sword.

Hardly any time passed before Muzien arrived, coming not from the wide, empty street but instead from atop the wall itself. With a flourish of his long coat, Muzien landed softly despite the great height, facing Thren from a mere twenty feet away. Unlike on their previous meetings, Thren felt confidence upon seeing his old master, and he made sure Muzien knew it.

"Glad to know you came alone," he said. "I was worried you'd feel the need for an escort after yesterday's humiliation."

Muzien's blue eyes burned with anger, but the elf kept his voice calm, his smile pleasant.

"Am I in need of protection?" he asked. "Certainly you are no threat to me."

Thren chuckled.

"Proud, even to the end. You wanted me, Muzien, and now I'm here. Would you care to tell me why?"

The elf crossed his arms behind his back, and he tilted his head to one side, analyzing his former student.

"Despite having the entire city under my control, you still resist me," he said. "Despite having failed at the task I sent you here to complete, you act as if you never failed at all. You confuse me, Thren, and the more I learn of you, and what you've done, the more confused I become. So here I am. I come to you as I should have when I first set foot in Veldaren: not with demands, nor condemnation, but merely questions."

"A noble offer," Thren said. "Though I wonder why I should give you even that. You have given me nothing but disrespect and insults, and only now that you're losing do you come to talk."

Muzien shook his head.

"Your ambush, outnumbering and surrounding me, still failed to kill me or crush my guild. Do not think you have won, Thren. You are still a nuisance, but one whose cost has become too great to ignore. I took as many lives as I lost yesterday, and I have far more lives to spare than you."

Thren chuckled.

"Yes, you did handle our ambush masterfully. I saw what you did with those tiles of yours, by the way, sending in men with hammers just after Victor's soldiers crossed over them. Very clever."

Muzien's face seemed to darken in the moonlight.

"So you are aware of the danger the tiles possess?"

Thren shrugged, deciding that was a game he no longer needed to play. Muzien had to know who was in control, to see whose hands truly held the fate of the city.

"Of course I am," he said. "This is my city, not yours, remember?"

Muzien's dark hand fell down to the hilt of one of his swords, then hesitated.

"I thought you must be the one," he said. "The Watcher is too weak of a fool to destroy everything if he cannot save it, but you...you still have a shred of the willpower I once saw in you as a child. Did you play Luther against me, or were you merely his puppet as well?"

"Luther played us all," Thren said, chuckling. "But I'd say you were played worse. I hold the key, Muzien. He gave it to me before I took his life. With but a whisper, I can bathe all of Veldaren with fire and destruction. You say you haven't lost yet. I say otherwise. I'm the one holding all the power, not you. Right now, you're just one of thousands who'd be caught in the blast."

"Luther gave it to you," he said. "Then you've had it from the moment you set foot into Veldaren...yet you never spoke a word. Why have you kept this a secret, Thren? Is your pride so great you hoped to defeat me without resorting to such threats?"

Thren clenched his jaw tight. That was an answer he could not give. At play here was not just the city, but also Thren's own echoing legacy. If Muzien had left immediately upon Thren's return, then things would have returned to the way they'd always been. But now the Watcher fought alongside him. Now the Watcher truly listened with open ears, and looked with open eyes. Sometimes fear and desperation were the best teachers.

"My reasons are my own," Thren said. "Luther was a fool, and now his weapon is mine. It's time you leave."

The darkened hand clenched into a fist, and Muzien openly glared.

"This madness is beyond even your limits. What is it you truly want, Thren? Do you want to be my heir again, and take your place at my side? Do you wish to rule as you did before, or usurp the throne I have carved for myself the past few months? Tell me. Let me hear it from your own lips."

Thren gestured north, to the distant gate through the city's wall.

"I want you gone," he said. "I will build a legacy for myself, and it will be free of your shadow. Go back to Mordeina. Either that, or stay, and burn with all the rest."

Muzien drew a sword, but before he could take a step, Thren pulled the golden amulet marked by a roaring lion from beneath his shirt and held it beside his lips.

"One word," he said, and he pointedly glanced to his left, where less than ten feet away was one of Muzien's many tiles of the Sun. "One word, and we're both dead. I'd suggest keeping your temper in check."

The elf hesitated, then with another glare, he jammed the sword back into its scabbard.

"You still haven't won," he said. "This is merely a stalemate. For all your boasting, you won't destroy the city and end your chance of ruling it."

"I beg to differ," Thren said. "If you stay, I will sunder the land. Better Veldaren as ash and dust than not in my hands, Muzien. I think that's a sentiment you understand all too well. Your situation is hopeless. So unless you want to be annihilated, accept defeat, and get out of my city. There is no way you can win this, and a hundred ways you will lose."

This was it, his final moment of victory. There was nothing Muzien could do to stop him. Every bit of power was in Thren's hands. With but a word, the elf died. How could he possibly resist him now? The Sun Guild would retreat from Veldaren, and in its vacuum, Thren would rise up to fill the void. He looked to his former master, seeking that fear in his eyes, that defeat, but instead Muzien grinned like a madman and laughed in his face.

"Hopeless?" he asked. "Far, far from it. You have but one

grand weapon, one you cannot wield with subtlety, nor precision. You have no middle ground, no repeated use. Your only threat is to destroy the city you seek to rule solely to spite me. I believe you're insane enough to do it, but not like this. You want to play games, Thren? You want to dance? Then go ahead. Continue with your schemes. Take the city from me. Earn your place. Earn your legacy. The only thing you accomplish by using that amulet is admitting your failure. You haven't won, Thren. You've only changed the rules of the game."

Thren felt his confidence starting to crack. Muzien wasn't afraid. Despite the danger, despite how with a single whisper, Thren could end all their lives…Muzien wasn't afraid. The determination on his face, the disgust…Thren almost spoke the word, almost destroyed them all, just to see that glorious second of panic and terror in the elf's eyes.

But the day before, they'd scored their first victory, and he'd done it fighting side by side with his son. No, there was still hope. There was still the rest of the game to be played.

"Why did you come here?" Thren asked, letting the amulet fall back beneath his shirt. "Why now? You don't need the wealth, and you don't need the reputation. You passed by two other nations on the way here, each worthy of your attention. Did you bring all your focus here to simply humiliate me? To show no disciple of yours shall ever surpass you? What brought you to my city, Muzien? What made you so determined to pry it from my hands?"

"Because you were my heir!" Muzien shouted. "I trained you, I molded you. Everything you are is because of my guiding hands. And then this…Watcher took it from you. Your thief war lasted for years, and every single day you failed to crush your foes, the weaker it made me look. How could I have you take over my empire if you cannot rule a single miserable city? You want to know why I am here, Thren? I am here to show that the greatest of humans is still nothing compared to me. I am here to erase whatever insult your existence has done to my name, all so I may start over. You are a failure of an heir, and in killing Grayson, you slew the only other man who might have been worthy. From the beginning, then, I must start. From this cesspool of miserable lives, from this wasteland that you call home, I will find another person worthy to succeed me, because the one thing I know more than anything else is that you are not worthy."

The elf spit out those last words as if hurling them at a wretched beggar. For years Thren had hated Muzien, denied him, and still those words pierced his flesh like daggers.

"You were the closest thing I ever had to a father," he whispered. "If I am unworthy, then it is by your own failure. You hypocrite. Would you take all credit for my successes, then cast me aside for my failures? As if that cleanses you? As if that hides your shame? You're wrong. It only reinforces it. I'm going to kill you, Muzien. When you die, it'll be because I rose above your teachings, surpassing every pinnacle you thought you'd perfected."

The elf smirked.

"Feeble dreams of a pathetic man," he said. "Cherish every breath you take, Thren. They're numbered."

Putting his back to him in mockery, showing how much of a threat he truly thought Thren to be, Muzien strolled down the street he still claimed to own. Thren watched him go, his temper boiling over.

"Ash!" he screamed after him. "I will leave you with ash and bone. This city will be your funeral pyre!"

Clutching the amulet, feeling its hard metal through his shirt, he almost gave in. A scar, he'd promised his son. He'd leave a scar upon the world that would never heal. Given the destruction he could unleash, the lives he would end, how deep might that scar run? Tighter and tighter he held it, feeling his hand beginning to shake. His guild was still in pieces, and despite all the power he wielded, his foe showed no fear. To his eyes the city was already ash and bone. What reason was there to go on?

Have hope, he told himself through his rage. *It might be only a glimmer, but it is still there.*

"I'm not your heir," he whispered, the calm of the night settling over him, soothing him. "I'm too old and tired to carry that mantle. But not my son."

His son. Thren looked to the city, imagining the Watcher prowling the rooftops, remembering the awesome skill he'd displayed in battling Muzien. How different might things have been if Aaron had never fallen for the sweet lies of Ashhur? How great might his son have become if he'd chosen to rule the city instead of pretending to save it?

"How badly did I fail you?" he whispered aloud, a weight on his shoulders, a weight he'd felt for nine years, growing even heavier. "Are you too far gone?"

When he'd stood upon that hill not far from the Stronghold, commanding Haern to take his life, he'd thought all hope of reuniting his family lost to him. But something was different now. At long last, his son was seeing how cruel the world could be.

Throwing back his head and straightening his shoulders, Thren bore the weight as if it were not there. Mind to the future, he strode down the same street Muzien had walked, determined to show the same lack of fear. Muzien's aura of invincibility was gone, the elf's victory no longer inevitable. Time to gather the old guilds. From the ashes they'd rise, and loudly declare the underworld would suffer no gods. A king, though, they would accept a king, and for once Thren dared hope it would not be his head that bore the heavy crown.

CHAPTER  18

Terrance stood at the door to the garden, hesitant to step outside, when Zusa found him.

"Is something the matter?" she asked.

Terrance startled, then blushed at his reaction.

"I'm sorry," he said, staring at the floor. "And no, nothing's wrong. I have something Alyssa requested. Could...could you give this to her?"

He offered her a slender wooden box not much bigger than his hand. She took it, surprised by its weight given its small size.

"Thank you," Terrance said, bowing low. "She's been out there for hours, ever since the funeral. I had a servant ask her if she'd like to come in, since the sun was setting and it was getting dark. 'It's always dark for me,' she said. I, uh, don't think I've quite seen her like this before."

"I'll see what I can do," Zusa said. "Try not to worry. Alyssa's strong. She'll endure like she always has."

Terrance looked relieved, and he bowed once more before retreating back into the mansion. Glancing down at the box, Zusa let out a sigh, then entered the moonlit garden. Following the stone steps through the roses and columbines, she found Alyssa sitting on a bench at the edge of a circle of birch trees. They'd buried Victor in the center of that circle, then marked the grave with a square stone tile dug into the earth. Alyssa's head was in her hands, and if she'd bothered to wear her eyes, they'd have been staring into nowhere. At least the weather was fine, the breeze warm and comforting against Zusa's skin.

"I've scoured the grounds three times," Zusa said, sitting down beside her. "Anywhere I might have sneaked through, I positioned another guard. Between all the rattling of armor and chatting guards, it might be louder now than during the day, but at least you and Nathaniel will be safe. Forgive me, Alyssa, but this never should have happened. I should have known Muzien would not take our involvement in the ambush lightly, and been ready."

Alyssa offered no reaction to her arrival other than a soft nod.

"Another attempt on my life," she said. "Another attempt on Nathaniel's. It won't ever stop, will it?"

"Is that what depresses you so?"

The woman shook her head.

"This one time? No. It's the history of them, Zusa. I feel it wearing on me. Always we are in danger. Always my enemies would seek to end my opposition by taking my life. Is there no other way they might strike against me?"

"You are the figurehead of an empire," Zusa said. "They could slay a thousand of our mercenaries and not do as much damage as they might by taking your life."

"I know," Alyssa said, leaning back into the bench, hands

resting in her lap. Her shoulders were so hunched, her tone so defeated, it made Zusa's stomach sick. "Trust me, I know."

"I've been talking to Victor's men," Zusa said, trying to force the conversation to something else. "Something about the battle in the square bothers me. Muzien had members of his guild rush the street with heavy hammers after the soldiers' passing, then strike those tiles of his he's placed throughout the city. That's where the explosions came from, which caused the majority of the casualties we suffered during the ambush."

"He trapped the tiles," Alyssa said. "Seems like something he'd do."

"Indeed," Zusa said. "But what if the rest of them are trapped as well? There are hundreds throughout the city, and if they're all as strong as what we—" She caught herself. "As what I witnessed, then thousands of lives are in danger."

"Only if Muzien has hundreds of men with hammers willing to sacrifice themselves to do it."

"I wouldn't put it past him."

Alyssa gave her a grim smile.

"Perhaps you're right. If you were to look into it, where would you go?"

Zusa shrugged.

"If it's magic, then Tarlak would make the most sense. A bit of coin would ensure he remained discreet regarding the matter."

"Discretion, from a wizard in bright yellow?"

"This world has seen stranger things."

This time the smile Alyssa gave her was sincere, and despite its fleeting presence, it did much to warm Zusa's heart.

"I kept my ears open while I was among them," Zusa continued. "No one suspects you in any way, and I doubt they ever will. Muzien looms too large over everything. In fact, the soldiers are hoping you'll remain true to your reputation and burn half the city to the ground attempting to slaughter the elf. He must have treated them well, or paid them well, for such loyalty. I must say, their desire for vengeance for their former master's death is admirable."

"They're fooling themselves if they think I have the heart for that anymore," Alyssa said.

"I think you fool yourself if you would believe that," Zusa argued. "No, I think you're wiser and more understanding of the consequences. Still, it might be worthwhile to let a few squads of soldiers loose into southern Veldaren, if only for appearances. Besides killing Victor, the Sun Guild also made attempts on your life and the life of your son. The worst thing you could be right now is timid."

"If we're to strike at them, we need to do it right," Alyssa said. "Can you find spots where the Sun Guild hides, then lead our men to them?"

"I can," Zusa said.

Alyssa nodded, letting the matter drop. The silence was thick, awkward, and filled with Alyssa's sadness. Zusa couldn't stand it, nor did she know how to fix it, which made her feel powerless. There was nothing she could do to change the past. Betrayal left the deepest of scars, and Alyssa had been betrayed far too many times in her young life.

"Terrance told me to give you this," she said after several minutes, gently placing the wooden box into Alyssa's hands. Her friend chuckled, and she did not open it, only held it.

"I shouldn't have killed him," she whispered. "Gods help me, what was I thinking?"

"You were thinking he'd drag your entire family down with his foolhardy quest for vengeance and power," Zusa said. "Just like I said he would."

"That only makes him a fool. That doesn't make him evil." She gestured to the gravestone before her. "That doesn't mean he deserved to die like he did."

"As if anyone gets what they deserve in this world," Zusa said, her words coming out far more bitter than she'd intended. "You were protecting yourself from his madness. Don't you dare feel guilty for doing what must be done."

"There had to be other ways," Alyssa said, and tears slid from her vacant eye sockets. "He'd have never betrayed me, I understand that now. Even to his death, he'd have remained loyal. But so many have turned on me, how was I to know? How was I to believe he could be different...and it's better to be the betrayer than the betrayed, right?"

She pulled open the lid to the box. Zusa could not tell what was inside until Alyssa dipped her hand within and removed the first of the orbs. They were shaped just like her glass eyes, but they were not painted in loving recreation of her original green irises. No, instead Zusa had to hold back her revulsion as Alyssa placed two solid black pieces of glass into her eye sockets. She looked like a thing of the night, a mockery of humanity, and the sorrow on her face only made it worse. If her eyes were windows to her soul, it frightened Zusa to think of what little remained within.

"I will not pretend at having sight when I am blind," Alyssa said, setting down the box beside her. "Nor will I pretend at happiness when I am mourning. Look at me, Zusa, and see it. Let everyone see what I've become. Even those who would protect me, I have killed. Everything I've sought to accomplish, I've failed at. Everything I've tried to build has crumbled. I'm a widow of my own choosing. Friends, family...who do I have, Zusa? My very life is poison, and everyone who dares get near me suffers for it. I'll never be able to trust anyone. No matter how hard I try, I'll never have anyone to..."

Zusa pushed her lips against Alyssa's, silencing such horrible thoughts. Holding Alyssa against her, she let the kiss linger, dared to put her other trembling hand against Alyssa's smooth cheek, brushing away the wetness of tears with her thumb. Through it all, Alyssa remained shocked still, neither returning the kiss nor pushing her away. When Zusa finally pulled back, she put her forehead against Alyssa's, their noses touching, and she gasped in a shuddering breath.

"You are never alone," Zusa said, and she felt tears running down her own face. Never before had she felt so naked, so vulnerable. "And you will never be unloved."

Those black orbs stared back at her, soulless, unreadable. As if in a dream, Alyssa reached up and put a hand on Zusa's shoulder.

"I'm sorry, Zusa," she said. "I...I don't know what to say..."

Each word was a knife. Despite all their years together, she'd never thought this moment would come, yet here she was, pushed away, rejected. Not since Daverik had she offered herself fully. Even with Haern it'd been purely carnal, a need for comfort and release. Gently came the resistance, but still it came, Alyssa's hands separating their bodies, her neck flushed, her face turning away in refusal of a second kiss that would never be.

Suddenly Zusa wanted to be anywhere in the world but there. Simply being in Alyssa's presence was unbearable, a reminder of her foolishness. She wanted to forget, to pretend nothing had happened, and sitting before those black eyes made it all but impossible. For a moment she even wished for her wrappings so they might hide her blushing neck and cheeks from the world.

"I should go," she said, rising from the bench. Her insides were performing loops, and she felt a wave of embarrassment smothering her.

"Zusa, wait," said Alyssa, reaching out blindly for her. Zusa shook her head, not caring Alyssa would not see.

"If your men are to assault the Sun Guild's hiding places, I should make sure they haven't moved them," she said, sniffling. "Just in case the ambush spooked Muzien."

Alyssa's hand dropped down to her side, and it seemed she struggled to find words.

"Of course," she said. "Stay safe, all right?"

Standing there in the moonlight, Zusa knew she could disappear into its shadows, and the freedom that offered was powerfully alluring. Still, she had to try one last time. She had to see the limits of her foolishness, even if it meant putting her neck out yet again.

"I love you, Alyssa," she said. "I always have. I always will."

There'd be no confusion now. No pretending it had never happened. Part of her screamed at how foolish she was, how stupid, but her pounding heart drowned it out.

Alyssa leaned back into the bench, looking more defeated than when Zusa had first come to her.

"I know," she said. "It's the one thing I've always known. I only wish I deserved it."

The chance was there, the ability to return her affection, even if only in words...but the words never came, and that was cruelest of all.

"Good-bye, Alyssa," she said. Turning to the western wall of the garden, Zusa ran without slowing, leaping into the shadow-bathed bricks and reappearing on the other side. Through the empty streets she ran, without sight, without thought, only seeking to cover distance, as if each step might somehow lessen the pain.

It didn't.

Faster, faster, cloak billowing behind her, she fled from what she could not outrun, until, legs burning and chest heaving, she slipped into an alley and flung herself against its wall. The mansion was far behind her, but it still didn't feel far enough. Beating her fists into the building's wooden side, she closed her eyes, let her tears fall.

"Damn it," she said, a whisper at first, then louder with each blow of her fist. "Damn it, damn it, damn it!"

Forehead still pressed to the wood, she did not see the man's arrival, only heard the softest rustle of his long coat.

"Hello, Katherine."

She whirled, knowing it already too late. A bag dropped over her head, followed by a rope about her throat. Arms grabbed her wrists and pinned her against the wall as the air burned in her lungs, and though it was in vain, she struggled anyway, fighting until the darkness took her completely.

CHAPTER

19

Haern had slept the entire day away, recovering from the constant battles and scouring of the city. After grabbing a bite to eat, he prepared his things and left. Not far from the tower was a gently sloping hill, and atop its soft green grass he sat and watched the sun set. Come dark, he'd return to the city, once more working with his father to bring the Sun Guild crumbling down. While at first it'd seemed an insurmountable task, this time they'd drawn blood, and proven Muzien was not the infallible demigod he pretended to be. Of all the damage that had been done, Muzien had done the most by preparing his public spectacle in the first place. As a frequent user of public spectacle himself, Haern decided he might need to pay particular attention to that lesson in the future.

The sun was almost gone when he heard the soft footsteps behind him. Glancing over his shoulder, he saw Delysia climbing the hill to join him. A twinge of nervousness hit his chest, and he did his best not to dwell on why.

"Is it all right if I join you?" she asked, stopping just short. He patted the grass to his left, and she crossed her legs and gently eased into a sit beside him. He'd always been comfortable in her presence, yet now there was a wedge between them, and no matter how hard he told himself to forget it, the wedge remained.

"It's been a while since I actually watched the sun set," Haern said. "Usually I'm running the other way, or it's hidden behind Veldaren's walls."

"It's been a while since you did a lot of things," Delysia said, reaching out to put a hand on his. "I'd say relaxing is one of them. Perhaps you should try it as well."

He laughed and shook his head. Inaction bothered him. Even taking the hours he'd needed to sleep had left him feeling guilty, let alone waiting for sunset, but Thren had sent a boy runner with a note while he'd slept, informing him where to meet come nightfall, and so he waited. There should be more he could do, he knew. He'd promised to protect the city, yet out there lurked a madman with the power to bring it all crumbling down into fire and ruin. To let things reach such a horrific precipice, to fail so terribly the people he'd sworn to protect...

"You've always been one for solitude and silence, but I know something's wrong," Delysia said. She looked his way, then patted his hand. "You've hardly said a word to any of us since Muzien's attack. If something's bothering you, then talk to me."

"It's going to get worse," he said, staring at the horizon. "Even if we somehow escape all this with Veldaren intact, hundreds will still die. How many of those deaths are on my hands?"

Delysia thought for a moment, and he appreciated that she did not give him an immediate, instinctual denial.

"I don't know," she said. "I don't know what brought Muzien here. I don't know what you'll need to do to secure peace. But Haern, don't you dare put the blood of the innocent on your hands when others are holding the knives. It's terrible enough when vile men do vile deeds, don't let them cast the blame onto others. It doesn't wash their own hands clean, nor stain yours."

She spoke what he needed to hear, and he tried his best to believe it.

"I may not bear direct responsibility," he said, "but all those people at the square...they died because Muzien wished me captured. Without me, they live. How do I not feel blame?"

"You took me from the aftermath before I could heal the dying," Delysia argued. "Would you have me shoulder the blame for their deaths?"

"No, that's ridiculous."

"Then why are you any more responsible?"

He had nothing to offer, so he let the words linger in the air, and he turned his attention back to the dwindling sunset. Delysia leaned closer against him, and though she appeared relaxed, he could sense her tension, her apprehension.

"Why didn't you let me stay?" she asked, finally voicing what had bothered her. "Those people, all those wounded... you should have let me heal them."

"Just like I should have let you heal Ghost?"

A cheap shot, and he felt guilty for saying it, but the frustration had weighed on him ever since that moment, and he could not bear letting it linger in silence on his shoulders. He thought she might snap at him. Instead she looked exhausted, all the anger of that moment drained out over the past few days.

"Why does it bother you so?" she asked. "What makes you

so angry that I'd rather have had him live than you taking your vengeance? Would you consider retribution more important than anything else you believe? Because I don't think you believe that yourself."

Haern rubbed at his eyes, maddened by the questions, mostly by his inability to answer them in any way that didn't leave him sounding like a child.

"It's because it's impossible," he said. "What you hope for this world to be, it just...can't. Giving mercy to murderers? Finding redemption in those who once raped and stole? It's a dream. A beautiful dream, but still a dream. The world isn't like that. There's no saving these people, no redeeming them from their cruel lives. I tried speaking of such things with my father, did you know that? He spit it back in my face. This world is filled with miserable people, some inflicting misery, and even more dwelling in its sick embrace. I don't see how I can be what you'd have me be, yet still survive."

"Why is it we who must break?" Delysia asked. "The evil of this world revel in their sin, then proudly demand all others accept it. They will never surrender, and so we must. They will never change, and so we must. 'See the world for what it really is,' they say. Hope is branded naïveté. Forgiveness is deemed a weakness. The only change they would foster is the crumbling of all things better men and women have built. Is that a world you wish to live in, Haern? Is that the world you fight for, a world where right and wrong are decided by bloodstained coins and the strength of the fist that holds them?"

"So you'd throw yourself against a wall of stone?" Haern asked. "Beat your head against it until it kills you? What is the point? Why suffer and die for something that will fail?"

"Because the smallest grain of sand can wear away a stone wall if given the time. Because every moment, I pray someone else will see, and demand this world embrace something better. Because with every drop I bleed, it might convince another that there is still hope. Would you refuse to give bread to a starving child, all because you cannot feed the thousand others that also starve?"

"I'm not talking about giving bread to a child," Haern said, shaking his head. "I'm talking of taking down Muzien the Darkhand, an elf who, outnumbered three to one by the finest fighters in Veldaren, still escaped unscathed."

Delysia wrapped him in an embrace with her right arm.

"Stop being paralyzed by the sheer size of the task at hand," she said. "Be motivated by it. I know you, Haern. Deep down, I know what you are capable of, and the great things you'd aspire to if given the chance. Would you give that all up due to the faults and failures of other men? If you do, then you've already let them win."

"The great things I'd aspire to," Haern said, chuckling. It felt like such a dark joke. "All I am, all I'm good at, is killing people. By killing the right people, I've managed to forge a peace. You beg me to spare lives, to look for forgiveness, to offer mercy... I see no way such things can make any difference in the pit that Veldaren's streets have become. There's only one way to succeed, and that's by being who I am. I'm the greatest killer Veldaren has ever known. I need no other aspirations."

He'd thought such admissions would hurt her, or frighten her, but they did not. Instead she leaned closer, her free hand pressing against the side of his face, and her eyes met his without any flinching or doubt.

"Do you know what I pray for every night?" she asked him. "Just before you leave, I pray that it will be the last night you're ever needed. I pray that you'll come home safe. Most of all, I pray that when you do come home, you're still the same man you were when you left. You're not the greatest killer Veldaren's ever known. You're its greatest protector. You've given so much, yet this world would take more, and more, dragging you down until you break. That's what I fear more than anything, Haern. And when I listen to how you talk, when I see you alongside your father, when I remember the tip of your sword at my neck when I went to heal Ghost's wounds . . ."

Tears had started to swell in her eyes, and she sniffled.

"Then I just pray harder," she said, looking away. "Pleading that Ashhur never takes from me the man I love."

Haern kissed her cheek, and when he rose to his feet, it felt as if boulders were strapped to his back, and he carried them with dead limbs.

"I'll be fine," he told her. "I promise."

"You shouldn't make such promises," she said. "Not unless you know you can keep them. I'm scared, Haern. I'm scared I'll lose you forever. Tell me you'll be all right. Tell me you'll return as who you've always been."

He swallowed down what felt like a hundred sharpened rocks in his throat. To save the city, he'd do whatever it took. Whatever must be done. *Monsters in the night*, he thought grimly.

"I would," he said, "but you'd sense the lie immediately, wouldn't you?"

She blinked, and twin tears ran down her cheeks.

"Go," she said. "The night needs you."

She needed him too, but Thren was waiting. Haern had a feeling Delysia knew that as well, and it added to the mountain of guilt that continued to grow on his shoulders. What started as a walk down the hill became a jog, then a sprint, as Haern outraced the demon in his thoughts, rushing back to the world he understood, the black-and-white shadows, the evil with their cloaks and coats, and his father who would lord over them all.

*   *   *

This time there was no confusion or fear when Nathaniel's dream deepened and his awareness of his surroundings strengthened. He let it carry him, guiding his consciousness through the sharpening dreamscape of his mind...or wherever his visions took place. At first there was darkness, just the shadowed silence of Veldaren floating beneath him as if he were a great bird, and then came a crack of light across the west. The sun was rising, and Nathaniel felt himself flying to the north.

Dawn comes, spoke a now-familiar voice, the firm, authoritative tone of Karak. *And with it rises an army of my savior.*

Something about the dream was different, strange, and then Nathaniel realized why. Time. It didn't race about him in a rapid, erratic manner. The sun did not rise like a leaf on the wind, nor fall like a stone. As Nathaniel soared over the green landscape beneath, broken by fields of grain and herds of pigs and sheep, he saw that they moved as on any other day. There was a sense of truth to everything, of firm reality that had been lacking in his other dreams.

"All this," he said. "Is this happening now?"

It is. Your mind moves where the body cannot, for there is something I would have you see.

Beneath him the land grew steadily steeper, gentle hills turning sharp and tall. What little he saw blurred as his pace increased, his vision tearing through the sky with such speed it left him breathless...at least, it would have, had he felt the need to breathe. The sharp wall of hills smoothed away, and his path curled more to the west. Clouds zipped beneath him, puffy and white. Nathaniel wanted to reach out to them, to discover if they felt soft like cotton, as they appeared, but he had no hands to move, no physical body at all, just his sight.

Then, as rapidly as it had begun, his speed lessened, and he dipped lower and lower, weaving through another stretch of hills, these more yellow than green, the short grass broken by scattered juts of rock through the tough soil. Nathaniel felt apprehension growing in him, an intense repulsion toward whatever he approached. He knew where he was going, had been there before in his dreams. Before he could dwell on it further, the hills ended, and the ravine began. It was enormous, hundreds of feet deep. His movement halted when he was just on the edge, and he felt the formation of a phantom body to accompany his mind. The heat of the sun, the blowing of the wind, he felt on skin he could not see. Doing his best to keep invisible feet planted, he peered down into the grand chasm, which stretched out for miles to the north and south. Far, far below he caught a glimpse of a river: a puny, lazy thing that seemed a total mockery of the depth and breadth of the chasm it had carved.

Nathaniel looked across the chasm to the west, and just as in his dreams, he saw an army gathered. Unlike in his dreams, it was not bathed in shadow, nor did the soldiers' eyes glow red like monsters'. From such a distance they looked human, albeit taller and stronger, their skins a sickly gray. Even from afar he could tell they were armed to the teeth, and that they numbered in the thousands, the army stretching out from the edge of the chasm like a great tail. And standing in the very center was the man with the ever-changing face. His eyes did not burn, but his irises shone as if they were glass, and within them raged a wildfire. They were tiny dots so far away, but Nathaniel could somehow see the man clearly, watch how the features of his face shifted and twisted, so slowly, so fluidly, that Nathaniel could never be certain what had changed.

My prophet, Karak whispered, and his voice was filled with love.

"Even in death, the faithless may be made to serve," cried the prophet, his voice echoing throughout the ravine. It all was so terrifyingly familiar, except no longer did the fog of dreams cloud over it all. No, he saw it with crystalline clarity as shapes began to crawl up both sides of the chasm. Hundreds, if not thousands, squirming like ants, climbing like spiders. Second after agonizing second Nathaniel watched, their forms growing closer and clearer. They had once been humanoid, and they were dead. What little meat remained upon them was rotted and black, easily scraped off by the cliff wall. Bone and cloth dug into the sides of the rock, scraping until they found purchase. Magnified a hundredfold, the scraping sound was a saw across Nathaniel's spine, yet there was nothing he could do. His phantom body would not move no matter what he attempted.

Higher and higher, no resting, no delaying. Sometimes one would lose its firm hold and fall, yet the others showed no reaction. They had no eyes for him to see fear within, no muscles to tire. Higher and higher, always higher and higher, until they came crawling over the sides. Nathaniel tried to flee, and thankfully he was lifted above them so the rotted bodies would not pass through his ethereal form.

"Are they his army?" Nathaniel asked as the dead continued to reach the top of both sides. It felt strange to ask questions knowing that a god would answer, but there was no denying Karak's overwhelming presence.

Not his army, Karak's voice echoed in his head. *His tool.*

Nathaniel watched as a rope soared from the prophet's side to the other, its length crossing the chasm. As it landed, he saw that the rope had been tied to a long piece of bone, which shimmered with dark magic, burying itself into the rough rock. Once it was firmly in place, the dead began to move anew. They crawled across the rope, swarming toward the center with slow, steady movements from both sides of the ravine. The only sound they made was from the popping and rattling of their bones and joints. Once they met in the middle, they grabbed onto one another, arms interlocking, mouths closing over legs. From both sides they climbed, fitting themselves into place, propping up some, linking together others, bone twisting into bone.

For ten minutes Nathaniel watched, each one a shivering torment of rattling and breaking. When it ended, a bridge of the dead spanned the chasm, and with a triumphant bellow the army began its march across, three abreast. If the soldiers were afraid of the drop, they showed no sign of it, so great was their blood lust. The prophet remained behind, watching the others pass, and Nathaniel was grateful. He feared to be in that man's presence, even in spiritual form.

As the army crossed, Nathaniel felt his vision beginning to break. Colors dimmed, as if a thin cloud floated in the way of the sun, and the sound of the army dulled. Nathaniel looked about as it seemed his world crumbled, and in the distance he saw the strangest sight: a winged horse, flying in circles high above the ravine, with a rider clad in green and brown. Nathaniel stared, and he'd have furrowed his brow if he could. The vision collapsed further, turning to gray and black. All sounds ceased, all physical sensations ended, as if a blindfold were over his eyes and mud pushed into his ears.

And then he opened his eyes, and saw he lay on his back in his bed, his room pitch-black but for the faintest moonlight seeping in below the curtain. His lungs burned, and he felt a desperate need to breathe, but he dared not make a noise. The presence remained, powerful, humbling.

The time approaches, Karak whispered into his ear. *An end to chaos and the beginning of a new age of order. Play your part,*

Nathaniel. Keep the gems of the chrysarium close. When my might roars free, the sinful of this city will learn to fear the name they have mocked and despised since before I was ever imprisoned.

Like moisture evaporating beneath a hot sun, so did Karak's presence dissipate, seemingly thinning instead of leaving at once. Upon its absence, Nathaniel finally gasped in air, and he felt his heart pound in his chest as if he'd run a hundred miles. Filled with a sudden need, he reached underneath his pillow and grabbed the nine gems of the chrysarium he'd hidden there. They were like ice to his touch. When he pulled them out and held them, each shimmered with color. Relief flooded through his body as their glow settled across his skin.

"Keep me safe," Nathaniel prayed as tears ran down the sides of his face. "I'll do it, just keep me safe, and Mother, and everyone else . . . keep us safe, and help me sleep."

Eyes closed, he let the gems give him comfort, and when he dreamed, he was amid the marching legion, eyes to the rainbow sky, free from worldly struggles. A wonderful dream. A dream he never wanted to end.

CHAPTER 20

Zusa awoke to find herself chained to a wall and bathed in light. Seven torches burned in a semicircle, each one equidistant from her. Her wrists were bound behind her with metal shackles, the short chain attached to them hooked to something on the wall she could not see. Blinking at the brightness, Zusa fought through a momentary spell of dizziness. She had to regain her surroundings. She had to recover before...

"Welcome back to the waking world, Katherine."

Muzien's voice rolled over her like a wave, killing what little hope she'd had of escape. He knew of her ability to manipulate shadows, had seen her use it to execute the former members of the Spider Guild. There was too much light, the manacles on her wrists were too tight and too low, forcing her to a crouch. The master of the Sun Guild stood beneath one of the torches, which was suspended from the wall of the small room by a metal hook. His arms were crossed over his chest, and though his pose was relaxed as he leaned against the wall, there was nothing calm or controlled about the awful hatred in his eyes.

"Or should I call you Zusa?" he continued when she refused to acknowledge him. "I thought I'd rescued whoever you were before the religious dogma and abuse changed you, but apparently I was wrong. You're still a slave, though the god you serve appears to have changed. You bow before the Gemcrofts now, don't you?"

Zusa refused to give him anything. It hardly seemed to surprise him.

"I've dug into your past," he said, coming closer and kneeling down so he could stare at her level. "Not hard after knowing of your connection to the Gemcrofts. You see, there's these... whispers about Alyssa I never quite understood. A wrapped woman who helped seal her ascension by killing Yoren and Theo Kull, a lurking specter who watched after her, guarded her. I thought them merely stories or rumors, ways to make her mercenaries seem more special than they were. But you... you've been the one at her side, haven't you? Her loyal shadow, her little lapdog?"

She kept her mouth shut, but her glare was answer enough. Muzien let out a sigh, and he rose back to a stand.

"So disappointing," he said, beginning to pace, hands deep in the pockets of his coat. "Twice I've had you imprisoned before me, but I fear this second meeting will not go as well as the first. You had such *potential*, Zusa. The way you kill, it is such savage beauty to behold, yet to turn on me in my hour of need, as if a mere mask and hood would prevent me from recognizing your masterful grace... it's as baffling as it is insulting."

His darkened hand touched her chin, forcing her to look at him.

"I hold no doubt you've cast aside your faith in Karak; you

never lied to me on that. But for you to be in Alyssa's pay doesn't feel right. You can't have betrayed me just for coin. I could give you more with far less risk, and you're a wise enough woman to know that. Power? I am true power, while Alyssa is a fading light. So what answer is left, Zusa? Come, surely you are willing to save yourself the pain and torture I would inflict upon you to have my answer. What is it that Alyssa offered you?"

Zusa pulled away from his touch, closed her eyes, and did her best to ignore his words, his presence. Crouching her body in tighter, she leaned against the wall, pretended to be far, far away. She'd been taught how to endure torture in her training as a faceless. Muzien would be better at it than most, and he certainly could break her in time. Her only hope was that time was something Muzien did not have. Cheek pressed against the rough wood, she thought of her visit to Angelport, her youth with the other faceless; anything other than Alyssa, and the answer to Muzien's question.

A sharp blade pressed against her throat, then a hand grabbed her hair to yank her gaze back to him.

"I am not one you should ever ignore," he told her, eyes so close she could almost feel the anger and disgust rolling off him. "You've betrayed me, Zusa, and you have no idea how terrible a choice that was."

"You think I'm afraid to die?" she asked him as the blade pressed tighter against her flesh. "Do it. Cut open my throat."

His lips pressed against her ear.

"No."

He let her go, put away his blade.

"I want my answers," he said. "And I will get them, one way or another...though I feel I already have one of them. You aren't afraid of dying; that much is obvious. You didn't betray me for coin, nor for power. So that leaves two possible solutions as to why you would remain so loyal to Alyssa, even now refusing to turn against her when facing torture and death. Either you feel you are in her debt... or you love her."

Zusa tried to remain perfectly still, to let the comment wash over her as if it meant nothing at all, but the wounds were too fresh. Alyssa's words hammered in her head. Muzien watched her like a hawk, searching for the slightest bit of information, and it seemed something in her reaction caught his notice. His eyes narrowed, and he halted his pacing.

"It'd be a powerful debt indeed to have earned so many years of loyal service," he said. "But love...I wonder, Zusa, is love what keeps your lips sealed? Not surprising, really, given how love's irrationality answers so many of my questions. I'm curious...does Alyssa love you back?"

Out came his dagger, and before she could react he'd already cut off a lock of her hair. Seeing her hair held in his blackened fingers unnerved her to no end.

"Love and loyalty," he said. "We'll discover just how deep each goes when Alyssa discovers you're my prisoner. Will she ransom for your life, Zusa? Offer an exchange? Send out soldiers? Or will she leave you here to die alone and unworthy of the risk...?"

"You damn fool," she said. "The city isn't yours, Muzien. It isn't now, and it never will be. Thren, the Watcher...they'll kill you. It's only a matter of time, and when it happens, I can't wait to watch every single thing you think you've built come crumbling down."

At last it seemed she'd struck a nerve. His darkened hand grabbed her by the neck, squeezing hard enough to choke. His flesh...it was so hot, so cracked, it seemed a demon of the Abyss held her, not an elf.

"This city," he hissed into her ear, "this overcrowded pit of humans, is mine. The only fools here are those who would resist the inevitable."

He let her go, and she gasped in air despite the horrible ache in her throat. Muzien put his back to her, just for a moment, and when he turned around he was his calm, cool self again. If anything, he looked to be in a better mood.

"You've given away your loyalty at last," he said, smiling at her. "You love Alyssa, don't you? It's almost...adorable, really. Like seeing a lovesick puppy licking at her master's boot. You never thought she loved you back, did you? I hope not. That would only make your betrayal of me all the more pathetic."

"Fuck you," Zusa spit. "Just kill me so I don't have to listen to this nonsense."

Muzien smiled, and he waved the cut piece of hair before her.

"If I thought you beyond saving, I would, but you're not. You are a complicated thing, which means the complications must be removed so you might reach your true pinnacle. Alyssa, and your love of her, is one of these complications. So that means we need to discover just how much Alyssa loves you, and how dedicated she is to your release. Once I have my answer, I'll capture her just like I captured you. I'll bring you two together, and then I'll make you watch as I cut into her. I'll make you watch as she bleeds, and screams, and begs for death. And when I've wrung every drop of enjoyment from her suffering, I'll hand you the blade. Then, when the only mercy you can offer her is a swift execution, we shall see just how much you truly love her. There is still hope for you, Zusa. There is still a future where you wield your skill and power in service of a worthy master. But it won't be with a divided heart."

He brushed her face with his blackened hand, the heat of it sending a wave of repulsion traveling down her spine.

"A worthy master," he whispered. "All your life you've sought to serve, first Karak, then his priests, and now Alyssa Gemcroft. It's all you know, isn't it? You're a woman of loyalty, of devotion...but you've been casting diamonds before the feet of beggars. It isn't too late to open your eyes. A worthy master, Zusa. That's all you've ever lacked, but one is before you now."

"Never," she said. "Kill me, torture me, do whatever sick act you can conceive. I will never serve you."

He smiled that dangerous smile of his.

"My dear Zusa," he said, "never is such a very long time. Thren will soon make another move against me, and when he does, I will kill him, and the Watcher as well. When those two die, and Alyssa's body rots on the floor beside you, there will be no one left to resist me. The city will be mine, and once that happens, I will have all the time in the world to teach you the meaning of loyalty."

He slapped her across the face, gently, almost playfully, and then strode toward the door on the far side of the room.

"You swore your life to me," he called out over his shoulder. "Never forget it, because I assure you, I never will."

The door opened and slammed shut, and then Zusa was alone with the bright light of the torches and the burning terror of her thoughts, both equally cruel, both unwilling to let her escape.

CHAPTER
 21

Antonil Copernus stared at the bodies as his soldiers cut them down from the fountain. Their blood mixed with the fountain's waters, coloring it a muddy red. There was no need to check, but as the four were dragged out onto the stone, Antonil ordered the soldiers to do so anyway. Opening the shirts of his dead soldiers, they found the four-pointed star carved into their flesh, some on the chest, some on the abdomen. Just like the three men the day before, and the two before that, all starting with the king's adviser, Gerand Crold.

"More and more every day," said one of his soldiers, a young man obviously shaken by the sight.

"Which is why we must remain vigilant," Antonil said, clapping him on the shoulder. "One day it will be zero, because we'll have finally broken the Sun Guild and their master."

"Begging your pardon, sir, but the Darkhand doesn't seem like the type to be broken."

The corners of Antonil's mouth twitched, the only hint he'd give of his inward wince at the words.

"Inform their families," he ordered, turning north toward the castle and marching away. He tried not to dwell on the soldier's fears as he moved through the quiet evening streets, but he failed. No, the Darkhand did not seem like the type to be broken, yet despite their resurgence in guarding the streets, along with over a dozen men they'd arrested bearing the symbol of the Sun, the city had not been consumed by fire and destruction. No, instead they continually found members of the city guard hanging from the fountain, and something about it felt...petty. Not grandiose. Not a statement. Just a petty resistance to a change the Darkhand could not stop. Despite the deaths, it gave Antonil a sliver of hope.

Not that it did much to help his mood. Distant change was not something the king was fond of, and every day Antonil was forced to endure the young brat's terrified ranting. Every day the king insisted they return to ignoring the Sun Guild, and every day Antonil responded the same way.

"This city can only have one king, and if you cower now, it will not be you."

If there was anything Edwin was afraid of, it was losing his tentative hold on power. So Antonil insisted the man would remain safe in his castle...and did not mention the tiles lining its outer walls, tiles that could bring the whole thing crumbling down in a heartbeat.

Sometimes those incapable of handling the truth are best left in the dark, he thought as he neared the castle. *Such a damn shame our king has to be one of them.*

As he reached the steps, he heard a commotion behind him, and when he turned he saw a lone soldier running as fast as his armor would allow, resulting in a rather obnoxious rattling of plate and chain. Frowning, Antonil stepped in his way and raised a hand.

"At ease," he said. "What is the rush?"

The soldier was a man Antonil recognized, whose station was at the western gate. His face and neck were covered with sweat, and after a bow, he spoke in short, quick sentences while attempting to catch his breath.

"I've a message for the king," he said. "Well, not a message. A request."

"A request for what?" Antonil asked. "And from whom?"

The soldier looked torn between amusement and frustration, and he swallowed before answering.

"Perhaps it's best I met with you first, sir," he said. "There is an elf at the western gate of our city. He wanted in, but we denied him. Seemed the safest thing to do until we asked. So he's outside waiting with his, uh, horse. Won't tell us what he wants, only that he'll speak with the king."

Antonil frowned.

"Do you think he'll speak with me?"

The soldier shrugged.

"When it comes to elves, does anyone know anything? Maybe yes, maybe no. But when it comes to our *king*, well . . ." The soldier paused, and he blatantly looked over Antonil's shoulder to the castle. "I know who'd be more willing to listen, and who'd do a better job speaking, when it comes to an elf."

They were dangerous words, and a sentiment that had been growing over the past year, particularly since Muzien's arrival and the king's complete unwillingness, or inability, to control his own capital city. Antonil knew he'd need to eventually clamp down on the open admission of such feelings, but deep down, he felt a total lack of energy to put toward such an effort. Perhaps when things calmed down, assuming they ever did.

"Go back to your post," Antonil said. "I'll see if this elf will speak with me. Whoever he is, he has no right to appear unannounced and demand an audience with His Majesty."

"Of course," said the soldier, bowing low. Spinning on his feet, he marched back down the street, and after a moment's hesitation, Antonil followed.

It's not like things can get much worse, thought Antonil. *We're due for good news, I'd say. Maybe he's here to bring back one of their own...*

Other elves scouring the city to drag Muzien out by his feet was an amusing thought, but sadly impossible. The king would never allow so many elves into his city, not after what had happened in the southern city of Angelport.

Back through his city he marched, and he took pleasure in noting far fewer marks of the Sun Guild on the people. Prior to the bloody battle at the fountain, his men and women had grown brazen, but now...now there were only the tiles proclaiming the Sun Guild's power. Antonil felt a shiver at the remembrance of what they could do, and he did his best to push it from his mind. Such things were currently beyond him, and he had to pray that somehow things would turn out fine in the end.

At the western gate, Antonil saw a larger-than-usual gathering of his men, no doubt ogling the elf on the other side.

"Get back to your posts," he told them as he pushed through, exited the enormous gates, and stepped out to greet his strange visitor.

It was the elf's horse that first grabbed Antonil's attention, not the elf himself. The beast was magnificent, tall and strong, and head to hoof colored a brilliant white. From its back grew enormous wings, which were currently folded in and pressed against its sides. With its huge eyes, it watched Antonil as he approached, and when its elven master bowed his head in respect, so too did the horse.

"Greetings," said the elf. "I am Dieredon, scoutmaster of the Quellan elves. With whom do I speak?"

He was tall, tanned, his long brown hair carefully trimmed and braided away from his face. Though his tone and expression were serious, his voice lacked the smugness and condescension Antonil had expected.

"My name is Antonil Copernus, and I am responsible for the safety of His Majesty's city," Antonil said, and despite an initial hesitation, he bowed his head also. *So what if he is an elf of a foreign land?* decided Antonil. A little civility might go a long way. Dieredon patted the horse beside him, then gestured to the castle in the distance, just barely visible beyond the top of the wall.

"Do you come speaking for your king?" he asked.

A tricky question. Antonil didn't want to lie, nor did he wish to be dismissed or ignored due to his station.

"No, I do not," he said. "But I am the closest you will reach to speaking with the king in this lifetime, Scoutmaster, so whatever message you have come to deliver, you may deliver it to me instead, and I will relay it to His Majesty if I deem it important."

The elf tilted his head, and then, to Antonil's shock, he laughed.

"Important?" he asked. "I come to aid your city, yet you would demean my potential words and insult me with politics and denials to meet your king? Perhaps I should just leave you to your fate, if you would be so insulting."

"Wait," Antonil said before the elf could turn to leave. "I did not mean to speak so harshly. I only wish to convey the fears of His Majesty. His ears will not be open to you, nor his mind, nor his heart. But I am here, and I will listen, and whatever message you carry I will do what I can to make sure he listens with mind, heart, and ears open...because it will come from human lips."

What he spoke was borderline traitorous, he knew, but beneath the elf's ire he sensed something terrible lurking, and had to know what. Besides, there were no other ears listening. For some reason, should Dieredon tell the king what he spoke, well...it'd be his word against the word of an elf. There'd be no contest. As for his plea, it seemed to have worked, for Dieredon's face softened.

"Forgive me," he said. "I'm a fool if I would pretend at my kingdom being any more free of prejudices than yours, and even if it were, I will not leave you to your fate due to my pride. An army approaches, Guard Captain, thousands of orcs gathered together under one banner, and they'll be at Veldaren's walls within days."

Antonil's entire body froze.

"An army of thousands?" he asked. "That's impossible."

"Surely you know their numbers exceed that in the Vile Wedge," Dieredon said. "Though perhaps you don't, given your isolation here."

"No, not that," Antonil said, shaking his head. "They are all trapped within the Vile Wedge. Even with the Citadel's fall, there is no way for them to cross the grand chasm unless they travel so far south they must pass through the Hillock, if not the Kingstrip beyond that. How could an army of foul monsters cross such a distance unnoticed with those numbers?"

"There is a space the orcs call the Bone Ditch," Dieredon said. "It is the most slender gap of the canyon, and they've used it as a burial place for centuries. They had…aid in crossing the Bone Ditch, and then skirted north of the Hillock and the waters of Sully Lake. They now approach the King's Forest. You must prepare your defenses, and summon whatever troops you can."

The King's Forest? Even if they're just reaching its northern stretches, that means…

"Three days at best," he muttered. The elf hadn't been exaggerating. He felt the blood drain from his face. "By Ashhur, three days? That's not enough time, Dieredon. Even if we had a standing army waiting for us at Felwood or the Green Castle, it'd take us that long just to have our messengers arrive. The only defenders we'll have are those already within our walls!"

"And how many men is that?" Dieredon asked.

Antonil began to answer, but realized he was taking everything at the scoutmaster's word. What if he was lying, or trying to sniff out the strength of their defenders?

"Not as many as I would like," he said, standing up straighter. "But enough to handle these orcs. They're strong but stupid beasts, and that is all they are. Without ladders and siege weapons, they will break upon our walls. Let them hack at our gates with their axes and swords. It will do them no good."

Antonil caught the look the elf gave, and it troubled him deeply.

"Unless you know something I do not," he added, trying to pry it out of him.

The elf crossed his arms, and whatever standoffish attitude he'd had was wiped away. Instead he spoke with a sudden earnestness and honesty that left Antonil stunned, and oddly flattered.

"I should have been here sooner," he said. "But I feared to let their army out of my sight, and then they moved with far greater speed than I anticipated. Someone is with them, Antonil. I have seen him only in glimpses, clothed in black, but I fear he is a necromancer. He is how they crossed the Bone Ditch, and I believe it is his guidance that has kept the orcs in check. They raid only the nearby farmlands to feed themselves, and have avoided any large cities, or the Green Castle. They're coming here, and they come with a purpose."

"He is still just one man," Antonil argued. "How much power can one man, even a necromancer, possibly wield?"

Dieredon stared him straight in the eye.

"Enough to bring your walls and gates crumbling down. I do not expect a siege, Antonil. I expect a massacre, and I pray it is of the orcs, and not the other way around."

The elf bowed low, then hopped up onto the back of his winged horse. Antonil stepped closer, feeling dumbstruck, his tired mind frantically trying to make sense of all he'd heard.

"Will you track them still?" he asked, hoping he might gain more information about their foes as they approached.

"No," Dieredon said, shaking his head. "If I press Sonowin hard, I might reach Nellassar in time to muster the Ekreissar to come to your aid. It won't be easy, but there's a chance..."

"I understand," Antonil said, and he bowed low. "And thank you. Even if there is no time to summon soldiers, we may still save the outlying villages from the raiding orcs. You've saved many lives this day."

"And if the goddess is kind, I will save many more," Dieredon said. "Peace be with you, Antonil."

His horse—Sonowin, Antonil assumed—let out a loud snort, and then its wings unfolded, spreading out fifteen feet to either side. With a great whoosh of air they beat once, twice, blowing back Antonil's hair before he retreated. The creature began running away from the walls, wings still beating, and then it soared into the air, looping about once before heading southeast toward Nellassar, the forest kingdom of the Dezren elves.

Antonil watched until it was a white dot indistinguishable from the clouds, then pulled his attention back down to the ground. An army of orcs, arriving with no time for him to muster troops, and aided by a mysterious necromancer?

"Damn it," he said, then with more gusto, "Gods fucking damn it!"

There was no time, no time to do anything if what the elf said was true. Worst was how he could not even wait to confirm his story. Waiting meant wasting precious time, and Antonil could think of no reason for Dieredon to lie. What could it possibly gain him? Spinning about, he rushed through the great doors of his city.

"Sir?" asked one of the guards.

Antonil ignored him, picking up his pace. Instead of heading toward the castle, he walked along the wall, toward the nearest of the many guardhouses stationed throughout the city. The building was squat and square, jutting out from the interior of the wall. When Antonil stepped inside, there was barely room for him among the several men seated within at the lone table. Along all the walls were swords and armor for the men to use on their patrols. Seated at the head of the table, ax still strapped to his back, was Antonil's good friend, the battle-scared veteran Sergan.

"Come to share a drink with us?" the older man asked.

"Out," Antonil said, looking to the others. "I must speak with Sergan."

The others quickly obeyed. Sergan leaned back in his chair, scratching at his beard.

"Something the matter?" he asked.

"The scoutmaster for the Quellan elves came to speak with me," Antonil said, deciding to keep it as brief as possible. "An army of orcs has managed to cross the Bone Ditch, and they're on their way here as we speak."

Sergan blinked.

"All right. How much time we got?"

"Three days at best, though two seems more likely."

The man slowly rose from his seat, and he finished off the drink before him.

"Well that sucks Karak's hairy cock, doesn't it? What's the plan?"

Antonil glanced over his shoulder and saw the soldiers lingering near the door, so he kicked it shut.

"We need to avoid a panic," he said. "Find the most reliable men you can, and get them riding north. Every bit of farmland, every village, if they're within striking distance of the King's Forest, they need to be emptied out."

"Want them to take shelter here?"

"No," Antonil said, hating his answer. "We may fall under siege, and if so, food will be scarce enough as it is. Get them to go west, or east, it doesn't matter, so long as they're out of the army's path. After that, get those riders to Felwood, the Green Castle, even Kinamn. All of Neldar needs its armies raised. If they besiege us, they'll have a chance to break it, and if not, and we fall..."

Antonil shrugged.

"At least they'll be ready when the army moves on."

Sergan's eyes glazed over, and Antonil could tell he was tracking routes and mentally assigning men to them.

"Fuck," he muttered. "You sure this elf ain't lying? This will be a whole lot of hubbub for nothing if he is."

"I'd give anything to have him be lying," Antonil said. "But

I don't think he is. We have to do whatever we can to prepare. Start recruiting anyone and everyone to join the guard; use the skirmishes with the Sun Guild as the excuse."

Sergan blinked, and his mind focused more on the immediate.

"All this secrecy," he said. "It's making me suspicious that you don't plan on telling His Majesty. I take it you don't think it's a good idea?"

Antonil paused, and then, unable to help himself, he burst into laughter.

"Telling him will do far more harm than good," he said. "Let the brat remain ignorant in his castle. He'll only interfere if he knows what's happening, and worse, he might prevent us from doing anything because the warning came from an elf and not, well, anyone else. When the army arrives, he's welcome to cower in his room while the rest of us save the lives of his people."

Sergan saluted.

"Understood," he said. "I'll get started on the riders."

Antonil saluted back, then made for the door.

"Do what you can, and as fast as you can," he said.

"Where are you going?" Sergan asked.

Antonil grinned at him, for he'd realized a way he might confirm the army's existence after all.

"I'm going to get us a wizard," he said, then exited so he might hurry to the Eschaton Tower beyond the walls.

CHAPTER 22

"Are you sure this isn't a trap?" Haern asked as he and his father lurked outside the fenced Roseborn Cemetery. They'd spent the previous night in disguise, sneaking into the various taverns and slums of the city to spread their message: they wished to meet with the highest-ranking survivors of the former guilds. Now the sun had finished its descent, and their time for meeting had almost come, the two lying on the rooftop of the grave keeper's home just opposite the cemetery's entrance.

"It might be," Thren whispered, and he glanced over at Haern and gave him a smug grin. "But would it matter?"

Haern shook his head.

"Most likely not."

"Then stop worrying about it."

It seemed wiser to worry about an ambush than to ignore the possibility, but Haern let the matter drop. If there was an ambush, it'd been set up carefully. As the people arrived one by one, Haern had looped the cemetery thrice while his father remained watching the gate. No groups of the Sun Guild remained lurking that he could find. That word of their meeting had failed to reach Muzien's ears was a strong signal that his power in Veldaren was waning. Just a week before, such an attempt would have certainly ended in disaster.

"We've waited long enough," Haern said, and he rose to a stand. "Anyone else who wanted to come would have already."

Thren stood as well, and reaching down, he held the rooftop with his left hand and then used it to swing to the ground. Straightening his clothes after landing, he glanced over to Haern, who followed.

"Keep your hood up, and keep it dark," his father said. "I need you mysterious and intimidating. Even if you don't say a word, your presence, and what it means, will speak volumes."

"You just have to be in charge, don't you?" Haern said.

Thren shrugged.

"I just don't want you messing things up. This crew will be antsy, and most likely thinking about how turning on Muzien will get themselves killed. If they're here, it's out of hope I can convince them otherwise. They want me to make them believe, and I can do that…but only if you keep your mouth shut."

"No promises," Haern muttered, grabbing his hood and willing its shadows to deepen. That done, he followed his father through the rickety gate, hands on his swords at all times.

There were nine of them gathered in a loose circle at the center of the cemetery, a few Haern recognized, and more he didn't. All of them wore the four-pointed star somewhere on their shirt or coat, and they looked miserable being there. They'd been muttering among themselves, but when Haern and Thren stepped into their midst, they all fell silent. Haern kept his body hidden by his cloaks, and he turned his gaze to each one so there would be no doubt as to who he was.

"I'm surprised to see you here, Martin," Thren said to a man with a heavily scarred face who was leaning against a slender tree, one of very few that grew throughout the cemetery. "Given how you betrayed me to Muzien when I first returned to Veldaren."

"I did no such thing," Martin replied, and he looked rather bored with the accusation. "I waited for a note or whisper of a plan, and none came until now. About time, I'd say."

Thren chuckled, and he turned to the rest. As far as Haern knew, Martin was the only former member of the Spider Guild. Of the others he recognized only Quentin, a lanky man who'd been third-in-command of the Serpent Guild. The others, if they'd been members of the Shadow Guild, or the Wolves, or the Hawks, had been so low in importance he did not remember them, assuming he'd learned their names in the first place. A clear sign of the damage Muzien had inflicted on the underworld. Under different circumstances Haern would have been pleased.

"Do the rest of you speak for the remnants of your guilds?" Thren asked them.

"Those still interested in making things how they were," said a skinny blond man, his frame dwarfed by the heavy coat he wore. "Can't say for certain how many that is, given how dangerous it is to talk of the old times."

"Right now, I'd say we're few," a woman beside Quentin added, a tattoo on her neck revealing her former allegiance to the Serpent Guild. "Too many pockets are filled compared to before Muzien's arrival. Are you here to offer us a return to the glory days, Thren?"

"I am," Thren said.

"And what might those glory days be?" Quentin asked. "Back to when we warred against the Trifect, losing men and women as fast as we recruited them? Or back to when we were glorified bodyguards squabbling over the scraps the Trifect paid us? Muzien might be sick in the head, but he's brought us power we haven't had in decades, and we don't need to remain slaves to the fucking Watcher to keep it."

Haern frowned, and he had to bite his tongue to remain silent. Such talk could derail whatever progress they hoped to make. His father knew that as well.

"You're right," Thren said. "You're slaves to Muzien instead, but I'm sure your ego can handle worshiping an elf over the Watcher. As for your petty gripes, keep them to yourself, Quentin. If you thought it hopeless, or did not yearn for better times, you wouldn't be here in this cemetery, so unless you have something worthwhile to say, cease your ego stroking and shut the fuck up."

Quentin reached for his sword. The woman beside him grabbed his arm to hold him still.

"We're not here to fight," she said, glaring at them both. "We're here because too many will die otherwise."

Haern lifted an eyebrow. This was interesting…

"What do you mean?" he asked, ignoring Thren's glare.

The woman glanced at Quentin, but neither seemed willing to speak, and so Martin did.

"We're all hearing rumblings of Muzien pulling out from Veldaren," he said, and the others nodded in agreement. "Nothing official, but most everyone seems certain it will happen at some point."

"You act as if this would be a terrible thing," Thren said.

"It wouldn't be," Martin said. "Except Muzien's discussing taking tithes before we do."

Haern felt his heart skip a beat. He looked to the others, and they all kept their eyes to the dirt, as if afraid to meet his.

"Tithes?" he said. "Like the tithes he took in the marketplace? The tithes you no doubt were a part of?"

"Enough," Thren said, glaring.

"He's right, though," Quentin said. "He wants more tithes, and on a scale that's frightening."

"I'm not sure he plans on leaving afterwards," said the blond man by the tree. "But the tithes, those I'm certain of. You've got to understand, Thren, we all have families here, friends, relatives. Most of our lowest ranks are children, or hold other occupations. They don't want this, none of us do. A bit of extra coin, or a chance at power, that's one thing, but this?"

Tithes, thought Haern. *He wants his tithes . . .*

Glancing about, and seeing no tiles, Haern realized that they might be in the only place in Veldaren safe from the wrath Muzien could unleash upon them. He wasn't sure if that made him want to laugh or cry.

"A rebellion's stirring in his ranks," Thren said after they all fell silent. "That's what you're telling me?"

"Only with those here from Veldaren," Martin said. "Those who came with him from Mordeina couldn't care less."

Thren nodded, and there was no denying the excitement growing in his voice.

"Then the time is now," he said. "You swore your loyalty to a mad king to spare your lives, but that won't protect you anymore. He must be brought crumbling to the ground, and we have the power to do it. Rise up, throw on your cloaks, and defy the Darkhand with every breath in your lungs. Let this outsider learn the folly of his pride and arrogance."

"Brazen words," Quentin said. "But how do we know it will work? And how do we coordinate such an uprising?"

"It will work because I am with you, and not against you," Haern said. "Muzien built his power in my absence. I am here now, and I will not let it stand. Tell the underworld your Watcher will aid you in returning things to as they were. Even if you doubt Thren, do you doubt me?"

Haern felt the immediate change in the air. Muzien might carry a towering reputation, but Thren and Haern had spent their lives cultivating auras of fear in Veldaren. For their power to be united? Suddenly the Darkhand's newly forged empire didn't seem quite so invincible.

"This is not some last-ditch desperate attempt," Thren told them. "This is the true might of our city rising up in defiance, and we will crush everything Muzien has built in one single blow. Spread word throughout the underworld. Tell those who once belonged to your guilds that very soon I will give my signal to the entirety of the city. When you see it, toss aside the Sun, throw on your cloaks, and in the name of the Spider, slaughter all who will not do the same."

"And what might that signal be?" Martin asked.

Thren grinned at him.

"You will know it when you see it. Until then, be ready. This will be bloody, but we will emerge stronger than ever before."

"Hold up," Quentin said. "I don't remember any of us saying we agreed to go along with your plan, not that there's much of a plan to begin with, and I as sure as the Abyss didn't agree to join your Spider Guild."

Haern felt the air immediately turn electric. Quentin's hand had never left his sword, and the stubborn look on his face made Haern nervous. Thren turned to him, but if he was worried, his bemused smirk hid it well.

"You don't have a choice," he said. "If you don't agree, and swear it with your lives, then consider it appropriate we are in a cemetery."

"You'd force us to your side with a blade at our throats?"

Thren laughed in Quentin's face.

"As if Muzien recruited any differently," he said. "Swear loyalty to the plan, starting with you, Quentin. Let the gods themselves curse you if you betray us to that damn elf."

The others exchanged glances, and far too many hands were drifting down to the hilts of weapons for Haern's liking. Despite who was before him, Quentin didn't seem intimidated in the slightest.

"You always thought you ruled over us," the man said, drawing his two swords. "Like your guild was hot shit while we were just rats. We bled and died fighting the Trifect because of your pride, leaving us vulnerable to the Watcher's rise. Muzien may leave or stay, but no matter what happens, I'll take my own chances instead of following you into yet another war because your bruised ego can't stand the thought of someone else ruling Veldaren instead of you."

The two faced one another in the moonlight, Thren with his arms crossed, Quentin with his blades ready. The rest watched, tense, curious as to the outcome of the battle. Haern remained back, trusting his father to handle an upstart like Quentin, and instead watching to ensure no one else attempted a cheap shot at Thren while he was locked in a fight.

"You think you can take me down?" Thren asked. "I can't decide if I should be insulted, or if you're just insane."

"You'll have plenty of time to decide after you're dead."

Quentin rushed forward, trying to catch Thren off guard. A painfully futile attempt, and Haern knew it the second the man leaped off his feet. Thren took a single step back with his left foot to brace himself, and in a smooth motion, he pulled his short swords free of their sheaths and swept them in an arc before him, batting aside Quentin's dual thrusts. Pulling them back around, he forced Quentin to retreat from his sudden flurry of slashes. None were meant to be fatal, Thren clearly playing with him. Within moments thin cuts lined Quentin's face, which was flushed a deep red, whether from exertion of frustration, Haern did not know.

"Weren't you to kill me?" Thren asked, parrying a frantic thrust with his left hand and smacking Quentin across the cheek with the flat of his other blade. "Then why am I not dead yet? Come, Quentin, surely you weren't boasting out of your ass?"

Instead of attacking, the man retreated further, throwing a plea to the woman who'd come with him.

"Help me, Michelle," he said. "He can't take the both of us!"

The woman shook her head.

"This is your fight," she said. "You finish it."

Quentin's eyes widened in fear as Thren stalked forward, swords twirling in his hands. Apparently deciding it better to die in a mad rush than flee, Quentin barreled forward with the grace and skill of a charging bull. Thren sidestepped the mad swings, then spun on one foot, the other kicking Quentin hard in the stomach. The former Serpent rolled to the ground, one of his swords falling from his limp grip. When he came to a stop, he retched in a weak attempt to suck in air. Thren remained still, ignoring the man completely and instead addressing the others.

"Have you forgotten who I am?" he asked. "Have you forgotten all I've done? I've come to *save* you from Muzien, and you'd treat me like a child?"

Quentin pushed himself onto his knees, fingers digging into the soft earth of the cemetery. He glared as Thren pointed a bloody sword his way.

"Last chance," Thren said.

Quentin opened his mouth to speak, but no words came forth. Instead his upper body constricted, as if he were choking. His eyes bulged, and he convulsed again, a dry heave that was horrible to hear. Haern stepped back and readied his swords, horrified by the sight. Wisps of shadow swirled about Quentin, rising up from the grass to seep into his skin. As they all helplessly watched, Quentin clutched at his throat, let out a single agonizing shriek, and then vomited up a stream of blood that seemed to stretch on and on unending. At last he stopped, plopped facefirst into the red puddle before him, and lay still. In the ensuing silence, Deathmask's laughter was like a cry of thunder.

"Surely you all did not think I would miss such an important meeting?" the man asked, sitting on the highest branch of the slender tree. Haern felt the hairs on his neck stand on end. He'd checked that tree multiple times, never once seeing anyone within it. That Deathmask could avoid him so easily was unnerving to say the least…not to mention the awful display that had been Quentin's death.

"Was that necessary?" Thren asked, gesturing to the bloody corpse.

"Hardly anything I do is 'necessary,'" Deathmask said, grabbing hold of one branch to swing down to another before hopping to the ground. He wore no mask over his face, nor the cloud of ash levitating about his head to intimidate his foes. Even without them the man was still an imposing figure, his eyes sparkling with sick pleasure. "But enjoyable? Fitting? I'd like to think so. Quentin was an oaf, and you were a fool for giving him another chance. We are *all* on our last chances so long as Muzien lives."

If Thren had thought that only the Watcher's presence could

galvanize the rest, Haern realized he'd sorely underestimated Deathmask's influence. The Ash Guild, despite its size, was the sole survivor of Muzien's takeover of Veldaren. For him to also throw in his allegiance with Thren and the Watcher gave their plan legitimacy even the most doubting of men could not deny.

"You will aid us then?" Thren asked as he sheathed his swords.

"I'll aid in crushing the Sun Guild," Deathmask said. "But I won't be your puppet, and I won't ever serve you with the slightest bit of loyalty. In fact, I'm going to say none of us here will. When the Sun Guild collapses, the Spider Guild won't be inheriting the city alone. The Wolves will rise again, as will the Serpents, the Shadows, and perhaps even a few new-colored cloaks will grace our streets. But we won't be yours to rule. Either you accept that, or discover if I'll be as easy to defeat as that idiot Quentin."

For the second time in mere moments Thren stared down another man in that cemetery, but they all sensed the difference. Haern kept his hands on the hilts of his sabers, not expecting to need them. A man like Deathmask was too random and dangerous a foe to take on, especially with so little to gain.

"The underworld will only rise up if they may return to the guilds where they once belonged," Haern said, hoping to defuse the situation before it might become worse. "If you want to conquer Veldaren, Thren, you'll need to do it the old-fashioned way: one street at a time, and only after Muzien is rotting in the ground."

Thren kept his gaze locked with Deathmask's for a moment more, then looked away.

"So be it," he said. "Do you all accept?"

One by one the others nodded.

"Good." Thren turned back to Deathmask. "Then when I

give my signal, bring the Sun Guild crashing down, and make it glorious."

Deathmask bowed low in mockery.

"Muzien isn't the only one who knows how to put on a good show," he said. Waving to the others, he strode toward the exit of the cemetery. After an awkward hesitation, the others followed. Haern joined Thren's side, watching them go.

"That went well," Haern said when they were out of earshot.

"I thought I asked you to keep your mouth shut."

"Did you ever hear me agree?"

Thren shook his head, then reached into his pocket and pulled out a rolled-up scrap of paper.

"What is this?" Haern asked as Thren handed it over to him.

"For your wizard friend. It's a simple request, one he should be able to handle. Get it back to me as soon as you can."

Haern tapped the paper against his palm.

"This is your signal, I take it?" he asked.

"It is."

Haern put it into his own pocket, then joined his father in step as he headed for the cemetery's rickety gate.

"Where are you going?" Haern asked.

"Somewhere to alleviate my foul mood."

"A whorehouse?"

Thren let out a chuckle.

"Anywhere owned by the Sun Guild," he said. "My swords are still hungry."

More killing, so casual, so easy. Troubling still was how little that realization bothered Haern. Falling back a step, he turned left when his father turned right.

"Have fun," he called over his shoulder. "I'll give Tarlak your request. I'm sure he'll be mightily pleased."

Thren waved without looking. Giving one more look about

the various rooftops and alleys to ensure no one watched or waited in ambush, Haern rushed west to the Eschaton Tower, and it seemed his every step was lighter than the last.

This was it, the final strike against Muzien. Either they'd bring him down, or die trying. Though it should have brought him fear, he felt only relief. Despite all the risks of failure, he'd have the fate of the city resting on the blades of him and his father. As he climbed the city's wall and then descended the other side, he knew, deep down in his gut, there was no other way he'd rather it be.

Haern had expected everyone to be asleep when he entered the tower, and was surprised to see Tarlak waiting for him in his chair before the fire. He held no drink, which immediately made Haern nervous.

"I hope you weren't waiting up on my account," Haern said as he shut the door behind him.

"Sadly, I was," the wizard said. "We've got a problem."

He gestured for Haern to have a seat, and so he did on the nearby couch. Settling into the cushion, he removed his hood and popped his neck.

"What's the matter?" he asked. "Are Delysia and Brug all right?"

"They're fine," Tarlak said. "They're both worried about you, of course, but that's not what this is about. Antonil came to visit earlier today, and he wasn't carrying good news. Apparently an army of orcs somehow crossed the Bone Ditch and is marching its way here while happily pillaging all the nearby towns."

"That's not..." Haern rubbed his eyes, picturing the landscape and trying to make sense of it. "Forget it, so assuming that's true, how much time do we have?"

Tarlak let out a bitter laugh.

"There's no assuming involved. It's not hard to find an army of orcs with a bit of scrying magic, given how their race isn't what I'd call subtle or elusive. And by my guess? If we're lucky, they'll be here two nights from now."

Haern slumped into the couch, hands falling to his sides.

"That's not enough time," he said.

"Thanks for stating the obvious. Antonil was practically begging me to help defend the walls. Your name came up a few times, too. Seems he thinks you'd be a good frontline soldier. I offered Brug instead, but no luck there."

Haern shook his head, and he closed his eyes, mind still racing.

"You misunderstand me," he said. "I mean when it comes to Muzien. We need more time for word to spread. Everything is almost in place for an all-out rebellion. This has to succeed, for there won't be a second attempt if we fail."

"An army of muscle-bound brutes marches toward our doors, and you're worrying about rogues and guilds? Surely this can wait until after."

Haern snapped open his eyes and rose from his seat, unable to resist a need to pace the floor.

"Think about it, Tar," he said. "Muzien views himself as ruler of the city. Tell me, what do you think he might do if an army of orcs smashes through the gates?"

"Truth be told, I have no clue," Tarlak said. "And neither do you."

"That's a lie and you know it. There's already rumors he's planning to pull his guild out of the city, and he won't do so without leaving a giant funeral pyre to soothe his wounded pride. And even if he isn't planning on leaving, what do you think Muzien will do if he thinks the city will fall? Do you think he's the type to let someone else have it?"

"Might be better for everyone involved that they die in a fiery explosion than let those orcs have their way with them," Tarlak mused. "And what prevents him from doing the same damn thing because of your little insurrection?"

Haern turned, met Tarlak's stare, and refused to back down.

"Nothing," he said. "But I'm tired of cowering in fear of him. When we rise up, I'm hoping his pride prevents him from activating the tiles, and that he tries to crush us personally instead. If he does, then we'll have our chance to kill him and end this permanently."

"And by 'we' do you mean you and Thren?"

Haern let out a sigh.

"Yes, I do. Is that a problem?"

Tarlak shrugged.

"I don't know. How could allying with Veldaren's most infamous lunatic possibly be a problem? It boggles the mind."

"Be serious, Tar."

"I am!" The wizard shot up from his seat. "You're not just playing with fire; you're rolling around in it while bathed in lantern oil. Night after night you're out there with him, prowling the streets, killing, plotting. Is it really so wrong of me to fear a bit of the father might be rubbing off on the son?"

Haern swallowed, and despite his friend's seriousness, he couldn't help but chuckle.

"So you're not going to be happy about this request, then?" he asked, handing over the rolled-up scroll Thren had given him. Tarlak snapped it from his hands, opened it, and quickly skimmed the contents.

"Dramatic little bugger, isn't he?" the wizard mumbled, then rolled it back up. "I take it Thren wants this made posthaste? You know there's stone tiles capable of destroying the entire city out there I should probably be studying instead, right?"

"And I know you're no closer to rendering them harmless than when you first started," Haern said. "We won't save the city that way, not with what little time we have. We save it by overthrowing Muzien, who holds the key to their destruction. You know I'm right, too, or you wouldn't be as upset as you are."

"I'm upset because I'm worried I'm going to lose my friends and family," Tarlak said. "You could at least acknowledge that. The city's not equipped to handle an enemy force with so little preparation, and you are facing off against a foe that, barring our recent fun at the fountain, has never once been defeated. Bad doesn't begin to describe this, Haern. Bad doesn't scratch the surface."

Haern reached out and put a hand on his friend's shoulder.

"We'll endure," he said. "We always have, and we always will. This invading army, there's only so much I can do against it with my swords, especially compared to the magic you and your sister wield. But Muzien and the Sun Guild...we cannot let them continue to hold a blade over our heads using those damn tiles. My plan is in motion, and during the confusion, I think we can save the city from their hands. Can you trust me to handle them, while you handle the threat from outside the walls?"

Tarlak let out a sigh, and he brushed away Haern's touch.

"Yeah," he said. "I can. Won't like it, but I can. I'll get Thren's toy made tomorrow. First I need to get some sleep, and I suggest you do the same. I have a feeling there's long days and nights ahead of you."

A snap of his fingers, and the fire dwindled down to just embers.

"Good night, Tar," Haern said as the wizard climbed the stairs.

"Good night, Watcher."

In the growing darkness Haern stayed, still struggling to process the new threat. There was just no space in his mind, no way for him to worry over it with the threat of Muzien looming over everything.

"One enemy at a time," he muttered, removing his sword belt and plopping onto the couch. "Is that so much to ask, Ashhur?"

Of course it is, he chuckled to himself. Closing his eyes, he felt his exhaustion weighing on every one of his limbs, and despite how young the night was, he fell asleep with ease.

CHAPTER

 23

Sef Battleborn paced before Alyssa in the middle of their dining hall, his heavy footsteps on the carpet her tool to track his movements. The man was far from happy, but given the overall state of things in Veldaren, Alyssa thought that was to be expected.

"It's been two days," Sef said. "If we're to retaliate and have it mean something, it has to be now. The longer we wait, the weaker we appear, and the more insulting it is to Victor's memory."

Alyssa choked down her sigh. Sef had been Victor's most trusted and second-in-command, and due to that relationship, she'd given him responsibility for many of her house guards, as well as all the mercenaries still sworn to allegiance to her. Risky, given how little she knew of Sef, but the act had done wonders in solidifying her control over Victor's assets, as well as hiding her guilt. Still, the problem with Sef's loyalty to Victor, Alyssa had discovered, was, well, his loyalty to Victor.

"Getting Victor's men killed does disservice to Victor, not the other way around," Alyssa argued. "Any such drastic measure must be made with care and control."

"Care we'd take, if the circumstances were better. If your... friend, Zusa, had returned to us with the information you'd promised, we'd already be on the move."

Alyssa winced, and she lifted her cup to her lips to hide the slip. As she drank, she tried to imagine Sef from what she remembered. He'd been a large man, thick around the chest. A beard, she decided, he'd also had a beard, and not without a significant portion of gray. She had a feeling he was stroking that beard, if not pulling on it in frustration.

"Calm yourself," she said. "You'll add more gray to your beard if you remain like this."

His pacing halted, just long enough for her to know the comment had hit home. *Good*, she thought. Even the little details went a long way in winning people over.

"Forgive me," Sef said. "Inaction and I do not get along very well. If you'd rather we wait to serve vengeance to the Sun Guild, I will accept that, but please, let us at least begin our own inquiries as to their dens and hiding places. We may not find anything, but at least I won't feel like I am sitting here on my hands."

It was a simple enough request, and Alyssa waved him off.

"So be it," she said. "You have my permission. Only information, Sef, and only through petty bribery. No promising a fortune, and no torturing and cutting off limbs, either. We don't want them scattered or actively hiding, not if we can help it."

She heard Sef's boots clap together, and she assumed he'd bowed, so she made the smallest of nods in return.

"May you have a pleasant evening, milady," he said. "At your leave?"

Another wave, and he left her alone in the dining hall. Sipping more of her green tea, Alyssa tried to fight down her bubbling concern for her friend. She'd heard nothing of Zusa since she fled their last awkward encounter. Given how she was going back in disguise into the underworld of Veldaren, it made sense that it might take more than a few days to finish her efforts, as well as get away safely. But even as Alyssa told herself this, she did not believe it, not for the slightest second. Was she dead? Wounded? In hiding, her identity revealed? Alyssa didn't know, and she didn't want to know. Despite her worry, at least she could still lie to herself, and believe that Zusa still lived.

One of the doors to the dining hall opened, and Alyssa tilted an ear toward it.

"Mistress, you have a visitor," said a servant. "Guard Captain Antonil Copernus."

"Bring him to me," she said, ignoring the tightening of her throat. What news might Antonil bring? Did he anticipate the carnage that Sef wanted her to unleash? Or perhaps he'd discovered news he wished to deliver personally, perhaps about a dead servant he knew was close to her...

"Greetings, Lady Gemcroft," she heard Antonil say from the door, and she smiled as sweetly as she could.

"Greetings, Antonil," she said. "Please, come join me, and if you have the time, I'll have a servant fetch you something to eat or drink."

"Time is something I sadly have little to spare," Antonil said, his voice traveling closer. "I...forgive me, I should have come sooner to extend my condolences. Victor was a good man, and a better man than this city deserved. I am sorry for your loss."

Awkwardness bubbled up inside her, the same awkwardness she'd been struggling with since Victor's death. Should she feign sorrow? Those close to her knew there'd been no real romance between her and Victor. How many tears were appropriate? What words should she say about the man she'd murdered in secret? She'd found carrying on had served her best, for her eyes spoke volumes, the sorrow in their darkness conveying far more than she ever could.

"Thank you," Alyssa said, keeping her voice flat. "And yes, he was a good man."

Antonil coughed, and she realized he was pacing before her just as Sef had. Did it have something to do with her eyes, or was it just a military sort of thing?

"I wish I had a better way to broach this subject, but I don't, so forgive my abruptness," Antonil said. "Given the situation, I will keep this quick. I believe an army of orcs from the Vile Wedge approaches our city, and I need as many soldiers as possible to man the walls and hold the gates. Your husband once promised me aid should I ever need it, and I come to you praying you will accept a similar obligation."

Alyssa's mouth dropped open, and she blinked multiple times across her glass eyes.

"Excuse me?"

"I know it sounds insane, because it is, but it's also true. I expect them to arrive tomorrow night, leaving us very little time. I've made what preparations I can, and I'm coming to you in private in hopes of preventing panic from spreading throughout the city. With the men I have, I can't even guard the entirety of the wall. My hope is to keep them near the gates, where the fighting will most likely be. Even then, my soldiers on the ground will be terribly few. I need men with experience, who know how to fight and won't break in fear. I need your mercenaries, Alyssa, as many as you might spare. If a gate falls..."

Alyssa held up a hand, stopping him.

"Servants should be waiting just outside the door," she said. "Order one to fetch Sef Battleborn. I want him to hear this."

As Antonil did so, Alyssa reached for her tea, then decided against it. What madness was this, she wondered? An army of wild brutes? Did they not have enough to worry about in Veldaren? When Antonil returned, he sat opposite her at the table, and she heard him chuckle.

"You know," he said. "A drink might not be a bad idea after all."

Beyond thanking the servant who came with his glass, Antonil said little as they waited. Alyssa brooded silently, thinking over the numbers of her remaining forces. Three hundred of Victor's had survived their attempt to ambush Muzien, and they'd combined with the two hundred house soldiers and private mercenaries Alyssa had carried prior to the attempt. A significant fighting force indeed, but could she risk sending so many? What happened if Muzien considered the chaotic battle the opportune time to enact his own revenge?

The door opened, and Sef announced himself before stepping in.

"Antonil, I don't know if you've met before," said Alyssa, "but this is Sef Battleborn, former soldier and friend of Victor's, and my newly appointed master of mercenaries. Go ahead. Tell him what you've told me."

Antonil repeated his warning. When he finished, she heard Sef laugh.

"Well then," he said. "It seems fate has a fucking sense of humor when it comes to timing. What is it you want from us?"

"I want you and your men to hold the western gate," Antonil said. "If Alyssa agrees, of course."

"Alyssa?"

The master of the Gemcroft household sighed. Despite the

weight she felt bearing down on her, the guilt and the frustration, she knew what was right.

"Every soldier at my disposal is yours," she said. "If you are
correct, and an army marches against us, I promise my men
will be there without fail."

"Excellent," Antonil said, rising from his seat. "Your gen-
erosity may save thousands of lives, and I cannot thank you
enough."

Alyssa dismissed such praise with a wave of her hand.

"I'm not here to receive glory for doing the right thing," she
said. "Nor do I act selflessly. I live within these walls, too."

"Perhaps," Antonil said. "But I thank you nonetheless. Now
if you'll excuse me, I have work to do." She heard a rattle of
armor, something, hands perhaps, clapping together.

"Hope to fight with you soon," she heard Sef say.

"You as well."

More rattling, and then the door opened, leaving Sef alone
with Alyssa.

"I take it my scouting of the streets will be put on hold?" Sef
said once Antonil was gone.

"I see why Victor kept you around," she said, smiling despite
herself. "You're so skilled at deciphering the obvious."

Another knock on the door, followed by a servant's clearing her throat and calling Alyssa's name. Alyssa fought down
another sigh. What now?

"Yes?" she asked.

"I found . . . it seems someone left you a . . . gift, milady," said
one of their younger servants. Alyssa frowned, confused. A gift
from whom?

"Bring it here," she told Sef. "And what is it?"

Sef's heavy footsteps thumped over to the door.

"It's a small box," he said.

"Fascinating," Alyssa said dryly. "And inside?"

She heard a popping of wood, followed by a grunt.

"Well?" she asked.

Still Sef hesitated.

"It's...it's a note," he said. "And a lock of hair."

Alyssa's heart skipped, and she felt the room about her suddenly closing in. Reaching out her hand, she accepted the lock, felt its smoothness on her palm.

"Read it," she said, voice falling to a whisper.

Sef cleared his throat, then began reading aloud.

"'The game is just starting, Alyssa, not ending. Your turn. Do you still have the heart to play?'"

Alyssa lifted the lock of short, soft strands, twirled them in her fingers.

"What color is it?" she asked, already knowing the answer.

"Black," Sef said. "It's Zusa's, isn't it?"

Tears gathered at the bottoms of her glass eyes as Alyssa clutched the lock tightly in her fist.

"Another change in plans," she said. "I want dozens of your men scouring the city looking for her. Spend coin, break bones, and cut off as many fingers as it takes to loosen people's tongues. I want to know where she is, Sef, and I want to know now."

"If it's the Sun Guild, people don't talk, not even..."

Alyssa bolted from her seat, and reaching out, she found the collar of his shirt and then yanked him closer.

"*Make* them talk," she said, staring at him with her black eyes.

Sef cleared his throat.

"This may take time. What about Antonil's request? What shall we do when the army arrives?"

"For his sake, pray we find Zusa before then."

"As you wish," he said. "But I have to ask...what makes you think she is not already dead?"

Alyssa let him go, and she lovingly brushed the lock of hair with her fingers.

"Because if she were, Muzien would not have sent me her hair," Alyssa said. "He'd have sent me her head. Now go. You have a job to do."

Sef bowed, then stomped away, already shouting orders before the door to the dining hall closed. Alyssa remained standing, her body shaking, her blood turning to fire in her veins. Teeth clenched, she was flooded with such shocking strength it felt like she awoke for the first time in ages.

"How dare you?" she whispered, remembering Muzien's arrogance when he'd come to visit her in her bedroom. "You think you can take those close to me? You think you can escape my reach?"

She'd once threatened to burn the city to the ground in her quest for vengeance for her son. That same desire flooded her, and with each passing moment it grew. Striking a fist against the table beside her, she felt a plate break, a shard of it cutting into her hand. Grabbing the plate, she flung it at the wall, heard its satisfying shatter.

"I will not have my love wielded as a weapon against me," she vowed with a soft whisper. "I will not let another piece of my life die as part of a game. This ends now, I swear it."

Your turn, echoed the words of Muzien's note, spoken in Sef's baritone voice. Despite her doubt and exhaustion she'd revealed to Zusa, despite all her broken words, the swallowing darkness and parade of betrayals, and despite the blood that dripped down her wrist to stain her dress, Alyssa found herself smiling.

Do you still have the heart to play?

As it turned out, the answer was a resounding *yes*.

CHAPTER 24

All things considered, Deathmask had seen stranger ways to request a meeting, but this was probably his favorite. The message was in a back alley of the Ash Guild's sliver of remaining territory, written using the blood of a dead member of the Sun, whose body lay slumped directly beneath.

Tonight. Same cemetery.

It was signed with the Watcher's eye. Deathmask chuckled, then shrugged his shoulders.

"Well now," he muttered. "How could I refuse such a thoughtful invitation?"

After gathering the rest of his guild, Deathmask returned to the cemetery where Thren had detailed his plan to overthrow Muzien and his Sun Guild. Finding it empty, Deathmask leaned against the slender tree he'd hidden in, Veliana at his side.

"We'll scout outside," Nien said.

"Would hate to have an ambush," Mier said.

Deathmask waved them off.

"You don't think this would actually be a trap, do you?" Veliana asked as the two raced off in opposite directions.

"Course not, but it will give them something to do."

"Why?" asked a voice from above them. "Do you think it will take me that long to arrive?"

Deathmask chuckled as the Watcher leaped down from the highest branches of the tree, landing softly before them with a flourish of his cloaks.

"Cute," he said. "I guess I should have thought to check my own hiding place."

The Watcher was usually an amusing one to banter with, but not tonight.

"I need to talk to you about tomorrow," he said.

"There's really not much to talk about," Deathmask said. "Thren gives his signal, whatever that is, and then we go about slaughtering everyone dumb enough to keep the symbol of the Sun on their person. If you're worried about us having second thoughts, I assure you . . ."

"That's not it," the Watcher said, cutting him off. "I don't want you to aid us in overthrowing Muzien. There's somewhere else I think you'll be needed more."

Deathmask glanced at Veliana, who lifted an eyebrow to show she was equally confused.

"All right," he said. "And where might that be?"

"Along the walls. There's an army of orcs approaching, and I think we'll be better suited with you using your magic to defeat them."

It took a bit more effort than it should have to hide his surprise.

"Well then," he said. "That's . . . unexpected. And how did an orc army arrive at our doorstep without anyone noticing?"

The Watcher shifted where he stood, something Deathmask caught as a sign of unease.

"We've known for a few days," he said. "We've been trying to keep it to ourselves until people must be informed."

"I'm glad you consider us so vital to have waited so long," Veliana said, echoing Deathmask's own sentiments.

"Few days or one, it still is ridiculous," Deathmask said. "How did they get so near?"

"From what I was told, a necromancer is with them, guiding them and keeping them under control. He is the one I fear might give us trouble. Tarlak will do what he can, but with your help, I feel confident together you two cannot be defeated."

Suddenly Deathmask's pleasant night wasn't so pleasant. Frowning, he tried to hold back the bite to his words.

"You know nothing of who this necromancer is or what he can do, but you're confident we can handle him? I'm not sure your knowledge of arcane and divine magic is able to fill a thimble, let alone make such judgments."

"I'm only trying to do my best," the Watcher said. "I'd like the people of this city to survive this whole mess relatively unscathed. The least you could do is think of others for once."

A bit of purple flame sparkled from Deathmask's fingertips.

"You've delivered your message," he said. "Now leave."

The Watcher hesitated a moment, then bowed low. Without another word, he dashed toward the exit of the cemetery. Deathmask didn't bother to watch him go, instead marching toward the western section where the newest graves were dug. Given the events of the past few months, there were more than enough to choose from.

"What are you doing?" Veliana asked him as she followed.

"Finding myself a body."

Identifying a fresh grave was easy enough, and he crouched

before it, fingers sinking into the loose soil. There was power in the bodies of the deceased, power he would use.

"What bothers you so?" Veliana asked as she stood beside him, arms crossed over her chest. "A few thousand orcs with no real way to breach the gates or climb the walls should be easy prey given the city's defenses."

"It's not the orcs," Deathmask said as he felt the veil of magic slipping over his eyes. "It's the necromancer who's with them. I must confirm it for myself."

Veliana asked him something else, but her words came as if from a thousand miles away, stolen by a rushing wind that grew louder and louder as Deathmask's mind sank into the darkness. He saw nothing, just swirls of gray and black, until they opened up like an eye he might peer through. Around him were trees, tall husks of gray, their color sapped away by the magic of his sight. Marching through those trees, weapons swinging casually from their hands, were orcs. Their skin, already gray, looked ashen in his sight. They sang some sort of marching song, the words warbled in his ears. Deathmask felt an innate sense of location, somewhere far north of the city.

Where are you? Deathmask thought as he flew through the forest as if he were a mosquito, lifting, dropping, weaving through trees and brush and orcs. His direction was the lone source of color he saw, a rift of red and purple visible through the trees. Closer and closer, with a speed that even birds could not dream of achieving, he approached the necromancer. Deathmask could hardly believe it, but he was nervous, and caught himself almost wishing to end the spell before arriving. Such a realization about himself was insulting enough to keep him going, magical sight bursting through the very trunk of a tree to behold the leader of the orc horde.

He wore a simple robe, like that of a priest, its color a stunning black. Shimmering over that black, like ice over a tree branch in winter, was a swirling aura of color that pulsed among red, purple, and blue. The sight of it made Deathmask sick to his stomach. Looking to the face beneath the shrouded hood, he expected a man or woman. Instead he saw a rotted husk. Its skin was thin and peeled back, like a corpse left out for days in the sun. No lips covered its teeth, which, in a strange contrast to the decrepit state of the rest of its body, were a clean white. Just peeking out from the arms of the robe were skeletal fingers, and it seemed its fingertips were constantly aflame.

Most notable of all were the eyes. There were none, not such as any normal person might recognize. Instead they were swirling orbs of fire burning within the recesses of the skull, tightly compacted and releasing not a hint of smoke. Red veins of magic pulsed within them, encircling the fire, constantly giving it life.

And then those eyes met Deathmask's. The skull tilted to one side, as if curious.

Begone, it said, and when it opened its mouth, it had no tongue, just a dank black hole from which the deep, rumbling speech escaped. At those words Deathmask felt a horrific jabbing pain throughout his mind, and with a scream he fell back, hands pulling away from the earth to end his spell. For long agonizing moments, he lay there, staring up at the night sky as pain pulsed throughout his head as if he were in the grip of the worst migraine in the history of mankind. It took several minutes before color returned, and several minutes after that, he felt capable of speech.

"I'll be fine," he said, trying to ease the worries of the other three of his guild with him. Veliana took his arm, and he accepted her help so he might stand.

"What did you see?" she asked.

Deathmask shook his head.

"I saw who I thought I'd see," he said. "Karak's damn prophet. That little worm has been a pain in Dezrel's side since its earliest days, and it looks like he's not done stirring up trouble. No doubt he's the reason the orcs were able to cross the Bone Ditch, and I have a feeling that orc army isn't marching alone."

"So we help?" asked Mier.

"It seems we should," said Nien.

"We should," Deathmask agreed, rubbing at his eyes in a vain attempt to dismiss the blobs floating before them. "But not at the gates like the Watcher's hoping, nor against Muzien. Karak's prophet is outside the walls, and while everyone's worried about the orcs out there, we have an unchallenged enemy lurking in here."

He took a step, failed miserably. Veliana caught him, and as she helped him back to a stand, he smiled her way.

"Would you be a darling and help me walk to Ashhur's temple?" he asked. "There's a few things I need to discuss with their high priest."

Veliana tightened her grip on his arm.

"If you insist."

By the time Deathmask walked up the marble steps, he'd mostly recovered from the mental blow the prophet had dealt him, which was good, because he had every intention of going inside alone.

"It will be awkward enough by myself," he told the others before leaving them at the bottom of the steps. "You three will just make it worse."

At the door he knocked twice, then waited to be let in.

The door opened a crack, and Deathmask smiled down at the young lad peeking out.

"Yes?" the boy asked.

"I'm here to speak with High Priest Calan," Deathmask said. "And when he asks why, tell him it's about Karak's most faithful lunatic. He'll understand."

"He might be asleep."

Deathmask rolled his eyes.

"Then wake him."

The door shut, and Deathmask spent the time with his eyes closed, trying to meditate the last of his nausea away. Leaving the body to witness visions from afar was always a risky venture, and to be struck down while doing so was incredibly unpleasant and disorienting. Part of Deathmask wondered if his cramped stomach had more to do with unease at how easily he'd been dismissed rather than the dismissal itself. The door opened, and he was glad for the distraction so he'd not have to dwell on that thought.

"Come in," the boy said. "Follow me."

They passed through the main worship hall, which was surprisingly quiet and somber, with the light dim and the place empty. Then came the living quarters deeper in the temple, the way lit with lanterns. Instead of to what Deathmask assumed to be Calan's room, they went to a very small, cramped room with the door already open. The boy bowed, then hurried away. Deathmask stepped inside to find the high priest kneeling beside a clearly sick man who also wore the robes of the priesthood. His face was coated with sweat, his skin pale, his forehead covered with a wet cloth. When Deathmask entered, Calan was busy using a second cloth to wipe away the sweat from the sleeping man.

"If you were worried about waking me, don't," the priest

said, glancing over his shoulder. "It seems I will never have a full night's rest in this city. No, I've been tending to poor Kirk here for the last hour, waiting for his fever to break."

"Why not use your magic to heal his illness?" Deathmask asked.

"The paladins had strict rules regarding what could and could not be healed," Calan said. "But for myself, I consider it a useful lesson. Daily my students heal the sick masses that come to them, and the strain wears on them greatly. Having them experience the ills they themselves heal helps keep things in focus, and remind them of how much good they actually do."

"But why watch over him yourself? You have men and women at your beck and call that surely could suffice."

"I consider that a useful lesson for myself," he said. "Very useful, given how I spend all my days with men and women at my beck and call."

Deathmask shrugged. Humility wasn't something he thought too highly of, but that was hardly an argument he felt like having now. No, he had business to attend to.

"If you would, Priest, there are things we must discuss."

Calan slowly rose to his feet and turned around, finally giving Deathmask a good look at the man. He was old but surprisingly alert, especially given the time of night. His face was oval, his features smooth and rounded. A friendly face, Deathmask decided, welcoming and harmless. Despite such a late interruption, he looked strangely amused.

"I recognize the robes you wear," the priest said. "You're from the Towers, am I right?"

"I was, but that is for another time," Deathmask said, cutting off the discussion before he could be forced to relive more unpleasantness. "So we might skip most of the formal trivialities, I am Deathmask, I rule the Ash Guild, and I am not one to waste my time with the gods unless given no choice, so that should impress upon you the importance of my being here. I've come bearing warning, and if you're wise, you'll listen well."

Calan chuckled.

"With such an introduction as that, how could I not listen?" he asked. "But perhaps let us take this elsewhere? I would hate to wake poor Kirk here."

Together they stepped back out into the hallway, the priest shutting the door behind them. Other than the rows of dim lanterns, they were alone.

"The lad said something about Karak's most faithful lunatic," Calan asked. "Would you care to elaborate on that?"

Deathmask crossed his arms and met Calan's stare. There was no weakness in his beady blue eyes, no fright at Deathmask's appearance, no intimidation or worry at whatever the warning might be. Good. Perhaps the man had a spine after all.

"How much do you know of Karak's prophet?"

A corner of the priest's mouth twitched.

"More than I would like," he said. "Jacob Eveningstar, the first man, beloved child of Karak since the earliest days when we were first given life from the dust. He's adopted many names since, though we in the temple know him as Velixar. Our own historians have not written of him in my lifetime, which has led some to believe he has finally passed on. Others insist he is a myth, or a moniker adopted by faithful servants of Karak to make it seem he lives forever. Now I have answered your question, may I ask what he is to you, and why you come asking of him?"

Deathmask smirked.

"I ask because he marches upon this city with an army of orcs he's gathered from within the Vile Wedge. He is no myth, Calan, no false identity. At the council, our wizards have met with him many times over the decades, usually in failed attempts to garner wisdom from his ancient, rotting brain. We've tracked him when we can, which isn't often, but it appears he is no longer content to hide and manipulate from afar."

Calan leaned back against the door, and it looked like a hundred pounds had been attached to his shoulders.

"He is a man to be feared," the priest said. "But we will challenge him should he threaten the people of this city. Thank you for your warning, for it shall serve us well."

Deathmask shook his head, and he wagged his finger at Calan.

"You don't get it," he said. "I'm not here because of Karak's prophet. I'm here because of the *others* who follow Karak. When the prophet marches upon our gates, what do you think his powerful, secretive priests will do, hrm? Do you think they'll sit back and watch events unfold like good little impartial observers? I don't think so, Calan. The moment Karak's priests realize who has come knocking at the door, they'll do whatever they can to sabotage the city's defenses to let him in. Even if I have to do it alone, I will do my best to stop them, but this is a foe your kind is far better equipped to handle. So when tomorrow night arrives, can I depend on you to keep us all alive?"

Calan ran a hand over his bald head.

"You care not for the gods," he said. "And even within these halls, I have heard your name whispered, as well as the deeds of your Ash Guild. Why come to me? Why would you risk your life fighting a dangerous foe like the priests of Karak when you have so little to gain? You could flee this place with ease, so why stay?"

Truth be told, Deathmask thought it a very good question, and taking in a deep breath, he let out a long sigh.

"Because Veldaren is my home," he said. "The only one I've known since I was exiled from the Council of Mages. The games we play here, I very much enjoy them, but the prophet and his followers would smash the board entirely. Honestly, I'd prefer neither god interfere with the affairs of Dezrel. Since that doesn't appear to be an option, I might as well pit one against the other in an effort to minimize the damage. The last thing I want to imagine is what would become of Veldaren if it were ruled by priests and prophets of Karak."

"Would it not be better to just admit that sometimes even a man like you does the right thing?" Calan asked.

Deathmask shrugged.

"Consider me too cynical to believe that. Now will you aid me or not?"

Calan outstretched his hand, and after a moment, Deathmask took it and accepted the handshake.

"We will," he said. "If the prophet arrives as you say, the might of Ashhur will rise against Karak's followers. It will only be a cage to prevent their interference, but should they choose to resist..."

"It'll be a brutal, devastating battle, I know," Deathmask said, grinning as if the idea entertained him. "But if it comes to that, trust me, on that night, it will be but one horrific battle of oh so very many."

CHAPTER 25

Haern had finished preparing the last of his things when Tarlak stepped into his room. Throwing a rucksack over his shoulder, he stood and lifted an eyebrow as the wizard offered a slender clay tube.

"Here it is," Tarlak said. "I hope Thren appreciates the effort it took to make that thing. To activate it, just break the seal at the top and then point it at the sky."

"Seems simple enough," Haern said, glancing over the tube. One end was smooth and filled with clay, while the other had multiple runes carved across the top, similar to those that ran along the side of the cylinder.

"Just don't forget," Tarlak said. "If either of you burn your faces off because you can't follow simple directions, I'm not accepting any of the blame."

Haern slipped the tube into the pack on his back, chuckling as he did.

"You, taking responsibility?" he asked. "I wouldn't think of it, Tar."

Tarlak grinned, the joy not even close to showing in his eyes. Stepping past him, Haern hesitated a moment, feeling awkward, and then he clapped the wizard on the shoulder.

"That army should come barreling out from the forest soon," he said. "Make sure you, Brug, and Del are somewhere safe when that happens, all right?"

"*Safe* might be a relative term, but will do," Tarlak said. "Antonil wants us at the gates, so that's where we'll be. We'll have to rely on you to take care of all that other fun stuff, like Muzien and exploding tiles."

Haern shot him a wink.

"I'll try not to disappoint."

Tarlak's arm barred his way before Haern could exit, and the wizard did not bother to pretend at joy or amusement. His words were serious, as were his face, his eyes.

"You do what must be done, you understand me?" he asked. "Either Muzien dies, or all of us burn. I know how fast he is, how incredibly dangerous he is with those blades. You'll have to be better. You'll have to be faster. Let nothing hold you back, and I mean *nothing*, not fear, not pain, not guilt, not even death. This dire madness ends tonight."

Haern pushed aside his arm, and he wished he had words to match Tarlak's intensity.

"I'll give all I have," he said. "I don't know any other way."

He exited his room and descended the stairs, hurrying down them two at a time. Barging out the doors, he had barely gone three steps before he heard Delysia call his name.

"I always know when you're nervous," she said. "That's when you try to leave without saying good-bye."

Haern turned to face her, a practiced smile on his face, an

easy joke on his tongue. The smile vanished and the joke died unspoken when she stepped close, wrapped her arms around his waist, and pressed her lips to his. His shock lasted only a moment before he closed his arms around her and returned the kiss. When Delysia finally pulled back, she took in a soft breath and released him so she might put her hands on his chest. Her red hair fell forward, shrouding her face, making her confession feel all the more intimate.

"I'm scared of tonight," she whispered. "Scared of what you'll be asked to do. Come back to me, Haern. Remember who you are, and why you fight. Can you promise me that?"

With his hand he tilted her chin up so she would gaze into his eyes. She was so vulnerable. So afraid. He wished just once she could forfeit the innate ability to sense truth and lie given to her by Ashhur. He wished just once he could tell her a comforting lie instead of the naked truth.

"I don't know if I can," he said. "Not given all I must do. But I promise to try."

He kissed her again. It did not last as long as the first, for she seemed content to sink against him, her head pressing into the cloth of his shirt. Her hands still clutched his clothes, and he felt the stress and nerves within him loosen as he hugged her close.

"I'll be here for you," she whispered. "Always and forever."

Gently he pulled away from her and then trudged across the grass toward the road leading to the city. It took all his concentration to focus on other things instead of glancing back over his shoulder, and revealing to Delysia just how nervous he was about the looming nightfall.

Along the road Haern adjusted the pack on his back. He wore simple street clothes, his cloak, sabers, and gear wrapped up in the pack. Given all he might have to do that night, Haern didn't have the heart to scale the wall. No, like any other traveler he passed through the city gates, not long before they would be shut for the night. The sky was dark above him, the sun hidden behind a thick wall of clouds that had come rolling in from the north. So far as Haern had learned, whispers of the approaching army were just that, rumors and whispers, yet still the air was thick with tension. Perhaps Haern was projecting his own worries, but in the dull gray light, it seemed the people looked hurried and edgy, eyes constantly flicking to nonexistent things at the corners of their vision.

Haern went to the heart of the city, and at the crossroads before the ancient fountain he could not deny the lingering fear. Too many rushed along to their destinations, and people did not linger in their conversations, if they stopped to have them at all. It felt like a city under siege, yet not a single enemy was at their outer walls. Of course there were plenty of enemies within, and perhaps deep down they all could sense the coming violence...

With the thick clouds, it seemed night would come early, and Haern found himself a secluded alley and removed his pack. First came his soft leather vambraces, then an outer shirt of a far darker color than the brown he currently wore. Next he secured his belt, and slid both sabers into their sheaths. His fingers lingered on the hilts, their weight a comfort as always. He'd come to view his sabers as friends, trustworthy beyond measure. Part of him wished he still had the pair Senke had given him. That he dwelt on such past times made him more uneasy. Taking his cloak, he slung it over his shoulders, let it fully envelop his body. While it was one cloak, it was also three separate, interlocking parts, allowing his arms greater freedom as well as giving him the ability to misdirect his foes by moving one piece differently from the rest.

Last was his hood, which he held in his hands, staring at it. The Wraith's hood, stolen after his death as a reminder that Haern was not a god among men, not their lord and ruler as the Wraith had wanted him to be.

"Remember who you are," he whispered. Not a god, not a lord or ruler. Then what was he? As he pulled the hood over his head, and its comfortable shadow fell across his face, he admitted he no longer knew. What did he fight for? Whose lives did he save by his killing? What peace did his sabers bring?

Eyes closed, he touched the hood, deepening its magic to hide his features. The mystery of his identity heightened his opponents' fear, giving him power through the unknown. Rising to his full height, he tucked Thren's signal into his pocket, then reached up to a nearby window. The climb was simple, and easily he reached the top. Given how tightly the many homes were packed together along the streets of Veldaren, and how flat their wood and stone rooftops were built, they fostered a second world come nightfall, one beyond the reach of guards and soldiers. Into that world Haern entered, weapons at the ready, visage bathed in shadow, person safely wrapped in his cloaks.

He was Veldaren's Watcher, its midnight protector, son of its underworld's most infamous master, and across the rooftops to his father he ran.

Thren waited for him across from a seedy tavern, lying flat on his stomach on the roof of a wine shop on the opposite side of the street. Rain had begun to fall, soft and gentle, and Haern hoped it would not interfere with the signal Thren had requested.

"Almost thought you'd abandoned me," Thren said as Haern joined him on his stomach, overlooking the tavern. It looked bright and bustling inside, the outside guarded by a single man who appeared drunk off his ass.

"And leave you all the fun?" Haern asked, shaking his head. "Someone needs to make sure you don't misbehave."

Thren grinned at him, the toothy grin of a predator.

"Tonight we both misbehave," he said. "Do you have my signal?"

Haern pulled the tube out from his pocket and handed it over.

"Break the seal and then point it upward," he instructed.

Thren sat up, looking the tube over before holding it before him.

"What's the plan?" Haern asked him before he could start.

"We give everyone a few minutes to see and react," Thren said as the rain momentarily died down. "Then we go barging in and slaughter all who are foolish enough to remain loyal to the Sun. Down there is one of Muzien's few remaining strongholds, and from what I've learned, it's where those who came with him from Mordan most frequent. If the elf's not in there, I'm sure we can find someone who knows where he's at. Are you ready?"

Haern clenched his hands into fists to prevent them from fidgeting against his saber hilts.

"I am," he said.

Thren drew a dagger, jammed the tip into the center of the clay seal, and then held the cylinder above his head. Haern watched, curious as to what the signal might be. For a moment nothing, and then a great red flash burst from the end of the tube with such force Thren had to brace himself with his free hand. Into the darkened sky streaked an enormous glowing ball, sparks trailing along its path as if it were a comet. Higher and higher it soared, and then it exploded in a great red plume that rolled in all directions, filling the sky with red smoke, the backdrop of clouds taking on the hue of dried blood. Four yellow sparks zipped through the air before burning out, leaving behind the painfully familiar symbol of Muzien's guild, that of the four-pointed star. It shimmered there, the golden color startling against the red...and then it began to change.

Each of the four points faded away, as did the lines connecting them. Replacing them was an illusion carefully created by Tarlak, that of a spider slowly uncurling its legs. Its body was made of smoke, its legs shadow, its entire form outlined in the still brightly burning red smoke. The symbolism was clear, and with the display seemingly as big as the city itself in the sky, impossible to miss. Despite the rain returning with fresh strength, the hovering spider remained, lording over the city, declaring it his.

"Your wizard did a fine job," Thren said, discarding the tube and returning to his stomach so he might peer over the building's edge to watch the tavern. Haern watched as well, curious if Thren's plan would succeed. To have so many rise up simultaneously, having not given Muzien any warning to counter, seemed almost ridiculous. But then again, no matter how many tiles he scattered throughout the city with his symbol, Muzien would always be a foreigner. Given how the majority of the underworld were motivated by fear and greed, their turning both against Muzien seemed entirely plausible.

The drunk guard outside was still sober enough to see the display in the sky, and he rushed inside. Haern tensed, straining his ears to hear. People within shouted, and two men rushed outside to look. One said something to the other, and at the second's response, the first drew his dagger and stabbed his companion in the throat. It should have been shocking behavior, but it made Haern's blood run cool, while Thren beamed.

"It starts," his father whispered.

The man outside tossed aside his coat, then raced down the street, away from the tavern. Rain beat down on upon the corpse, mixing with its blood into a growing puddle before the tavern door. More shouts came from inside, the sounds of wood breaking, glass shattering. Thren rose to his feet, and the man looked so eager, so *alive*.

"Come," he said. "Let us crush them all."

Haern wished he didn't feel the same excitement. Grabbing the side of the rooftop, they both swung down, landed lightly on their feet, and drew their blades. In perfect tandem they ran, gaining as much speed as they could in the short distance. Like monsters of the night they blasted into the tavern, Haern slamming open the door with his shoulder while his father smashed through one of the windows, a shower of glass heralding his arrival. Haern surveyed the entire tavern in a heartbeat, welcoming the feeling of time slowing down while the pounding of his heart surged. Over a third of those there had tossed aside their long coats, with several even fighting bare-chested due to the Sun Guild's symbol having been sewn onto their shirts. All eyes turned their way, and Haern allowed a grin to spread across his face at the fear he saw in them.

Thren landed before a group of three, and he tore into them with ruthless efficiency. The nearest died before turning at the sound of the breaking glass, the other two barely getting their weapons up in time to temporarily avoid death. Haern ignored the fight, instead focusing on a tall man lifting a crossbow from the other side of the bar. Leaping feetfirst, he dropped beneath the bolt, which whizzed past his head, and then crushed the man's windpipe with his heels upon impact. Haern landed atop the bar, a hard jolt to his chest that would certainly leave a bruise, but he had no doubt he'd recover far faster than the man he'd kicked.

His instincts flared a warning, and he rolled aside as a short sword thunked into the wood of the bar. Haern slashed wildly, cutting its wielder across the face, and then pushed off the bar and onto his feet. Two others joined the first, the three all holding short swords and bearing the four-pointed star on their coats.

"Are you mad?" Haern asked them, ignoring the ache in his side. "Have you forgotten who I am?"

"Muzien'll kill us if we flee," said the center of the three, his speech whistling from several missing teeth.

"I'll kill you if you stay," Haern shot back.

They seemed not to care, and they simultaneously lunged, trying to spear him from all directions. Haern spun, deflecting all three with both his weapons. The motion sent his cloak billowing upward, and he used it to hide how low he dropped to the ground. Before they could react he sprang into them, sabers crossed in an X as he crashed into the man on the left. Legs pumping, he bowled him over, cutting across his stomach as the man hit the ground. Intestines burst out like coiled springs. Dying screams in his ears, Haern spun, each sword blocking an attack. Sidestepping left, he brought both weapons to bear on one man, the expert precision of his strokes easily knocking his foe's short sword out of position. The man tried to retreat backward, as if sensing his own vulnerability, but Haern lunged into him with a ferocity that would have made his father proud, burying his left saber up to the hilt in the man's chest.

Haern released it as the last of the three tried to stab him in the back. His saber curled down and about as he turned, lifting the thrust so that it passed harmlessly above his shoulder, and then Haern struck the man hard in the throat with his free hand. The windpipe crunched inward against his fist.

His foe doubled over hacking as Haern yanked out the second saber. The sounds his foe made were awful, ragged gasps as he sucked in air followed by whistling hisses as he released what thin breaths he could manage through his missing teeth.

"Consider this a mercy," Haern said as he plunged a saber into the man's heart.

Kicking the body to the ground, Haern looked to the corner to see his father finishing off his own group. One last member of the Sun remained, and Thren beat aside his flailing defenses and then slashed his short swords across the man's abdomen, splashing the floor with gore as his stomach opened and his innards plopped free. Thren wiped at his face with his shoulder in a vain attempt to clean his eyes, then nodded at Haern.

"Downstairs," he said, as if oblivious to the horrible display at his feet.

Those not dead or dying had fled, and Haern strode through the now-empty tavern to the door behind the bar and yanked it open, revealing six rickety stairs leading to the basement.

"How many down there, you think?" Haern asked as Thren joined his side.

"Does it matter?"

Haern shrugged.

"How about this one, then: that door down there, does it open inward or outward?"

Thren grinned, all the long years and lines seeming to fade from his face.

"Inward," he said. "The honor's all yours. I'll be your shadow."

The stairway was too narrow for them to run side by side, so taking the lead, Haern raced down the steps, gaining speed, and at the bottom he flung himself shoulder-first into the door. The wood snapped, the hinges groaned, and whatever lock was on the other side could not hold against the force of his impact. As the door flung open, Haern dropped to a roll, and his prescience was rewarded by four crossbow bolts soaring above him. Coming up from the roll, sabers ready, he found five men standing together in what appeared to be little more than a well-stocked cellar, the members of the Sun all armed with daggers and swords.

Haern's hesitation lasted for a single heartbeat, and then after him came Thren, bursting into the cellar with the energy and devastation of a tornado. Side by side they assaulted the five, cutting, thrusting, overwhelming them so they could only retreat. Haern saw the stunned horror in their eyes as he parried a frantic counter, their realization at how terribly outclassed they were when it came to the art of killing, and he knew the battle would not take long. Their confidence, their spirit, was already broken. Taking down the flesh was merely perfunctory after that.

Haern pushed two of his foes back farther, frightening them with blurs of steel that were merely feints. As they retreated, he turned to the middle of the five, catching him trying to sneak a thrust into Thren's side. Out went his saber, and it came back bloodied. Seeing the space the other two left him, Haern risked turning his back to them for the briefest moment. Sensing the coming aid, Thren lunged to one side, turning the attention of his foes even farther away, and Haern came crashing in unopposed. He cut the throat of one, and the other managed to duck just in time so that instead of taking out her throat he merely slashed across her cheek.

Leaving her to his father, he brought his attention back to the other two, and was mildly disappointed to see them attempting to flee. Haern was faster, and his sabers found their backs before they reached the stairs. Yanking them free, he looked to the final member of the Sun, who was cornered by his father.

"I surrender!" the woman said, hurling aside her dagger. "I'll join, I swear, I swear I'll…"

Thren cut out her throat anyway, and as the body fell, he kicked her once in the chest in contempt.

"The writing's in the damn sky," Thren told the dying woman. "What worth are you if you can't understand until it's too late?"

Haern watched the life leave her eyes, and he echoed Tarlak's words in his mind again and again to harden his heart against the cruel image.

Do what must be done, you understand me? You do what must be done…

"Not even guilt," Haern whispered, and he cleaned the blood off his sabers using a dead man's shirt.

"What's that?" Thren asked, cleaning his own blades.

"Nothing," Haern said. "Where to next?"

Thren sheathed his short swords, frowned at a cut on his arm, and then gestured up the stairs.

"To the streets," he said. "Let's see if we can witness the fruit of our labors."

They climbed the stairs into the empty tavern, and Haern stepped out first, followed by Thren. In the soft rain, they could still hear the occasional scream, and the darkness made the various fires easy to spot. Looking to the rooftops, Haern saw a man running, the dark green cloak of the Serpent Guild flapping from his back. To his left Haern spotted another trio, two men and a woman, and all of them bore the color of the Spider Guild. Thren's smile blossomed, and when the three rushed to Thren and bowed low, his satisfaction was almost sickening.

"Muzien likes to say the sun always rises," the woman said. "But it also sets. Night has fallen upon Veldaren, Master Felhorn. Give us our orders."

The title gave Haern chills that even the gray cloaks of the Spider could not.

"Hunt down all who remain loyal," Thren told them. "From the highest of nobles to the lowest of the low, I want those with the Sun on their bodies executed."

"What about you?" asked one of the men.

"He's with me," Haern said. "And we have the highest of the highest to find."

Thren cast a look over his shoulder, and he seemed terribly amused.

"Indeed," he said, returning his attention to the first of many to rejoin his guild. "I'll be fine, now go. Shed blood in my name."

They did as they were told. Instead of watching them go, Haern ran back across the street and climbed to the rooftop they'd first lurked upon prior to the assault. Feeling the rain beating down on him, he held a hand up over his eyes and peered across the city. He saw shapes everywhere, though how many were real and how many were imaginary distortions of the rain, he couldn't guess.

"You left none to tell us where Muzien is," Haern said as Thren joined him on the rooftop.

"He'll show himself," Thren said.

"What makes you so confident he will?"

Before he could answer, the ground shook from an explosion not far to the south. Purple fire roared into the air, accompanied by black smoke and a tremendous blast of sound. Eyes twinkling, Thren pointed toward the distant fire and grinned.

"I think we found our invitation," he said, and before Haern could call it insane to run into a certain ambush, Thren dashed across the rooftops, aiming to do just that.

More dying screams reached his ears through the rainfall.

Not just thieves. Bakers. Smiths. Clerks. Stablemen. Prostitutes. Any who bore the four-pointed star upon their breast, or painted it above their doorways, all died as the resurging tide of the old guilds burst open doors and climbed through windows, cloaks that had been hidden or tossed now hung proudly from their shoulders. It felt like the Abyss had risen up to swallow Veldaren, and Haern clenched a fist tight as he did everything to convince himself it was justified.

"What must be done," he whispered.

Legs pumping, cloak billowing, Haern followed his father into the storm.

CHAPTER
26

No enemy was yet in sight when Antonil ordered Veldaren's city guard and stationed soldiers to arm themselves for battle. Their foes would arrive that night; he was certain of it. And as the clouds deepened, bringing rain in from the north, he could not shake the feeling they were borne on an unnatural wind. Come nightfall he stood above the western gate, eyes to the distant King's Forest, as the few hundred men under his command joined him on the wall.

"What happens if this army doesn't show?" Sergan asked beside him as the soft rain fell.

"Then I'll claim it was an exercise," Antonil said. "Gods know we could use the practice."

When the symbol of the Sun erupted above the city, only to be consumed by the Spider, murmurs spread all across the wall. Antonil watched, a foul feeling deep in the pit of his stomach.

"What does it mean?" Sergan asked him as they both peered up at the sky.

"It means exactly what it looks like it means," Antonil said. "The Spider Guild's rising up against the Sun Guild. Of course they'd pick tonight to do it, while not a single city guard will be out there to stop them. Tonight's going to be ugly, Sergan. While we fight our battle at the walls, there will be another raging inside them."

"Try not to think on it," Sergan said, pointing north, and he was hardly the only one to notice. "The scum of the city can butcher each other to their heart's content; we have our own enemy to worry about."

From the forest the army emerged. At first they were distant dots of gray, blobs of a different color from the rest of the night. As the army continued to march, coming closer, those on the wall better saw their armor, their drawn weapons. They carried no torches, for they had no need of them, given their racial ability to see in darkness as well as daylight. Antonil envied the ability as his own men struggled to keep their torches lit against the rain. Even from such a great distance, they could easily hear the thrumming of drums and a chorus of war chants sung by deep voices.

"No wagons or catapults," Sergan said, squinting in an attempt to see them better. "But if they're coming out of a forest, they'll have had plenty of choices for a solid battering ram. Unless they built a cover for it, though, our archers will tear whoever's carrying it to pieces."

Antonil nodded, keeping unspoken Dieredon's fears about what the necromancer could do. Up and down the wall he heard his men calling out, and he was proud of how much was in mockery of the approaching army. The fear was there, hidden but controlled. So long as it stayed that way, Veldaren had a chance.

"What the...?" Sergan asked, voice trailing off as he pointed dumbly.

From deep within the forest sailed thin dots of deep-purple fire, bursting from the trees in a direct flight toward Veldaren's skies. The men around him braced their shields or lowered themselves to take cover, for it seemed as if they were projectiles... but then they arced, and shifted, continuing to fly without dropping. Antonil stared along with all the others, baffled as to what approached.

"Sir?" Sergan asked, but Antonil didn't know what to say. The shapes were growing closer, and lit so brightly by the purple fire, he swore he could almost make out...

And then the screams hit. A thousand of them, horrific wails, as if the tortured souls of the very Abyss were given a chance to let loose all their torment and agony. The blistering cacophony descended upon them from above. Antonil felt his heart skip in his chest, felt terror clawing at his throat. There was no reason for it, no rationale; he simply felt terror, helpless, crippling terror, and he knew he was not the only one. All around him, his soldiers cowered along the wall, holding their ears or covering their eyes.

"Fight it," Antonil screamed, trying to muster strength against this supernatural horror. "Fight it, fight it!"

Slowly he felt the fear ebbing, and he looked up to see the orbs flying directly above them. They were skulls, he realized, those of the dead the army had butchered on its march toward the capital. Their flesh was peeled away but for the tiniest of bits that still clung to the bone, flapping in the ethereal fire that burned and burned. The skulls took circular flight over the gate, some dipping down low to soar mere feet above his soldiers as if to toy with them and their fear. Others looped into the city, sending their horrific screeches piercing through Veldaren's streets.

Through sheer will Antonil rose to his feet, and he banged his sword against his shield in a vain attempt to counter the wailing.

"On your feet," he screamed to his men, and he pushed through the ranks, striking his shield again and again. "On your feet, you cowards. Going to piss yourselves over a little screaming? It's just a damn trick, now *on your feet*!"

Slowly his men returned to their senses. Antonil's heart felt as if it were racing a hundred miles a minute, but the fear was receding, the screams no longer carrying the same edge. Up and down the wall he continued, calling to his men, commanding them to stand. It felt hopeless, as for every man he convinced to stand, two more remained whimpering, but he had to try. Lightning cracked above, and glancing up, he saw that the fire of the skulls had dimmed. As the orc army continued its approach, the skulls winked out one by one, falling lifeless to the ground, where they shattered on the stone streets and walls.

It was as if a vise had been removed from his throat. Those who had cowered now stood, embarrassed, angry. Antonil slapped men on their backs, still shouting, barely aware of what he said and knowing his men would not truly hear, either. The tone was what mattered, the force of his words, the power of his conviction. They would live. They would fight. They would win.

"They better hope they have more than cheap tricks if they want to get inside these walls," Sergan said as Antonil returned to the wall above the western gate. Antonil looked to the field and road outside the gate, where the army was massing. With the dark and the rain, he couldn't begin to count. His best estimate put them at several thousand. Solid numbers, but unless they had ladders and rams, the walls would still hold.

A hand tapped his shoulder, and Antonil realized Sergan was trying to get his attention while also pointing to the sky.

"Looks like our friend is back," Sergan said.

Sonowin looped above the city, the white of the horse's body and wings a startling contrast to the dark storm.

"You're in charge," Antonil said as the horse looped lower and lower toward the nearby city district. "I'll be back shortly, I promise."

"Don't take too long," Sergan called after him as Antonil descended the stairs. "I'd hate for you to miss all the fun!"

From his lower perspective, Antonil did the best he could to watch where the flying horse landed. He counted the homes as he passed them, trying to remember where he'd last seen the white beast fly. Finally at one of the alleys on his left he turned in, hoping he'd guessed correctly. Being away from his men at such a crucial time upset him to no end, but the elf would not come flying in amid the rain and the chaos without good reason.

Come bringing good news, Antonil pleaded in his mind as he stopped halfway through the alley, which was disappointingly empty. Letting out a sigh, he started to move, then heard a whistle from above. Looking up, Antonil chuckled, then lifted his sword in a salute. From the rooftop leaped Dieredon, landing lightly on his feet.

"Greetings, Dieredon," Antonil said as he pulled off his helmet.

"Greetings to you as well, Guard Captain," Dieredon said as he took a step back and then kneeled in respect. His long hair was wet and sticking to his face, and he looked about as haggard as Antonil felt. "Though I fear greetings are all I may offer you."

It took little imagination to understand what the elf could

mean. Antonil pointed toward the west wall as the distant army of orcs let out a great communal roar.

"We can't defeat them on our own," Antonil shouted to be heard over the din. "Where is our aid?"

Dieredon shook his head, and the softest hint of sadness pulled at his features.

"The Ekreissar will not aid you," he said. "We have been forbidden. Ceredon insists this is a minor skirmish, and nothing more. We are not the keepers of man."

"Minor skirmish?" Antonil asked. "What about the necromancer traveling with them? You're the one who said he was dangerous, that he might bring down our walls all on his own."

Another communal roar washed over the city, louder, closer.

"I know." Dieredon said. "Forgive me, Antonil. I will watch, and I will pray. Whoever started this war will not go unpunished."

The elf whistled, and Antonil glanced up to see Sonowin landing atop the nearby roof, wings fluttering to flick off the building rain. Dieredon bowed one last time and then leaped, kicked off the side of the building, then twisted to catch the side so he might pull himself up. Antonil watched him mount the horse, feet rooted to the ground until at last the elf took off into the dark night, quickly vanishing amid the storm. Once Dieredon was gone, he felt free to let out how he truly felt.

"Damn it all!" Antonil shouted, slamming his mailed fist into a wall. They were alone now. The mockery of the skulls showed they faced no normal army, yet their walls of wood and stone would have to hold. Still shaking his head, he stormed back to the gate, muttering curses. Upon arriving, he saw that the ground forces were still terribly thin.

"Where the bloody Abyss are Lady Gemcroft's mercenaries?" he cried to no one in particular. With so many on the wall, only two dozen stood before the solid wood-and-metal gates, the most Antonil could spare. He'd expected several hundred to join him. It seemed Alyssa had different ideas. Did she plan on keeping them with her at her home? What did it matter if the whole city burned so long as her mansion endured? Antonil was used to such thinking from the highborn, but he'd hoped for better from her. Apparently he'd been wrong.

"What, are we not good enough for you?" a familiar voice shouted over the din.

Antonil turned to see Tarlak pushing his way through the soldiers so he could hurry down the stairs of the wall, his yellow robes looking ridiculous contrasted with the black and blue of the night. For some reason it made Antonil smile, and eased his anger and stress.

"Forgive me," Antonil said. "I didn't think a wizard for hire would be the most reliable of defenders."

"Are you kidding, we're the most reliable of all," Tarlak said, closing the distance and offering Antonil his hand. "Though we need to work on the 'for hire' part. So far as I know, we're not getting paid..."

"Later," Antonil said. "Are you alone?"

"Del and Brug are up there," Tarlak said, jerking a thumb toward the top of the wall. "Both should prove more useful than you might expect. Well, Delysia will be, anyway. What is it you want me to do?"

Antonil stared dumbly for a moment, then shrugged.

"I've never commanded a wizard before," he said. "I don't even know what all you can do."

"Think more in concepts, then. Defense? Offense? Walls, gates, fire, ice, what?"

Antonil gestured to the wall, and the chorus of war chants and drums on the other side.

"Orcs bad, humans good, do what you think is best. Is that basic enough?"

Tarlak snapped his fingers, and a bit of fire sparked from them.

"Kill as many as I can," he said, grinning. "Got it."

Despite himself, Antonil smiled.

"I think we all have those same orders," he said.

"If you two are done sucking each other off, there's a battle to fight up here," Sergan shouted.

Antonil secured his shield on his back, then hurried up the stone steps to the wall, the wizard following just behind. Upon reaching the top, Antonil overlooked the thousands of orcs, who were preparing a charge. They looked so similar to men, just more muscular and broad-shouldered. The shade of their skin was most noticeable, a pale likeness of flesh, as if all color and life had been drained from their bodies. Some wore crude armor, but they were few, with the majority wearing war paint, skulls, and straps of leather. Each orc looked capable of handling two men at once in battle, and given how they outnumbered them so terribly...

Tarlak nudged him with his elbow, pulling him from such thoughts.

"Behind the army," Tarlak said, lowering his voice as if afraid of being overheard. "What is that?"

A thin line formed the very rear of the orc forces. It was difficult to tell, but they did not appear to be orcs. As to what they could be, Antonil had no guess. In the center of the line, though, was a man or woman clothed in solid black, not even their face visible due to a heavy hood.

"That'd be the necromancer leading them," Antonil whispered back.

The wizard let out a grunt.

"Interesting," he muttered. "I might not kill as many orcs as I'd like if whoever that is out there decides to come play as well."

Antonil clapped him on the shoulder.

"You're like any other soldier now," he said. "Do your duty, and we'll be fine."

"If you say so, but don't hold any delusions about being my commanding officer..."

He stopped, unable to be heard due to the great cry the orcs let loose while simultaneously smacking their weapons together and stomping their feet. Thousands, Antonil saw, so many thousands, and with another cry they surged toward the city.

"The gates better hold," Antonil muttered so that only Tarlak could hear.

"Don't see any reason why they won't," the wizard replied. "What are the orcs going to do, beat it down with their bare hands?"

"Seems like it. Here they come. *Arrows, loose!*"

The rows of archers on the walls released arrow after arrow as the army of orcs came barreling forward. A great cry accompanied the charge, deep, throaty roars easily drowning out any shouts of pain from those brought low by the shafts. Antonil watched the arrows fly, taking grim satisfaction in watching the wounded drop, quickly trampled by the orcs who came stampeding after. Volley after volley they fired. With so many in the fields before them there was no need to aim, only release as fast as possible.

Beside him, Tarlak rubbed his hands together, nearly overcome with glee.

"Just a little bit of fire along the walls and we'll all be heading back to bed within the hour," he said. That glee vanished when a red dot appeared from the back line overlooking the battle. Tarlak cocked his head, watching as it grew, and then his eyes spread wide.

"Oh shit," he said, then turned about to scream at the dozen soldiers bunched up before the gates. "*Get out of the way! Move!*"

Antonil turned back, then saw that the red dot was a roaring inferno of fire surging toward the city in a great beam. It burned through the orc army, consuming bodies as if they were oil-soaked cloth, and then slammed into the city gate. The beam never slowed. The wood exploded, shrapnel shooting in all directions. The soldiers behind the gate screamed as the molten rock flowed over them, melting through their armor and shields. Their dying screams were terrible but mercifully short, death claiming them swiftly. Then, just as suddenly as it had appeared, the beam vanished, leaving only a trail of smoke and scorched earth.

The way was clear, and the orcs let out a great cheer, not caring about their losses.

"Down, now, form a line!" Sergan screamed. "We can't let them in!"

Antonil stared in shock, knowing he should act but unable to. The way was clear. Just like that, all their walls, all their preparations, meant nothing. The way was clear.

"Snap out of it," Tarlak shouted as he joined the surge down the steps. Antonil grabbed him before he could get away.

"You protect us from him," he said. "We can fight the orcs, but that foe is beyond us."

Tarlak paused, then nodded. That done, they both rushed to the ground, Antonil taking his place in the center of the formation of shields and swords. Through the blackened stone and broken pieces of the gate, they watched the orc army come barreling in with wild abandon. Antonil spared a glance over his shoulder, hoping for a miracle, but hundreds of reinforcements were not marching down the street to save them. They were alone.

Thanks, Alyssa, he thought bitterly. *You're our city's savior.*

"Hold!" Sergan shouted from the front line, a wall of shields on either side of him. "Hold!"

The walls nearly empty but for a few scattered archers, the remainder of the forces gathered to hold the gate, a mere four hundred against thousands. The challenge was overwhelming, the narrowness of the entryway their only hope.

"They broke our gate," Antonil shouted, mere seconds before the army slammed into them, and the bloody chaos began. "Let's build a new one with their dead!"

CHAPTER 27

Every hour someone came to change the torches that bathed Zusa in light. She remained chained to the wall, her wrists rubbed raw by the metal of the manacles. She'd tried wriggling free, but they were far too tight, and it seemed her fingers were always tingling, just shy of falling asleep.

"Time to eat yet, Scar?" Zusa asked the man, middle-aged and with a long scar across the top of his head that left a gap in his short brown hair. He was one of several she saw consistently coming down into her little prison, and she had yet to learn his name despite repeated attempts. Eventually she'd named him herself, the reference to his obvious deformity annoying him, and Zusa found amusement in that little bit of power.

"I haven't decided yet," Scar said, lighting a fresh torch using the old one, then setting it into its holder.

"How about a bath? You know I look forward to it."

The man glared and remained silent. Zusa leaned back her

head, closing her eyes as she smiled. Muzien, in his insanity, seemed to truly believe he could win Zusa over with time. Despite her imprisonment, she'd been treated well, fed meals twice a day and given water to drink whenever she requested it. Every night someone, always a woman she noticed, would come to remove her clothes and then bathe her. She'd clean the shit and piss, washing it away with buckets of water and plentiful rags, and then scrub until Zusa was clean, relative to her surroundings. Her original clothes remained in the far corner, just within the reach of the torchlight, while the outfit she currently wore was one of the many they'd changed her into after bathings.

She'd thought to escape during the bathing, but the bather never seemed to have the key to her manacles, and she saw no way to escape them even if left unguarded. If only she could find a way to snuff out the damn torches...

"I'm not the one in charge of wiping your ass," Scar said, moving on to the next torch.

"Do you want to be?" she asked. "I know some men like that sort of thing."

He rolled his eyes in disgust. Zusa continued to watch, wishing she could get more of a rise out of the man. Once she decided on an attempt to escape, being able to manipulate her lone guard could prove vital. By the Abyss, if she could get him close, get him angry and careless, that might be all she would need, for swinging from his belt was a single large key, and she felt certain it was for her manacles.

As Scar was finishing swapping out the last of the torches, the door on the far side banged open, and Zusa flinched at the sudden noise. Two men rushed in, one she recognized, one she did not. The familiar one was a fairly squat man with green eyes, missing teeth, and an impressively large nose. She'd begun calling him Wart, due to the many that grew on his hands.

"What the fuck?" Scar asked, glaring at the two. "Nearly burned my hand off 'cause of you."

"Everything's gone to shit," Wart said, tugging at the collar of his shirt. "Thren made this giant spider illusion over the whole city, and it's triggered something fierce. Seems our entire damn guild has turned traitor. Had to kill two of our own just to make it here without dying."

Scar stood frozen where he was, mouth hanging open.

"Jace?" he said, and the tall man with Wart nodded his head.

"It's bad," he said, and he swallowed as if he tasted something foul between his teeth. "We might need to start thinking about abandoning the Sun Guild if we want to live."

All three of them fell silent for a moment, until Scar muttered a curse under his breath.

"Let me see this," he said, pushing past them so he could exit through the door. Jace and Wart remained down there, arms crossed, looking lost and confused. The rug had been yanked out from underneath them, and it amused Zusa to no end seeing how lost they looked without their precious Muzien to guarantee them safety.

Scar came back down the stairs, and he appeared angrier than before.

"Cheap tricks," he said. "That's all it is, cheap tricks to go with one last desperate attempt at power. We'll ride this out, the three of us, until Muzien gets things back under control."

"You don't get it," Wart argued. "There is no getting this under control. You think I'd be this scared if it were only a few casting aside the pointed star? You two are Mordan outsiders, but I'm from here, right here, and I got a spider tattoo hidden on my arm. You want to know what Thren'll do to me if this overthrow succeeds, and I'm not a part of it?"

"Muzien will do you ten times worse if you turn traitor now," Scar argued. "And if you're from here, then you know how easily we took over these streets. We won't lose them, not when Muzien hits back."

From the far corner, Zusa interrupted them with her laughter.

"Which killer will you run to like the scared children you are?" she asked them. "Which one will you bet your life on succeeding? Guess right and live, guess wrong and die like the traitors you are. I'm the one in chains, yet my life is safer than yours."

None of the three seemed too pleased with that fact.

"We can't stay," Jace said. "No matter which side we join, too many know about this place. I say we cut our losses and run. Take neither side, and see if we can hide in the chaos. When things settle down, we'll join with the winner, and no one will be the wiser."

"We leave, and abandon her, there's no rejoining Muzien," Scar said. "We might as well cut her throat and then toss on the gray cloaks of the Spider."

Zusa grinned at them despite the chilling of her blood. Suddenly the conversation was not quite so amusing.

"Then let me go," she said. "Say I escaped while you were distracted. Do you think it'll be the first time I have done so? I'm a complication, so let me out, and you can do whatever you wish."

The three exchanged a look, and she sensed the unspoken debate flowing through them.

"You're right," Wart said, the first to break the silence and turn her way. "You *are* a complication, and I'm thinking we remove that complication right now."

He drew a dagger from his belt, and Zusa struggled to remain perfectly still and not reveal her growing panic.

"Don't be stupid," she said. "Alyssa Gemcroft will pay a princely sum to have me back. Take us somewhere safe, ransom me to Alyssa, and then flee with your newfound wealth to somewhere neither Thren nor Muzien has a presence."

Scar grabbed Wart by the sleeve, halting his approach.

"The reason we're holding her is because of the Gemcroft bitch," he said. "She might not be lying about that ransom."

"What?" Wart asked. "We've gone from keeping our heads down and waiting for a winner to suddenly negotiating ransom with one of the Trifect? That's the damn *opposite* of laying low. I'm not looking to make a profit out of tonight. I just want to live. You can't spend coin if you're dead."

He pulled his sleeve free, then pointed his dagger at Zusa.

"Do you think she's just a normal woman we can drag around? There's a reason we've got all those torches burning about her. She's some sort of witch or trickster, and the moment those manacles are off her wrists, we're all dead. I say cut her throat, find a place to hide, and wait until we know exactly what the fuck is going on. If she's so important to Alyssa, then maybe we can sell Muzien out to her once this all settles down, and we're ready to run."

"No matter who wins tonight, we can claim the winner was the one who killed her," Jace added.

Scar glared back and forth, happy with neither. Zusa could sense his willpower breaking. Arms pinned behind her, she could think of no escape if they turned on her, no way to survive. She tried to let her panic fuel her determination, give some sort of influence to her words.

"You'll be making a mistake," she said. "If you let me live, and agree to a ransom, I'll make no attempt to escape. I'll have no reason to break my word, not if you don't break yours."

It wasn't enough. The men were scared, and they didn't want to take any risks. She tried to think of another angle, but what was there besides coin? She couldn't offer them her body. They could rape her corpse if they truly wanted to, and besides that, the three seemed more interested in long-term survival than short-term gratification.

Scar opened his mouth to say something, but then the shrieks from outside came. All three dropped to their knees and put their hands over their ears, wincing as if in terrible pain. Zusa closed her eyes and shivered as the wails washed over her like water. It seemed as if the screamers were mere inches away and on all sides as they let loose their agony. While the others looked baffled, Zusa felt the taint of Karak within each cry, and she did her best to fight against it. Even held captive, she would do all she could to deny her former god and any power he might hold over her.

Several more times they sounded, each time like needles to her skin. There was no rational thought to the fear, no reason, just the sound of horrible torment and a gut belief that somehow she would soon suffer in the same way. What released the cry, or what Karak could have to do with anything, Zusa had not the slightest clue. It seemed the other three in the room didn't, either.

At last the wailing ceased, and the ensuing silence was almost beautiful. Feeling as if she'd just run a dozen miles, her body lifted and fell with her deep breaths as she glared at her captors.

"You three are all in over your heads," she told them. "Just flee. Flee from here as fast as you can if you want to see the sunrise."

Before any could respond, the door swung inward again, and a woman wearing a long coat of the Sun stepped inside.

"Soldiers!" she cried. "We need you, now!"

Scar looked to the others, then nodded at their unspoken question.

"Go," he said. "I'll handle this."

The chains holding her hands behind her back were incredibly short and low to the floor, forcing Zusa to kneel. As the rest rushed out the door, and Scar slowly approached while drawing his dagger, Zusa forced her knees up and her feet underneath her. No matter what happened, she was going to fight him. Eyes on his, she watched every step, and she wished she could project her very will as a blade to slay him.

"This is your own fault, you know," Scar said. "You turned on Muzien, and you got yourself caught. There's no one else to blame, so you can spare me that glare."

He towered over her, blade in his right hand, light from the torches illuminating the ugly scar across his head.

"Just make it quick," she said, every muscle in her body tense.

Squatting down so his face was even with hers, he smirked, his dagger hovering before her chest.

"If you insist," he said.

Her knees were up before her, covering much of her body, and when Scar thrust the dagger, she hopped as best as her constricted body could manage. As her body began to fall, she jerked her knees all the way up. Instead of burying itself in her heart, the dagger pierced her kneecap before scraping to one side, blood splashing from the long, thin cut. The pain was intense, but Zusa made not a cry, her mind brutally focused so that nothing mattered but the quick, precise movements of her chained body.

Upon hitting the ground, she snap-kicked, extended her leg as far as it could go. Her toes jammed into Scar's windpipe, and as much as it hurt her foot, she knew it hurt him far worse. The impact of the hit caused him to fall backward on instinct, but because he'd extended himself for his dagger thrust, the arm holding the weapon was much closer than the rest of his body. Thrusting out her legs again, abdominal muscles screaming from the movements after such long inaction, she closed her thighs around his wrist. Legs curling about his arm, she yanked the man to the floor. He was unable to brace himself, and his head snapped against the wood. She felt his arm slacken in her grip.

Not dead, she thought. *Dazed at best.*

With no way of grabbing the dagger that lay upon her thighs, she released her grip on Scar's arm and stretched out her foot, trying to use her toes to hook the key ring attached to his belt. She brushed it once, unable to secure it on her big toe, before Scar let out a moan and rolled away from her. Panicking, she tried to kick him in the throat, but he continued rolling. Zusa stared at the dagger between her legs, which had fallen during her attempts. No scenario existed in which she could somehow wield it against her captor.

"You bitch," Scar murmured, slowly pushing himself onto his hands and knees. He looked her way, and she saw the already swelling purple bruise on his forehead, saw how bloodshot his eyes were. When he spoke, his voice was raspy and painful to listen to, but he was able to draw breath, which was all that mattered.

Scar struggled back to a stand, and safely out of kicking distance, he stood over her, panting.

"You bitch," he said again, louder, stronger. His eyes, which had been glazed when he first looked her way, regained their focus. His hands curled into fists, and she knew whatever hope she'd had of escape was gone.

"What sort of demon are you?" Scar asked.

"Just a trickster or a witch," she said, praying that her death would be quick. She smiled despite feeling like she wanted to throw up. "I thought you knew that."

He looked to the dagger between her legs, decided against it, and instead staggered to her pile of clothes in the corner. He reached into the pile and withdrew one of Zusa's original daggers. Holding it tightly, blade downward, he stalked back toward her with a sick gleam in his eye.

"I did," he said. "You little trickster. Let's see how well you kick when you have no feet."

The door banged open, and both turned to see Wart's body tumbling down the stairs. Scar froze, suddenly unsure, and then in stepped a soldier wearing a blessedly familiar tabard, sword in hand, fresh blood on both his blade and his armor.

Scar, apparently coming to a decision, dropped the knife and lifted his hands into the air.

"I surrender," he started to say. He never had the chance to finish the offer. The soldier took two steps and slashed out the man's throat. Body crumpling to the ground, the soldier knelt, retrieved the key, and then went to Zusa's side as more soldiers tramped down the steps and into the room.

"Lean forward," the soldier said. Zusa did so, and he reached behind her and unlocked the manacles. The moment she heard them snap open, she pulled forward and let out a single sob. Her muscles screamed from the movement, but it felt so good to have her arms no longer trapped behind her. Accepting the soldier's offered hand, she stood on wobbly feet. At the door, the last of the armored men entered, one of them holding Alyssa's hand as he led her into the room. Zusa felt her breath catch in her throat, and she thought of every single second of the last time she'd seen her.

"Zusa?" Alyssa asked, her eyes still the solid black they'd been on their previous meeting.

"I'm here," Zusa said, voice sounding weak to her own ears.

She didn't know what to expect. She didn't know how her

friend would react after rejecting her earlier advances. Tired mind a swirling mixture of exhaustion, shame, and relief, Zusa felt paralyzed with indecision. She almost dropped to one knee in respect to thank Alyssa, but there was no chance to do so.

Alyssa took two rapid steps, then burst out in a run toward the sound of her voice. Arms flinging open, she hit Zusa at full speed, latching on to her with trembling strength. Zusa caught her, and unable to stand, she fell back a step to brace against the wall. Alyssa's fingers dug into her back, and tears ran down her face. When Zusa opened her mouth to say something, anything, Alyssa silenced it with a kiss.

"I'm sorry," Alyssa whispered when she finally pulled free. "I'm so sorry for all I've done, and tonight, I'm making it right. I'm taking Nathaniel, and we're leaving this damn city. I won't lose you again, not ever, do you understand me? Of all the things I've failed, I won't let your love be one of them."

Tears ran down Zusa's cheeks as well, and she pressed her palm against Alyssa's beautiful face, smiled down at her.

"Thank you," she said. "Now please, I feel disgusting. Let me change into something clean."

Gently pulling from Alyssa's embrace, she passed through the path the soldiers opened for her to the other side of the room, where her clothes remained piled. Not caring that the men might watch, Zusa hurried out of the simple shirt and pants one of Muzien's women had put her in, then slipped on the outfit she'd first built in a fit of anger at Alyssa. Doing her best to put such a frustrating memory behind her, she put on the pants, pulled the shirt and cloak over her head, and then tightened the belt. Sliding the daggers into their sheaths, she felt whole, felt herself, and she returned to where Alyssa waited and took her hand.

"Let's go home," Zusa said.

"It's not that simple," Alyssa said as they filed up the stairs and out into the streets wet with rain, which continued to fall. "An army's come, and Antonil needs my men."

Her mercenaries, all five hundred of them, were gathered about where Zusa had been held prisoner, the cellar of a nondescript home. They'd fully surrounded the place, and several hundred were waiting in formation in the street.

Zusa pulled her hood over her face to protect it from the rain.

"Where are we going?" she asked as they took their place in the very heart of the formation.

"To the west gate," Alyssa answered.

Their march was slow, and Zusa tried to relax as they made their way. Ahead of them she heard the constant beating of drums, and several times the invaders let out deep-throated war cries that made even the hardiest of men with them seem nervous. Zusa almost suggested that she and Alyssa be dropped off at the mansion, but would either be much safer there than surrounded by the armed mercenaries loyal to her?

Zusa decided perhaps not. From what she could see, several fires burned throughout the city despite the rain, plumes of dark smoke rising up to the storm clouds. Twice they passed dead bodies lying at the entrance to a home, the scenes carrying the look of executions given the undressed state of the victims.

"Is this Muzien's doing?" Zusa asked upon seeing a third.

"Is what?"

"The bodies," Zusa answered, feeling foolish. "There's dead bodies at the entrances of several homes."

Alyssa shrugged.

"Let the underworld eat each other for all I care. This city is no longer my own."

Zusa had a feeling that would be easier said than done, but she did not argue the point. It felt good just to be walking, and to have her arms swinging at her sides instead of locked behind her back. The good feelings lasted until she heard a voice cry out to them from the rooftops.

"Lady Gemcroft!"

The squad froze, and dozens of soldiers looked up to where a handsome man with brown eyes and dark hair knelt on a rooftop. Based on the color of his cloak, he was a member of the Ash, one of the twins, she realized.

"Explain yourself!" one of the commanders of the mercenaries shouted, drawing his blade in anticipation of an ambush. Instead the thief swung down to the ground, unafraid of the many armed men clearly unhappy with his arrival.

"Lady Gemcroft," he repeated, getting as close as he could to Alyssa before a wall of soldiers stopped him. "We need you at the southern gate!"

"Guard Captain Copernus said he needed us at the west," Alyssa said.

The soldiers tried to push him aside, but the man resisted.

"It is not Antonil who needs you," he cried. "It is your son!"

Alyssa froze, and Zusa felt her grip on her hand tighten tenfold.

"My son is safe at home," she said, but it sounded like even she did not believe it.

"No, he's not."

Alyssa motioned for her men to make way. Guessing her intent, Zusa led her so that Alyssa was dangerously close to a dangerous man.

"If this is a lie, I will have my men string you from your innards from the top of a lamppost," Alyssa said. "Now where is my son?"

The Ash Guild rogue licked his lips, then grinned.

"Follow me," he said. "And tell your men to ready their swords. They'll be needed."

CHAPTER

28

Thren finally slowed his run as he neared the explosion caused by one of Muzien's tiles, and Haern was happy he had. Besides giving Haern a chance to catch his breath, it also meant Thren didn't plan on just blindly running into what was certainly an ambush.

"You're not tired, are you?" Thren asked, looking at him sideways.

"I can fight for hours more," Haern said, and he wasn't lying. "Worry about yourself."

Thren shrugged, dismissing the matter as quickly as he'd brought it up. The two were beneath an awning erected before a tannery, momentarily safe from the soft rain. Peering out from underneath, Thren stared at the lingering smoke of the explosion, which continued unabated by the rain.

"If it's an ambush, he'll want to spring it when we're completely surrounded," Thren said, musing aloud. "That means his men must be hidden so we do not see them on our approach."

"He'll also have to be ready from all directions," Haern added. "There's no way for him to know where we'll be approaching from."

Thren frowned, thinking.

"They'll be inside at least two different buildings," he said. "Possibly even the ones that tile just wrecked. I bet they have a few on the rooftops as well, just decoys to make us think the ambush isn't as heavily manned as it is."

"You act as if you can read his mind."

Thren glared at him.

"I was his pupil for many years, Watcher. I have a feel for how he thinks. Right now he's hoping we come rushing in across the rooftops, kill the few up top, and then drop down to the street to investigate. Which means we're going to do the opposite."

Haern joined him in looking at the smoke, which rose on the other side of two more buildings.

"And what is that?" he asked.

Thren drew his swords, stretched his back.

"Stay low, stay together, and scour the nearby buildings while leaving the scouts up top alive and unaware."

Haern couldn't help himself.

"And what if Muzien anticipated you seeing through his plan and prepared an ambush for us doing just that?"

Thren let out a snort.

"Then he's the god he pretends to be, and trying to outthink him will be like chasing our own tails. Forgive me for not buying into the elf's legend. He's not perfect, he's not infallible. That's what tonight is all about, Watcher. Tonight we prove that bastard's mortal."

Haern drew his swords, and he saluted his father.

"To noble goals," he said, grinning.

Together they ran, crouching low to keep their profiles as minimal as possible. Upon crossing the street, Haern slid around the side of the tall building, back pressed against it. Given the darkness and the rain, seeing him would be all but impossible. Above him was a window, and he turned about, put a boot on Thren's offered hands, and then leaped to catch its windowsill. Pulling up, he crouched on the windowsill and peered inside. The room was incredibly dark, but the magic of Haern's hood let him see as if soft starlight bathed the interior.

He was in an upstairs storeroom filled with crates stuffed with various metal bits and screws. On the other side was a second window, and peering out of it with his shoulder pressed against the wall was the dark outline of one of Muzien's thugs. Carefully Haern crept down from the window and then slowly crossed the distance. Given the little light coming from the windows, he knew only sound could give him away, and between the boots Brug had made him and his own lengthy training, no sound would be made. Bathed in darkness, he felt his Watcher persona stirring. Tonight was a night for murder, an art he had long perfected.

Once he was a few feet away, Haern drew his dagger and held his breath. So far the man still peered out the window, no doubt hoping to catch a glimpse of Thren or the Watcher. Now much closer, Haern could see he was incredibly young, maybe fifteen at most. Strangely enough, he was very softly whistling, no doubt thinking the storm would overwhelm the noise. The song was even cheerful, not nervous as Haern had first assumed. To kill him was to end the song. Haern knew this should give him pause, perhaps guilt, but instead the confidence of it angered him further. All across the city, men and women were dying. At the gates soldiers fought for their lives.

In the streets the old guilds were rising up, slaughtering the new that had taken their place. Yet here, in this hollowed section of the city, members of the Sun waited for him and Thren like it was just a game? As if victory were already assured?

Sickened, and with his pride wounded, Haern burst into movement. He clamped a hand over the man's face, then jammed the dagger into his back. The whistle turned into a gargle. Yanking out the dagger, Haern thrust it again and again, each stab more vicious than the last as he felt the Watcher persona fully take control. Dragging the limp body away from the window, Haern gently let it drop, then returned to the window he'd entered from. Thren remained outside it, patiently waiting.

Leaning out, Haern offered him his hand. Thren leaped, caught it, and then climbed up with his feet as Haern pulled.

"Just one?" Thren whispered once he was inside.

"Up here, anyway," Haern whispered back. "The stairs are over there. Can you see them?"

"I can't," Thren said. "But I don't need to. Lead the way, and I'll follow."

To the stairs they went, Haern realizing that his father had grabbed the bottom of his cloak and was using it to guide himself. At the top of the stairs, Haern peered down and saw that someone must have lit a small fire or torch given the way red-and-yellow light flickered against the wall, casting shadows. None appeared to be of men or women, leaving Haern with no clue as to how many were downstairs. Moving down three steps, the farthest he could go before he might be visible to those downstairs, he tensed for action. They'd need to act fast, just in case the numbers were far greater than they expected.

Wait, he mouthed to Thren, who was one step behind him. Just in case the light from downstairs was not enough, he held out his right hand, blocking Thren's way. Tensed and ready to run, Haern waited, knowing it shouldn't be long. When lightning flashed, filling both floors with momentary light, Haern rushed down the steps two at a time. Thunder rumbled, and combined with the rain, he hoped the noise might mask their descent. Upon hitting the bottom, he pivoted, leaping with sabers leading.

Four members of the Sun were gathered in a store, two men waiting at the door across from Haern, two more holding crossbows as they peered out the nearby windows. A lantern burned from a hook in the center of the ceiling, casting amber light across the two rows of shelves. It seemed they had not heard their approach, and Haern grinned with grim amusement at their intense concentration. As he crossed the room, he hopped atop the shelf, which was pleasantly thick and sturdy. A spare glance behind showed Thren climbing the other, and together they crouched along. Halfway there, they stopped when Thren was directly beneath the lantern.

On your signal, Thren mouthed as he reached up to touch the lantern. Haern nodded, and he could not help himself. He counted to three, then let out a soft whistle, the same song as the man upstairs. Out went the lantern, flooding the store with darkness.

"Shit," he heard one of them cry, coupled with the *twang* of a crossbow string. Haern heard it strike the wood of the far wall, no doubt somewhere near the staircase. They didn't realize how high up they were, how fast they rushed toward them. Thren leaped first, and Haern followed, the two descending upon the four before they could realize the danger they were in. Haern extended his legs, his heels slamming into the chest of the other crossbowman. The body crumpled beneath him. Just to be sure, Haern jammed his sabers downward until they both hit flesh. The man to his right swung at Haern's face, but he dipped below, yanking free his sabers and then whirling, both blades cutting across his foe's chest and waist. As the rogue cried out in pain, Haern completed his turn, bringing his sabers back down, this time across the neck and shoulders.

The man crumpled, and having finished his opponents, Haern looked to see Thren having done likewise, one of his short swords still sticking out of the back of a Sun member lying facedown beside the window.

"Did they hear us?" Thren whispered. Haern almost admired how quickly he could put the dead out of his mind, always focused on the task at hand.

"I'm not sure," Haern whispered. They'd only allowed a single cry of pain. Swiping clean his sabers on a dead man's coat, he leaned against the wall and peered out the window. He saw only an empty street, the two buildings on the other side appearing dim and empty. Not far to his left was the destruction left by the exploded tile, the street turned into a crater, the nearby buildings crumpled into ruin. They, too, were dark. The realization made Haern's nerves tingle.

"This was the only one with a lantern," Haern said.

Thren caught his meaning immediately.

"Drawn like moths," he said. "Upstairs, now."

This time without need for stealth, they ran as fast as they could, and by the time Haern set foot on the bottom stair he heard the door to the store bang open. A crossbow bolt thudded into the wall behind him as he followed Thren into the upstairs storeroom. The windows both had grappling hooks attached to them from the outside, but so far no one had made the climb.

"Take the windows," Thren said. "I'll hold the stairs."

"Sure, claim the easy job," Haern said, rushing the window to his left. As a woman grabbed hold of the sill and started to pull herself up, Haern took advantage of his momentum and leaped into a kick. His right heel slammed into her chest while she was still halfway inside, and against such force she could not maintain her grip. With a cry she fell back outside, returning to the rain and the dark. Landing on his side, Haern ignored the jolt to his elbow, rolled to his feet, and then leaped to the other window. An ugly man with the four-pointed star on his chest hopped into the room, and he drew his daggers just before Haern tore into him, making a mockery of the man's defenses. Two vicious hits, and the man staggered back to the window. Feinting a thrust to put him out of position, Haern cut across his groin, the pain breaking whatever concentration the man had had. When he instinctively doubled over in pain, Haern uppercut him with the butt of his saber, then stabbed. His sabers buried themselves halfway to the hilt in the man's chest, and with a kick, Haern sent him tumbling out the window to the ground below.

Haern was tempted to cut at the rope of the grappling hook but knew he had no time. Rushing to the other window, he caught sight of Thren battling two at once, using the limited space and his height advantage to keep them bottlenecked at the top of the stairs. Trusting him to hold, Haern engaged the two Suns who had made it inside. They stood shoulder to shoulder, trying to form a defensive perimeter to protect the rest who climbed. Despite how young they looked, each had seven rings in his left ear. *Skilled for such youth*, Haern realized. The Sun Guild was throwing its very best at them in one last-ditch attempt at victory.

That number stops at seven, Haern thought as he spun. With such little light, he knew the twirling of his cloak would be an indecipherable jumble of gray and black. They tensed, unsure where his attack would come from and not knowing he had fallen to his knees.

Swiping sabers wide each way, he jammed the blades through their boots and into the tender flesh just below their shins. He yanked the weapons free as he pulled back, spraying blood across the floor. The two unable to evenly brace their weight, Haern assaulted the one on the right, beating him away from the window with a flurry of slashes. When the other tried to aid him, Haern immediately switched targets, parrying a thrust high and then kicking him in the stomach. The window now unblocked, Haern pivoted, stabbed the throat of a third still trying to climb through, and then returned his attention to the one on the right. One hand pushed aside the frantic attempt to block, the other plunged a saber into the man's chest. As he dropped, Haern left the saber embedded, drew a dagger from his belt, and then flung it across the room. He'd hoped merely for a distraction, but luck was with him, the throw embedding the dagger in the eye of a man pulling himself up from the other window. The body slumped over, half in, half out.

"Running out of time!" Haern yelled to Thren as he blocked a swing, juked one way, then pulled his other saber free. His opponent tried to press the attack, but Haern was already on the move, just a ghost in the room the other could not hope to follow. Dashing one way, then another, he caught him off guard with a kick to the groin, then a second kick to the chest. The man stumbled back, hitting yet another trying to climb through the window. Haern left them entangled and ran to Thren's side.

There were four on the stairs, two of whom had managed to make it to the very top step and even height with Thren. It was taking all of Thren's skill to keep them at bay, parrying and thrusting with his short swords, their battle illuminated by a single torch carried by a man at the bottom of the stairs. When

Haern joined, however, it went from a close battle to a slaughter. His father taking the left, Haern the right, they cut the two down, then sent the bodies tumbling into the others.

"Follow me," Haern said, dashing to the left window. The entangled pair had just managed to make it inside, and Haern crashed into them like a whirlwind. The first fell, a gaping hole in his throat, while the other managed to barely avoid death by leaping to his left...and right into Thren's charge. His father brought him down with ease, and with the window free, Haern put a foot on the ledge, stepped out, and spun to grab the rooftop. Pulling himself up, he rolled onto his back and gasped in air. His heart pounded in his chest, yet they weren't close to finished.

Thren joined him a moment later, dropping to both knees as he also fought for breath.

"They won't follow through the windows," he said. "Too easy to defend. They'll come from the other rooftops."

"Makes sense," Haern said. "Question is, how many?"

"Does it matter?" Thren asked. "We'll have our answer soon enough."

Haern sat up, then hopped to his feet. Twirling his sabers, he pointed east.

"This side's mine," he said. "You take the west. Fall back to the middle if you cannot hold."

True to Thren's assumption, the remaining members of the Sun Guild scaled the two adjacent buildings, gathering on the flat rooftops in preparation for an assault. Haern saw four on his side, and a glance over his shoulder showed five at the other. Terrible numbers, but they'd need to cross the gap between the buildings. An easy feat under normal circumstances. With Haern and Thren protecting the way? Hopefully that would prove far more fatal.

"What are you waiting for?" Haern shouted when the four remained where they were. "The fun's over here, not over there!"

One of them raised an arm, and Haern realized they were synchronizing their attacks from both sides. *Not a bad idea*, Haern thought, though it gave him and Thren even more time to catch their breaths. All in all, a trade he'd gladly take.

The fist dropped, and the four ran. They'd been bunched together, but upon receiving the signal, they spaced out so that they covered the building from corner to corner. Haern pulled back a step, knowing he could not protect the entire stretch of the wall, which meant he had to make sure the first exchange of the battle was lethal, before they could surround him.

No doubt they'd assumed he'd stay near the middle, but just before they leaped, Haern dashed north. He saw the panic in the farthest of the rogues, saw how the woman tried to bring her weapon to bear. It only botched her landing, her left ankle twisting upon contact with the roof. As she fell, Haern was ready, dropping to his knees and then bracing his sabers. The woman rolled straight into him, as if for an embrace, and the movement impaled her on his blades. Lifting her up to a stand, Haern stared into her dying eyes. He looked for malice, or for fury, but he saw only fading surprise and shock as her blood poured across his hands. Berating himself for such weakness, he kicked her body off the rooftop, then turned to the others. Only three now, and he let the magic of his hood dim, let them see the grin on his face. He felt no joy whatsoever, but they need not know that. Let them see a monster reveling in battle. Let them see the blood of their friend upon his sabers, and be afraid.

When he attacked, two met the charge, the third hesitating out of fear. Better than he'd hoped. Haern never slowed, and when the men planted their feet and swung, Haern dropped to his side, sliding beneath them on the rain-slick rooftop. Back on his feet in a heartbeat, he rushed the frightened, solitary man, who had retreated to the rooftop's edge.

"No, wait!" he shouted, green eyes wide, scraggly red hair drenched with rain. It was so strange to hear. Wait? For what? Did he want mercy? Was he hoping to somehow survive after all his guild had done? Haern kicked him in the chest, sending him tumbling off the building. He didn't watch him fall. When he heard the sickening crunch of the body smacking the hard stone below, Haern envisioned the breaking bones, and he saw the shocked look on the face of the woman he'd killed moments earlier. Was that how greatly Muzien had won over these men and women? Did they think death could never come for them so long as they wore the four-pointed star?

Haern whirled, remembering the other two, but it seemed they'd chosen safer prey. Thren had fallen back to the center of the rooftop as Haern had ordered, two of his five dead, the other three methodically cutting and thrusting in rhythm so Thren could not manage a counter. With two more rushing in from his blind side, he'd be a dead man. Haern had to be faster. Picking up speed, legs pumping, he let out a scream and prayed his father would obey.

"Thren, turn!"

His father disengaged a step from the three, then spun to face the other two. His back was vulnerable, but as Thren blocked the attacks of his ambushers, Haern came crashing in from the other side. Mind focused to a razor's edge, Haern spun and blocked, parried and twisted, his blades dancing in a weave the three could not hope to match. One fell, heel sliced out, and then a second dropped, a red smile opened on his throat. Haern never lost momentum, stabbing the wounded man in the heart as he leaped over him, parrying a frantic thrust of a dagger, and then plunging both sabers into his final opponent's chest. Pushing for a few steps, he twisted his sabers free as he shoved the body with his heel, sending him tumbling off the rooftop to die in the rain on the street below.

Turning, he saw his father standing above the corpses of the final two. Given how perfectly still he remained, how stiff his arms and tense his legs, Haern thought Thren had taken a wound, but then he followed his gaze to the nearby rooftop.

Standing alone, rain beating down against his long coat, was Muzien the Darkhand.

He said nothing, only stood there watching as the soft wind of the storm played with the bottom of his coat. Slowly Haern joined his father's side, and they both readied their weapons. Here he was. At long last, they faced the elf who had held the entire city hostage.

"What is he waiting for?" Haern asked in a low voice.

"For us to approach," Thren said. "It's his way of challenging us, seeing if we'll accept."

"He'll kill us the moment we try to leap over."

Thren shook his head.

"That isn't like him. That elf's pride won't let him kill us except in a fair fight."

"Two against one? Hardly sounds fair."

Thren grimaced.

"Trust me," he said. "It's fair."

He broke into a steady jog, and after a moment's hesitation, Haern followed. Together they reached the roof's edge, leaped over, and then landed before the master of the Sun Guild, who at last showed a sign of life.

He smiled.

CHAPTER

29

The symbol of the spider consuming the sun had just graced their skies when Deathmask arrived at the temple to Ashhur, the rest of his guild in tow. He was pleased to see Calan waiting for him underneath the awning of the temple, along with what appeared to be the majority of the priests and priestesses. Deathmask walked up their marble steps, giving not one thought to the rain. Rain, darkness, shadow...they only gave him more tools to spread fear.

"It seems this is a night for strange bedfellows," Calan said, offering his hand to Deathmask while looking up to the symbol of the spider slowly fading away before the crimson clouds.

"Let the underworld decide its new king," Deathmask said. "We have more important matters to deal with. Are you and your kind ready?"

Calan turned to those with him, about twenty in number. While Calan looked calm as ever, the rest were clearly nervous, and Deathmask hoped it would not affect their abilities should it come to battle.

"We are," Calan said.

"Good," Deathmask said. "Follow me."

He hopped back down the steps, where Veliana and the twins waited.

"I'm not comfortable with this," Veliana said, joining him in stride.

"You don't need to be," Deathmask said as he hurried through the rain toward Karak's temple. "You just have to look pretty, be dangerous, and follow orders. Being comfortable is currently a perk we're not allowed to have."

He glanced over his shoulder and saw the trail of priests and priestesses in their white robes falling behind and growing scattered.

"Pick up the pace," he called to them. "Or is a bit of rain too much for your old bones?"

"One day, when you are old, you will see how terrible it is for your bones to hate the rain," said Calan, who had caught up with him, the effort leaving him slightly out of breath.

"My dear priest," said Deathmask, "I highly doubt I will ever have the privilege of growing old. I prefer far too interesting a life."

Calan let out a soft laugh that might have been a cough.

"I cannot decide if I pity you or envy you," he said.

"I'd understand either, so go for both," Deathmask said, and he shouted once more for the priests to pick up their pace on the way to Karak's temple.

They were halfway there when the first of the shrieks came over the walls. Deathmask dropped to his knees, feeling as if he'd been punched in the gut. Hands to his ears, he glared at the sky, and the wailing skulls soaring in it.

It's just a spell, he told himself, trying to fight the effects. *Just a spell, you pathetic worm, now stand up.*

His legs refused, however, his hands shaking even as they covered his ears. Clenching his teeth, he tried again, pushing away any thought of the sound, denying the magical chains that were being lashed to his body. Before he could try again, a soft ringing met his ears. Chanting. Singing. Looking to the priests, he saw that their hands were raised, soft whispers of light rising up like smoke from their fingertips. Upon his hearing their words, it seemed the cries of the skulls were very far away. This time when he tried to stand, he did so with ease, as did the rest of his guild.

"Karak only desires obedience and order," Calan said, staring at the skulls with clear distaste. "He does not care how he achieves it, even if he must use fear and destruction."

The eldest of the priests continued singing their chant to Ashhur, while the younger among them shrugged off the lingering effects. Deathmask dwelt in amusement at the irony of his leading such a glowing procession of song and light. The skulls now ignored, they continued down the street until they reached the large but vacant-looking mansion that was the disguised temple of Karak. Deathmask saw that several priests, all fairly young, stood at the corners of the building.

"They've been keeping watch since sundown," Calan explained as the young priests came running upon spotting their group.

"I see."

Beckoning the stragglers over, Calan gave the entire procession their orders.

"Spread out, all of you, just like you were told. Lift your hands to the sky, and deny the darkness."

Deathmask leaned over to Veliana as the priest gave his orders.

"Stay hidden," he told her. "And keep the twins with you. If things go bad, I want you three to have the element of surprise. Just stay hidden until I make a move myself, got it?"

Veliana's foul look told him how unhappy she was with the idea, but she did not argue, nor did Mier and Nien. The three ran west, to the large mansion beside the temple, and scaled to the top. Trusting them to act wisely, Deathmask joined Calan's side. The old priest stood before the closed gates of the temple courtyard, hands at his hips. While many of the others sang hymns or offered prayers, Calan remained silent.

"Will you not worship like the others?" Deathmask asked.

"There is a time and place for everything," Calan said. "And for now, my heart is on the challenge at hand."

"When do we attack?"

The priest shook his head.

"We will not. I told you, this is merely a cage."

Deathmask chuckled.

"We'll see how Karak's priests like being caged, then. Will you call for them?"

Again Calan shook his head.

"They know we are here, and they will answer the challenge. It comes down to strength and will, and I pray we have enough of both."

Deathmask would have preferred assaulting immediately instead of forfeiting the element of surprise, but he'd long ago learned his influence over men of faith was limited at best. Staying at Calan's side, he watched the rest of Ashhur's faithful surround the temple, keeping an even spacing between them. Their singing grew louder, and given how it made Deathmask uncomfortable, he could only imagine what it felt like to Karak's worshippers inside. Nails on glass was his assumption.

The singing continued for several minutes more. Deathmask remained tense, certain the priests inside were forming a plan of attack. Under no circumstances did he believe, even for a moment, that Karak's minions would willingly accept imprisonment on such an important night. Dipping his fingers into the bag of ash tied to his side, he almost put up his floating mask, then decided against it. Intimidating a priest of the dark god, the brutal Lion of order? There was little point in that. Still, should push come to spellcasting, Deathmask trusted himself to have a trick or two neither party had seen before.

With a deep rumble, the door to the temple opened.

"About bloody time," Deathmask muttered. "Not sure I could handle any more singing."

Six priests stepped out, wearing the dark robes of their order. They all appeared to be in the later stages of life, hair gray or thinning. Some wore pendants of the Lion, others chains of silver and gold on their wrists and bare ankles. None looked to be in a good mood, but neither did they seem particularly afraid. The six kept silent, only shifting so that three each were on either side of the temple door. Then came the seventh, and Deathmask knew immediately he was their leader, Pelarak. Besides the air of authority he carried, the chains around his neck signified his role as high priest. Deathmask knew little of him despite his time studying at the Council's libraries and paying off informants throughout Veldaren.

Pelarak stepped out from the others, and he lifted his arms. The priests of Ashhur quieted their song so Pelarak's words might be heard.

"What foolish spectacle is this?" he asked. Though his frame was short and slender, he sounded larger than his body should allow. Stronger. More intimidating. "You dare sing your songs of weakness and frailty so that they reverberate throughout the house of the strong? You dare spit in the face of the god who built this city, the god who would lift mankind up from the pit it has created for itself? Tell me why you have come, then leave us in peace."

Calan stepped forward, arms at his sides and head held high. In many ways, he and Pelarak seemed so similar, men who might have been brothers if not for the gulf between their faiths. Except that while Calan looked welcoming, and as if he could not hurt a butterfly, a hard edge seemed to lurk in Pelarak's features.

"Peace is all we seek," Calan said. "We have not come to fight, but we will if we must. Battle rages on the walls, and we cannot allow you to interfere. Remain in your temple until the night has passed, and then we shall leave you be."

Pelarak looked to the priests surrounding his temple, then brought his attention back to Calan.

"Your greater numbers are irrelevant," he said. "And what is it you fear we will do in the battle? Aid in our own city's destruction? We fight against the chaos of life, child of Ashhur. We do not foster chaos. You have no purpose here. You accomplish nothing, now go before Karak's might must be revealed to you."

Calan's voice was surprisingly steady given what he demanded.

"Show me," he said, and it seemed even Pelarak was caught off guard. "Show me Karak's might."

Deathmask drummed his fingers against his sides, almost itching to cast a spell. Was Calan insane? Or did he yearn for a fight despite his earlier claims? Taking a few more steps away from the priest (just for safety, of course), he watched in anticipation for…what exactly, he was not sure. The might of Karak? What did that even mean? Were the two about to duel? Deathmask had to fight off the urge to glance up at Veliana and the twins on the rooftops to his left. If things got crazy, which he had a feeling could be a very serious possibility, he hoped the three would remain disciplined enough to wait for his signal to interfere. The last thing he wanted was to have his guild screw up something it didn't understand.

Pelarak took two more steps so that he was at the foot of the stairs, then stretched out his arms to either side, palms upward as if in supplication to the skies above.

"So you ask," said the priest. "So shall you receive."

The dark, empty-looking mansion suddenly changed. Behind Pelarak was now a towering edifice of black marble. Obsidian statues of the Lion reared up all throughout its garden, and above its door was a skull of the beast, teeth stained red with blood. The place seemed to pulse with strength, the sight of it placing a worm of doubt in Deathmask's stomach, doubt that grew when Pelarak dropped to his knees before the temple and raised his arms higher.

"I stand before the face of doubt," Pelarak cried to the heavens. "Karak, my god, give me your strength. Give me the might of the Lion!"

It seemed the night grew darker, all color fading from the world. The six priests behind him began a dull chant, the words indecipherable. The temple seemed to pulse once, and then the rain grew silent. Whatever songs Ashhur's priests had been singing ended, for Deathmask heard them no longer. The sky above filled with stars despite the rain, which continued to fall without any apparent source.

"Behold the Lion," Pelarak said, and it seemed the world trembled at the proclamation. "Behold the waiting Truth at the end of life."

Deathmask knew he stood on one of many dark, paved streets of Veldaren, but his mind refused to acknowledge it. Beneath his feet whirled a million stars, intermixed with shapes and colors similar to suns and clouds, only of a size vast beyond his comprehension. Firm ground remained beneath his feet, yet it felt as if he were floating, lost in the void. And then he realized the void was alive, breathing, grumbling, *roaring*.

The Lion had come. Deathmask saw its eyes before him, each one larger than the temple. His stomach twisted. Not larger than the temple. Larger than the world, larger than a million worlds. They burned with fire, and the gaze seemed to strip Deathmask down to naked flesh and bone, taking account of his life and dismissing it within a single beat of his heart.

Before the infinite expanse, they were but specks of dust resting upon the tiniest of fleas that crawled through the celestial fur. Through his hands Pelarak wielded the Lion's power, guiding its claws, controlling the teeth made of stars and shadow. When the priest rose to his feet, letting out a primal cry of anger, the Lion roared with him. Down its gullet Deathmask saw a million souls crawling in a futile attempt to escape, their shrieks of ache and torment so loud he felt he was trapped with them. When he breathed in deep, he smelled charred flesh and tasted burning meat on his tongue. On and on went the roar, terrifying in its ceaseless fury. Before such a display, he knew they had no chance to defeat it. Whatever tricks he wielded were nothing before such all-encompassing majesty. They'd awoken a foe that knew no equal, that feared no spell, that could not understand defeat. Also awoken was an emotion Deathmask had not felt in a very, very long time: terror.

All he could think to do was bow, and he was not the only one. Many of the priests of Ashhur did the same, crumpling to their knees as if someone had slashed out their heels.

But Calan did not. He took a step toward the temple and lifted a single, glowing hand.

"Enough."

His word was a shock wave that shook the world. A wave of light rolled off him in all directions, and as it passed over the rain the drops themselves froze in place, hovering in midair. Deathmask let out a gasp, feeling as if fresh air had been poured into his lungs. Another step, and a glow spread throughout the priest's garment, softly enveloping his face and hands.

"Behold the illusions," Calan said, and it seemed that with every word he spoke the light upon his body shone brighter. "Behold the lies. Behold the fear."

Everything—the power, the certainty, the worldly dominance—it all crumbled. The stars collapsed, the wailing souls ceased. The eyes of the Lion became nothing, and high above, the dark clouds returned. No longer did fire burn in the distance, no longer did the smell of burning flesh reach his nose.

"Behold the emptiness denied."

Another shock wave, and the last of the godly beast vanished with a fading cry. The rain fell as it always had, and the patter of its landing upon the streets and rooftops returned. Calan pointed to the temple, and at the simple gesture, the ground cracked between them like a spreading vein, breaking the obsidian stone steps. All seven priests of Karak dropped to their knees, unable to stand. The priests of Ashhur returned to their feet, and they lifted their hands heavenward as they began to sing anew.

"Your role this night is done," Calan told the seven. "Go into your temple, and do not leave it."

And then, to Deathmask's shock and relief, the priests did just that.

"Never tangle with priests," he muttered to himself. "Should have listened to you, Vel."

He glanced over his shoulder to where the rest of his guild were supposed to be hiding, curious if they had witnessed the same thing as he. It seemed they had, for Veliana was shaking her head at him, looking more disgusted than before. Even

Mier and Nien appeared rattled, their weapons drawn and twirling in their fingers.

Running his hands through his hair, Deathmask rejoined Calan's side as the other priests resumed their songs.

"You handled yourself well," the priest said at his arrival.

"I'm not sure I agree," Deathmask said, thinking off his terror and hopelessness.

"I've seen grown men weep and soil their garments before such demonstrations of power," Calan said, shaking his head. "Many of my own fell to their knees just the same, and they have the strength of their faith to cling to in their despair. What do you have, to have not broken as they did?"

"I have nothing, not even my own name," Deathmask said. "Maybe that's the trick, to have nothing?"

The priest smiled a tired smile.

"Perhaps," he said.

Deathmask nodded to the temple as several more of the priests joined them, gathering toward the front now that the confrontation seemed to be over.

"Plenty of time to go before all this madness settles down," he said. "At least it's good to know all the priests are locked up safe and tight while we figure everything else out."

"Not all of them," one of the priests said, earning him Deathmask's full attention. He was one of the younger ones who had been watching over the temple while awaiting their arrival, Deathmask realized.

"Would you care to elaborate?" he asked.

The young man turned to Calan, who nodded for him to continue.

"A few left just before you arrived," the young man said. "Since they weren't many, just five of them, we stayed hidden like we were told."

"You've done fine," Calan said, putting a hand on the man's shoulder in an attempt to ease his worries. Deathmask, however, had no patience for such things.

"Where did they go?" he asked. "What direction did they turn?"

The man pointed down the street.

"They went all the way to the end, then turned south," he said.

South? Deathmask took Calan by the arm and pulled him away from the others.

"Nearly all of Veldaren's soldiers have gathered at the west gate," he said in a low voice.

"Which leaves the south gate vulnerable," Calan said, finishing the thought. "I'm sorry, I cannot spare any of my men. We must stay here, and ensure those within the temple do not attempt to break through our line."

Deathmask let out a groan. This was stupid. This was insane. Worst of all, this was completely not like him. But if the southern gate were to fall, and the rest of the city fell with it...

"I'll make sure it holds," he said, and before Calan could say a word, he whipped about, motioned for the rest of his guild to join him, and then began jogging. He was halfway to the turn by the time they descended the building and caught up with him.

"Where are we going?" Veliana asked.

"To the south gate," Deathmask said. "To make sure no idiot priests open a door for our lovely invading orcs."

"No," Veliana said, and she stopped. Deathmask clenched his teeth to hold down his groan as he turned to face her.

"What was that?" he asked.

"I said no. We're not soldiers."

"You're good at killing," Deathmask said. "That's close enough."

"We don't fight wars, and we don't put our lives on the line for others without reason." Veliana crossed her arms. "Do you really think this city has a chance to fall? These walls have stood for centuries. Let the king's men handle this."

Deathmask knew others would be upset by being challenged so brazenly, but that was the reason he adored Veliana so in the first place. She spoke her mind, and more often than not, she was correct, but not this time.

"Listen to me," he said. "Were you not paying attention when the skulls flew over the walls? This isn't a normal army, they aren't led by a normal leader, and the orcs aren't the kind to conquer a city in any civilized sense. This is extermination we all face, the obliteration of everything we've ever built. I don't feel like running for my life tonight. Do you? Do any of you?"

The twins stood at either side of Veliana, faces eerily calm.

"A dead city is a boring city," said Mier to her.

"A *profitless* city," added Nien.

Veliana rolled her eyes.

"Sometimes you make me miss James Beren so much," she said, referring to the Ash Guild's former leader.

"Consider this protecting our investments if it makes you feel any better," Deathmask said as he resumed his jog down the road. "And you'll have to tell me about James some other time."

Most everyone was staying inside their homes, doors locked and windows shuttered, which gave Deathmask a blessedly empty street to race down. Under different circumstances it would have made a wonderful night to enjoy. If only it would stop raining, he could at least pretend things were fine and happy. Not that he'd have long to pretend as he and his guild raced toward the vulnerable southern gate.

So far it seemed the entirety of the battle had been focused on the western gate, with only a token guard left behind. Of that token guard, all appeared to have been slain, two corpses on the ground and a third man lying with his body hanging half off the ramparts above. Deathmask couldn't tell how they'd died, but he had a pretty damn good guess who was responsible.

Five priests, four men and one woman, were arranged in a line before the shut gate, arms raised skyward. They were chanting the words of a prayer or spell, and Deathmask knew he could not let them finish it. Dipping his hand into the bag of ash clipped to his belt, he pulled out a handful and cast it into the air. Half of it swirled about his face, hiding his visage. The rest swirled forward with incredible speed, as if borne on the winds of a mighty storm. When it surrounded the five priests, they breathed it in, and immediately they began to hack and cough. It would not kill, Deathmask knew, but it would cause them momentary difficulties, which was all it'd take to disrupt the spell they cast.

"Take them down, quickly," Deathmask ordered as he came to a halt while the other three rushed ahead. At close quarters his guild would tear the priests apart. Getting there, though, was the trick. As shadows coalesced around the hands of the priests, Deathmask slammed his wrists together and unleashed a spell of his own. A ball of flame shot from his palms, arced over his guild members, and then struck the ground directly before the five. Upon contact it exploded into nine more balls of flame, which bounced forward, long tails of fire trailing after them. The priests were forced to protect themselves, calling upon Karak's magic to deny the flames and banish them before they could be burned.

The tactic was merely a stalling one, and before he could cast another spell, the priests countered with their own. Waves of shadow rolled forth from their hands, their collective chants giving it power. Deathmask summoned a magical shield, but the shadow pierced it with ease and washed over his body. Immediately he felt his strength waning, his emotions ebbing. Ahead of him the twins crumpled to their knees, as if without the energy to stand. Only Veliana managed to avoid it, having leaped aside and rolled into an alley as the waves went sweeping by.

We're too vulnerable, thought Deathmask. Of the five, three continued chanting, keeping the curse strong as it bound the Ash Guild, while the other two drew daggers from their belts and approached Mier and Nien, who knelt completely defenseless. Gritting his teeth, Deathmask forced himself to focus, to push through the deadening of his mind and the weakening of his limbs. He dropped to his knees, then fell to his stomach, but he didn't care. He had to focus. Push the words from his lips. Build the power within him into something dangerous. Give it form.

"It seems tonight is a night of sacrifices," said the closer of the two as they neared the twins. His skin was wrinkled and pale, his eyes gleaming cyan. One bony hand reached for Mier's hair, the other clutched a long bone-hilted dagger eager for blood. "Karak be praised."

Veliana leaped back out from the alley, daggers ready for the kill, but the two nearest seemed ready for her arrival. The second priest with the pale man, a portly fellow with an ill-kempt beard, lashed his hand at her as if pushing away a fly. The air distorted between the two, the passing of a spell, and then Veliana let out a cry as she halted in mid-leap. It seemed her entire body had been chained to the ground, and her arms and legs pulled back painfully as her momentum halted. With a yank of the priest's arm, she was flung to the ground as if pulled by a dozen unseen arms. Unable to brace herself, Veliana let out a single terrible cry as her face struck the stone street, blood splattering from her mouth and nose upon impact.

Push through! thought Deathmask as the pale priest paused a moment to watch Veliana fall, then lifted Mier by the hair, the bone knife pressing against the soft flesh of his throat. Reaching out a trembling hand, Deathmask focused on the corpses of the two soldiers on either side of the far trio who maintained the weakening spell. While he'd never consider himself a necromancer, Deathmask was well aware of the power contained within the bodies of the recently dead, and the lingering energy of a murdered soul. Harnessing that power and flooding it with his own fury, he clenched his fingers into a fist, detonating the corpses. They exploded with a shower of gore and bone, with such force they rent and twisted the metal of the armor they'd worn in life. The shrapnel tore into the three priests, slashing open their skin and knocking them into one another.

Their concentration broken, the weakening spell faded. Strength flooded back into his limbs, and most importantly, into those of the twins. Mier grabbed the hand holding the dagger to his neck, pulling it away. Nien was up in seconds, his own daggers at the ready. As Mier held him still, his twin cut a line across the pale priest's throat, then whirled, ramming the dagger up to the hilt in the chest of the portly man who had struck down Veliana.

Meanwhile the remaining three priests of Karak staggered back to their feet, dark magic swelling on their fingertips.

"Help her!" Deathmask screamed. After a split-second hesitation, Mier dashed left while Nien charged the remaining three. Scooping Veliana up into his arms, Mier sprinted to the side of the street as a bolt of shadow struck the ground where she'd lain, its impact forming a spider web of cracks throughout the stone. Deathmask let the sight of her bruised, bleeding face fuel his fury. Summoning fire nowhere near as hot as his rage, he hurled another blast from his fists. Its center burned solid black, the outer edges bright yellow, and it left a line of fire burning atop the street as it passed.

Nien, catching its approach from the corner of his eye, recognized the spell and dropped to his stomach at the last second. The three priests outstretched their arms, summoning a protection spell against the fire...but then the attack was no longer fire. The flames died, the black center icing over, hardening into stone and frost the size of a man. It blasted right through their protection, seeming to crack the very air itself, and then struck the centermost priest. The meteor of ice carried him through the air until he collided with the closed gate behind him, smashing his chest and waist, crushing him like the bug he was in Deathmask's eyes. A wet crack accompanied the hit, a truly satisfying sound.

And then Nien had closed the distance between them. His daggerwork was exquisitely efficient, stabbing through the closer priest's outstretched palm to cancel his spell, then opening a hole in his throat with a single thrust. The other reached out, shadows sparking from her fingers. She wasn't fast enough. Nien cut off those fingers, kicked her in the throat, and then plunged the bloody dagger into her belly. As she crumpled, Nien spit on her corpse.

Deathmask dropped his hands to his sides and let his magic leave him, let the circle of ash about his face drop down to his feet to be washed away by the pouring rain. Slowly he walked toward the little alley where Mier had taken Veliana, dismissing any fear that she was significantly injured. His Veliana was a fighter. It'd take more than a single spell to bring her down.

Inside the alley he found Mier doting over Veliana, who was

propped up against the wall. Her face was bruised, her eyes bloodshot, and she held a rag to her nose to halt the blood dripping from it.

"She's a lucky woman," Mier said, stepping away so Deathmask could have a look. "Her nose is broken, but she kept all her teeth."

"I don't feel lucky," Veliana said, and she winced. "Gods, it hurts to talk."

Deathmask put a hand on her shoulder as he knelt before her, smiling.

"Well then," he said. "I know which god to thank for the coming days of blessed peace."

If glares could kill, Deathmask would already be ten feet in the ground. Laughing, he pulled down his cloth mask and kissed her on the forehead.

"Thanks, Vel," he said softly.

"This was stupid," she responded, voice slightly muffled by the bloody rag.

Deathmask winked.

"So you said already."

Turning about, he exited the alley to find Nien grinning at him.

"I got four," he said.

"Just one here," Deathmask said. "Guess I'll be buying you drinks tonight, if we can find a bar that's open."

He looked to the dead bodies of the priests and priestess, shuddering to think how much worse the battle might have gone if someone with the power of Pelarak had been among them. And then he frowned, baffled by what he saw. A one-armed boy was climbing the stone steps to the wall above the gate. He held his arm before him, hand clutched tightly around something that was glowing a rainbow of colors through the cracks between his fingers.

Nien joined him, and he hesitated upon seeing the boy, as surprised as Deathmask.

"Who the bloody Abyss is that?" he asked.

A one-armed child dressed in fine clothing? Deathmask couldn't say for certain, but he did have a guess.

"I think that's Alyssa Gemcroft's son," he said. "But why is he..."

And then the boy raised his hand high, releasing a terrible explosion of blinding white light, and it seemed all the city trembled.

CHAPTER 30

Nathaniel was huddled on his bed, gems of the chrysarium in his hand, when the otherworldly wailing pierced through the storm. Closing his eyes, he curled over, gems clutched to his chest, as he felt shivers steal control of his body. He cried, and it made him feel like a child, but there was nothing he could do. The sound was so awful, so filled with pain and agony, he would give anything to have it stop.

Calm yourself, whispered a voice, and immediately Nathaniel felt his terror easing away. *You only hear the suffering of sinners.*

He sat up a little bit straighter and looked down at the gems through his blurred vision. They were glowing, each and every one of them, shining as if a star were trapped within their centers. The colors washed over him, and he felt at peace. The distant wailing grew fainter, weaker, and easily ignored. Once more he knelt in the presence of Karak, and Nathaniel closed his eyes and tried to speak with the respect owed to a god.

"I'll try, Lord," he whispered.

Are you afraid?

Lying would be foolish to do, as well as insulting. So he told the truth.

"Yes, Lord."

Karak's voice echoed throughout the room, firm and wise.

I can take that fear from you, but only if you let me. Will you open your heart to me, Nathaniel? Will you give yourself to me, all your body, all your heart, and all your mind?

Had he not already? Karak had warned him of the attack on their house, had saved his life and the life of his wounded guard. He'd given him an opportunity to live up to everything his mother asked of him, elevating him to potential savior of the city. What more proof must Karak demand?

Lifting the gems up before him, he gave his answer.

"I will."

The gems grew warm in his hand, and it seemed comfort flowed through them up his arm. His shivering ceased as the sensation spread to his chest and then up his neck. His head grew lighter, less focused, as if he were suddenly in the midst of a dream.

Now is the time, Karak whispered into his mind. *Rise up, and be strong.*

Nathaniel slid his feet off the bed, then hopped to the floor. He wore his long loose bed robes, and he was surprised to see they were soaked with sweat. Was the heat of the gems truly so great? But he didn't feel it. He hardly felt anything beyond the comfort of the gems.

"What must I do?" Nathaniel asked, dismissing such thoughts.

Dress yourself, then leave the mansion. Your task lies beyond its walls.

Nathaniel stripped naked so he might wear something more appropriate. Each movement was steady and slow, emphasizing the feeling of a dream. He almost thought it might be, and he looked to his bed. Empty. For some reason that convinced him. If he were asleep, he'd be in his bed. He wasn't, so he must be awake. If his mind was muddled, it was only due to his own fear and weakness, which the gems were thankfully muffling.

To change, he had to put the gems atop the dresser. The moment they left his fingers his panic returned. The wailing from outside had stopped, but it didn't seem to matter. He felt afraid, felt certain that enemies were closing in on him from all sides. He dressed as fast as he could, yanking on his pants and then flinging on a shirt. It was still bunched around his chest when he reached out and grabbed the gems, knocking two to the floor.

"Better," Nathaniel mumbled. At their touch he felt their comfort return, and such a minor inconvenience like shrieking skulls could not irritate him. Why had he panicked? Why had he feared for his life? Karak was with him. Karak would always be with him. Bending down, he scooped the other two into his hand, held them tight. Finally ready, he went to the door, used the tips of his fingers to turn the knob, and then stepped out.

The vast majority of Alyssa's mercenaries and house guards were out with her, attempting to rescue Zusa from whoever had taken her. She'd told him this before leaving, insisting he remain safe inside, and lying to his face that no one would dare hurt him while she was gone. Too many had broken into their home for him to believe that. When he looked up and down the hall, he saw it was empty. What few soldiers remained were all patrolling outside the mansion. Who would protect him? The servants? Even they'd been sent home, given no explanation, though Nathaniel had known the reason. An army was approaching, Karak's army, the liberators of the oppressed, and his mother wanted them to be with their families when it arrived.

Nathaniel made his way to the front door, hurrying as fast as his legs could carry him. He knew he should be planning ahead, trying to figure out a way to escape the notice of the guards, but he did not. Karak had told him he would be the one to open the way. What hope did a few hired soldiers have to stop the plan of a god? He opened the door with confidence and stepped out onto the stone path leading to the front gate.

Two men watched the door, one on either side of him, and both seemed perplexed by his arrival.

"Little master?" the one to his left asked. "You should be inside. This rain'll give you a cold."

"The kid's just scared to be alone," said the other.

Nathaniel peered at them both, saw neither seemed alarmed. Good. Then they wouldn't be ready. When the first reached down to take him by the shoulder, Nathaniel burst into a run, the chrysarium's gems held securely against his stomach. He heard the men shout, but the surprise was enough for him to gain distance, and they in their armor would have trouble keeping up. *Faster*, Nathaniel urged himself, the comfort that encompassed his mind dipping slightly. *Go faster, run faster, move, move!*

The stone path flew beneath him as he raced toward the gate. Three more men waited there, and hearing the commotion, they turned to see Nathaniel's approach. The iron gate was locked, and the way the three drew their weapons, he knew they had no intention of letting him past even if they would not actually hurt him. With just one arm and no time, he saw no way to scale the fence or slip past the guard. But it wasn't his wisdom he was relying on.

Trust in my power, Karak spoke into his mind. *Let me open the way.*

The gems in his hand were hot now, incredibly hot. Twenty feet from the three guards, he skidded to a halt, and he dropped all but one of the gems, an emerald pulsing a green that seemed deeper than the mightiest of pines, purer than the thickest fields of grass. Before the soldiers could decide what to do, Nathaniel flung the single gemstone at the gate. It landed amid them, bounced once, and then Nathaniel had to look away from the sudden explosion of light.

Wind blew against him, he felt the ground shake, but he focused on none of it. His hands were empty, and he needed the gems, *craved* them. They were his protection, the weapon of Karak, his key, his shield. And they were his, only his. They still pulsed with light and heat, the rain that fell upon them turning to mist upon contact. They would not burn him, though, for it was his touch they were meant for. When he had them safely back in his grasp, he stood and ran, thinking nothing of the carnage he passed through, the blackened ground, the torn and twisted metal, the dying men with their armor broken and their exposed flesh bleeding.

I will save everyone, he thought. *I will be the one to open the way.*

Nathaniel looked back only once to see several soldiers chasing him. Sprinting faster, he moved without thinking, seeking only to turn and shift at random intervals. He passed by several alleys before choosing one, immediately left it at the first opening to his right, then crossed the new street he emerged onto, sliding his thin body through the slender gap between two wooden buildings. All the while he heard shouts, directions, but they were losing him in the darkness and the rain. They had no clue where he was going, nor for what reason. But he did.

The southern gate. The image of it pulsed in his mind, hovering before him as clear as day. No matter which way he turned, he knew the direction of it, could have pointed at it blindfolded if he must. The distance was great, but he could manage if he kept running, if he ignored the burning in his lungs and the aching in his limbs. The moment he thought of their pain, the heat of the gems pulsed, and the pain faded.

Thank you, he thought as he finally made it to the main road running north and south through Veldaren. The gems pulsed once, as if in acknowledgment. Wiping his face with his elbow to try to clear away some of the mud and rain, he returned to sprinting, this time not quite as fanatical. He'd make it, he felt certain of that. Never mind the bodies he saw littering either side of the road, many wearing either colored cloaks or the four-pointed star. Never mind the distant drums and cries of battle. The way was clear, and if it wasn't, Karak would make it clear. His god, the one who had granted him power, offered him a future of peace and calm. He'd never lie to Nathaniel, never betray him. The light of the gems was almost blinding, and he nearly lost himself in its euphoria.

They dimmed, his mind gained a sliver of clarity, and he saw the gate before him. There must have been some sort of battle, he realized. Soldiers lay dead at the gate, and near them were corpses in long dark robes. Though they were strangers to him, the sight flooded his heart with a terrible ache, coupled with overwhelming rage.

Those were my faithful, Karak spoke to him. *Slain in my service. You must accomplish what they could not.*

Granted new strength, Nathaniel raced to the stone steps, trying not to look at the bodies, a distant part of him fearful of the anger that filled his chest when he did. One at a time he climbed the steps, and he held the gems so tightly he felt his hand hurting, and when he glanced at his fingers he saw tiny droplets of blood dripping down.

Behold, Karak spoke, denying him a chance to dwell on the injury he'd inflicted upon himself. *Mankind perfected*.

Nathaniel had reached the top of the wall, and when he gazed out upon the fields that spread from beyond the gate, he saw the thousands standing at attention. They were a minuscule representation of the legion Nathaniel remembered from his vision. Men and women of all ages, all sizes, standing in perfect rows. They gazed upward, uncaring of the rain, glimpsing things through the clouds Nathaniel could only wish to see again. Nathaniel felt tears run down his face as he felt his mind slipping through their ranks. He sensed no pain, no fear. They did not hunger. They did not thirst. They would never strike down their brother, nor betray their sister. Such a perfect, simple, harmonious peace.

"Because of me?" he whispered, as if in disbelief that he might somehow have caused such a creation. The heat of the gems in his hand was an unrelenting fire, and from within them he heard Karak's voice speak with an excitement he'd never before heard.

Let the gems go, Nathaniel, Karak ordered. *Make open the way*.

They flared a brilliant white, but Nathaniel did not close his eyes. All sight was replaced with the image of himself, sitting on a throne, a silver crown resting on his forehead. Most important of all, his amputated arm had returned, healthy as ever, rendering him whole. This promise of Karak, this offered gift, Nathaniel would give anything to have it. Letting out a mindless cry, he tossed the gems into the air, off the wall to the ground before the sealed city gate. They landed, one by one, until the very last.

The explosion that followed was the loudest thing Nathaniel

had ever heard, a cacophony of cracking stone, twisting metal, and shattering wood. Beneath him he felt the wall lift up as if in the grip of giants, and then he was flying. Suddenly deaf, he landed amid silence, rolling at dizzying speed. Pain flared throughout his body, particularly his hand. When he came to a stop, he let out a sob. His fingers ached, his face and arms were scratched, his clothes torn. Rolling onto his stomach, he tried to regain his senses. He lay in the wide street, corpses and rubble on all sides of him. What had once been the southern gate was now a gaping hole in the wall, and through it he watched the approach of Karak's perfection.

Only it wasn't perfection. Rotted men and women lumbered in from the fields, pale flesh hanging loose from their bones. Open wounds marked their faces, some missing hands, eyes, others whole sections of their bodies. No blood poured from them, no pus oozed out of them. A few were little more than dust and bones, and still they came, step after step. From those clouded eyes he saw no anger, no fear or lust…but he saw nothing else, either. They were dead, mindless, moving husks without any shred of life. If there was life within them, it was buried down deep, locked away in the undead prison that was their very own bodies. Karak ordered, and they obeyed. That was what mattered. That was *all* that mattered.

Whatever comfort Nathaniel had felt was gone. Whatever peace, it faded away as he witnessed the terrible lie that was Karak's truth.

This? he thought. *This is Karak's desire for all mankind?*

Slowly his hearing returned, and with it came scattered shouts and preparations for defense, all drowned out by the rattling, clanking horde pouring into the city.

"No," Nathaniel whispered, tears streaming down his face. "No, no, no, please, I didn't know. I didn't know!"

They were almost upon him. Huddling into a ball, his hand atop his head, Nathaniel closed his eyes and waited for his life to end.

Has this whole world gone insane? Deathmask wondered as he staggered back to his feet. He'd lost his balance come the explosion, the entire southern gate blasting inward as if smashed by the fist of a god. His eyes were still filled with spots from the brightness of it, a combination of light, fire, and smoke that had been overwhelming in the darkness. Ignoring the discomfort, he watched as through the rubble and smoke an army of undead marched upon the city. The sight only confirmed to him that, yes indeed, the world had gone insane.

"Get Vel to safety," he told the twins. "We've got incoming."

"Fuck you," Veliana said, pushing off the wall to a stand. "It's just a broken nose. I can fight."

Deathmask knew she lied, but he had no time to argue.

"Fine," he said. "Follow me. Try to sever limbs and break the spine. They'll shrug off everything else."

He led them out of the alley to the center street, and it took all his strength to keep his composure while facing the approaching throng. He counted at least a thousand, if not more, and they were already beginning to flood through the opening straight toward them. They had only moments...

"Guard the sides," he told them. "I've got the middle."

They obeyed, not knowing what he planned or even meant, and it filled Deathmask with pride that he commanded such trust. Staring down the undead army, he took in a deep breath. He'd never been the strongest at the Council of Mages. He'd never commanded fire the size of entire fields, never been able to conjure strange monsters larger than buildings or summon windstorms of such power they could peel the flesh from a man's skin. But he'd been crafty, using what power he had to its extremes. Most of all, he'd learned whatever spells suited him, uncaring whether they were considered fair on the field of battle, or in poor taste when it came to a wizard's duel. That was why he'd frightened them. That was why they'd been so eager to see him exiled. No one higher in rank could ever sleep comfortably at night knowing he might have set his eye on them during his steady, unrelenting climb.

And now that he faced a foe that could feel no pain, could lose no blood, and could fight on despite missing whole limbs? Deathmask grinned behind his gray cloth mask. Now he'd have to get creative.

Putting his palms together, he opened them, and a swirling orb of white electricity blinked into existence. Such a tiny thing, no bigger than his eye, but it took a tremendous amount of energy to conjure it. With a gasp Deathmask sent it hurtling toward the opened gate. Thin lines of light sparked off it as it traveled past the houses, coupled with audible pops and cracks as if it were a thunderstorm trapped within a marble. It flew over a dozen undead that had already entered the city, Deathmask trusting Vel and the twins to handle them, then passed through the broken remains of the gate and into the army beyond.

Deathmask clenched his fists, and the orb detonated, pulsing out a second sphere of translucent black energy. The tiny white orb remained in its center, thick arcs of lightning flashing out to the edges of the dark sphere. From all directions air rushed into the orb, the strength of its pull frightening. The dead already within its reach crumpled, their bodies crushed under a weight unimaginable as they were pulled into the center. Pale flesh ripped and disintegrated, bones turning to dust as they swirled into that sparking orb. Deathmask focused on keeping it going, pouring his energy into it as the spell ripped the undead down to the very fabric of their being.

As he'd hoped, Veliana tore into the undead who'd been inside the city prior to the spell, using her speed to her advantage. He didn't like how uneven she appeared on her feet, despite how brilliantly she fought. Her daggers weren't the best weapon to use against the dead, but she surrounded them with a faint violet fire, a spell he'd taught her in the early days after taking over the Ash Guild, and it aided in cutting through the bones of her foes. He also saw one of the twins beside her, keeping her from being overwhelmed, but Deathmask was too drowsy to know which of the two he was. As for the other, he could not find him, nor could he spare the mental faculties to look.

Dozens of walking corpses poured into his spell, and with each passing second the toll on his body increased. At last he felt his mind tearing, felt the air in his lungs ready to rip out through his chest, and he let the spell end. The sphere shimmered, then vanished as quickly as it had erupted. A sound like thunder accompanied the vanishing, and just like that, the way into the city was clear once more.

"Hold them back," Deathmask shouted. He took a step, stumbled, pushed to his feet and continued. "Hold them back!"

"Bloody how?" one of the twins shouted. He kicked at the flailing corpse of a young woman, his heel taking its head clean off. The body staggered back, and Veliana struck it from the other side, both daggers severing the spine halfway up. The undead thing collapsed, all motion leaving its rotted body.

"I don't know," Deathmask said, fire growing around his hands. "Just…be creative."

With a wave of his hand, a wall of flame spread across the broken entrance to the city. Another wave, and a second appeared, the two spaced apart by just a few feet. The fire would mean little to those entering, for they would feel no pain, nor fear, but it'd peel away their flesh, putting a strain on the prophet holding them together. Deathmask hoped it'd hurt, or piss him off, so that at least their eventual deaths might have accomplished *something*.

The remainder of the first wave was cut down by Deathmask's guild, a paltry victory considering the many more who marched into the twin walls of fire. At least it gave him a second to think. Killing the thousands of undead wasn't feasible, but if he could somehow seal the gap...

The child responsible for the whole mess suddenly ran past him, and Deathmask reached out to catch him by the collar.

"Nathaniel?" he asked, and based on the boy's reaction, it confirmed his suspicion. Deathmask hurled the child before him, the boy collapsed to his knees, and Deathmask jabbed a finger in his face.

"Stay and watch," he said. "This is your mess, so if we fail to clean it up, at least have the courtesy to fucking die along with us."

The unending wave of undead staggered through the walls of fire. The flames licked their weathered clothes, peeling back rotted skin and setting their bodies alight, not that it bothered them in the slightest. Nathaniel turned to see the macabre sight of burning men and women lurching forward while letting out soft, deep moans, and his flesh paled. For some reason this made Deathmask feel better, and he snapped his fingers. The broken pieces of the gate shimmered, the thick, heavy stones darkening as shadows coalesced around them. Deathmask felt a strain on his mind akin to that of using his arms to lift something far too heavy, but he would not break.

The first of many enormous stone segments lifted into the

air, then flung toward the gap. It landed with a resounding crash, smashing the dead beneath it as it rolled once before coming to a stop. A second followed, not much smaller than the first. It crushed even more, a large part of it landing atop the twin walls of fire. With the entrance shrunk, the undead bunched together, their flow into the city slowed.

"Bit by bit," he hummed to himself as he grabbed another chunk. "That's how you build a home, brick by brick."

He was about to fling another section when he saw Veliana fall. She'd ducked underneath flailing arms when another of the undead beside her kicked her in the head. As she tumbled, the two burning corpses rushed on, teeth snapping, fingers reaching. Immediately abandoning his spell, Deathmask flung his arm forward. A bolt of shadow flew from it, and he quickly followed it up with a second. The bolts slammed into the chests of the dead, and the sound was like breaking stone. The impact blasted both of them to the rubble of the gate, shattering their rib cages. Veliana rolled, found her feet, and then came back up swinging. Every step was a retreat, for too many were coming through despite having to climb and crawl through the rubble of the broken gate.

As Deathmask prepared another spell, one of the twins suddenly appeared at his side.

"Welcome back, Mier," he said. "Come to die with us?"

"It's Nien," the twin replied. "And I didn't come alone."

Nien rushed ahead to join his brother, and over Deathmask's head vaulted a strange woman in gray. Her feet barely touched the ground before she leaped again, tearing into the dead with vicious precision. It took a moment, but he recognized her as Alyssa's pet and protector, Zusa. The four linked up in the street before the entrance, Veliana and Zusa on the ends, the twins in the center, a wall of spinning steel fighting back the dead. Against any normal foe, Deathmask would have put his money on them, but when a stab to the eye or a slash across the throat did nothing to your opponent, things were a bit more dire.

Lifting his arms, Deathmask began a spell, then pulled his arms downward to complete it. From the sky streaked a burning meteor, the stone half Deathmask's size. It slammed into the center of the gate rubble, blasting stone in all directions and crushing over a dozen of the dead. The momentary respite allowed the four to retreat a few steps, breaking necks and smashing skulls along the way. For every one they killed, it seemed two more poured into the city, unafraid of the destruction that had come before.

"What in the world were you thinking?" Deathmask asked Nathaniel. He received no answer from the frightened boy.

Feeling the beginnings of a headache lurking in the corners of his mind, Deathmask was preparing another spell when he heard a great many voices shouting behind him. Sparing a glance, he saw hundreds of armed men racing down the street, their weapons and shields held high.

It was the most beautiful thing Deathmask had ever seen.

"I could kiss you, Nien," he said to Nien as he turned his attention back to the fight.

Dismissing his walls of fire, Deathmask cracked his knuckles as he tried to formulate a new plan. Amid the chaos, a soldier grabbed Nathaniel and pulled him to safety. On either side of him, the soldiers rushed on, slamming into the army of undead while releasing a boisterous cry.

"Was this your doing?" someone asked him, and he turned to see Alyssa Gemcroft holding her son in her arms.

"Spare me the accusations," Deathmask said. "Your son is the one who blew up the gate."

"I meant keeping him alive."

He chuckled.

"Oh. That. Yes, I'll take credit for it, plus any payment you feel necessary. Now have your men keep the dead contained, and let me do the rest."

"They know their orders."

Deathmask watched as the fight took a whole new turn. With their numbers bottlenecked by the wall, not enough could make it through the broken gap to overwhelm the trained soldiers, who hacked at the undead with steady strikes. Should any get too close, the soldiers used their shields to push them back and gain space. Any soldier who faltered was immediately replaced. Such a pleasant sight, but Deathmask knew it was risky to let it go on for too long. He couldn't guess the numbers of the dead, and they would not tire, nor would they be frightened by the sheer wall of bodies building up near the entrance.

A wall of bodies...

"This should be interesting," he said, and he grinned. Black light pulsing from his hands, he let his mind drift, and with magical sight he overlooked the many, many corpses scattered all throughout the entrance. Most were lacking in power compared to a fresh corpse, but the bones and flesh were there, the building blocks of life. Casting his spell, power flowed out of him with frightening speed. He gasped, and it felt as if he were drowning, but he continued, fingers hooked in the necessary formations. More and more he felt it building, like lightning preparing to strike, and with a terrible cry he released his power in a wave visible only to those with eyes attuned to the world of magic.

The bones from the fallen corpses suddenly flooded with life, and they shot toward the gap in the wall as if fired from a bow. Ribs, thighs, teeth, skulls: they all snapped and flew, the larger pieces rolling along the ground if necessary. The bones struck other bones, dug into the dirt, broke against stone, but still they came, still they collected. Neither the living nor the undead were safe as the wall formed. One unfortunate soldier caught too close screamed as his ribs burst through his own armor.

A worthy cause, Deathmask thought with a wince as many of the undead outside the wall shattered into pieces and flew into the gathering wall. The sound was horrific, so much clattering and snapping, but at last the macabre creation was done. A solid wall of bone blocked the way, twice as high as a man. From the other side, he heard the undead futilely beating against it. The way was shut, and unless someone interfered, it would remain shut.

Deathmask let out a gasp and collapsed onto his back. Running his hands through his hair, he closed his eyes and felt the rain beating down upon him. All the while he laughed.

"Death?" he heard Veliana ask, and he opened his eyes to smile at her.

"Not tonight," he said, accepting her offered hand. "Gods be damned, not tonight."

CHAPTER

31

Even when Thren and Haern landed on the rooftop with him, Muzien kept his swords sheathed, showing no fear at their presence. If anything, Haern was convinced it made his smile grow all the larger.

"So it comes to this," the elf said, and he lifted his arms wide as he gestured to the city all around him. "Like petulant children you two refuse me, throwing your tantrums and striking at those nearby, as if it might accomplish something. I offered each of you a chance to join my side. You could have had power. You could have ruled like you once ruled, only in my name instead of yours. Is your pride so great? Are your eyes so blind you cannot witness the inevitable?"

"I see nothing inevitable here," Thren said, slowly sidestepping so he and Haern might be on opposite sides of the elf. "No, what I see is a broken guild, and a guildmaster about to die."

"You see your own reflection," Muzien said.

"And you would call *us* blind," Haern said, voice soft, focus razor-sharp. No matter that he remained empty-handed. The elf was dangerous, and Haern would not be caught off guard. "Look around. The guilds have risen up against you. By tomorrow no one will dare wear your mark. It'll be as if you never stepped foot within our city."

"Our city?" he asked. "Does it belong to the two of you now? I often wondered why Thren never crushed you as the years wore on. Did you two think to *share* the city? Was that your compromise?" He shook his head. "It doesn't matter. Whatever success you think you've had, it dies tonight. Let the matter be settled, perhaps as it always should have been from the very start."

They had him flanked, but still no signs of worry. Part of Haern wanted to lunge before Muzien drew his blades. Part of him was terrified to begin the battle at all. He'd fought this foe before, in a brief exchange that had left him humiliated. Only outnumbering him three to one, with Zusa aiding them, had they defeated Muzien at the fountain ambush...and Haern sorely wished Zusa were with them now.

Slowly Muzien shrugged off his long rain-soaked coat. Beneath was a simple black shirt that left bare his long, lanky arms. His body was thin but his muscles were tightly corded like a feline predator's. With total confidence, the elf drew his swords and then settled into a low stance, with all the urgency and speed of one engaging in a practice duel. The movements showed his complete control of his body, like that of a dancer. Haern prayed he could match such grace.

"It doesn't matter if you've slain every single member of the Sun Guild," Muzien said. "Watcher, alone you conquered this city. Thren, alone you built the Spider Guild into an empire. Alone, I will outshine you all. This will be the crown upon my legacy, forged with your bones and painted with your blood."

He extended his darkened hand and beckoned them close. "Come and die."

They leaped at once, Haern and his father, their swords swinging. Muzien spun with such grace it seemed to mask how fast his movements were. Both of Haern's strokes rang against steel, blocked by a single blade. Around and around the elf spun, his other blade moving to block the next set of hits as if he'd known before Haern did where they were to strike. Another block, and this time Haern tried to push closer, to force Muzien to turn his way instead of continuing his spin.

It worked far better than Haern had expected. Muzien's twirl ended, and he jumped at Haern, his two long swords chopping down at each collarbone as Thren's simultaneous slash passed mere inches away from the elf's exposed spine. Haern fell back, sabers barely able to cross in time to block. The ringing of the two hits was so close together they seemed like one, and then before Haern could react, Muzien had already turned, parrying a killing thrust from Thren. His heel shot out, catching Thren in the chest. As his father stumbled away, Haern returned to the offensive, denying the elf a chance to finish him off.

Muzien brought his attention to him fully, and for a few seconds their blades danced, and Haern felt as if he stood a chance. He feinted low, then swung both weapons high. Knowing they'd be blocked, he kept his body moving, improving his positioning. When the weapons made contact, Haern swept his right leg, hoping to send Muzien tumbling to the ground. Instead the elf hopped above it, snap-kicked Haern in the chest, and then dashed away, somehow sensing Thren's futile attempt to stab him in the back though Haern himself had never seen the approach.

Haern and Thren were now side-by-side, and together they rushed Muzien instead of allowing him a reprieve. Each blade seemed to have its own mind as Muzien battled them both. Haern attempted a double thrust when he thought the elf out of position. Instead Muzien parried them upward with one sword, rotated toward him, smacked the twin sabers higher with his other blade, and then finished the turn to face Thren directly, swords moving in opposite directions to safely redirect both of his father's attempted strikes.

Press on, Haern told himself as he did just that. He felt the rain falling upon him, heard its soft patter, but it was all distant, his concentration at a razor's edge. The only time he'd felt similar was during his battle with the Wraith in Angelport, and the two foes were certainly comparable, yet somehow Muzien seemed faster, stronger. Heart hammering in his chest, Haern paused a moment to let Thren force Muzien into a block, then leaped at him again. Muzien stepped away, retreating toward the building's edge, and Haern felt a glimmer of hope at how the elf had to remain on the defensive at all times. Just as Haern knew the slightest mistake could mean death for him, so too could it for Muzien.

The sound of their steel was a constant chorus as father and son trapped Muzien at the rooftop's edge. The elf's blocks were growing more desperate, and several times he had to push Haern or Thren back to gain himself distance prior to shifting attention to the other. Eyes on his foe and nothing else, Haern kept himself at a perfect balance, always threatening, never vulnerable. As Muzien countered one of Thren's slashes, forcing him to retreat, Haern launched himself into a flurry of four strikes. Muzien blocked the first three, but the fourth slipped through, cutting into his chest and nicking a rib. Blood sprayed as the elf let out a pained cry.

Haern tried to finish him, but the elf ducked low, rolled left, and then burst underneath Thren's downward stab. Tumbling headfirst, he sprang back to his feet and spun about to face them from the center of the rooftop.

"I'd hoped raw skill would be enough," Muzien said as blood trickled down his shirt from the shallow wound. "It seems not to be."

"Sorry to disappoint," Haern said, and he nodded at his father.

Thren took the lead, leaping with both swords slashing in a downward-angled arc. Haern followed a step, then dashed to his right before leaping in, hoping to cut down Muzien from the side. The assault from both directions should have pushed Muzien to his limits...but then somehow it seemed he became two, body splitting to assault each of them. Haern twisted in midair to plant his left foot to halt his momentum so he might defend himself. Sabers up, he blocked the elf's slash...only to see the image fade away like smoke the moment their blades connected.

The real Muzien struck at Thren hard, viciously tearing into him. There was no subtlety or maneuvering, just pure strength that Haern's father was hard-pressed to match. Haern rushed to his aid, only to see Muzien hop backward a step, then split again, one thrusting toward his father, the other toward Haern. With no choice but to react, Haern swept his sabers wide to parry the thrusts, fully expecting to banish a second illusion. Only this time he heard the clang of steel hitting steel, while his father scattered an illusion with his rapid counter.

Fighting down panic, Haern tried to plant his feet and refocus, but then Muzien's image shimmered, vanished. Having seen it before, Haern reacted without thinking. When the elf had fled their previous fight, he'd teleported directly forward, and Haern assumed the same thing would happen now. Instead of trying to turn or block, he tucked a shoulder into a roll. He felt movement against his cloaks, one of Muzien's swords tearing into it, but he was just barely too far. When he finished the roll he spun, crouched low, ready to face the elf head-to-head.

Only instead the elf was pacing before Thren, who was trapped against the edge of the rooftop.

"Is this the best you can do?" Muzien asked him.

Haern burst into a sprint as his father engaged him one-on-one. Their blades danced, a beautiful display Haern wished he could have watched at a time when neither of their lives was on the line. Muzien scored a single cut across Thren's arm before Haern joined in, attempting to stab him in the back despite knowing it would never work. Somehow the elf would know, and be ready. He always was.

The next few moments for Haern were surreal in their clarity and speed. Together he and his father attacked the elf from both sides. After every block, every parry, the elf's image would split. One would scatter the moment their weapons made contact, but Muzien continued to bounce between them, always on the offensive. Left with no choice but to treat each one as real, Haern scored over a dozen fatal blows on mere illusions, and Thren likewise. Back and forth they raged, no give, no gain, their numbers advantage neutralized. Haern scattered an illusion, ducked below the swing of a second illusion, dismissed it with a slash across the thigh, and then found himself under assault by a wicked thrust-and-slash combo. He shifted aside to avoid the thrust, blocked the slash, and then swung for the elf's throat.

Muzien twirled away, ducking beneath another cut by Thren as he did, and then leaped at them both. Each blocked, Haern's opponent vanishing into smoke, Thren's striking him hard enough to make him collapse to one knee. Instead of going to aid him, knowing he'd be countered by either an illusion of Muzien or the real thing, Haern grabbed a throwing knife from his belt and flung it through the air. As he suspected, twin images of Muzien separated, one striking at Thren while the other attacked Haern. The dagger pierced the elf through the chest, his image scattered into smoke, and then the dagger continued on, burying itself in the real Muzien's left arm.

It was the first true score of the battle, and while it should have left Haern elated, it only made him nervous. Muzien retreated to the far side of the rooftop, yanking the dagger from his arm as he did. As the blood ran down, he glared at them, no more amusement, no more smiling.

"Ever the meddler, aren't you?" Muzien said to him. "Like Thren's, your skills are greater than any human has a right to possess. I trained Thren, but who trained you, Watcher?"

"You don't deserve to know my name," Haern said, glancing at his father. "Let alone the name of my teacher."

Thren nodded, having returned to his feet and joined Haern's side.

"You're bleeding," Thren told his former master. "I thought your victory tonight was inevitable?"

Muzien flashed a smile, as temporary as the flashes of lightning across the storm clouds above.

"Bleeding is not the same as dead," Muzien said. "I would think by now you would have learned the distinction between the two."

The elf twisted one of the many rings on his darkened hand, took two steps backward, then settled into a stance.

"Now would you like to fight, or would you prefer to continue boasting about a victory not yet attained?"

The way he'd twisted the ring made Haern cautious, and only that caution kept him from being impaled. Instead of breaking into a sprint, he took a single, measured step forward, and then the elf's image blurred momentarily, only to reappear mere feet away. Muzien was already swinging his swords, completely ignoring Thren and instead going for Haern's throat and chest. Without the forward momentum he'd anticipated, Muzien had to take a single extra step, and that heartbeat of time was enough for Haern to fall backward, weapons rising to block. The elf's swords slammed into his sabers, pushing them aside to open him up to a kick. Haern turned his body aside, but that only partially deflected its power.

Muzien's heel crushed into his throat, hard enough to leave him gasping. Haern rolled along the rooftop, a vain defense against the expected assault that never came. Instead Muzien paced before Thren, swords held loosely at his sides.

His smile had returned.

"So hard you fight against me," the elf said as he launched himself at Thren. Every stroke was perfection, strong when it appeared soft, fast when it appeared slow, a feint when Thren was ready, a vicious strike when he was not. On his knees, Haern watched with spots growing in his eyes as he gasped. Each breath was quick and uneven, and accompanied by the taste of blood.

"Where was this effort when the Trifect humiliated you?"

Thren tried to go on the offensive, but his thrusts looked slow compared to the elf's dazzling speed. Two quick parries, and suddenly Muzien was on the offensive again.

"Where was this pride when the Watcher dethroned you?"

Muzien hit him with three straight dual chops, the third banging Thren's block out of the way. Out went one of the swords, cutting across Thren's chest, the other shoving downward the attempted defense. As Thren let out a cry, Muzien punched him in the face with the hilt of his blade. Thren dropped to his stomach, one of his short swords scattering across the wet rooftop. He crawled toward it, and a kick to his stomach was his reward.

"How have you failed so greatly?" Muzien shouted at Thren, towering over him as Haern struggled to stand. The elf beat his father with his fists, his feet, savaging him with both body and words. "You have nothing, no guild, no family, no heir, only a name that has crumbled into ruin. Every accomplishment has become dust, every act of worth like water on desert sand. What hope do you have of being remembered? You will be forgotten, Thren, your life, your death, your family, all forgotten!"

Haern coughed hard enough he thought he might vomit. He willed his throat to open, his lungs to calm. Amid the torture, Thren reached out for the blade he'd dropped. When his hand closed about the handle, Muzien jammed his heel down onto his knuckles. Thren screamed, tried to swing with his other blade. The elf smacked it away as if it were a bothersome fly, then, just to humiliate him, struck both sides of his face with the flat of his sword.

"What is it you live for?" he asked. "What is it you bleed and die for? You're a puppet continuing to dance after the strings have been cut. I can think of no worse joke than that."

"I can think of several," Haern said, his voice hoarse.

Muzien glanced his way, and instead of appearing concerned by his recovery, he seemed annoyed.

"You're still breathing," he said, crunching his heel down harder on Thren's hand. "Must I remedy that?"

"You're welcome to try," Haern said, wishing he felt as confident as his words suggested.

Muzien kicked Thren in the cheek for good measure, then approached, his swords twirling in his hands. Their eyes locked, and Haern felt himself being judged anew, and as expected, coming up lacking.

"To think this city quivered in fear of you," Muzien said. "You're worse than Thren. At least my disciple built an empire for himself, however short it might have lasted. You have the same skills, the same speed, yet you lurk in hiding, with a false name and a covered face. If only you had slain Thren and ruled in his place, or accepted my offer to become my new heir. Now your legacy will be a tributary that runs into the river that is my own."

"Gods, you're full of yourself," Haern said, eyes seemingly on Muzien's hands while truly focusing on the elf's feet. "And trust me, I'm used to..."

Muzien's legs tensed, and Haern was already bringing his sabers up to block before the elf even moved. Their weapons connected, and Haern felt how much weaker the left arm was than the right. The effects of the wound, the pain...knowing it affected Muzien allowed Haern to go on the offensive, constantly swinging in his sabers from that side, forcing Muzien to compensate. The arm was slowing, weakening as it bled. Their blades danced, Haern scored another cut across the thigh, and then Muzien retreated to gain distance.

The retreat was only to use his dual image trick, but as Haern watched the elf split in two, leaping in opposite directions so they might close in from both sides, he saw one holding his weapons at equal height, while the other let his right hand dip. Trusting his instincts, Haern ignored the first completely, and he refused to let Muzien reclaim the offensive. Haern turned and leaped right at him, the two connecting in midair with their weapons crossed. They spun, shifted, kicking and punching as they both crashed to the rooftop.

Haern rolled away, having managed a satisfying elbow to the elf's face. When he rose to his feet, Muzien did the same, glaring as blood dripped down his chin.

"You're no longer entertaining, Watcher," Muzien said. "This ends now."

"That it does," Haern said, settling into a stance, his feet loose, his sabers ready. "You're all out of tricks."

"Am I?" Muzien asked, twisting one of his rings.

The elf's body shimmered for a moment, and then he ran both left and right, six mirror images of himself forming a circle encompassing Haern from all sides. Once he was fully surrounded, every image leaped into the air, swords pulled back for the plunge. Haern remained still, feeling as if time itself were slowing. The six were perfectly similar down to each strand of hair, their movements exact copies of one another's. There was no difference, no difference at all. Except the gentle wind that teased Muzien's wet hair and clothing did not come from six directions.

Just one.

Despite his instincts, his fear, Haern forced himself to ignore all others, to not flinch or react. At the last possible moment he spun, one saber thrusting, the other swinging high and wide. Five killing thrusts sank into him. One he parried, and it was not smoke or illusion he struck, but solid steel. Muzien fell, unable to shift his momentum, and Haern's other saber sank up to the hilt in the elf's gut. His body collapsed, both swords held out wide, wrapping about Haern as if seeking a final embrace.

"I am Veldaren's Watcher," Haern whispered into his ear as the elf bled out against him. "And I will be remembered."

Before Muzien could respond, Haern yanked free his sabers, spun, and slashed twin gashes across his throat. The elf opened his mouth, closed it, eyes wide with shock. Even as he died, Haern saw him unable to believe he could be defeated. It filled his veins with ice, his stomach with disgust.

"Not a god," he said, reversing the grip on a saber. Falling to one knee, he rammed the tip through Muzien's eye, pushing until he felt the saber press against the back of the skull.

"Just a corpse."

Haern pulled out his saber, and as he slowly sank back from exhaustion, he heard his father speak his name.

"Watcher..."

CHAPTER

32

At first Delysia thought the defenders would be overwhelmed when the gray-skinned tide came slamming in with raised axes and swords. Their numbers were so great, and they were both taller and stronger than the city's soldiers. The defenders had shields and a narrow space to hold, though, and when the tide reached the entrance it slowed as the orcs jostled one another, fighting for order. Even that minor cut to their momentum hurt the effectiveness of their charge, and without armor, they had no protection against the swift, steady blows from the soldiers. Above them the archers rained down arrows, chipping away at the massive numbers beyond the wall.

For a moment Tarlak and Delysia remained silent and watched the battle, only Brug having joined in. Antonil's men fought bravely, and they used the limited space to the utmost effectiveness. Brug did himself proud, for in such close quarters, and against such reckless foes, he could punch and slash with his thick daggers and rely on his armor to keep him alive. Antonil lorded over it all, shouting out orders, directing the reinforcements to wherever the line of soldiers began to bend, sometimes even physically yanking men back himself when he saw they were wounded and would not hold.

And then the initial rush was past, the surge of fear and excitement replaced with the brutal, ugly cutting of throats and hacking of limbs. Rebuilding the wall with the dead had been no idle boast by Antonil, for as the orcs died at the broken entrance, their corpses became obstacles those behind had to stumble across, and with each one that fell, the wall grew higher, the footing more treacherous.

Minutes passed, and still the fight went on, the orcs having to pause to drag away their dead so they might charge anew. So far the human soldiers had suffered drastically fewer deaths. They also had far fewer lives to give. Delysia wondered why her brother remained out of things, but before she could ask, he turned to her and ducked his head closer so she might hear him.

"The necromancer's so far staying out of things," he said. "The moment I start flinging fireballs, I doubt that stays the same. But if we can be clever about this..."

He pointed to the sky, hurrying through words of magic. At the spell's completion, he flung down his hand, and from the storm clouds shot a thick bolt of lightning that crashed down into the center of the orc army. A grin on his face, Tarlak did it again, this time on the far corner of the battlefield. Delysia winced against the brightness, and she wondered about the efficiency of such a tactic.

"It won't be enough," she told her brother after a third.

"I know," he said. "Just testing. He's not shielding his army against magic, which means this might have a chance."

Tarlak rushed forward, pushing his way through the soldiers so he might reach Antonil's side. Delysia followed, a gut instinct telling her she needed to stay with her brother at all times, for when the necromancer finally turned his attention on Tarlak, he would need her aid.

"Let them through!" Tarlak shouted once he was close enough to grab Antonil's pauldron and yank him around.

"Are you mad?" Antonil asked, gesturing behind him to where his men were desperately fighting to keep the bottleneck going. "This is the only hope we have!"

The wizard shook his head.

"If it looks like you'll hold, or seal the gap, that necromancer out there will just blow another hole through a different part of the wall. Let them inside, Antonil. Let them think they've won!"

Antonil leaned down so he might lower his voice.

"And then what?" he asked.

Tarlak glanced Delysia's way.

"Leave that to us."

It was an incredible gamble, and Delysia did not think Antonil would accept the risk. It seemed, however, she had underestimated the trust the guard captain had in the wizard.

"I'll pull everyone back, forming a perimeter," he said. "We won't last long, not without aid, but we can keep several hundred pinned in at the least. Will that suffice?"

Tarlak nodded.

"It will."

Antonil jabbed the wizard in the chest.

"Gods help me, I'm putting the lives of all my soldiers in your hands," he said. "Don't let me down."

"I give you permission to haunt me throughout all eternity if I fail," Tarlak said, and despite the grim atmosphere, he grinned. Antonil shook his head, hardly sharing his humor.

"Damn wizards," the man muttered before lifting his sword above his head and shouting orders, screaming for his men to fall back into a defensive perimeter. As he did, Tarlak grabbed Delysia's hand and pulled her along, running deeper into the city.

"What are you planning?" she asked him as they ran.

"It's not much of a plan," he said. "Get the orcs inside, out of sight from the necromancer, and then blow them to bits with the nastiest spells I've got until he catches on. Hopefully by the time he does, there won't be much left of his army."

With the wall, the bodies, and the rain, it would indeed be tough to see anything from afar. That was assuming, of course, the necromancer watched with normal eyes, but she decided there was no point in voicing such a concern. The plan, what little of it there was, had already gone into motion. The city's defenders steadily retreated, their deeper ranks spreading out. With each step they lashed at the orcs, slaying them by the dozens. With their little armor, all they had to rely on was their strength and their numbers, and so far they had not been given a chance to bring either fully to bear. Antonil's men continued to spread out, forming a great ring of mail and blades, but it took longer for the orcs to fill the gap, having to stumble through the broken corpse-filled gate. Delysia lost sight of Brug, the shorter man hidden among the hundreds of others, and she prayed he would survive the night.

At last the ring reached the farthest it could without breaking. Two men deep, the soldiers did their best to fight the orcs to a standstill, letting their enemies' blows rain down upon their shields before retaliating. Delysia felt her breath catch in her throat, the bloody battle mere feet in front of her, but before she could join in, Tarlak grabbed her shoulders and turned her so she might look him in the eye.

"I need your help on this," he said. "Do you understand? I

know you hate killing, but if any of us are to survive tonight, it has to be done."

The night she'd helped rescue Haern from the Stronghold flashed through her mind, immediately coupled with a sense of revulsion.

"I don't know if I can," she said, softly enough she wondered if Tarlak would hear her amid the clashing of swords, the screams of the dying, and the constant fall of the rain.

"Yes, you can," Tarlak said, turning his attention back to the battle. "You're stronger than you know."

Fire danced around his hands as he began his spell. Delysia watched, feet feeling as if they were made of stone. No, she did know her strength, perhaps far better than Tarlak could believe. She was not naïve enough to think this battle could be avoided, nor to believe there would be any reasoning with such a vile race. The power given to her, she wanted to use to heal, not to hurt, not to destroy. To let such a cruel world force her to kill, to turn her into what she'd sworn to Haern never to become again…

The first spell leaped from Tarlak's hands, a ball of flame that soared over the defenders' heads before dropping down. It detonated, sending out a rolling ring of fire in all directions. The orcs it passed over screamed, the flesh from their necks to their knees charring, exposing pink muscle and inner organs that spilled across the ground. Pushing himself through two soldiers so he might have space, Tarlak followed it up with a blast of lightning that struck an orc mere feet away who was trying to decapitate him with an ax. It leaped five more times, tearing into the orcs, each leap accompanied by a loud *crack*.

"Come on!" Tarlak shouted over the rain as he flung two smaller balls of flame, each one striking an orc in the chest and dropping him to the ground. "Come on!"

Arcane power swirling around his hands, he lifted them above his head and then slammed them together. The ground rumbled, and then in a straight path between Tarlak and the broken entrance the ground rose and then dropped, cracking the stone and upending all combatants in the way. Over a hundred orcs found themselves on the ground, helpless as Antonil's soldiers surged in, cutting them down before quickly retreating as the seemingly unending tide from beyond the wall rushed through to replace their numbers.

Two more bolts of lightning followed, Tarlak firing them as fast as his fingers could manage. Delysia watched him, her guilt steadily increasing. Such a pace would exhaust her brother, but he did not slow. He couldn't. Shards of ice flew from his palms, their tips razor-sharp, and they slashed through the attackers with ease. The space before the entrance had become a horrific mess of blood, bone, and gore, yet it seemed the tide would not relent. More ice, and then Tarlak switched back to fire, unleashing a torrent from his palms that shot out as if from the belly of a dragon, consuming a dozen of his foes. All around Tarlak the soldiers cheered him on, lifting their swords and shouting his name when he struck down a trio with a long lance of ice that impaled them together, even when they crumpled in death.

"Too much," Delysia whispered, watching him falter a spell and have to try a second time before summoning a bolt of lightning from the sky to strike the center of the penned-in orcs. "You're doing too much."

At last he fell back, dropping to his knees and holding his forehead. Delysia wanted to go to him. She wanted to bring her healing magic to his aid, to banish his exhaustion, but their foes, despite the tremendous assault they had suffered, still poured inside undeterred. Her role in this battle, it wasn't watching, and it wasn't healing. Not yet.

Something in her snapped, and she suddenly felt very cold. It was cowardice to leave it all in the hands of others, to let Tarlak and Brug and Haern and hundreds of soldiers be the ones to stain their hands with blood in an attempt to keep everyone safe. Not when she could help them. Not when she could share the burden, for no matter how heavy it was, she could bear it. After all, her brother was right. She was strong, and the army invading her city was about to find out just how strong she could be.

Delysia broke into a run, feeling incredibly calm despite the carnage around her. Past her brother she ran, and when she reached the thin line of soldiers she moved them aside with a mere wave of her hand. Faster and faster she pumped her legs, racing toward the heart of her opponents' formation, wanting every bit of momentum she could muster. They would not stop her. They would not defeat her. She barely felt the rain. She barely heard the battle cries, the wounded, the dying. Antonil's men were trying to reseal the hole in the wall, smashing toward it with their shields while enduring the retaliation of their foes. They would not succeed, not without help. Her help. A group of six orcs saw the gap she'd opened and rushed toward her, weapons raised, mouths bellowing out a cry she did not hear. They did not scare her. They only made her run faster.

Just before they could strike, she flung her arms wide and shouted Ashhur's name. The ensuing shock wave blasted the nearest orcs to the ground as if they had been struck by the most tumultuous of winds. Her momentum halted as light shot out from her body in all directions. From her back spread a shimmering set of wings comprised of holy light, and controlling them was as natural as moving her hands. Delysia stepped forward, but her feet were no longer touching the ground. Her body moved ahead nonetheless, and her wings lashed out ahead of her, elongating, becoming blades that sliced through the orc bodies as if they were straw. The blood and gore could not stick to the light, and as the orcs howled, she surged forward, lashing them again with her wings.

"You are not welcome here," Delysia said, and she felt her voice was not her own. "Begone from this city."

She pointed a hand, and from her finger blasted a beam of light twice the size of a man. It tore through their ranks, disintegrating anything it touched. Many orcs flung themselves against the wall of soldiers, tearing at them with wild abandon instead of facing her. Others reacted like rabid dogs, rushing her no matter how reckless it might be. Delysia felt nothing as she struck them down, not even slowing the movements of her feet as she propelled herself toward the gate while hovering above the ground. Whips of light cracked from her hands, searing flesh and shattering bone. She was almost to the gate, and with a thought she sent a wing corkscrewing in, ripping apart the dozen who had tried, and failed, to flee in time. As the wings retracted, the stunned soldiers on either side regained their wits and rushed to seal the gap.

Delysia turned, her wings becoming ethereal, their light rising up to the sky like shimmering smoke. The orcs still within the city were quickly cut down by the remaining soldiers, barring the scattered pockets that had broken through the ring and fled beyond. Delysia felt the ground touch her feet, and the sound of the rain grew in her ears. With a gasp she took in a breath, and it felt like she woke from a dream. All around her, soldiers gave her a wide berth as they moved to solidify their defenses, which was good, for it felt as if the slightest breeze could have toppled her.

Tarlak caught her before she finally fell.

"Easy there," he said as she let him hold her. Her arms and legs felt intensely weak, her head filled with cotton.

"Are we safe?" she asked.

"Seems so," he said. "It looks like the attack has stalled. I doubt the remaining orcs are excited about fighting after they've watched so many of their own slaughtered."

"And Brug?"

"The idiot's still on the frontlines, angry and kicking."

Delysia smiled.

"Good," she said. "Now let me go."

Just as quickly as the weakness had hit her, it was gone, her strength slowly returning to her body. Gently pulling herself free of her brother, she stood apart a few paces and ran a hand through her soaked hair, much of which stuck to her face and neck.

"That'll teach that bastard necromancer not to mess with the Eschaton," Tarlak said, and he made a rude gesture with his arms toward the city entrance. "So what do you think, are we due for a reward, or a *really* large rew—"

He never finished the sentence. Tarlak screamed as he dropped to his knees, fingers clutching at the sides of his face, fingernails digging into his skin so hard thin drops of blood dripped down his cheeks as he raked them up and down. The pain in his voice was terrible to hear. When she reached out for him, he slapped her hand away.

"Don't," he said, crumpling, as if trying to shrivel down as small as possible. "Don't...don't touch me..."

His entire body had begun to quiver. Fighting down her rising panic, Delysia closed her eyes and whispered a simple prayer. When she opened them, her vision was attuned to the realm of gods, the natural world turning shadowy and dark. Shimmering an alternating violet and crimson were a dozen snakes latched on to her brother's body. Their eyes were rubies, their scales obsidian. They twisted and curled about him, sliding through his robes as if the cloth were made of air. Only their heads did not move, for they had sunk their ethereal teeth into Tarlak's face and neck. At those spots Tarlak scratched, his hand passing through them like shadows. Every few moments Tarlak's veins pulsed a bright red, the light visible even through his flesh and clothing.

What curse is this? Delysia wondered, baffled by the sight of it. Some strange evil of Karak's, she knew, but how could she break it? There was only one way she could think of, and that was simply to bathe her brother with Ashhur's grace and pray the curse could not withstand it. Despite his resistance, she grabbed Tarlak by the front of his shirt and knelt down.

"You will endure this, do you hear me?" she told her brother. "You're stronger than this, now fight it!"

There was no way to know if he heard her, so she trusted him to resist. Pleading to Ashhur, she summoned the strength within her, flooding her hands with light. With normal sight it would have appeared as a white glow, but to her god-sight it was a brilliant knife that she plunged into her brother's chest. Tarlak gasped as her physical hands touched his body, and then the snakes released, slithering with stunning speed. Delysia felt pain spike up her body as they dug their fangs into her hands, quick jabs before slithering back into her brother's flesh. From each one a trail of smoke floated through the night, traveling back to their master who gave them power and life. Delysia thought to cut the strands, but there was no guarantee it would end the curse. Even worse, she feared it might bring death to Tarlak instead of the mere agony the cursed snakes caused.

"Begone from him," she said, pulsing more of her power into her brother's body. The snakes writhed, and she heard a dozen screeches, like those of wounded birds. Instead of the prayer's exorcising them, the visible manifestations of the curse sank into him, burrowing their heads down into his flesh as their shimmering tails tightened their grasp. Delysia felt herself running short of breath as she continued to pray. Her words caused the horrible things to clench tight, dig deeper, bite harder. Tarlak screamed on his back, thrashing wildly against her touch.

At last she was desperate enough to try cutting the threads. She reached out to the shadowy tendrils, clutching one with her hand. The moment she did, a flash of darkness passed over her eyes, and she heard a voice rumble deep within her mind.

You are nothing, little girl, merely a feeble child playing in the realm of gods. It will cost you dearly.

"A feeble child?" she hissed as she felt herself growing dizzy. "Then prove it, you fiend. I'm not scared of you."

At first laughter was her only response, so full of loathing and mockery she felt her neck flushing. The curse sank deeper into Tarlak, and it filled him with such pain he arced his back and flung aside his arms so far she feared he would break his own bones. The scream that tore out of him was unearthly in its power, terrifying in its agony, and then with a dozen raptor cries, the snakes leaped from his body and into hers.

Delysia's turn to scream. Even the little concentration it took to keep the god-sight enabled left her, and she found herself crumpled on the ground, trembling as she looked through tearstained eyes at her curled fists. The cursed vipers had been biting her there, but she saw only her own quivering hand. But the pain was real, so very real. Equally terrible was the presence of Karak, like a cold shadow cast across her body. It left her feeling isolated, alone, denied the comfort of her god as she writhed in agony.

"Del?" she heard Tarlak ask. He sounded as if he were just waking up from a deep sleep. "Del, no, what did you do?"

The pain shifted, curling through her body, attacking her lungs, her heart, her throat. Her eyes burned, and she closed them, unable to shake the image of two obsidian vipers latching on to her eyeballs. Face to the ground, she shuddered as the rain fell upon her, and she'd have given anything for that water to wash away her consciousness.

Feeble child, the prophet's voice echoed in her mind. *A man or woman can die from pain, if it is great enough. The mind breaks, unable to handle such levels of torment. That fate awaits you, Priestess. I will drag you to the very brink, and then beyond. You'll die screaming, pissing yourself like a newborn babe as you claw out your eyes. By the end you will be a broken husk, a fitting testament to Karak's fury. This city may not be mine, but I have waited for centuries, and I can wait for centuries more. But how long can you endure? Days? Hours? Minutes…*

The pain heightened. It didn't seem possible that it could, but it did. Despite her closed eyes she saw a thousand exploding spots fill her vision. While only a dozen had bitten her brother, now she felt as if there were a thousand sinking in their fangs, flooding her with their venom. Every inch of her skin was on fire, every bone in her body aching, every breath she took seeming certain to be her last.

You feel the fires of the Abyss, feeble child. No mortal can withstand their caress.

She heard Tarlak calling for her, distant, unimportant. Rational thought seemed lost to her, her mind able to focus only on the terrible, all-encompassing pain. She didn't know where she was. She didn't know her own name. And then she felt herself go numb, fully numb, as the presence of the dark god bathed her mortal form.

There is still respite, he whispered, his voice deeper than the prophet's. *Even in death, there is time to reach out your hand…*

The momentary respite from the pain allowed her to gather her thoughts, and she let out a single, pitiful laugh. If it was possible to stun a god, she felt she'd done it, for neither Karak nor the prophet spoke his ugly words in her mind. Gritting her teeth, she coalesced her thoughts so she might voice her denial. The effort was incredible. The mere act of opening her mouth meant enduring a thousand beestings across the muscles of her tongue and throat, but she would not be silenced.

"No."

Every shred of her will, every last remnant of her power, she poured into that single word. With everything she would deny him. With everything she would fight the cruelty he sowed, the darkness he fostered. The pain returned, as furious as ever, but she clung to that word, assigning to it her very identity. Her name was Delysia, and even if she was but a feeble child, she was not Karak's child, and would never be.

Death comes for you, Priestess. My time for games is ended.

The prophet's voice.

"No."

She was on her knees now, her awareness returning. It was raining, her clothes were wet, her hair sticking to her face. Wave after wave of agony coursed through her. She beat her fists against the hard stone of the road as she screamed it out again.

"No!"

Light shone from her fists, and when she struck them again, the stone cracked, spider webs racing for hundreds of feet in all directions from the blow. She heard a ringing, high-pitched and piercing, but it felt wonderful to her ears. Lifting her hands, she watched smoke drift off them, spreading into the night air for only a few feet before dissipating. Ashhur's power flooded from her chest to her extremities, and she reveled in its presence. A whisper, and she returned her vision to the realm of gods.

The snakes crawled about her body, but they were twisting

in pain, mouths opening and closing in feeble attempts to bite. Clasping her hands together, she lifted them above her head, then flung them down as she stood to her full height. Light flashed from every inch of her skin, and she heard the cursed things shriek, then cease to be. The tendrils connected to the prophet snapped and withdrew, curling like the legs of a dying spider. And then, with a sudden intake of air, her sight returned to normal, and it seemed her ears resumed working again, for she heard the patter of the rain with sudden, startling clarity.

"Never," Delysia whispered as she dropped to her knees, chest rising and falling as she gasped in air. "Never yours."

"Del!"

She barely had time to brace herself before Tarlak flung his arms around her in a hug. Despite every muscle in her body feeling sore, she laughed and pressed her face against his chest.

"I'm all right," she whispered.

He pulled back, kissed her forehead.

"And it's a good thing, too," he said. "Because if not, I'd have killed you for pulling such a reckless stunt."

Awareness continuing to grow, she saw the remnants of the battle all around her, the gathering soldiers, many of whom stared at her with a mixture of fear and awe. Crossing her arms over her knees, she pressed her head against them and let herself finally cry, the tears as much for relief as they were a reaction to the trauma she'd just endured. Tarlak held her for a few moments, and she sensed he had something he wanted to say. Given the many who lay dying all around her, she had a feeling she knew what. That he would ask it of her, trust her to endure it despite all he'd seen, warmed her tired heart.

"You've already done so much," he told her. "But there's still more to do if you can manage it."

"I know," Delysia whispered, head lifting from her forearms.

Tears were in her eyes, and she wiped them away. There would be time for weakness later. "Help me up, will you?"

Rising to his feet, he grabbed her wrist and pulled. When she stood, she felt her exhaustion fading, burying itself deep down until it could be dealt with later. Brushing strands of red hair away from her face, she staggered to the wounded. Her first few steps were weak, and she nearly stumbled. When she reached the nearest, a man bleeding from a horrible stab to his stomach, she dropped to her knees and put her hands directly against the tear in his flesh.

"Stay still," she said, hoping her hoarse voice could be heard over the rain and commotion.

It seemed he heard, either that or her presence was enough to calm his cries and make him lie still. Closing her eyes, Delysia prayed the first of what she expected to be very many prayers. Holy light shone around her hands, she heard a distant ringing, and then she opened them to see the wound healed, the blood drying and flaking away from the fresh white scar.

"Thank you," the man said, and he looked ready to kiss her.

Delysia smiled at him, tried to stand. Her legs quickly betrayed her, and she fell back down onto the hard stone. Within seconds Tarlak was there, grabbing her arms.

"I'm fine," she said. "Just...stay with me in case I'm not, and see if you can bring the wounded to me instead."

"Sure thing," Tarlak said, and he shouted out the order. As the injured men lined up, some limping, others being carried, Delysia dropped back to her knees and began to resume. Brug joined her and Tarlak from further up near the gate, and he tapped the wizard in the side with a gauntleted hand.

"Ready to go back to the tower and guzzle down something incredibly alcoholic?"

"Sorry, Brug," Tarlak said. "I don't see much reason to celebrate."

"The city's safe, and we're still alive," Brug said. "Sounds like reason enough to celebrate to me."

Delysia put her hands onto the stump of a man's left arm, felt the bone and blood moving underneath her fingers. It'd take a lot of time to heal, time she didn't have. Deciding to simply seal the wound, she offered a quick prayer, then motioned him away. While waiting for the next injured, she glanced over her shoulder, looking back at the rain-soaked city, a city filled with deathtraps bearing the four-pointed star. A city whose fate Haern fought to wrestle from the hands of a maniac.

"We're not safe yet," she said softly, and it seemed the thunder rolled in agreement.

CHAPTER

 33

Haern glanced over his shoulder as he knelt before Muzien's corpse, saw his father standing on the far side of the rooftop. There was no reading that hard face, that impassive stare, but it seemed he had nothing to say. Turning back to the corpse, Haern sheathed his sabers and then began to search the body. He wasn't entirely sure what he was looking for, just something magical, perhaps bearing the four-pointed star to signify its link to the tiles that remained scattered throughout Veldaren. Once it was in his hands, the city would be finally be safe, so long as Tarlak and the others held the gates...

"You won't find it," Thren said.

Haern froze, and he felt dread race from the center of his chest to his extremities, constricting his neck, tightening his gut. Slowly he rose back to his feet and turned to face Thren.

"What do you mean?" he asked, already fearing the answer.

From underneath his shirt Thren pulled out a golden amulet

that hung from his neck by a long thin chain. Carved into its surface was a roaring lion, Karak's favored symbol. There was no need to explain. What else it could be?

"How?" Haern asked, his voice low, still hoarse from the kick to his throat.

"Luther gave it to me before I killed him," he said. "As well as the word needed to activate it."

Haern dared not move, not until he knew what this change meant. His father controlled the fate of the city, not Muzien? Then the deception, the lies, claiming Muzien held it and not him...

"Why would Luther give it to you?" he asked.

Thren twirled the amulet in his fingers, drops of blood from his nose dripping across its gold.

"Because I was strong enough to do what must be done," Thren said. "The king's throne hides ancient doors to ancient worlds, and that prophet at our gates would doom us all if he reaches them. If the gates fell, I was to destroy everything to spare Dezrel from enslavement to Karak and his priests. Those tiles were never meant for evil, Watcher. They were meant to do what must be done to protect all of mankind. I would think someone like you would understand that. After all, how many have you slaughtered in the name of 'protecting' the common folk of Veldaren?"

Haern felt his mind reeling.

"But Muzien destroyed several other tiles," he said. "He knew."

"Only too late," Thren said, slipping the pendant back underneath his shirt. "His pride blinded him, and at last he paid the price."

"Why did you lie to me?" Haern asked. "Just so I'd help you kill Muzien?"

"I lied so you'd see what we could accomplish together,"

Thren said as he slowly paced before him, the rain pouring down upon his bruised face. "I wanted you to realize how even the greatest fall before our combined might."

"It doesn't matter," Haern said, and he shifted, trying to keep his muscles limber. "Our time together is over."

"Not if you don't want it to be," Thren said. "I was Muzien's heir, and with his death at our hands, my right to rule will only be reinforced. The Sun Guild may be crushed here, but all throughout the west, the remnants will eat each other trying to decide on a new leader. I can rally them, unite them, while you remain here, the city of Veldaren yours to rule and protect as you see fit."

"I won't do it," Haern said, shaking his head. "I want nothing to do with the guilds."

"Then what is it you do want?" Thren asked.

"Peace, for those who live here."

His father laughed, and he stretched his hands out wide as he gestured to the city.

"What do you think Muzien brought?" he asked. "All the guilds, he subjugated. The Trifect, he cowed. The king, he terrified into inaction. We *had* peace, a peace broken only by our hands. That is the way of this world. The strong rule the weak, and we are the strong. Your pretended truce only upset the balance of things, but it's gone now, and through this chaos we might give birth to something better. Something proper."

He jammed a finger at Haern.

"If you want peace for Veldaren, then take it. Help me rebuild the Spider Guild, and I will appoint you its leader as I travel west. You'll never defeat them all. You'll never make this city safe, because for every greedy bastard you kill, two more are ready to pick his corpse clean. But if you lead them? If you control them, decide their truces, and strip power away from all other pretenders? Then this city will know peace. It will be by your hands, and under your name."

Haern heard the words, the insidious logic, and he had no answer. All he did...what was the point? Was it for revenge against his father? If he wanted peace, if the result was all that mattered, then what reason did he have to reject such an offer if deep down he believed it would be work? Lord of Veldaren's underworld, without the need to prowl the rooftops and slaughter so many to maintain his fearful reputation...

"What more could you want?" Thren asked, and Haern could hardly believe the pleading he heard in his voice. "Assume the throne you were always meant to have. There is no one better deserving of such a crown. The Spider Guild is yours. *Veldaren* is yours. Take it."

Haern wanted to. He felt the future hovering before him, tantalizing in its possibilities. With but a word, he could finally rule the underworld. No more prowling. No more games and bribes. The peace Muzien had forged, Haern could make it last. With Thren as his ally, who would dare resist them? Even the Darkhand had fallen. The fear inspired by the Watcher would rule supreme, overcoming Thren's, the guilds', the king's...if only he stood at his father's side.

His father. Haern looked to him, and he felt a thousand memories rush through him. His lessons. His training. A childhood of books and loneliness. And in it, he remembered how Thren had clutched in vain at power, bit by bit slipping through his fingers. The way it had driven him. The sacrifices it had cost him. Delysia had opened Haern's eyes to a better world, and his father's arrow had shown him the underworld would swallow that better world if given the chance. If truly forced to decide, which would Haern embrace?

In his mind's eye he saw himself in a future where he ruled

Veldaren, cloaked in gray, a Spider on his chest and bloody swords in his hands. In that future there would never be a day when the city no longer needed him, not after he lifted it in his hands and declared it his. In that future there would be no difference between him and his father.

Haern faced Thren, and he gave an answer he should have given the very moment the question was asked.

"No," he said. "I am a servant, not a king. I will never take your place."

Thren remained perfectly still, and he swallowed as if nails were in the back of his throat.

"So be it," he said, clutching the amulet through his shirt. "If I cannot have a legacy to continue beyond my death, then let my very death cause all of Dezrel to shudder."

Panic spiked Haern's heart as he realized what his father meant to do.

"Wait!" he shouted.

"For what?" Thren asked. "You heard Muzien. I have nothing left, and I am too old to build anew. Even if I reformed the Spider Guild, it'd never be what it once was, especially not with you lording over everything. I would rather the city learn, once and for all, the punishment it must suffer for turning against me. Better it as ash than in the hands of others."

"Stop it," Haern said, taking a careful step closer. Thren appeared dangerously unhinged, the most emotional Haern had ever seen him. Even the day he'd come home after Marion's death, he'd not looked so broken. "This is insane!"

"What other way is there? What other legacy might I hope to have? This path I've walked has cost me everything: my friends, my wife, my children. I have no family, no heirs. Even my own son, he's lost to me now..."

"Your son..."

He dared not question it, dared not doubt. The game was at its end. Haern slowly reached up to the sides of his hood. Pulling back the soft cloth, he peeled away the protective shadows, revealing his blond hair and naked face. He said nothing, only stared at Thren as his father stared back, jaw trembling, hands shaking. It felt like an eternity before he finally spoke, and when he did, his voice shook with rage.

"My son," Thren said, tears falling from his eyes as he spit out the words, "died in a fire. He died betraying *everything* I ever taught him. What it meant to live, to rule. What it meant to be family. Don't you get it, Watcher? *I have no son.* He is lost to me, and is never coming back."

Still silent, Haern lifted his hood back over his head as water rolled down his face.

"Give me the amulet," he whispered. "Then get out of my sight."

Thren shook his head as he drew his swords.

"If you want it, you'll have to cut it from my neck."

The warm night suddenly felt so very cold.

"Don't make me do this," Haern said. "Please, it doesn't have to be this way."

His father settled into a stance, short swords held at the ready before him.

"Since the day you first scrawled your mark, this was meant to be. Damn my cowardice for waiting so long. My life or yours, Watcher. Draw your blades."

Haern did so, settling into the very same stance as his father, left hand out, right hand held back for a parry or thrust.

My life or yours. So terribly simple.

Thren burst forward, both blades pulling back to swing, and Haern felt his instincts taking over. He met the charge, refusing to let his father establish any momentum. Their blades connected, Haern blocking the combined strike, then digging in his left heel and sweeping with his right. Thren leaped over the kick, tucked into a roll when he hit the ground, then shot back out of it. Both short swords thrust for Haern's waist, one coming in much faster than the other so Haern could not parry both aside with a single blade.

Falling back, Haern batted away each in turn, feeling dangerously close to losing his balance. Thren pressed on, slashing with one hand while attempting to thrust through an opening with the other. Every moment, Haern had to remain aware of the positioning of his weapons, to avoid using the easiest block or parry if it meant using the one Thren expected. Blades dancing, Haern pushed himself on, screaming at himself to move faster, to anticipate each and every maneuver.

Digging in his feet, Haern suddenly halted his retreat and flung himself forward. Thren tried to counter, but Haern parried one thrust out wide while his other saber moved high, blocking the downward chop before it could gain any strength. Suddenly at close proximity and with his weapons out of position, it was Thren's turn to fall back. With each step he shifted himself slightly to the left or right while frantically flinging his short swords in the way of every stroke. Haern tried to keep him on the retreat, denying him a chance to steal the offensive, but only ended up overextending himself. Thren batted aside a weak thrust, stepped in close, then crosscut.

With no way to block in time, Haern arched his back, then let himself fall. The blades sliced the air above him, then looped around for downward thrusts. Haern crashed his blades together, forcing his father's short swords to come together as well, then twisted his head to the side. Thren's swords stabbed into the rooftop, the cold steel missing Haern's neck by less than an inch. Now in a terrible position, Haern swung his legs, hoping to force his father to retreat lest he be tripped. Instead Thren let go of his swords, leaving them embedded in the rooftop, and leaped over the trip attempt. A bold gambit, but with Thren still towering over him, there was little Haern could do to take advantage.

As Thren landed, Haern chopped, hoping to catch his father reaching for his short swords. Thren shot out his right heel, kicking Haern in the stomach. Breath blasting from his lungs, Haern forced the weapons to continue, slicing a shallow wound across Thren's extended leg. Thren gritted his teeth to hold in a scream, then kicked off with his other leg. All his weight pushed down on Haern's stomach as his father pirouetted above him, snatching both short swords in a brilliantly fluid motion. The turn continued, arms twisting so that the sharpened edge of both swords slashed for Haern's neck.

The moment Thren began the spin, Haern knew his intention, knew he could not position his swords in time to block, nor would cutting Thren's leg do enough damage to prevent the maneuver. So instead he let his arms fall limp, curled his legs in as tightly as possible, and then shot them out like an uncoiled spring. Both heels slammed into Thren's groin just as he was completing the turn, the power of Haern's kick lifting his father off his feet and sending him tumbling away, his attempted killing stroke averted by a hair's width.

Haern rolled onto his hands and knees, then stumbled to a stand. His stomach ached, but he felt comfort knowing his father hurt worse. Thren had fallen onto his back, and he twisted onto his stomach and let out a cry of pain as he slammed both sword hilts against the rooftop. He'd fight through it, Haern had no doubt, which meant he needed to capitalize immediately. Ignoring the pain in his gut, he closed the gap between them, sabers swinging. Thren rolled, swords lashing out to parry, rolled again as Haern chased. The movements were too erratic, Haern's chase too slow, and he felt a terrible sting across his knee as one of Thren's blades struck true. Haern's next step was uneven because of it, an opening his father did not miss. Thren ceased retreating, pulled up onto his knees, and thrust with his right arm, his entire body extending forward to maximize both power and reach.

It should have pierced him through the gut, but Haern swept it high and wide with his right saber. The tip cut through his cloak, nicked a rib as it opened up a gash across the side of his body. Blood flowed, Haern screamed. He twisted to one side while simultaneously attempting to cut through Thren's arm at the elbow. Thren was ready, blocking with his other sword while pulling back the first. Up from his knees he shot, unleashing stroke after stroke. His sudden fury was overwhelming, and Haern had to push himself to his limits just to match it. Their blades sang as the rain fell down upon them, steadily worsening their footing.

Several times Haern thought himself dead, and his speed was the only thing that saved him, a block coming up just in time, a dodge pulling his neck away so that it left only a scratch instead of a fatal gash. Heart pounding so hard it felt as if drums were beating in his ears, Haern abandoned any pretense of going on the offensive. His father had become something else, something savage and beyond human. Every block left Haern's arms aching, his every defense steadily picked apart until he was vulnerable. Haern sought only to survive, to endure the wrath. *Where was this fury when we fought Muzien?* he wondered. Or did Thren hate the Watcher even more than the former master who had abandoned him in disgrace?

Haern retreated until he was at the corner of the rooftop with nowhere to go but down. He could flee, he knew, perhaps drop and hope to survive the fall, but he would not let that be how their battle ended. Holding his ground, Haern matched Thren stroke for stroke, preferring his skill to be what decided their duel instead of whether or not he landed with a twisted ankle. He braced himself with his left leg, felt it slip, and dropped to one knee. Both short swords crashed down at him, and he crossed his sabers into an X to block. Thren poured his strength into them, trying to force through, to beat Haern down, but at last it seemed he had reached his limits. When Haern pushed back while rising to a stand, Thren could not stop him.

Just like that, the battle turned. Haern stole the offensive, and he refused to relent despite how his arms and legs felt made of wood. His lungs burned as he gasped in air, and he felt close to vomiting, but his father would only feel worse, having pushed himself to the breaking point and then beyond. The toll of the entire night, the exhaustion, the emotion, it'd come calling. Haern used no clever patterns, no little tricks. Instead he slashed at Thren over and over, simple, easily blockable maneuvers. Keeping him engaged. Force him to use more of his rapidly dwindling strength. Every swing met with weaker resistance. Every thrust got that much closer before the parry came.

Haern thought the battle a foregone conclusion by the time he had Thren cornered on the opposite end of the rooftop. His father blocked once, twice, then slipped to his knees. Defeat was in his lowered gaze, in his sagging shoulders. Haern pulled back to swing, letting exhaustion and rage blank his mind instead of dwelling on the killing stroke.

Except that when the sabers were whistling through the air, Thren looked up, and there was no defeat in his eyes. With one last burst of energy, he blocked the stroke, lunged to his feet, and used his other blade to keep Haern's sabers out of position. His knee rammed into Haern's already sore stomach, followed by a head-butt that flooded his vision with stars. Stumbling, Haern tried to pull back into some sort of defense, and only pure luck had him blocking a stroke coming in high toward his neck. He forced himself to keep moving, to rely on the lessons his father had given him on reacting when fighting blind. His sabers swung wild as he retreated, and he managed to catch another thrust. By the time Thren attempted a third, Haern had recovered.

Saber met sword, and this time Haern stepped in close, having caught Thren poorly positioned. His elbow struck Thren in the throat, and when his father retreated, Haern hammered both his sabers into him as if felling a tree. He didn't care at the nicks and chips he wore into his own weapons, didn't care that Thren's defense was poor and desperate, seeking only to keep his short swords in the way. Strike after strike, beating him down to his knees, unleashing upon him years and years of loneliness and betrayal. At last Thren's swords bowed, his arms too weak to raise a defense. Haern cut across Thren's left hand, kicked the right, then pressed his swords together and smashed his father across the temple with the bottoms of both hilts. Thren dropped, body limp, swords falling from either hand. He lay on his back, raindrops beating down upon him, his eyes half-open.

Standing over his father, Haern gasped air into his lungs. His entire body ached, he bled from multiple places, and he still felt a terrible need to vomit. Overwhelming it all was cold, vicious rage. Here was the man who had made a mockery of his childhood, who had slaughtered friends to prevent him from knowing a life beyond power, corruption, and death. The man who had denied him to his face. Did Thren know of anything better? Was there anything besides hatred, pride, and vengeance in his sickly heart?

There was a way to end it. To put every last bit of it behind him. The tip of his right saber pressed against Thren's throat. One cut. One single cut, that's all it'd take, and his father would bleed out beside the body of his mentor.

Thren's eyes seemed to gain focus, and he stared up at Haern with his battered and bloodied face.

"So damn blind," he said, voice raspy and weak.

Haern pressed the saber tip tighter to his throat, ensuring he would not try to move.

"Blind?" he asked.

"So blind. How can you not see? My shadow..."

"I'm nothing like you," Haern said, feeling his temper flare.

At that Thren let out a wet cough that might have been a laugh.

"So...damn...blind," he said, voice gaining strength. "You *are* me. Look at the blood on your hands. Count the dead. See the chaos you've unleashed upon Veldaren." He coughed again. "With my death there is no one left to challenge you. Do it, Watcher. Kill me, and rule Veldaren unopposed."

He closed his eyes and tilted his head back, as if welcoming the fatal sword thrust. Haern stood over him, his hand clutching the hilt so tight his knuckles had gone pale. In his heart he tried to deny him. They weren't the same. Haern didn't revel in violence. He didn't kill without mercy...yet he'd felt the thrill of battle as side by side he and Thren had taken on the Sun Guild's greatest. He'd helped torture their members. He'd helped the old guilds rise up to slaughter hundreds that night, and for what?

"You're wrong," he whispered, his words not just for his father.

"You do what must be done," Thren said softly. "For yourself, and for those you care for. As I have always done. I never had to justify it. I never had to question it. Why did you?"

He looked up at Haern, and tears were trickling down the sides of his face.

"Why did you have to betray me so?"

Haern felt the rain beating down on him, and he wished they were shards of glass that might tear into him, to rip out the pain and confusion and sadness he felt.

"I was the one betrayed," he whispered, and before Thren could respond, Haern struck him with his foot across the temple. His father let out a single soft cry as his head snapped to one side, then went silent. Haern stared down at him, watching the soft movements of his father's chest. Still breathing. Still alive.

Haern dropped to his knees, and his sabers fell from his hands. He felt all the guilt he'd numbed, all the lives he'd taken, come crashing back down upon him. How many killings were because of the vow he'd made as a broken child seeking vengeance? How many were because of his own pain, his own fears? Balling his hands into fists, he beat them against Thren's chest, striking him again and again as he cried over his body.

"I loved you," he shouted. "Why was that never enough? Why was *I* never enough?"

He'd slain his own brother chasing his father's approval, endured a thousand trials, pushed himself to the brink, all in hopes that he'd receive the love he knew he deserved. And it'd never come. To his father his life was a betrayal, and it would always be a betrayal. Haern buried his face into that familiar gray tunic, clutched the fabric with his fingers as he struggled to regain control. He'd thought those wounds healed. He'd thought he embodied everything his father hated, but Thren was right. The men they'd tortured and killed, all while he denied his guilt? The power he'd wielded, all while pretending to be a servant? There was no difference between them, not when they both sought to rule.

It was an overheard prayer by Delysia that had stayed his first true murder. It was during another prayer of hers that he'd witnessed the monster that was his father as he shot an arrow through her back. And after all that, what was it he'd told her?

A beautiful dream, but still a dream.

When had he given up hope? When had he let the world defeat him? Haern stared at the shell that was his father, and he felt just as hollow.

"Who I am," he whispered, echoing Delysia's pleading for him to remember. Now he knew. He was a scarred, lonely child still fighting to be loved. With his cloaks and sabers, he'd built a new life to hide from that truth. With his hands he'd killed hundreds. With his eyes he'd looked upon the city and declared it his. The lonely child wishing to be loved? He would not destroy that final shard of innocence. He would not shatter the last piece that kept him human.

"I won't kill you," he whispered. "I can't. I don't want to know who I'd become if I did."

Reaching underneath Thren's shirt, he grabbed the amulet and yanked it hard enough to break the slender gold chain. Amulet tucked safely into his pocket, he rose to his feet and limped to the rooftop's edge.

For one more day, the city was safe. In such a broken world, it would have to suffice.

He hung by one arm, then dropped to the ground. Grunting against the pain, Haern steadily limped west. By the sound of it, the battle at the walls was mostly over, the invading army defeated. Haern was barely aware of the buildings he passed and the streets he crossed. He didn't know where else to go, so he went to the western gate. His chest felt hollow. His head felt light. Step after step, he made his way, until at last he saw a gathering of soldiers before the ruined remnants of the gate, many of them wounded.

Amid them, healing magic glowing on her hands, her white robes stained with dirt and blood, was Delysia. Haern stopped when he saw her, feeling drained of energy and suddenly unsure. He'd needed to confirm she'd survived, but beyond that? He'd hurt her so many times now. Perhaps it was best to finally leave her be, to save her from the downward spiral of his own life. Her eyes met his, and he wondered if she saw his guilt, his crippling indecision. If she did, it didn't matter.

She came running.

Arms flinging around him, Delysia held him, her face against his chest as she let fall tears of relief.

"I've come back," Haern whispered, and despite how simple the proclamation, he realized it was true enough. His arms closed about her, holding her tight as his cloaks encircled them both, and there was comfort in their shadows.

EPILOGUE

A week later, as Haern prepared for nightfall, Tarlak stepped into his room and let out a cough to gain his attention.

"Just received word from the king," the wizard said, lifting a scroll in his left hand to punctuate the sentence.

"What about?" Haern asked as he finished pulling on one boot and grabbed the other beside him on the bed.

"Well, you being . . . you know, you. The Watcher. The king's agreed to honor the original truce, so long as the other guilds are willing to go along with it. Given how they're all in various shades of disarray, I can't imagine anyone risking both your wrath and the king's paranoia instead of taking the free gold."

"The Ash Guild might," Haern said, rising from the bed and pulling on one of his vambraces.

"I think even Deathmask has had more fun than he'd prefer over the past few months," Tarlak said. "Call it a hunch, but I believe he'll lay low for a while, and manipulate the different guilds as they form instead."

"It's not a bad idea," Haern said, putting on the second

vambrace. "I expect I'll be doing much the same. It seems all the old guilds are resurfacing, though mostly in name only. I need to make sure the rulers are at least somewhat sane, and will listen to reason. The last thing we need is some upstart deciding they'd rather have another war."

Haern pulled on his cloaks, the weight and feel of the fabric giving him a slight chill.

"There's also the matter of Thren," Tarlak said, clearly unhappy about broaching the subject.

"What about him?" Haern asked, keeping his voice indifferent despite lurking emotions quite to the contrary.

"Well, he's still alive. That's issue number one. Issue number two is what do we do about him? A repeat of the thief war would be what I would call a Very Bad Thing, and it's also possible he could use his reputation to gather the fledgling guilds under his control. Doesn't matter if he wouldn't have a chance of winning. That psycho tried to blow up all of Veldaren. What's a little underground war compared to that?"

Haern shook his head, and he wished he could better explain it.

"I think Thren is finally broken," he said. "So long as I'm alive, he won't try anything drastic beyond reinforcing his claim on the Spider Guild, and perhaps establishing dominance over the rest. I'll keep an eye on things, just in case, but I wouldn't lose any sleep over it."

The wizard shrugged.

"If you say so. Oh, and while I'm remembering…" He pulled out a golden amulet, a simple-enough-looking thing with a single roaring lion in its center. "Do you want it?"

Haern frowned.

"Don't you need that?" he asked.

"Not anymore," Tarlak said. "Unmade the last of the tiles

earlier today. It's a lot easier to disarm a lock when you have the damn key. They're as dangerous as kittens now, and the city guard's had fun breaking them with sledges and shovels. I'm guessing after all Muzien put them through, it's a rather cathartic exercise. The king also informed me of his gratitude in his note here. Shame gratitude does not mean mountains of gold. Anyway..." He offered the amulet. "Want it?"

Haern pulled Senke's old pendant of the golden mountain from underneath his shirt, put it back.

"I have the only amulet I need," he said. "Keep it as a memento if you'd like, or melt it down for the gold. It means nothing to me."

He pulled his hood over his head, let the shadows envelop his face. As he straightened it, Tarlak paused, giving him an odd look.

"Is this your first time going out since...?"

"Yeah," Haern said, interrupting his question. "It is."

Tarlak chuckled.

"Had a hunch. Delysia's waiting for you outside. Make sure you say good-bye to her beforehand, all right? You're the King's Watcher. That means showing my sister some manners."

Haern smiled, and he felt a bit of his nervousness ebbing. He put his hand on the wizard's shoulder, squeezed it tightly.

"Every time I've needed you, you've been there for me," he said. "I just want to thank you for that, Tar."

"Most welcome. Now get out there and do your job."

Haern nodded, descended the stairs.

"At *Veldaren*, I mean," Tarlak shouted after him, eliciting a chuckle from Haern.

As Tarlak had said, Delysia waited for him outside the door to the tower, arms crossed and a smirk on her face. She looked almost golden in the light of the setting sun.

"Is this going to become a regular thing?" he asked her as he shut the door behind him.

"I doubt it," she said. "You overestimate my patience if you think I'll be waiting for you every single night just to say good-bye."

Haern laughed, hoping to hide his own nervousness with good humor. It felt like there were a hundred things they had yet to discuss, and part of him wondered if he would ever tell her what had happened between him and Zusa. Doing so could hurt her, but keeping it silent made it feel like every moment with her was a lie. He didn't know how to reconcile it, didn't know what was right, and he hated how it left him awkward and silent. Perhaps it would grow easier as the memory faded, no different from that of Ghost's death.

"Just let me pretend you miss me that much every time I go," Haern said, forcing a smile to his lips. "Surely it can't be that far from the truth."

She smiled, one just as forced as his own. Trying to guess the reason, he assumed it had to do with his returning to his duties as the Watcher, and he did his best to head off any worries.

"I'll be all right," he told her. "Tonight's a night like any other."

"That's a lie, and we both know it."

So it *was* about his safety. He fought down a sigh. He could battle Thren Felhorn as well as the Darkhand, yet still she'd fear for his safety?

"If it will make you feel better, I'll remain low for a while, try not to get into any real skirmishes."

"That's not what worries me," she said. "You're going back to being the Watcher. What does that mean? After everything you went through a week ago..."

Haern stepped closer, and he found himself unable to meet her eye as he spoke.

"Whatever drives me, it's more than just peace for this city," he said. "I could have had that, if I wanted it. I could have become everything my father desired...but that's not who I ever wish to become. Who I am, who I choose to be...it has to mean something. It has to make all these sacrifices worthwhile. And I do know who it is I wish to be. I finally do."

He crossed his arms, uncrossed them, feeling so naked, so exposed, but he had to say it. He had to tell her, if only so he might silence the guilt eating at the back of his mind.

"I once asked you to be my rock, to be there so I knew who I was. That was wrong of me, Del. I never should have put the burden of my confusion and failures on your shoulders. That was nothing but cowardice. I want you to know that I ask nothing of you now. I ask nothing, expect nothing..."

Delysia grabbed the front of his shirt, yanked him close, and shut him up with a kiss.

"My love is a gift," she said. "And you don't need to ask for it, because it's already yours."

"But the risks I take, the battles...death will come for me, Del. Knowing that, how can I be so selfish and cruel? I never wanted to hurt you, and never wish to again."

Delysia wrapped her arms about him, holding him close.

"It doesn't matter," she said softly. "Wherever you go, I will always be waiting. If you should die, I'll wait, and I'll pray, and I'll look for your face when Ashhur takes me home. I'm scared of losing you, but I won't let that fear cost me the time we have together."

Haern smiled down at her, and he felt tears building in his eyes.

"I don't know what I'd do without you," he said.

"You'd only miss me for a little while," she said, standing on her toes so she might kiss his forehead. "And even then,

I promise, I'll be waiting. Now go and stalk the shadows, Watcher of Veldaren. You have a city that needs you."

Haern hugged her again, and he could not believe the relief he felt.

"Thank you," he whispered.

Gently separating their bodies, he pulled his hood low over his face and adjusted his cloaks.

"Safe travels, Watcher," she said, turning to leave. "I'll be here when you return."

"Always?" he asked her.

"Always."

With her smile in mind, he ran to the city, ran to the rooftops and the dark alleys that were his comfort, his battlefield, his home.

The very first time she'd entered the Gemcroft mansion, Zusa had rescued Alyssa from the cold prison built beneath. Now, as the rows of servants, soldiers, and wagons rolled out, she felt she had rescued Alyssa once again, not just from her mansion, but from the whole damn city of Veldaren. It had been a prison far more encompassing, and far harder to escape, but Zusa was determined to make this freedom last. The city of thieves and murderers would not control them anymore. It'd taken weeks of planning, shifting trade agreements and policies, appointing various stewards who would remain in the city, none of whom would have enough power to become a potential threat...

"Zusa!"

She turned, saw Nathaniel calling out to her from the seat beside his mother in their carriage, beckoning her.

"Will you join us?"

Zusa smiled at him, and normally she would have, but she'd

caught a familiar face lurking on a nearby rooftop, so instead she remained at the front door of the mansion, cupped her hands on either side of her mouth, and shouted back.

"I will soon enough! Keep your mother company for me."

Nathaniel beamed and bobbed his head in answer before snuggling closer to his mother. The sight warmed Zusa's heart. It'd taken days before Nathaniel had shown any sign of recovering from whatever he'd endured at the western gate. Karak had been involved, that was all Zusa had gleaned, and the knowledge soured her stomach. But upon learning they'd be moving to Riverrun, abandoning their family home in Veldaren, the boy had steadily improved. Truth be told, he acted like a great weight had been removed from his shoulders, and he was hardly the only one who'd had that reaction.

As the great caravan rolled west, Zusa calmly walked to the end of the property, locked the iron gate behind her, and then crossed the street. Curling around to the side of a building, she easily climbed up, finding the Watcher waiting for her on the slanted rooftop. He smiled at her from underneath his hood, then gestured to the caravan.

"I heard the rumors, not that I believed them," he said while crouched at the rooftop's edge. "I thought Veldaren was Alyssa's city?"

"If this city belongs to anyone, it's you," Zusa said, smiling. "Lady Gemcroft has finally decided the safety of her family is more important than putting up a powerful facade. We're leaving this sick, rotten city. If Nathaniel wants to return when he comes of age, so be it. Until then, we'll live in Riverrun."

Haern nodded as he watched the train of people and wagons roll on. Zusa sensed he was uncomfortable. Hardly surprising. They'd yet to speak of their night together. She'd been terribly vulnerable, and perhaps it had been the same way for him.

Given the shadows across his face, hidden even in the midday light, she had a feeling Haern was not one used to letting his guard down.

"Zusa," he said, still not looking at her. "About last time we..."

She grabbed his hand and shushed him.

"You gave me comfort when I needed it," she said. "Let it remain just that, and nothing more."

Except it had been more, and she almost said so, but it was not what he wanted to hear. He looked down at her hand holding his, then cupped it with his other before he stood.

"There's someone I think I love," he said. "She's gentle, good at heart...but given this brutal life I lead, the risks it'd bring her just by being with me..." He tilted his head at her, laughing to reveal his embarrassment. "It's sad, but you're the only person I know to talk about this with. Am I a fool to hope for some sort of happiness? Is it selfish of me to endanger her so?"

Zusa used her free hand to slowly pull back his hood to reveal his handsome face, his square jaw, his beautiful blue eyes. She wanted to see him like that one more time, to have a face to remember instead of his low hood and shadowed visage. Standing on her toes, she gently kissed his lips, then pulled back so she might meet his gaze.

"You're a kind, wonderful man," she told him. "Be with who you love, and damn any fear that keeps you apart. You deserve happiness in this life, Watcher. We all do."

That said, she pulled away from him and turned her attention to the Gemcroft caravan.

"I have a family to be with," she said. "I trust you'll handle Veldaren well enough while I'm gone?"

"I'll do what I can," he said, smiling at her. "And Zusa... thank you."

Pulling his hood back over his head, he climbed to the apex of the rooftop and then slid down from view. Zusa watched him go, and she wondered if she'd made a mistake in not telling him.

Down to the street she climbed, then ran to join Alyssa and Nathaniel in their wagon.

That night the three of them gathered around a campfire in the heart of the circle of wagons. Veldaren was a glowing candle in the distance, and the atmosphere was one of celebration. Alyssa had ordered several kegs opened, and her servants and soldiers drank themselves stupid. Zusa smiled amid the revelry, soaking in the joy despite feeling ill herself.

"You're going to love Riverrun," Alyssa told Nathaniel, who sat next to her, chomping on a chicken leg. "There are rows of falls, each with deep pools between them, that you can just dive and swim..."

"Does the boy know how to swim?" Zusa asked.

"I'm right here," Nathaniel said. "And yes, the *boy* does know how to swim."

"My apologies," Zusa said, dipping her head. "Next time, I will ask the boy directly."

He glared, but it was comical, overemphasized, and she laughed. That laughter quickly ended as she felt her stomach shifting, suddenly and with little warning. Turning aside, she let out a single cough before she vomited up much of her meal. The smell was awful, the taste of the greasy meat coming back up her throat no better. She coughed again, trying to recover her breath.

"Are you sick?" Nathaniel asked, and Zusa smiled despite the silliness of the question.

"With nothing you can catch," she told him.

"All right, it's late," Alyssa said, tapping Nathaniel on the back. "Go on and get to bed. We have an early start tomorrow."

Nathaniel kissed his mother's cheek, then wandered off toward the tent the servants had erected for him. Alyssa remained behind at the fire, glass eyes staring at Zusa from across it. Zusa wondered what she was thinking, how she might react.

"I remember my sickness when I carried Nathaniel, and it wasn't always in the morning," she said. "How long have you known?"

For a brief moment Zusa thought to lie, a ridiculous notion given how quickly it'd be found out. Stare locked on the fire, she felt strangely nervous and embarrassed as she answered.

"Not long," she said. "Two weeks ago my blood never came."

Alyssa rose from her seat, walked around the fire, and then sat cross-legged beside her. She leaned forward, hands clasped. No judgment. No anger. Just concentration.

"Do you know who the father is?" she asked.

Zusa nodded, said nothing.

"Will you tell him?"

It was the one question that had been raging in her mind for weeks. Zusa looked up, mind finally made, heart finally ready. Would she tell him? Would she add another burden to an already burdened man? Reaching out, she grabbed Alyssa's hands, gripped them tightly as she met her gaze and gave her answer.

A NOTE FROM THE AUTHOR

Well, that's it. Six books finished, and if you've made it this far, I'd like to think they all did something right to keep you reading to the very end. I'm not going to pretend it went as I expected it all to go, and there were plenty of characters (Ghost and Zusa in particular) who threw me for several loops along the way. I guess that's part of the fun, and the reason you go on the journey in the first place, right?

To those of you who have read the Half-Orc series, know that I did my best to keep continuity intact, but if there are any breaks or changes, treat this as the definitive version of that first battle in *The Weight of Blood*. The same goes for the fight in *The Cost of Betrayal* between Thren and Haern. Consider the ending confrontation here in Chapter 33 (and to a lesser extent, the final relationship between Haern and Delysia) to be what I've always felt these characters deserved. Hopefully they're also far more satisfying to you longtime readers than what I delivered in the Half-Orcs. I guess I'd also be remiss if I didn't at least address the potential question of "What the heck was up with the prophet?" The answer is in the Half-Orc books. I'll try to just leave it at that.

Anyway, after Thren and Haern tore into each other near the end of the last book, having their confrontation finally come to a head here was awesome. Brutal, and there might have been a few tears in this writer's eyes, but still awesome. No matter all he had gone through, a piece of Aaron Felhorn still remains, still wishing to be loved by his father. I've always thought of Thren as a monster, and there at the end, he finally reveals just how terrible a monster he really is. It's a scene I have had in my head for years now, a scene I was terrified I would fail to make as powerful as it was in my own imagination. God I hope I pulled it off.

As for the ending...to stave off the (likely many) e-mails I'm sure to get: yes, I do have plans to use that twist sometime far down the road. No, I make absolutely no promises as to how and when we might eventually get to see Haern and Zusa's child, nor in what manner, nor in what series. This is me leaving the door open the tiniest crack, just in case I ever decide to return. I hope you'll forgive me for taking the luxury while I have the chance.

Real quick obligatory thanks. Thank you, Devi, for being a fantastic editor throughout all six books, helping me shape this series while also never letting me forget how much room for improvement there is in all aspects. Thank you, Michael, for handling all the publishing stuff so I don't have to. Thank you, Rob, for listening to my rambling phone calls as I debate what the heck to do with Zusa or Alyssa.

Last, but certainly not least, I want to thank you, dear readers. Three-quarters of a million words later, you're still here with me. For such an investment of your time, I hope I have given you an exciting journey. I hope I've given you characters you cherish, characters whom, whether they lived or died, you'll remember for a long time after setting this book down and moving on to another. You came into my world, asking to be entertained, and I hope I repaid that privilege well with a damn fine story.

I've said it before, and I'll say it again—I'm living a dream, and it's because of you. There's no way I can thank you enough. But just because I can't, doesn't mean I won't try. So, from the bottom of my heart:

Thank you.

David Dalglish
July 2, 2014

extras

orbit

meet the author

Photo credit: Mike Scott

DAVID DALGLISH currently lives in rural Missouri with his wife, Samantha, and daughters Morgan and Katherine. He graduated from Missouri Southern State University in 2006 with a degree in mathematics and currently spends his free time teaching his children the timeless wisdom of Mario jumping on a turtle shell.

introducing

If you enjoyed
A DANCE OF CHAOS
look out for David Dalglish's new series, starting with

SKYBORN

Seraphim: Book 1

*Ever since the Ascension, the last remnants of humanity
live on six islands floating above the endless ocean.
The Seraphim are their elite guardians, defying gravity using
ancient wings and wielding powerful elements to wage war
in the skies. Kale and Breanna Skyborn share one dream:
to protect their island home of Weshern by becoming
members of the Seraphim. They join the Weshern Academy,
enduring hours of drills and training to master fire, ice,
and sword. They must learn quickly, for a nearby island
has set its hungry eyes upon Weshern. When the invasion comes,
the twins must don their wings and ready their blades
to save those they love from annihilation.*

PROLOGUE

Breanna Skyborn sat at the edge of her world, watching the clouds drift beneath her dangling feet.

"Bree?"

Kale's voice sounded obscenely loud in the twilight quiet. She turned to see her twin brother standing at the stone barricade that marked the end of the road.

"Over here," she said.

The barricade reached up to Kale's waist, and after a moment's hesitation, he climbed over, leaving behind smoothly worn cobbles for short grass and soft dirt. Beyond the barricade, there was nothing else. No buildings. No streets. No homes. Just a stretch of unused earth, and then beyond that... the edge. It was for that reason Bree loved it, and her brother hated it.

"We're not allowed to be this close," he said as he approached, each step smaller than the last. "If Aunt Bethy saw..."

"Aunt Bethy won't come within twenty feet of the barricade and you know it."

Wind blew against her, and she pulled her dark hair back from her face as she smirked at her brother. His pale skin had taken on a golden hue from the fading sunlight, the wind teasing his much shorter hair. The gust made him stop, and she worried he'd decide to leave her there.

"You're not afraid, are you?" she asked.

That was enough to push him on. Kale joined her at the edge of their island. When he sat, he sat crossed-legged, and unlike her, he did not let his legs dangle off the side.

"Just for a little while," he said. "We should be home when the battle starts."

Bree turned away, and she peered over the edge of the island. Below, lazily floating along, were dozens of puffy clouds painted orange by the setting sun. Through their gaps she saw the tumultuous Endless Ocean, its movement only hinted at by the faintest of dark lines. Again the wind blew, and she pretended that she rode upon the it, flying just like her parents.

"So why are we out here?" Kale asked, interrupting the silence.

"I was hoping to see the stars."

"Is that it? We're just here to waste our time?"

Bree glared at him.

"You've seen the drawings in Teacher Gruden's books. The stars are beautiful. I was hoping that out here, away from the lanterns, maybe I could see one or two before..."

She fell silent. Kale let out a sigh.

"Is that really why you're out here?"

It wasn't, not fully, but she didn't feel comfortable discussing the other reason. Hours ago their mother and father had sat them down beside the fire of their home. They'd each worn the black uniforms of their island of Weshern, swords dangling from their hips, the silver wings attached to their harnesses polished to a shine.

The island of Galen won't back down, so we have no choice, their father had said. *We've agreed to a battle come the midnight fire. This will be the last, I promise. After this, they won't have the heart for another.*

"It is," Bree said, wishing her half lie were more convincing. She looked to their right, where the sun was slipping beneath the horizon. Nightfall wouldn't be long now. Kale shifted uncomfortably, and she saw him glancing behind them, as if convinced they'd be caught despite being in a secluded corner of their small town of Lowville.

"Fine," he said. "I'll stay with you, but if we get in trouble, this was all your idea."

"It usually is," she said, smiling at him.

Kale settled back, sliding a bit further away from the edge. Together they watched the sun slowly set. In its glow, they caught glimpses of two figures flying through the twilight haze. Their mechanical wings shimmered gold as they hovered above a great stretch of green farmland. The men wore red robes along with their wings, easily identifying them as theotechs of Center.

"Why are they here?" Kale asked when he spotted them.

"They're here to oversee the battle," Bree answered. She'd spent countless nights on her father's lap, asking him questions. What it was like to fly? Was he ever scared when they fought? Did he think she might ever be a member of the Seraphim like they were? Bree knew the two theotechs would bless the battle, ensure everyone followed the agreed-upon rules, and then mark the surrender of the loser. Then would come the vultures, the lowest ranking members of the theotechs, come to reclaim the treasured technology from the fallen.

The mention of the coming battle put Kale on edge, and he fell silent as he looked to the sunset. Bree couldn't blame him for his nervousness. She felt it too, and it was that reason she couldn't stay home, cooped up, unable to witness the battle or know if her mother and father lived or died. No, she had to be out there. She had to have something to occupy her mind.

They said nothing as the sun neared the end of its descent. As the strength of its rays weakened, she turned her attention to the east, where the sky had faded a deep shade of purple.

The coming darkness unsettled Bree. Since the day she was born, it had come and gone, but it was rare for her to watch it. She much preferred to be at home next to the hearth, listening to her father tell Seraphim stories, or their mother reading Kale ancient tales of knights and angels. Watching the nightly shadow only made her feel...imprisoned.

It began where the light was at its absolute weakest, an inky black line on the horizon that grew like a cloud. Slowly it crawled, thick as smoke and wide as the horizon itself. The darkness swept over the sky, hiding its many colors. More and more it covered, an unceasing march matched by the sun's fall. When it reached to the faintly visible moon, it too vanished, the pale crescent tucked away, never to be seen until the following night. Silently the twins watched as the rolling darkness passed high above their heads, blotting out everything, encasing the world in its deep shadow.

Bree turned her attention to the setting sun, which looked as if it fled in fear of the darkness complete.

"It'll be right there," she said, pointing. "In the moment after the sun sets and before the darkness reaches it."

Most of the sky was gone now, and so, far away from the lanterns, the two sat in a darkness so complete it was frightening. The shadow clouds continued rolling, blotting out the field of stars that the ancient drawing books made look so beautiful, so majestic and grand. But just as she'd hoped, there was a gap in the time it took the sun to vanish beyond the horizon and for the rolling shadow to reach it, and she watched with growing anticipation. She'd seen only one star before, the North Star, which shone so brightly that not even the sun could always blot it out. But the other stars, the great field...would they appear in the deepening purple?

Kale saw it before she did, and he quickly pointed. In the

sliver of violet space the star winked into existence, a little drop of light between the horizon and the shadows crashing down on it like a wave. Bree saw it, and she smiled at the sight.

"Imagine not one but thousands," Bree said as the dark clouds swallowed the star, pitching the entire city into utter darkness so deep she could not see her brother beside her. "A field spanning the entire sky, lighting up the night in its glow..."

Bree felt Kale take her hand, and she squeezed it tight. Blind, neither dared move, instead remaining perfectly still as they waited. It would only be a matter of time.

It started as a faint flicker of red across the eastern horizon. Slowly it grew, spreading, strengthening. Just like the shadows, so too did the fire roll across the sky, setting ablaze the inky clouds that covered the crown of the world. It burned without consuming, only shifting and twisting. It took thirty minutes, but eventually all of the sky raged with midnight fire, bathing the land in red. It'd last until daybreak, when the sun would rise, the fire would die, and the smoky remnants would hover over the morning sky until fading away.

A horn sounded from a watchtower farther within their home island of Weshern. The blast set Bree's heart to hammering.

"They're starting," she whispered.

Both turned to face the field where the two theotechs hovered. The horn sounded thrice more, and come its halting, the forces of Weshern arrived. They sailed above the field in V-formations, their silver wings shimmering, powered by the light element that granted all seraphim mastery over the skies. Hundreds of men and women, dressed in black pants and jackets, armed with fire, lightning, ice, and stone that they wielded with the gauntlets of their ancient technology. Despite her fear, Bree felt an intense longing to be up there with them, fighting for the pride and safety of her home. Sadly it'd be five years before she and her brother turned sixteen and could attempt to join.

"Bree..."

She turned her head, saw her brother staring off into the open sky beyond the edge of their island. Flying in similar V-formations, gold wings glimmering, red jackets seemingly aflame from the light of the midnight fire, came the Seraphim of Galen. The two armies raced toward one another, and Bree knew they'd meet just above the fallow field, where the theo-techs waited.

Bree pushed herself away from the edge of the island and rose to her feet, her brother doing likewise.

"They'll be fine," she said, watching the Weshern Seraphim fly in perfect formation. She wondered which of those black and silver shapes was her mother, and which her father. "You'll see. No one's better than they are."

Kale stood beside her, eyes on the sky, arms locked at his sides. Bree reached for his hand, held it as the armies neared one another.

"It'll be over quick," she whispered. "Father says it always is."

Dark shapes shot in both directions through the space between the armies, large chunks of stone meant to screen attacks as well as protect against retaliation. They crashed into one another, and as the sound reached Bree's ears, the battle suddenly erupted into bewildering chaos. The seraphim formations danced about one another, lightning flashing amid them in constant barrages. Enormous blasts of fire accompanied them, difficult to see with the sky itself aflame. Blue lances of ice colored purple from the midnight hue shot in rapid bursts, cutting down combatants with ease. The sounds of battle were so powerful, so near, Bree could feel them in her bones.

"How?" Kale wondered aloud, and if he weren't so close she wouldn't have heard him over the cacophony. "How can anyone survive through that?"

Boulders of stone slammed into the fallow field beneath, carving out long grooves of earth before coming to a stop. Bree flinched at the impact of each one. How did one survive? She didn't know, but somehow they did, the seraphim of both islands weaving amid the carnage with movements so fluid and beautiful they mirrored that of dancers. Not all, though. Lightning tore through bodies, lances of ice with sharp tips punctured flesh and metal alike, and no armor could protect against the fire that washed over their bodies. Each seraph that fell wearing a black jacket made Bree silently beg it wasn't one of her parents. She didn't care if that was selfish or not. She just wanted them safe. She wanted them to survive the overwhelming onslaught that left her mind baffled on how to take it all in.

The elements lessened, the initial devastating barrage becoming more precise, more controlled. Bree saw that several combatants were out of elements completely, and were forced to draw their blades. The battle had gradually spread farther and farther out, taking them beyond the grand field and closer to the edge of town where Bree and Kale stood. Not far above their heads, two seraphim circled in a dance, one fleeing, one chasing. They both had their twin blades drawn. Bree watched, entranced, eyes wide as the circle tightened, and the combatants whisked by each other again and again, slender blades swiping for exposed flesh.

It was the Galen seraph who made the first mistake. Bree saw him fail to dodge in time, saw the tip of the sword slice across his stomach. The body fell, careening wildly just before making impact with the ground. The sound was a bloodcurdling screech of metal and snapping bone. Bree's attention turned to the larger battle, and she saw that many more had drawn their blades. The number of remaining seraphim was shockingly few, yet they fought on.

"No one's surrendering," Kale said, and she could hear the fear threatening to overtake him completely. "Bree, you said it'd be quick. You said it'd be quick!"

The area of battle was spreading wildly out of control. Galen seraphim scattered in all directions, loose formations of two to three people. The Weshern seraphim chased, and despite the nearing town, they still released their elements. Bree screamed as a pair streaked above their heads, the *thrum* of their wings nearly deafening. A boulder failed to connect with the fleeing seraphim, and it blasted through the side of a home with a thundering blast.

"Let's go!" Bree screamed, grabbing Kale's hand and dashing toward the barricade. More seraphim were approaching, seemingly the entire Galen forces. They wanted to be over the town, Bree realized. They wanted to make Weshern's people hesitate to fight with so many nearby. As the twins climbed over stone barricade, the sounds of battle erupting all about them, it was clear their seraphim would make no such hesitations. Lightning flashed above Bree's head, and she cried out in surprise. She ducked, stumbled, lost her grip on her brother's hand. He stopped, shouted her name, and then the ice lance struck the cobbles ahead of them. It shattered into shards, and Kale dove to the ground as they flew in all directions.

"Kale," Bree said as she scrambled to her feet. "Kale!"

"I'm fine," he said, pushing himself to his hands and knees. When he looked to her, he was bleeding from several cuts across his face and neck. "I'm fine, now hurry!"

The red light of the midnight fire cast its hue across everything, convincing Bree she'd lost herself in a nightmare and awoken in one of the circles of Hell. Kale pulled her along, leading her toward Aunt Bethy's house, where they were supposed to have stayed during the battle, waiting like good children for their parents to return. Hand in hand they ran, the air above filled with screams, echoes of thunder, and the deep hum of the seraphim's wings.

When they turned a corner, they saw two seraphs flying straight at them from farther down the street. Fire burst from the chaser's gauntlet. It bathed over the other, sending her crashing to the ground. Kale dove aside as Bree froze, her legs locked in place from terror. The body came to a halt mere feet away from her, silver wings mangled and broken. Her black jacket bore the blue sword of Weshern on her shoulder, and Bree shuddered at the sight of the woman's horrible burns. High above, the Galen seraph flew on, seeking new prey.

"Bree!" her brother shouted, pulling her attention away. He'd wedged himself in the tight space between two homes, and she joined him there in hiding.

"We have to get back," Bree insisted. "We can't stay here."

"Yes, we can," Kale said, hunkering deeper into the alley. "I'm not going out there, Bree. I'm not."

Bree glanced back out of the narrow alley. With the battle raging above the town, Aunt Bethy would be terrified at their absence. They were already going to be in trouble for not coming in like they were supposed to in the first place. To hide now, afraid, until who knew when it all ended?

"I'm going," she said. "Are you coming with me or not?"

Another blast of thunder above. Kale shook his head.

"No," he said. His eyes widened when he realized she was serious about going. "Bree, don't leave me here. Don't leave me!"

She dashed back into the street, racing toward Aunt Bethy's

house. As strongly as Kale wanted to remain hiding, Bree wanted to return to their aunt's home. She wanted to be inside, in a safe place with family. Let him be a coward and stay. She'd be brave. She'd be strong.

A boulder crashed through the rooftop of a home to her right then blasted out the front wall. Bree screamed, and she realized she wasn't brave at all. She was frightened out of her mind. Fighting back tears, she turned down Picker Street, where both they and their aunt lived. Five houses down was her aunt's home, and Bree felt her heart take a sudden leap. Her legs moved fast as they could carry her.

There she was. Her mother was safe, she was alive, she was...

She was bleeding. Her hand clutched her stomach, and Bree saw with horrible clarity the red gash her fingers failed to seal. She lay on her back, her silver wings pressed against the door to Aunt Bethy's home, a dazed look on her face. Beneath her was a pool of her own blood.

"Bree," her mother said. Her voice was wet, strained. Tears trickled from her brown eyes. "Bree, what are you...what are you doing out here?"

Bree didn't know how to answer. She fell to her knees, felt her pants turn wet from the blood. She reached out a trembling hand, wanting so badly to hold her mother but fearing what any contact might do.

"It's all right," her mother said, and she smiled despite her obvious pain. "Bree, it's all right. It's..."

Her lips grew still. She breathed in pain no more. Her hand fell limp, holding back her sliced stomach no longer. Bree touched her shoulder, shook her once.

"Mom," she said, tears rolling down her cheeks. "Mom, no, mom, please."

She buried her face against her mother's chest, shrieking out in wordless agony. She didn't want to see any more, to hear any more. Bree wrapped her arms around her mother's neck, clutching her tightly, not caring about the blood that seeped into her clothes. She just wanted one more embrace before the vultures came to reclaim her wings. She wanted to pretend her mother was alive and well, holding her, loving her, kissing her forehead before flying away for another day of training and drills.

Not this corpse. Not this lifeless thing.

A hand touched her shoulder. Bree pulled back, expecting to see her brother, but instead it was a tall Weshern seraph. Blood smeared his fine black coat. To her surprise, the surrounding neighborhood was quiet, the battle seemingly over.

"Was she your mother?" the man asked. Bree could barely see his face through the shadows cast by the midnight fire. She sniffled, then nodded.

"Then you must be Breanna. I…I don't know how else to tell you this. It's about your father."

His words were a dagger to an already punctured heart. It couldn't be. The world couldn't be that cruel.

"No," she whispered. "No, that can't be right."

The seraph swallowed hard.

"Breanna, I'm sorry."

Bree leapt to her feet, and she flung herself at the man, screaming at the top of her lungs.

"No, it can't. Not both, we can't lose them both, we can't…we can't…"

She broke, collapsing at his feet, her tears falling upon his black boots. She beat the stone cobbles until she bled, beat them as she screamed, beat them as high above, the midnight fire burned like an unrelenting pyre for the dead.

CHAPTER 1

"I keep telling you," Jevin said as they walked the stone road to the fishing docks. "You aren't ready."

"But you said when we turned sixteen we'd get to go with you," Bree insisted.

"And when is that?" Jevin asked.

"Next week."

The deeply tanned man threw up a hand, as if that answered everything. He carried dozens of heavy nets slung over his shoulder with his other hand. Jevin was a friend of Aunt Bethy, and he was quick to remind Bree and Kale of how close he'd been to their father as well.

"Peas in a pod," he'd tell them. "Until he joined the seraphim, anyway."

Bree had used that close relationship to guilt and charm dozens of gifts and favors out of the man, but as they passed through the gathering crowds of fishermen, she decided that connection might now be working against her.

"It's not that long to wait," Kale said, walking alongside her. "I'd rather practice on land a few more times anyway."

Bree had to choke down her exasperated groan.

"Of course you would," she said. "You're terrible at it."

Kale raised an eyebrow at her.

"Yes. That's the point. I'd rather not go crashing headfirst into the ocean because I don't know what I'm doing."

"I'm not sure crashing headfirst into dirt is any better..."

"Enough," Jevin said, interrupting them both. "We're not having this discussion. You want to fly, do it over the island."

She had a dozen retorts ready, but Bree held them in,

deciding it was not yet time to wage this battle. Idea growing, she obediently dipped her head and remained silent as they crossed into the docks. All around her were tanned men, their clothes faded brown and grey. Several long tables lined either side of the street, their surfaces coated with fish guts and gore as giant cleavers rose and fell, cutting off the undesirable parts as those beside them sliced with long knives, cleaning and gutting the catch of the day. The noise was one of hearty cheers, jokes, and laughter accompanied by thuds of steel and the constant roar of the unseen Fount below.

But most interesting to Bree were the men at the far end, where the docks ended and the sky began. With the morning so young, most were strapping on their wings, buckling belts, and adjusting the connected gauntlet on their left hands. At their feet were dozens of nets and sharpened harpoons. The wings themselves were short and stocky, designed for lift instead of speed. Bree and Kale had practiced with a set just like them, hovering several feet above the ground while Jevin watched protectively. The whole while, it drove Bree insane. It was like being a bird with clipped wings.

"Hey, Bryce," Jevin said, approaching a hollowed-out stone block where a bearded man stood within, arms crossed. "Morning going well?"

"No one's died, but the fish ain't catching themselves," Bryce said, deep voice rumbling. "So going as well as one can hope for without wishing on angels."

The big man turned about, scanning rows of wood shelves inside his structure, each one lined with the wing contraptions. He found Jevin's, pulled it off, and handed it over.

"The switch was getting sticky, so I replaced the spring," he said. "Best I can do before sending it off to Central for the theotechs to have a look."

"I'm sure it's fine," Jevin said, hooking his free arm through the two leather loops that went underneath the armpits. As he stepped away, Bree put her hands on the small barrier between her and Bryce.

"Mine, too," she said.

Bryce shot a look to Jevin, who gave a hesitant nod.

"Should start making you pay for this," the bearded man said, leaning down beneath the front shelf and pulling up a smaller set of wings from out of view. "Light elements don't come cheap."

"Thank God you aren't paying for it then," Bree said, accepting the wings. The Light element that powered the wings came from Central, and Weshern's Archon then allocated a set amount each month to training new fishermen.

"Rate you're using it up, I might have to anyway," Bryce said, but a grin was on his face. Seeing Kale lingering beside Jevin, he called out, louder. "You also going to fly today, kid?"

"Maybe," Kale said, smiling warmly at the man. "But only if Bree doesn't hog it all."

They traveled across the street and onto the wood planks, Bryce's roaring laughter at their backs. As Bree clutched the wing contraption to her chest, she glanced down. The docks were built onto the side of their island, overhanging the sky, and through gaps in the planks she could see glimpses of the clouds below. The sight gave her shivers of the good kind.

Jevin stopped them at an open spot near the middle, let his net plop to the wood, and then lifted his wings up and over his shoulders. He was a scrawny-looking man, his face long and gaunt, but his arms and chest were corded muscle. The wings could only carry so much weight, and while the stunted version the fishermen were given was designed to carry more than normal, it still had its limits. As a result, nearly all the men around were lean and fit, strong of arm and thin around the waist. The more fish they could carry each trip, the better their pay at the end of the day.

"Is it all right if I go first?" Bree asked her brother as Jevin began tying the buckles.

"You'd only argue with me if I said no," Kale said, and he grinned at her. "Go ahead. We both know you love the sky more than I do."

Bree mussed his hair, then began sliding on the harness of the wings. She'd never understand why Kale didn't love the sky like she did. They spent every single day of their lives with their feet touching the ground. The clouds, the wind, the world spinning beyond...how could you ever deny the allure? Putting an arm through one side, she shifted the wings onto her back and shoulders, then slid the other arm through. The weight settled comfortably. The wings were a rustic gold, hard and unmoving from their folded position. Everything else, though, was stiff leather and padded cloth. Two buckles went underneath her armpits, a large strip of leather dropped down her back and then latched around her waist, and the last two strips connected to those looped about her thighs before buckling tight. Bree went through the process, fastening one after the other, refusing Jevin's offered help.

"How do I look?" she asked when finished, standing tall and thrusting back her shoulders.

Jevin smiled at her.

"Like an angel," he said.

Bree glanced over her shoulder at the small, stunted wings now attached to her back. They were not designed to move, instead remaining perfectly in place during flight. It was the Light element that gave the wings the ability to fly, and that element was controlled by the left gauntlet attached to the wings.

Reaching over her shoulder, she shifted the wings to rest a bit more comfortably, then unhooked the gauntlet from its side. A slender tube ran from its bottom to the thick stump at the arch of her back, where the wings connected. Bree put her left hand inside the golden gauntlet, then tightened the buckles as much as they allowed. There was no doubt to her that the training piece had been designed with boys in mind, and it took every hole on the belt to get them snug.

"Flex your fingers," Jevin said, having watched her all the while. She did so, showing that the gauntlet fit fine and would not cause issues in flight.

"What next?" Jevin asked, running her through the check-list he'd taught her to prepare for any period of flight.

"Check the element," she said.

She lifted the gauntlet, where along the wrist was an opening covered by a sliver of glass. Inside, protected by the metal of the gauntlet, was a white prism shard: the Light element they used for flight. Various tubes and wires understood only by the theotechs connected to the prism, drawing out the energy of the Light element and pulsing it through the tube running from the gauntlet's edge to the wings. As Bree flew and the Light element was used, the color would slowly drain away, turning the prism gray. Peering through the thick glass, she saw the element was bright white, fully charged.

"Good," said Jevin. "Next, check the switch. Make sure it ain't sticking or being stubborn."

Bree knew all this, and on normal days she'd have grumbled at his belief that he must remind her. Not today. Today she felt a stirring in her stomach. Today, she knew, was different.

Built into the right side of the forefinger was a red toggle switch. Using her thumb, she could tilt it forward and backward, effectively increasing, or shutting off entirely, the push from the Light element that was sent to the wings. Back and forth she moved it, quick enough to prevent the wings from gaining any lift. The contraption thrummed, a deep, pleasant sound. The wings themselves shimmered a bright gold.

"Remember, stay above the docks," he told her as he picked up his net. "And try not to fly more than thirty minutes. Bryce gets pissed at me when you do."

He walked toward the end of the docks, and she followed. Jevin paused, and there was no hiding his frustration when he glared at her.

"What are you doing?" he asked.

"I'm going with you."

"No, Bree, you're too young to..."

"Josh Hadley is already fishing with his father, and he's fifteen. Do you think he's a safer flier than I am?"

Of course he wasn't, and the argument was hardly a new one for her. Still, Jevin was suited up for work, and with each second he argued, he was risking missing out on a good catch.

"Fine," he said. "Your aunt will kill me for this, no matter how many times I tell her it was your idea. Promise me you won't do something stupid."

"Jevin..."

"Promise me."

Bree rolled her eyes.

"I promise," she said.

Jevin hardly looked convinced, but he let it drop.

"Let's go," he said. They walked to the edge of the docks, where the wood came to an end. Peering over, Bree saw only clouds, big white puffy things drifting lazily along. The twisting in her stomach heightened, but her excitement easily overwhelmed it.

"Don't do anything stupid," Kale called out to her, stopping at a groove cut into the wood that marked where those without wings were not allowed to cross.

"I wouldn't dream of it," Bree called back.

"Liar."

Jevin took her by the elbow and guided her closer to the edge, chuckling at her brother's words.

"Remember," Jevin said, "scrunch your shoulders to rotate forward, pull them wide to rotate backwards. It'll help a little, but most changes of direction will depend on your own upper body strength."

Her mouth opened, the words *I know* on her lips, but he shushed her with a glare.

"This is serious," he said. "You may think it all obvious, but when something jostles your wings, and you're plummeting toward the water in a dead spin, even the easiest of things can be hard to remember. I've watched good men, fishers all their lives, react wrongly to things they didn't expect. It cost them their lives. So fly slow, fly straight, and stay away from the Fount. Got it?"

Despite the seriousness of his tone, she bobbed her head and smiled.

"Got it."

Jevin took in a deep breath, and for a moment she feared he'd change his mind, but he finally relented.

"Well then," he said. "Come along."

introducing

If you enjoyed
A DANCE OF CHAOS
look out for

A CROWN FOR COLD SILVER

by Alex Marshall

"It was all going so nicely, right up until the massacre."

Twenty years ago, feared general Cobalt Zosia led her five villainous captains and mercenary army into battle, wrestling monsters and toppling an empire. When there were no more titles to win and no more worlds to conquer, she retired and gave up her legend to history.

Now the peace she's carved for herself has been shattered by the unprovoked slaughter of her village. Seeking bloody vengeance, Zosia heads for battle once more, but to find justice she must confront grudge-bearing enemies, once-loyal allies, and an unknown army that marches under a familiar banner.

FIVE VILLAINS. ONE LEGENDARY GENERAL.
A FINAL QUEST FOR VENGEANCE.

CHAPTER 1

It was all going so nicely, right up until the massacre.

Sir Hjortt's cavalry of two hundred spears fanned out through the small village, taking up positions between half-timbered houses in the uneven lanes that only the most charitable of surveyors would refer to as "roads." The warhorses slowed and then stopped in a decent approximation of unison, their riders sitting as stiff and straight in their saddles as the lances they braced against their stirrups. It was an unseasonably warm afternoon in the autumn, and after their long approach up the steep valley, soldier and steed alike dripped sweat, yet not a one of them removed their brass skullcap. Weapons, armor, and tack glowing in the fierce alpine sunlight, the faded crimson of their cloaks covering up the inevitable stains, the cavalry appeared to have ridden straight out of a tale, or galloped down off one of the tapestries in the mayor's house.

So they must have seemed to the villagers who peeked through their shutters, anyway. To their colonel, Sir Hjortt, they looked like hired killers on horseback barely possessed of sense to do as they were told most of the time. Had the knight been able to train wardogs to ride he should have preferred them to the Fifteenth Cavalry, given the amount of faith he placed in this lot. Not much, in other words, not very much at all.

He didn't care for dogs, either, but a dog you could trust, even if it was only to lick his balls.

The hamlet sprawled across the last stretch of grassy meadow before the collision of two steep, bald-peaked mountains. Murky forest edged in on all sides, like a snare the wilderness had set for the unwary traveler. A typical mountain town here in the Kutumban range, then, with only a low reinforced stone wall to keep out the wolves and what piddling avalanches the encircling slopes must bowl down at the settlement when the snows melted.

Sir Hjortt had led his troops straight through the open gate in the wall and up the main track to the largest house in the village…which wasn't saying a whole lot for the building. Fenced in by shedding rosebushes and standing a scant two and a half stories tall, its windowless redbrick face was broken into a grid by the black timbers that supported it. The mossy thatched roof rose up into a witch's hat, and set squarely in the center like a mouth were a great pair of doors tall and wide enough for two riders to pass through abreast without removing their helmets. As he reached the break in the hedge at the front of the house, Sir Hjortt saw that one of these oaken doors was ajar, but just as he noticed this detail the door eased shut.

Sir Hjortt smiled to himself, and, reining his horse in front of the rosebushes, called out in his deepest baritone, "I am Sir Efrain Hjortt of Azgaroth, Fifteenth Colonel of the Crimson Empire, come to counsel with the mayor's wife. I have met your lord mayor upon the road, and while he reposes at my camp—"

Someone behind him snickered at that, but when Sir Hjortt turned in his saddle he could not locate which of his troops was the culprit. It might have even come from one of his two personal Chainite guards, who had stopped their horses at the border of the thorny hedge. He gave both his guards and the riders nearest them the sort of withering scowl his father was overly fond of doling out. This was no laughing matter, as should have been perfectly obvious from the way Sir Hjortt had dealt with the hillbilly mayor of this shitburg.

"Ahem." Sir Hjortt turned back to the building and tried again. "Whilst your lord mayor reposes at my camp, I bring tidings of great import. I must speak with the mayor's wife at once."

Anything? Nothing. The whole town was silently, fearfully watching him from hiding, he could feel it in his aching thighs, but not a one braved the daylight either to confront or assist him. Peasants—what a sorry lot they were.

"I say again!" Sir Hjortt called, goading his stallion into the mayor's yard and advancing on the double doors. "As a colonel of the Crimson Empire and a knight of Azgaroth, I shall be welcomed by the family of your mayor, or—"

Both sets of doors burst open, and a wave of hulking, shaggy beasts flooded out into the sunlight—they were on top of the Azgarothian before he could wheel away or draw his sword. He heard muted bells, obviously to signal that the ambush was under way, and the hungry grunting of the pack, and—

The cattle milled about him, snuffling his horse with their broad, slimy noses, but now that they had escaped the confines of the building they betrayed no intention toward further excitement.

"Very sorry, sir," came a hillfolk-accented voice from somewhere nearby, and then a small, pale hand appeared amid the cattle, rising from between the bovine waves like the last, desperate attempt of a drowning man to catch a piece of driftwood. Then the hand seized a black coat and a blond boy of perhaps ten or twelve vaulted himself nimbly into sight, landing on the wide back of a mountain cow and twisting the creature around to face Sir Hjortt as effortlessly as the Azgarothian controlled his warhorse. Despite this manifest skill and agility at play before him, the knight remained unimpressed.

"The mayor's wife," said Sir Hjortt. "I am to meet with her. Now. Is she in?"

"I expect so," said the boy, glancing over his shoulder—checking the position of the sun against the lee of the mountains towering over the village, no doubt. "Sorry again 'bout my cows. They're feisty, sir; had to bring 'em down early on account of a horned wolf being seen a few vales over. And I, uh, didn't have the barn door locked as I should have."

"Spying on us, eh?" said Sir Hjortt. The boy grinned. "Perhaps I'll let it slide this once, if you go and fetch your mistress from inside."

"Mayoress is probably up in her house, sir, but I'm not allowed 'round there anymore, on account of my wretched behavior," said the boy with obvious pride.

"This isn't her home?" Hjortt eyed the building warily.

"No, sir. This is the barn."

Another chuckle from one of his faithless troops, but Sir Hjortt didn't give whoever it was the satisfaction of turning in his saddle a second time. He'd find the culprit after the day's business was done, and then they'd see what came of having a laugh at their commander's expense. Like the rest of the Fifteenth Regiment, the cavalry apparently thought their new colonel was green because he wasn't yet twenty, but he would soon show them that being young and being green weren't the same thing at all.

Now that their cowherd champion had engaged the invaders, gaily painted doors began to open and the braver citizenry slunk out onto their stoops, clearly awestruck at the Imperial soldiers in their midst. Sir Hjortt grunted in satisfaction—it had been so quiet in the hamlet that he had begun to wonder if the villagers had somehow been tipped off to his approach and scampered away into the mountains.

"Where's the mayor's house, then?" he said, reins squeaking in his gauntlets as he glared at the boy.

"See the trail there?" said the boy, pointing to the east. Following the lad's finger down a lane beside a longhouse, Sir Hjortt saw a small gate set in the village wall, and beyond that a faint trail leading up the grassy foot of the steepest peak in the valley.

"My glass, Portolés," said Sir Hjortt, and his bodyguard walked her horse over beside his. Sir Hjortt knew that if he carried the priceless item in his own saddlebag one of his thuggish soldiers would likely find a way of stealing it, but not a one of them would dare try that shit with the burly war nun. She handed it over and Sir Hjortt withdrew the heavy brass hawkglass from its sheath; it was the only gift his father had ever given him that wasn't a weapon of some sort, and he relished any excuse to use it. Finding the magnified trail through the instrument, he tracked it up the meadow to where the path entered the surrounding forest. A copse of yellowing aspen interrupted the pines and fir, and, scanning the hawkglass upward, he saw that this vein of gold continued up the otherwise evergreen-covered mountain.

"See it?" the cowherd said. "They live back up in there. Not far."

———

Sir Hjortt gained a false summit and leaned against one of the trees. The thin trunk bowed under his weight, its copper leaves hissing at his touch, its white bark leaving dust on his cape. The series of switchbacks carved into the increasingly sheer mountainside had become too treacherous for the horses, and so Sir Hjortt and his two guards, Brother Iqbal and Sister Portolés, had proceeded up the scarps of exposed granite on foot. The possibility of a trap had not left the knight, but nothing more hostile than a hummingbird had showed itself on the hike, and now that his eyes had adjusted to the strangely diffuse light of this latest grove, he saw a modest, freshly whitewashed house perched on the lip of the next rock shelf.

Several hundred feet above them. Brother Iqbal laughed and Sister Portolés cursed, yet her outburst carried more humor in it than his. Through the trees they went, and then made the final ascent.

"Why…" puffed Iqbal, the repurposed grain satchel slung over one meaty shoulder retarding his already sluggish pace, "in all the…devils of Emeritus…would a mayor…live…so far… from his town?"

"I can think of a reason or three," said Portolés, setting the head of her weighty maul in the path and resting against its long shaft. "Take a look behind us."

Sir Hjortt paused, amenable to a break himself—even with only his comparatively light riding armor on, it was a real asshole of a hike. Turning, he let out an appreciative whistle. They had climbed quickly, and spread out below them was the painting-perfect hamlet nestled at the base of the mountains. Beyond the thin line of its walls, the lush valley fell away into the distance, a meandering brook dividing east ridge from west. Sir Hjortt was hardly a single-minded, bloodthirsty brute, and he could certainly appreciate the allure of living high above one's vassals, surrounded by the breathtaking beauty of creation. Perhaps when this unfortunate errand was over he would convert the mayor's house into a hunting lodge, wiling away his summers with sport and relaxation in the clean highland air.

"Best vantage in the valley," said Portolés. "Gives the head-person plenty of time to decide how to greet any guests."

"Do you think she's put on a kettle for us?" said Iqbal hopefully. "I could do with a spot of hunter's tea."

"About this mission, Colonel…" Portolés was looking at Sir Hjortt but not meeting his eyes. She'd been poorly covering up her discomfort with phony bravado ever since he'd informed her what needed to be done here, and the knight could well imagine what would come next. "I wonder if the order—"

"And I wonder if your church superiors gave me the use of you two anathemas so that you might hem and haw and question me at every pass, instead of respecting my command as an Imperial colonel," said Sir Hjortt, which brought bruise-hued blushes to the big woman's cheeks. "Azgaroth has been a proud and faithful servant of the Kings and Queens of Samoth for near on a century, whereas your popes seem to revolt every other feast day, so remind me again, what use have I for your counsel?"

Portolés muttered an apology, and Iqbal fidgeted with the damp sack he carried.

"Do you think I relish what we have to do? Do you think I would put my soldiers through it, if I had a choice? Why would I give such a command, if it was at all avoidable? Why—" Sir Hjortt was just warming to his lecture when a fissure of pain opened up his skull. Intense and unpleasant as the sensation was, it fled in moments, leaving him to nervously consider the witchborn pair. Had one of them somehow brought on the headache with their devilish ways? Probably not; he'd had a touch of a headache for much of the ride up, come to think of it, and he hadn't even mentioned the plan to them then.

"Come on," he said, deciding it would be best to drop the matter without further pontification. Even if his bodyguards did have reservations, this mission would prove an object lesson that it is always better to rush through any necessary unpleasantness, rather than drag your feet and overanalyze every ugly detail. "Let's be done with this. I want to be down the valley by dark, bad as that road is."

They edged around a hairpin bend in the steep trail, and then the track's crudely hewn stair delivered them to another plateau, and the mayor's house. It was similar in design to those in the hamlet, but with a porch overhanging the edge of the mild cliff and a low white fence. Pleasant enough, thought Sir Hjortt, except that the fence was made of bone, with each outwardly bowed moose-rib picket topped with the skull of a different animal. Owlbat skulls sat between those of marmot and hill fox, and above the door of the cabin rested an enormous one that had to be a horned wolf; when the cowherd had mentioned such a beast being spied in the area, Sir Hjortt had assumed the boy full of what his cows deposited, but maybe a few still prowled these lonely mountains. What a thrill it would be, to mount a hunting party for such rare game! Then the door beneath the skull creaked, and a figure stood framed in the doorway.

"Well met, friends, you've come a long way," the woman greeted them. She was brawny, though not so big as Portolés, with features as hard as the trek up to her house. She might have been fit enough once, in a country sort of way, when her long, silvery hair was blond or black or red and tied back in pigtails the way Hjortt liked…but now she was just an old woman, same as any other, fifty winters young at a minimum. Judging from the tangled bone fetishes hanging from the limbs of the sole tree that grew inside the fence's perimeter—a tall, black-barked aspen with leaves as hoary as her locks—she might be a sorceress, to boot.

Iqbal returned her welcome, calling, "Well met, Mum, well met indeed. I present to you Sir Hjortt of Azgaroth, Fifteenth Colonel of the Crimson Empire." The anathema glanced to his superior, but when Sir Hjortt didn't fall all over himself to charge ahead and meet a potential witch, Iqbal murmured, "She's just an old bird, sir, nothing to fret about."

"Old bird or fledgling, I wouldn't blindly stick my hand in

an owlbat's nest," Portolés said, stepping past Sir Hjortt and Iqbal to address the old woman in the Crimson tongue. "In the names of the Pontiff of the West and the Queen of the Rest, I order you out here into the light, woman."

"Queen of the Rest?" The woman obliged Portolés, stepping down the creaking steps of her porch and approaching the fence. For a mayor's wife, her checked dirndl was as plain as any village girl's. "And Pontiff of the West, is it? Last peddler we had through here brought tidings that Pope Shanatu's war wasn't going so well, but I gather much has changed. Is this sovereign of the Rest, blessed whoever she be, still Queen Indsorith? And does this mean peace has once again been brokered?"

"This bird hears a lot from her tree," muttered Sir Hjortt, then asked the woman, "Are you indeed the mayor's wife?"

"I am Mayoress Vivi, wife of Leib," said she. "And I ask again, respectfully, to whom shall I direct my prayers when next I—"

"The righteous reign of Queen Indsorith continues, blessed be her name," said Sir Hjortt. "Pope Shanatu, blessed be *his* name, received word from on high that his time as Shepherd of Samoth has come to an end, and so the war is over. His niece Jirella, blessed be *her* name, has ascended to her rightful place behind the Onyx Pulpit, and taken on the title of Pope Y'Homa III, Mother of Midnight, Shepherdess of the Lost."

"I see," said the mayoress. "And in addition to accepting a rebel pope's resignation and the promotion of his kin to the same lofty post, our beloved Indsorith, long may her glory persist, has also swapped out her noble title? 'Queen of Samoth, Heart of the Star, Jewel of Diadem, Keeper of the Crimson Empire' for, ah, 'Queen of the Rest'?" The woman's faintly lined face wrinkled further as she smiled, and Portolés slyly returned it.

"Do not mistake my subordinate's peculiar sense of humor for a shift in policy—the queen's honorifics remain unchanged," said Sir Hjortt, thinking of how best to discipline Portolés. If she thought that sort of thing flew with her commanding colonel just because there were no higher-ranked clerical witnesses to her dishonorable talk, the witchborn freak had another thing coming. He almost wished she would refuse to carry out his command, so he'd have an excuse to get rid of her altogether. In High Azgarothian, he said, "Portolés, return to the village and give the order. In the time it will take you to make it down I'll have made myself clear enough."

Portolés stiffened and gave Sir Hjortt a pathetic frown that told him she'd been holding out hope that he would change his mind. Not bloody likely. Also in Azgarothian, the war nun said, "I'm...I'm just going to have a look inside before I do. Make sure it's safe, Colonel Hjortt."

"By all means, Sister Portolés, welcome, welcome," said the older woman, also in that ancient and honorable tongue of Sir Hjortt's ancestors. Unexpected, that, but then the Star had been a different place when this biddy was in her prime, and perhaps she had seen more of it than just her remote mountain. Now that she was closer he saw that her cheeks were more scarred than wrinkled, a rather gnarly one on her chin, and for the first time since their arrival, a shadow of worry played across the weathered landscape of her face. Good. "I have an old hound sleeping in the kitchen whom I should prefer you left to his dreams, but am otherwise alone. But, good Colonel, Leib was to have been at the crossroads this morning..."

Sir Hjortt ignored the mayor's wife, following Portolés through the gate onto the walkway of flat, colorful stones that crossed the yard. They were artlessly arranged; the first order of business would be to hire the mason who had done the bathrooms at his family estate in Cockspar, or maybe the woman's apprentice, if the hoity-toity artisan wasn't willing to journey a hundred leagues into the wilds to retile a walk. A mosaic of miniature animals would be nice, or maybe indigo shingles could be used to make it resemble a creek. But then they had forded a rill on their way up from the village, so why not have somebody trace it to its source and divert it this way, have an actual stream flow through the yard? It couldn't be that hard to have it come down through the trees there and then run over the cliff beside the deck, creating a miniature waterfall that—

"Empty," said Portolés, coming back outside. Sir Hjortt had lost track of himself—it had been a steep march up, and a long ride before that. Portolés silently moved behind the older woman, who stood on the walk between Sir Hjortt and her house. The matron looked nervous now, all right.

"My husband Leib, Colonel Hjortt. Did you meet him at the crossroads?" Her voice was weaker now, barely louder than the quaking aspens. That must be something to hear as one lay in bed after a hard day's hunt, the rustling of those golden leaves just outside your window.

"New plan," said Sir Hjortt, not bothering with the more formal Azgarothian, since she spoke it anyway. "Well, it's the same as the original, mostly, but instead of riding down before dark we'll bivouac here for the night." Smiling at the old woman, he said, "Do not fret, Missus Mayor, do not fret, I won't be garrisoning my soldiers in your town, I assure you. Camp them outside the wall, when they're done. We'll ride out at first"—the thought of sleeping in on a proper bed occurred to him—"noon. We ride at noon tomorrow. Report back to me when it's done."

"Whatever you're planning, sir, let us parley before you commit yourself," said the old woman, seeming to awaken from the anxious spell their presence had cast upon her. She had a stern bearing he wasn't at all sure he liked. "Your officer can surely tarry a few minutes before delivering your orders, especially if we are to have you as our guests for the night. Let us speak, you and I, and no matter what orders you may have, no matter how pressing your need, I shall make it worth your while to have listened."

Portolés's puppy-dog eyes from over the woman's shoulder turned Sir Hjortt's stomach. At least Iqbal had the decency to keep his smug gaze on the old woman.

"Whether or not she is capable of doing so, Sister Portolés will *not* wait," said Sir Hjortt shortly. "You and I are talking, and directly, make no mistake, but I see no reason to delay my subordinate."

The old woman looked back past Portolés, frowning at the open door of her cabin, and then shrugged. As if she had any say at all in how this would transpire. Flashing a patently false smile at Sir Hjortt, she said, "As you will, fine sir. I merely thought you might have use for the sister as we spoke, for we may be talking for some time."

Fallen Mother have mercy, did every single person have a better idea of how Sir Hjortt should conduct himself than he did? This would not stand.

"My good woman," he said, "it seems that we have even more to parley than I previously suspected. Sister Portolés's business is pressing, however, and so she must away before we embark on this long conversation you so desire. Fear not, however, for the terms of supplication your husband laid out to us at the crossroads shall be honored, reasonable as they undeniably are. Off with you, Portolés."

Portolés offered him one of her sardonic salutes from over the older woman's shoulder, and then stalked out of the yard, looking as petulant as he'd ever seen her. Iqbal whispered something to her as he moved out of her way by the gate, and wasn't fast enough in his retreat when she lashed out at him. The war nun flicked the malformed ear that emerged from Iqbal's pale tonsure like the outermost leaf of an overripe cabbage, rage rendering her face even less appealing, if such a thing was possible. Iqbal swung his heavy satchel at her in response, and although Portolés dodged the blow, the dark bottom of the sackcloth misted her with red droplets as it whizzed past her face. If the sister noticed the blood on her face, she didn't seem to care, dragging her feet down the precarious trail, her maul slung over one hunched shoulder.

"My husband," the matron whispered, and, turning back to her, Sir Hjortt saw that her wide eyes were fixed on Iqbal's dripping sack.

"Best if we talk inside," said Sir Hjortt, winking at Iqbal and ushering the woman toward her door. "Come, come, I have an absolutely brilliant idea about how you and your people might help with the war effort, and I'd rather discuss it over tea."

"You said the war was over," the woman said numbly, still staring at the satchel.

"So it is, so it is," said Sir Hjortt. "But the *effort* needs to be made to ensure it doesn't start up again, what? Now, what do you have to slake the thirst of servants of the Empire, home from the front?"

She balked, but there was nowhere to go, and so she led Sir Hjortt and Brother Iqbal inside. It was quiet in the yard, save for the trees and the clacking of the bone fetishes when the wind ran its palm down the mountain's stubbly cheek. The screaming didn't start until after Sister Portolés had returned to the village, and down there they were doing enough of their own to miss the echoes resonating from the mayor's house.